ALPHAS IN THE WILD

ACTION ADVENTURE PARANORMAL ROMANCE
COLLECTION

ANN GIMPEL

Edited by
ANGELA KELLY
Illustrated by
FIONA JAYDE

CONTENTS

ALPHAS IN THE WILD

ACTION ADVENTURE, PARANORMAL ROMANCE COLLECTION

By
Ann Gimpel

~

~Hello Darkness~
~Alpine Attraction~
~A Run for Her Money~

~

Dark. Delicious. Unforgettable.
The hottest alphas live—and love—in the mountains.

~

Tumble into second-chance love, where magics collide,
mountain gods are out for blood, and aliens invade Earth.

COPYRIGHT PAGE

Re-released by Ann Gimpel and Dream Shadow Press in December 2015. This book has been substantially rewritten. *A Run For Her Money:* This book began as a short story by the same name published by Sam's Dot Publishing in March 2012. ISBN: 978-1-948871-24-2

HELLO DARKNESS

A SECOND-CHANCE PARANORMAL ROMANCE NOVELLA

By

Ann Gimpel

Tumble off reality's edge into a brutal blizzard where magics collide

Earth magics collide, forcing Moira Shaughnessy to take a chance on a man who hurt her so badly she never forgave him.

A ranger for the U.S. Park Service, Moira is in serious trouble. Fleeing from Ryan, her cheating husband, who's a Native American shaman, she stumbles into the arms of a man she never thought she'd see again. He hurt her once by choosing his magic over her. Would she be a fool to take a chance on him now?

Tim hasn't seen Moira in ten years. When her name shows up on his patient roster in the rural clinic where he's a doctor, he can't believe his luck. Deeply held secrets forced him from her side, but he's never forgotten her. Never stopped loving her. This time, he's determined to make different choices, even if it costs him his birthright as the next Arch Druid.

Pursuing very different motives, Tim and Ryan follow Moira deep into the backcountry, catching her in a crossfire between Celtic magic and Native American shamanism. A freak blizzard compounds her problems, taxing her survival skills to the max. Against the specter of almost-certain death, Moira has some hard choices to make.

CHAPTER 1

Moira Shaughnessy's booted feet hit the ground in front of the Family Medicine Clinic. Slamming the door of the dusty white Park Service pickup, she considered ignoring her boss's orders, peeling out of the parking lot, and heading for the Baxter Pass trailhead. She had a crew to oversee, goddammit. A work project to complete. But her boss, John, had been painstakingly clear, both yesterday at Park Headquarters in Three Rivers, and a mere ten minutes ago on the sat phone. Granted, he'd been far more pointed on the phone.

"It's not a suggestion, Moira," he'd growled. "This is a directive —from me. I want to hear from someone with MD after his name before I authorize you to head up that work detail. Do not set one foot on the trail before you receive my orders, e-sign them, and e-mail them back to me."

"But that's usually a formality—"

"Not this time. No buts. I made you an appointment at the clinic in Bishop that clears some of our crews. They're open until six. I already lost two rangers this summer in the Pinecrest fire. That was two too many in my book, so get your butt into that clinic."

Moira gritted her teeth. She'd thought she could avoid dealing with the whole mess by leaving the office early yesterday and taking one of the northern passes over the Sierra Nevada Mountains, but John tracked her down.

Phooey. I ran, but guess I couldn't hide...

It was downright annoying that her boss needed a doctor to reassure him she wouldn't collapse—or something—in the backcountry. For the briefest of moments, she felt like pounding her fist into the nearest tree, but then she pulled herself together. Nothing was wrong with her, except her slimy, cheating husband. Sure, she'd lost a few pounds since she left him, but she hadn't been all that hungry.

Problem was, John remembered similar struggles from years ago when she first started working as a park ranger. She hadn't eaten enough then, either, and grew far too thin. Just her luck, he'd been overseeing a backcountry work detail when she got woozy and fell off one of the mules.

Understanding surfaced; embarrassment followed. Her boss cared about her. That wasn't a bad thing. Anger bled out of her with a whoosh.

"May as well get this over with," she muttered.

Moira walked briskly to the clinic, pushed the door open, and headed for the counter. The antiseptic smell common to all medical offices hit her like a wall as she strode across the scrubbed linoleum floor.

"Yes?" A young woman with dyed red hair looked up from her computer screen with eyes so green she had to be wearing colored contact lenses.

"Moira Shaughnessy. I think you're expecting me. My boss called from Kings Canyon-Sequoia Park Headquarters."

The receptionist clicked a few keys. "Your insurance card, please."

Moira blew out a frazzled breath and dug through her fanny pack for her wallet. Once she found it, she extracted the plasticized Blue Cross card, handing it over. "I'm really in a bit of a hurry—"

"Here's your card back." The clerk gestured at the nearly full waiting room. "The doctor will be with you as soon as he can. He had a full schedule before he agreed to work you in."

"Is it okay if I go outside for a few minutes? I need to lock my truck. I, uh, didn't think I'd be in here for very long."

"Sure. So long as we know where to find you." The phone trilled, and the receptionist picked it up, Moira obviously forgotten. "Family Medicine, how may I help you?"

Moira let herself back outside. Too restless to return to the overcrowded waiting room, she paced up and down the parking lot. Fall had turned the aspen trees lining Bishop's streets to shades of red and gold that were quite striking, but all she could think about were the minutes ticking by. It was twelve miles from the trailhead to the top of the pass, and a couple more to where her trail crew was. Leaving today would be foolhardy at this point. She'd never even make the pass before night fell.

"Damn it!" She glanced at her watch. How long was this going to take anyway?

"Ms. Shaughnessy?" A man's voice sounded from behind her.

She spun, surprised out of her funk.

And stopped dead.

"Tim?"

Moira stared at the tall, rangy man with long, white-blond hair and ice-blue eyes. He was dressed in teal scrubs and sandals with a stethoscope draped around his neck. A broad grin split the clean planes of his face. She'd forgotten how heartbreakingly beautiful he was.

"I saw the name and hoped it was you." He held out a hand, but she remained frozen in place. "After all, how many Moira Shaughnessys could there be?"

She stood there, flabbergasted. What were the odds? She hadn't seen Tim O'Malley since they'd both graduated from U.C.

Davis. When she realized her mouth was hanging open, she shut it with a snap.

"Is that any way to greet an old friend?" One corner of his mouth turned down in an expression she remembered all too well.

"It's just… I mean I never expected…" She felt warmth rise from the open neck of her buff-colored uniform shirt. Heat suffused her face until she was certain every freckle was outlined in bright, living color.

"Hey, *mo ghrá*. I know we didn't split up under the best of circumstances…"

"No shit. And you can skip the *beloved* part." A familiar anger stirred, but she batted it aside.

"Moira, I'm sorry. I was sorry then, and I still am." He sounded so sincere, it tugged at her heartstrings. Part of her wanted to believe him, and part of her was afraid to.

"Grannie told me some of it—about the Arch Druid stuff. And you having to be celibate or something."

He creased his brow, the smile fading. "I'm glad she did. I was sworn to silence about Druid affairs." He cleared his throat. "In truth, I still am."

"What she told me didn't make it any easier. I tried to call you —a bunch of times."

"I know."

"Christ, Tim, it's been close to ten years."

He looked chagrined. "I suppose I know that too."

Her heart, already damaged from her sham of a marriage, squeezed painfully in her chest. She'd loved Tim once. And thought he loved her. They'd known one another since they were children growing up in the same sprawling Irish immigrant community.

"So what happened?" She eyed him, struggling for equanimity. "It's a long way from Druid to doctor. Or are you a nurse here?"

"Nope, I'm the doc. My training took up eight of the ten years since—"

The clinic door flew open. A harried-looking, overweight woman in white scrubs rolled her eyes. Her short brown hair stood up in spikes, and her muddy green gaze shot darts. "There you are. Dr. O'Malley, you have patients."

He waved her to silence. "Fine, Bridgette. I'll be in soon."

"But—"

He made shooing motions with both hands. "I said I'll be in soon."

Bridgette screwed her face into a disapproving frown. "Whatever," she snapped and banged the door shut.

Tim closed the few feet between them and laid his hands on Moira's shoulders. "Can I buy you dinner? Or maybe just a cup of coffee, if you're still mad at me and not willing to risk an entire meal."

"I'd like that, but I'm on my way to work. See…"

She took a big breath, and an annotated version of her story tumbled out. She mentioned her divorce and her lack of appetite, but skipped the low points about her marriage, figuring it wasn't really any of Tim's affair.

"Last time I wasn't very hungry was right after you and I broke up. I'd just started working for the Park Service. Unfortunately, John—that's my boss—has a long memory."

Tim listened until she was done talking, and then placed his stethoscope in his ears. "Take a deep breath." He moved the bell to several locations on her chest, and then had her turn around and positioned it on her back. "Your heart sounds healthy to me." He gripped her wrist, taking her pulse as he ran his gaze over her body in a familiar way that tightened her throat and made her belly clench with heat.

"What do you weigh?" He eyed her again. "Maybe one thirty?"

Moira nodded. No point in lying since he could drag her inside and plunk her on a scale. "One twenty-two."

"It could be worse. Have you had issues with anorexia since—" color blotched his cheeks "—well, since us?"

Moira shook her head. "I've maybe lost ten pounds this time round." She looked away. "The problem was a whole lot worse ten years ago."

"Moira." His voice cracked with emotion. "I'm sorry. Scarcely a day goes by—"

"Don't." The word tore out of her. "Just don't. I have to get to work. I'd never have stopped, except John insisted."

He stepped back a pace and nodded. "You should be fine, so long as you start eating again. What is it your boss needs?"

"A phone call, I think."

"Not a fitness for duty statement?"

She shook her head. "No. Nothing so formal."

Not yet anyway.

"Good, because that would require a real physical and some labs. Jot his number down for me." He pulled a small notebook out of a pocket and handed it to her, along with a pen.

As she gave it back, he caught her hand in his. "I've thought about you so many times over the years. I guess I always believed —" The color in his face deepened. "When will you be back through Bishop so we can talk? Or better yet, I've got a few days off after today's clinic. I could backpack with you. Meet you wherever you're—"

"Uh-uh." She shook her head. "It's against regulations to bring civilians, other than the trail crew, on Park Service work projects."

His blue eyes twinkled. She'd forgotten how intense they were, like a multihued ocean. "You told me you were heading over Baxter Pass."

"Yeah." She smiled back because she couldn't help herself. "So I did. I'm also telling you not to follow me."

He bent his head, and brushed his lips over hers. The kiss was so sweet and so fleeting, memories flooded her, and she pulled away, her heart doing flip-flops.

"If it won't be different this time, don't start." Her voice held a thin, strained note.

"Things will be different. I would've called you. Almost did a hundred times, but I felt so rotten about—"

"Dr. O'Malley." Bridgette clumped across the yard and grabbed his arm. "You have patients."

He shook her off. "When have you ever known me to leave before I've seen each and every one of them?"

"Never." She sounded sullen.

"And it won't happen today, either. Get back inside, and hold down the fort. If you could take vitals on everyone it would be a big help."

Bridgette's gaze moved from Tim to Moira. Pursing her lips in an unpleasant expression, she stalked back into the clinic.

Tim turned to Moira. "It was wonderful to see you again. Here." He scribbled something on one of the tiny sheets of notebook paper, tore it off, and handed it to her. "My cell. Call anytime."

"I just may take you up on that."

TIM WASN'T ready to go back into the clinic. His emotions were too close to the surface. He watched Moira's truck drive out of the parking lot heading south. The last time he'd seen her ate at him like an out-of-control cancer. They'd spent hours in his apartment arguing. Though he'd dissected it a hundred times, trying to figure out what he could've done differently, he'd never come up with anything useful.

He made a strong effort to stuff the memory into its subterranean hidey-hole, but it wouldn't cooperate. Since the professional objectivity he'd need to face a waiting room full of patients had just scattered like so much dust, he set off at a brisk pace intending to circle the block. He knew from experience that once that particular memory surfaced, he had to let it play itself out.

Bridgette and the clinic would just have to give him a few minutes more.

"I TELL you I'm done. Not just done. Fucking done."

Tears streamed down Moira's swollen, blotchy face.

"I've waited for you since I was sixteen years old, Tim O'Malley. That's six years in case you can't count. I didn't expect much back then, but we're nearly done with college. You won't do any more than kiss me. You won't live with me. You won't talk about getting married. Fuck! Why am I even bothering?"

She jumped to her feet and ran to a window, gripping the sill hard enough to whiten her knuckles.

He grabbed her arm. "I—I do love you, Moira. I've told you I want to save sex until after we're married."

"Well I don't. Besides, you never asked me to marry you."

"You're not being fair. There are things I can't tell you."

She whirled, her golden eyes on fire. "Fine. Keep your fucking secrets. And keep your fucking virginity. I talked with Father O'Brannigan—"

A chill marched down his spine. "You what?"

"You heard me. I had to talk to someone. Even he said it wouldn't be the end of the world if we had sex. He said God would forgive me so long as we got married. What's the problem? Do you like boys? Jesus, even the clerk at the corner store is hotter for me than you are."

"Mo ghrá—"

"Don't 'mo ghrá' me." She twisted out of his grasp. "Get out of here. Don't worry. I'll be gone by the time you get back."

"Moira—"

"For the love of Christ, just leave. If you ever loved me—" Her face crumpled and she sobbed helplessly, turning away from him.

Feeling like he was being torn in two, Tim stormed out of his apartment. The minute he got to the bottom of his steps, he began to run.

He loved Moira. Loved her with every fiber of his being. But he understood his duty to his Druid heritage too. Slated to be the next Arch Druid, he was forbidden physical congress with women. His magic needed to be honed to the highest possible level.

Sex would interfere.

Tim ran until sweat streamed down his sides, despite the chill of an unseasonably cool June in California. A full moon hung low, clinging to the horizon. It was a lover's moon. He cursed, drowning in irony. A lover's moon, but not for him.

He wasn't surprised when he ended up ten miles north of Davis at the Druids' priory. Despite it being three in the morning, he pulled the bell chain. Its somber chime matched his mood.

The intercom next to the carved oak door crackled. "What business brings you here?" It was a standard Druid greeting, though the speaker sounded half-asleep.

"I must see Liam. Now."

"Tim O'Malley. Is that you?"

Tim blew out a ragged breath. "Yes. Let me in, goddammit."

A tone sounded, and the door swung open soundlessly on well-oiled hinges. A man he didn't recognize hustled up the long hallway. "Master." He inclined his head.

"I'm no one's master. Go back to sleep. I know the way."

Liam McAllister's quarters were on the third floor of the rambling stone structure that had once been a Catholic monastery. Tim pounded up the stairs, his stomach so tight he wondered if he'd vomit. He'd just raised a fist to hammer on Liam's door when it opened, and the Arch Druid stood before him. If the older man had been asleep, it didn't show.

"Welcome, son." Liam held out his arms, but Tim shook his head. Without waiting for an invitation, he stomped into the spacious quarters lined with leaded glass windows on two walls. The moon mocked him, front and center in those windows.

"You have to release me from my vows."

Liam drew his thick eyebrows together. "You must know I cannot do that. You didn't take vows. You were born to your calling."

Tim spun to face the man who'd been like a father to him. Long, white hair framed his bearded face. Bright blue eyes radiated concern. The Arch Druid was tall—of a height with Tim—and wraith-thin. Black robes flowed around him.

"But it's not like I'm the Dalai Lama." He took a breath to steady himself. "You don't understand. I love Moira. It's tearing me up that I can't have her. Christ! I can't even tell her why I can't make love to her— or marry her."

Liam nodded slowly. He reached a kindly hand toward Tim. "Actually, you are a lot like the Dalai Lama. 'Tis the goddess who picks our progression. Would you care to sit, son? I believe a spot of spirits might calm you."

"Irish whiskey won't solve this."

Liam made a snorting noise. "A dram of good Irish whiskey will solve practically anything. Or at least soften it till it feels more manageable."

He pulled a decanter close and poured amber liquid into two cut-crystal shot glasses, pushing one toward Tim. "You will be able to wed once your training is complete, and you sit in my place."

Battling frustration, Tim drained his glass. The whiskey burned going down. It matched the fire in his soul.

He trained his gaze on Liam. "You don't understand. That may have worked hundreds of years ago. Not anymore. Look at you. Goddess willing, you'll live another twenty or thirty years. Maybe more. By then Moira will be long since married to another. Hell, she could be a grandmother." He banged a fist on one of the tables scattered about the room. A lamp rattled ominously, and he reached to steady it.

"Please," Tim begged. "At least let me tell her why I can't wed her."

Liam shook his head. "I cannot do that. The workings of our society have always been secret. 'Tis how we've shielded ourselves from the machinations of the Church."

"The Church isn't still out to get us. Not actively, anyway."

Liam turned on him, blue eyes ablaze. "Thinking like that will land you in trouble. Have you not followed their exorcisms? Or their dogma? And 'tis not just the Catholics I'm talking of here. What do you believe clerics think of those like us who call magic, engage in astral travel, and commune with gods, spirits, and the dead?"

Tim's shoulders sagged. He felt like a sail with the wind knocked out of it, attached to a ship that would never find port. "That we were evil."

Liam nodded. "Organized religion's raison d'être *is to rid the Earth of wickedness. Moira is Catholic. She goes to confession. I tell you, son, we cannot risk it. 'Tisn't been so very long since they killed one of us. Surely you recall Sean Newbry. 'Twas scarcely an accidental drowning. His astral self came to me whilst he was dying."*

"And?"

"The parish priest caught him in the midst of a blood offering ceremony, talking with Earth spirits. Sean was certain the cleric followed him since he'd taken care to go deep into the Sierra foothills."

Tim fought a sinking feeling. "You said drowning."

"Are you certain you want the grisly details?"

"Yes."

"Four priests waylaid him late one night, bound him, gagged him, tied a heavy weight about his waist—"

"Enough." Tim sat heavily. He dropped his head into his hands and remembered what Moira told him about talking with Father O'Brannigan. What a fucked up mess this had turned into. He still cared about Druidry, but did he care enough to give up Moira for the rest of his life?

"Tim?" Liam asked after a long silence.

He looked up. "No matter how I slice and dice this, I don't want to live without her. Hell, I don't know if I can."

"I understand." A considered intake of breath and Liam continued. "I gave you permission to attend medical school. That was a concession as I'd rather you were here by my side. Then you came up with that idea about a public health degree.

"Mayhap it would be best if you didn't see Moira—or even call her— at least for a while. Try to immerse yourself in your studies. Believe me, son, when I tell you the goddess takes care of her own."

A sob rose from the depths of his soul. Mortified, Tim tried to swallow the next one down. He stuffed a knuckle in his mouth and bit down hard.

"'Tis all right. Life does not give us easy choices." Liam got to his feed, walked around the table, and patted Tim's back. "There is no shame in tears."

FORCING himself to return to the present, Tim took a deep breath, and then another. He wasn't twenty-two anymore. He could stand up to Liam if it came down to it. He pulled open the side door to the clinic and went to the tiny staff room, where he knew he'd find the afternoon's schedule posted. Despite reliving painful memories, he felt more alive than he had in years.

The goddess had brought Moira back into his life. Things would be different this time. He'd see to it, even if it meant confronting Liam and walking away from Druidry forever.

CHAPTER 2

*M*oira didn't remember walking to her truck or getting into it. As she drove south on Highway 395, her mind was full of Tim. Since she had the time—no way she could leave until John authorized it—she pulled off on a side road just past Big Pine and went for a walk. The desert, with the White Mountains to the east and the Sierras to the west, was dotted with sagebrush. A few late-season wildflowers were still blooming. In an uncharacteristic burst of silliness, she picked an Indian paintbrush and stuck it behind one ear.

Her grandmother always told her Tim would come around, but Moira grew tired of waiting. He had secrets. Big ones. Every time he got that closed look that meant he wouldn't answer her, a part of her shriveled and died.

They'd started hanging around together even before high school. Things became more serious during college, but he hid behind a wall whenever she tried to get close. Slapped it up so fast, it made her head spin. And he'd never been willing to do more than kiss her, no matter how hot the two of them got.

She remembered the haunted look in his eyes when she asked about living together. Or getting married. Or having kids. They'd had a really ugly fight one night. She'd said a lot of things she wished she could take back. Even accused him of being a closet gay. College graduation was two weeks after that, and she hadn't seen Tim in the years since. She'd tried to call him, off and on, for a long time, but he never picked up the phone or responded to the messages she left. She'd even written him letters where she apologized for her harsh words. They never came back, but he never answered, either.

Moira stopped walking. Tears flooded her eyes. It was hard to believe the things he'd said earlier today. It sounded like he still cared about her, even after all this time.

"This could be a slippery slope," she murmured. "I have to be careful."

The breakup with Tim spawned her first bout of food issues. The psychologist had explained it to her, but understanding didn't make it go away. Her problems weren't about eating, but about control. Since Moira hadn't felt she had any control over her relationship with the man she loved, she'd exerted control over her body by refusing it needed fuel.

It took many months to crawl out of that hole, but she had. Starting the Park Service job helped a lot. Ranger jobs were hard to come by. She'd beaten out over a thousand other applicants who applied for two available positions.

Once she felt more competent, her appetite recovered, and she'd been fine.

Until Ryan.

Crap. There have been two men in my life. One wouldn't ever fuck me, and the other one didn't take the preacher seriously when he recited our vows.

Moira kicked at a rock.

Ryan Ravenshead.

What was it about shamanistic men that drew her like a moth to a flame? For Christ's sake, Tim was raised to be a Druid. And not just any old Druid. Grannie had whispered he was in line to be the next Arch Druid, master over the order. If he'd been a garden-variety Druid, she supposed they would've fucked like rabbits, gotten married, and raised a bunch of kids. All those Celtic holidays were full of sex. Like Beltane, for example. And Lithia, the high summer festival.

Then there was Ryan. He was supposed to take over as shaman for his tribe, except he was such a lazy sack of shit, his father passed him over in favor of another. That hadn't stopped him from practicing magic, though. Far from it. Except his spells developed a twisted edge once he knew he'd never be the tribe's magic man. Even without any supernatural powers of her own, she'd felt their perverted taint in the air. And she'd heard Singing Bear castigating his son on more than one occasion.

"Humph." She shrugged. "Don't suppose I'm going to solve that one today. Do we ever truly understand why we fall in love with anyone?"

A ground squirrel popped out of a hole, stared at her, and chittered madly.

She laughed. "If you know something about love, by all means spill it."

The furry creature dove back underground.

"Sorry. Didn't mean to scare you off." She squatted, looking down the hole. She'd never really loved Ryan, but she had been lonely. He'd filled a void and introduced her to sex. She'd been a virgin when she met him. If it wasn't for that, she might not have been sucked into his web so easily.

Straightening, Moira turned and walked back to her truck, surprised by how much better she felt. She pulled bread and cheese out of a cooler and made herself a sandwich to eat while she drove. It was easier to eat if she was doing something else. That way, food consumption was relegated to more of an automatic process, and her internal mavens didn't predict gloom and doom for every crumb she swallowed.

~

TIM SPUN the combination dial on the medication safe. That done, he walked out of the clinic and locked the dual dead bolts. With the recession in full swing, the clinic had been broken into regularly. The locks helped cut down on burglaries as did the alarm, which he set next.

He caught a glimpse of himself in the side mirror of his car, not surprised he was grinning like a fool.

It was pushing nine at night, but he wasn't the least bit tired. His good humor had been so apparent through his afternoon and early evening clinics that several regular patients commented on it. So much so, he wondered how he usually came across to them.

Not like a fellow in love, that's for sure.

Tim reached down to rearrange himself. His cock had been ecstatic to see Moira. It reminded him of that over and over by pushing uncomfortably against the front of his pants. Scrubs fit loosely and had a tie waist, but an erection was almost impossible to hide under them. He'd donned his long lab coat and buttoned it, once he understood he'd never be able to coax the damned thing into submission.

He even ducked into the men's room during the afternoon, hand curving around himself practically before he got the stall door closed. Shutting his eyes, he imagined Moira naked, her masses of golden hair falling in a tangle to her slender waist. Not that he'd ever seen her without clothes, but he could imagine what she looked like. His fantasy only got as far as closing his mouth around one of her nipples and feeling it harden under his tongue when his cock erupted in his hand. He'd thought that would hold him at least until the end of the day, but he'd started to swell again almost immediately.

Medical school and residency had been real libido killers. Whenever his long-denied sexuality threatened to surface, he volunteered for another twelve-hour shift that often morphed into twenty. He hadn't been able to control his dreams, though. In them, Moira kissed him, licked him, and fucked him with abandon.

Tim started his car and headed for the modest two-bedroom apartment he rented on the western edge of town. His clinic job in Bishop was courtesy of the United States Public Health Service, and they didn't pay much better than what he'd earned as a resident.

Until Moira's grandmother, a talented hedge witch, had died three years ago, he'd kept surreptitious tabs on Moira through the old woman, swearing her to secrecy. So he'd known about Moira's relationship with the Indian, but not her marriage. Tim clutched the steering wheel in a death grip. It had taken everything he had not to race to her side after she took up with another man and beg her to reconsider, but he wasn't any freer than he'd been the day she walked out on him.

Not really.

He nearly missed his driveway and hit the brake so hard his body lurched against the seatbelt.

"Damn it!"

He rubbed his collarbone, undid the belt, and got out of the car. He'd always been ambivalent about becoming Arch Druid. The dark side of magic revolted him. And the price of maintaining celibacy—and silence—until after his investiture was too high. It had cost him Moira.

Though Liam finally gave him permission to find a life outside Druidry, it came with conditions. Liam's heavy Irish accent still rang in Tim's mind. "I expect you to return to us, son, once you've had a taste of the other world. I'll not be dying till I see you seated in my place."

Tim trudged up the stairs and into his apartment. Despite everything, he still couldn't believe his luck running into Moira again.

I should have called—

Yes, but I didn't have anything better to offer her.

That's not what I told her today, he thought guiltily.

His cell phone rang. Tim looked at the caller ID and felt his eyes widen. It had been years since he'd seen that number, but he'd never forgotten it. Could the call be coincidence?

There are no coincidences, an inner voice reminded him. *Everything is driven by the gods.*

He tapped the answer icon with fingers that weren't all that steady. "Liam?"

A familiar chuckle warmed him. "So you remember an old man, do you?"

"Of course. When I saw the number, I was afraid—"

"Someone was calling to tell you I'd passed beyond the veil. Not quite yet, son."

"Thank the goddess. I—"

"Be quiet and listen. I told you I would let you return in your own time. That promise still holds, but I have had a sending. It came on All Hallows' when the wards betwixt the worlds are thin. You are in danger. That woman you used to love is mixed up in this somehow."

An iron bar of tension settled between Tim's shoulder blades.

No, not coincidence at all.

He tried for decorum, but couldn't stop the words from rushing out. "I saw Moira today for the first time in years. Please, Liam. I must be free to tell her what I am, and I must be free to wed her if she'll have me. I couldn't stand it if she walked out on me again."

Tim heard a weary intake of air. "We have been over this ground before. You'll recall that I told you—"

"I recall exactly what you told me. Liam, you need to hear me out. I love you like a father, but if I have to sever my ties with you and Druidry to have Moira in my life, that's what I'll do."

Tim's stomach tightened. This was it. The confrontation he'd been avoiding for years. He sucked in a jagged breath. The inside of his lungs felt raw, as if he'd inhaled ground glass. "I'm scarcely a youngster anymore. By the time you were my age, you had four children. Or was it five?"

"Aye, but I was Arch Druid."

"Not the point."

"You would turn your back on your heritage?"

Well, would I?

Moira flickered before his eyes. His golden girl, all hair and eyes and flashing temper. His ambivalence toward the destructive side of Druid magic rose to taunt him. He'd have to master it to sit in the Arch Druid's chair.

Still, it was hard to just say *yes* and be done with it. If he were brutally honest with himself, he always thought he'd move into Liam's role—just a whole lot later down the line—and with Moira by his side. He bit hard on his lower lip.

Why was Liam forcing his hand?

No. I'm forcing his.

"Maybe there's some middle ground," he began cautiously. "If I could tell her the truth and be free to...to do more than kiss her—"

After a silence that was so long Tim looked at the display to see if they were still connected, Liam said, "If you bed her, you will be as good as wed. It will link your souls through all lifetimes. 'Tis part of the Arch Druid's legacy."

Yes, I know.

Tim clutched his iPhone so hard, the metal dug into his hand. "Did you just give me permission—?"

"Not exactly."

"What then?" Tim blew out a breath he didn't know he'd been holding. "You're squeezing the life out of me, Liam. I don't want to walk away from you, but I will if I have to. There's a part of me that owes you loyalty and is willing to take on the burden of being Arch Druid. But a bigger part wants Moira and a normal life."

"I was afraid of that." Another pause. The air in the room

warmed. Tim sensed the Arch Druid's presence. The next words sounded in his mind.

"I have prayed and discussed this with our Council and the goddess, Gaia. I had planned to get hold of you. The sending hastened my time line."

"You're here, aren't you?"

A chuckle. *"If my astral self meets the definition of here."*

Tim clicked the phone off and set it down. He didn't need it anymore. "Tell me the outcome of those discussions." He swallowed, girding himself for the worst. If he had to strip-mine something from his life, it would be Druidry, not Moira.

"Mayhap if you had a wife, 'twould hurry you along getting back to your true calling."

Tim wasn't certain he'd heard right. "I think you just gave me permission to break my celibacy and follow my heart."

"I did."

His eyes stung. He squeezed them shut. This was a time for joy, not tears. "How much can I tell Moira?"

"Only enough so she'll forgive you."

"What about my magic?"

"You are considerably older now. 'Tis a gamble, but not so great a one as it would have been ten years ago. We shall hope for the best."

The warmth in the room surrounded Tim. It felt a lot like a hug. His face split in a broad grin. "Thank you, Liam. If you were truly here, I'd hug you back."

"What's that American term?" The Arch Druid laughed, the sound rich and warm. *"I'll take a rain check on that, son."*

"Sure thing. Uh, Liam, one last thing. I think my true calling is medicine."

Liam chuckled again. *"You might be surprised. There is a reason the goddess sent me that vision. Take care of yourself."* The warmth of his sending winked out.

Tim danced a jig around his living room, then raced to the

bedroom, dragged out his backpack, and started tossing things into it.

On his umpteenth trip to the closet, something caught his eye, and he closed his hand around a hand-hewn staff of rowan wood. Liam had told him it was carved out of downed branches from the One Tree. Before Tim went on hiatus from the order, he'd used the staff to call and focus his magic. It had been lying in the back of one closet or another for a very long time.

The wood warmed instantly under his touch. "Okay." Tim placed the staff on his bed next to his pack. "You're in. We leave at first light. You can masquerade as a walking stick."

He could've sworn he heard the wood chortle deep in his mind.

CHAPTER 3

*M*oira moved briskly up the rocky trail. She'd slept —or tried to—in the back of her car at the trailhead and dreamed about both Tim and Ryan. Morning arrived far too soon. One advantage of getting going, though, was that the specter of Ryan's infidelity retreated when she was on the move.

Sleep's overrated, she thought wryly, tugging at the waist belt of her regulation-issue backpack to tighten it. She sighed as some of the weight moved off her shoulders. Despite employing women rangers for better than fifty years, Park Service gear was still designed for men. Moira blessed her broad-shouldered, slim-hipped build. If she'd had a girlier figure, she'd have been out of luck—and miserable.

She scanned the familiar Sierra backcountry in an effort to move beyond the muddle her mind had become. She was close to timberline, the few trees twisted and stunted by their fight to survive at altitude. Open, shale-covered terrain spread around her. She named off the surrounding peaks in her mind, all of which she'd climbed at one point or another.

It was early November, and the wind at nearly ten thousand feet held a definite bite. She had cold weather gear in her pack, but she hoped it wouldn't snow. Fresh snow would fill in the holes between good-sized talus blocks littering the mountains, making them impossible to see. A turned ankle was a reality she couldn't afford right now with John breathing down her neck. It would be embarrassing—never mind a career-killer—to use her sat phone to call for rescue because of a stupid mistake. The Park Service rewarded self-sufficiency in its rangers.

Moira grimaced, imagining the humiliation of trying to explain what should've been an avoidable injury.

Stop it. Hasn't happened. The last thing I need right now is to borrow trouble.

She peered at lenticular clouds floating high above her head, at the mercy of the jet stream. They were always harbingers of bad weather.

A particularly vicious gust of wind attacked her braid. Long, blonde hair plastered her face, and she stopped to shove the errant strands out of the way. Spying a house-sized boulder, she sheltered on the lee side, shucked her pack, and hunkered behind the rock to gather her hair together. Once she wasn't moving, Ryan's face rose to mock her. Unfortunately, so did the rest of him, all naked six foot four inches with his cock buried in some nameless redhead he'd shoved up against their living room wall.

"Not *my* living room anymore," she ground out between gritted teeth. Moira willed her mind to stop playing the fucking tape loop, goddammit, but it wouldn't cooperate. Ryan's chiseled Native American features, dark braids, and intense dark eyes stared at her. Shock etched into his face once he realized she'd come home early.

And caught him red-handed. Or red-dicked as the case may be.

Rage, a constant companion ever since *the incident*, tightened her guts into a painful knot. Bile rose, burning the back of her throat. Moira hoped her lawyer was taking care of all the particulars. She'd given him a list of everything she wanted, aside from the clothes and personal effects she'd grabbed after sending the redhead packing. She hadn't been back to her house in the weeks since *it* had happened. And she didn't intend to go there ever again. She'd moved into the barracks at Park Headquarters. It wasn't bad, actually. She'd lived there before she started hanging around with Ryan.

Nope, she just wanted her things and her more than half. Let the bastard refinance if he had to. Most of the down payment on their house had come from her.

California's a community property state, one of her internal mavens reminded her.

Community property or not, there was no way she was sharing any of her federal retirement. She'd been quite clear with the attorney on that point. After all, she and Ryan had only been married for a few months. Hopefully the brief time they'd lived together before that wouldn't work against her in court.

Her mind drifted to Tim. Now he was a much more pleasant topic to contemplate…

Whoa there, sweetie. Rein it in. I don't know enough to toss my eggs into that basket. Not yet, anyway.

Cold seeped into her back from the rock she rested against. Moira flexed her fingers. They were cold too. She shook her head, hard. "I know better," she muttered as she shoved to her feet so she could get moving again. It was too cold to stay put for long, unless she layered up on clothing.

The trail was deserted as she chugged toward Baxter Pass. Odd that she hadn't seen any other backpackers. It was late in the season, but still…

Her orders to oversee the trail crew had finally come through in an e-mail from John early that morning. She'd clicked all the appropriate boxes, added her electronic signature, and sent it back to him.

She would've been on the move well before dawn since she was awake, but in light of his insistence about the doctor, she waited for official authorization. A ten-year veteran of the Park Service, she had enough seniority to stay in the backcountry if she chose—rather than being chained to a desk—but not quite enough to pick her assignments. She didn't want to sully her track record by being insubordinate.

She thought about the roster tucked in her pack. She knew some of the crew, but about half of them were fresh recruits. Trail crews were always a mixed bag. Some were serious, Sierra Club types who were hard-core environmentalists. Some hated people, viewing the backcountry as a refuge, and then there were the ubiquitous druggies. They brought their own stash—never mind it was against Park Service regulations. She always worried one of the latter bunch would have a major meltdown on some hallucinogen and start killing people.

Moira shivered. Reaching up, she zipped her buff-colored fuzzy jacket all the way to her chin.

Something wet landed on her face. A snowflake. The sky looked threatening enough to really dump. For a minute, she considered stopping again to dig out her weatherproof parka and pants and then decided against it. Speed was her friend. She needed to crest the pass before the weather turned really rotten. At twelve thousand feet, Baxter Pass was a low point on a long, exposed ridge. Not a good place to be caught in the middle of a storm. Moira laid into her afterburners. Even uphill, carrying a fifty-pound pack, her long legs could churn out better than three miles an hour.

An hour passed. Then part of another.

Only two more sets of switchbacks, and I'll have it.

Her breath came fast in her throat. Thin, cold air burned her lungs, but she was used to it. A side benefit of pushing herself hard was it thrust Ryan and his betrayal out of her mind. Of course, he had lots of excuses. She was never home, and he had *needs*. She snorted derisively. Well, she had needs too, but you didn't find her spread-eagled across her desk for anything with a dick between his legs.

She wasn't exactly sure when she'd fallen out of love with Ryan, but it hadn't been all that long after the wedding. She winced as the truth struck home. Sex was always great, but in every other respect he was a self-centered boor who blamed everyone in the world for his own shortcomings—like his inability to hold a job, for one.

Her mind strayed to his incredible body. Broad shoulders, well-defined muscles, dazzling abs, and a high, tight ass. Mildly disgusted with herself, she realized she'd put up with a lot to maintain her connection to his sculpted body and knowing fingers, mouth, and cock. They'd had sex almost every day—sometimes twice, if she wasn't working—and she missed the feel of a man's body stretched against her. Her nipples pebbled into hard points, rubbing against her sports bra. When she realized her pace had slowed, Moira forced herself to think about something else.

Ryan was bad for her. She'd known it for a long time, and getting away from him was the best thing that could've happened to her. In retrospect that nameless redhead had done her an enormous favor.

Yeah, well if I ever run into her again, I'll be sure to let her know. Moira laughed wryly.

A fine mist, swirling with snowflakes, had all but obscured the last thousand vertical feet of trail, and she couldn't see much of anything. No point in getting careless—and maybe walking off the trail's steep edge—just because she was distracted by man problems. Moira shoved the last vestiges of Ryan out of her mind, hoping he'd stay gone this time.

She was grateful she'd been over this pass before. It could be confusing near the top where the trail angled right, just before curving down to the alpine basin holding Baxter Lakes. She raised her hands to her face and blew on her fingers. Gloves would've been nice, but she was only about an hour from her destination; she didn't want to take the time to dig through her pack for them. As long as she kept moving, there was no danger of frostbite or freezing to death.

Whooshing, even louder than the incessant howl of the wind, dragged her gaze upward. A flock of ravens flew overhead, stark against the white mist. She tried to remember what she knew about avian migration patterns. Usually, by this time, most birds had left the high country since they needed trees to survive the cold months.

Wonder what they're doing here?

She pushed a vague sense of unease aside and plunged down the trail, grateful to have the pass behind her. A thin coating of snow crunched under her heavy boots. After about half a mile, the fog thinned. It was barely snowing anymore, and what had fallen was melting. Her stomach growled. She glanced at her watch. Nearly eight hours had passed since she'd eaten.

Uh-oh. Not good.

She glanced at the lakes below and thought she could see the trail crew's camp, but wasn't certain. It could just as easily be a group of large white boulders.

Her stomach rumbled again, complaining about its empty status, particularly since she'd just covered over twelve miles and climbed six thousand feet.

Okay, okay, I'll stop, she reassured it, grateful it was sending hunger signals again.

She pulled her parka out of her pack and arranged it on a flat rock to shield her pants from moisture. Balancing the pack against her legs, she sat and dredged through it for the clear plastic canister with her food. As she ate salami, cheese sticks, and crackers washed down with Gatorade, she smiled to herself.

Mountaineering food was a long way from haute cuisine, but it did the job.

A squawk from behind startled her. Moira whipped her head around to look, and her mouth fell open. At least a dozen ravens stood on the trail, paired off in some sort of weird formation. She thought about the bunch she'd seen in the sky and wondered if these could possibly be the same ones. Her heart sped up, hammering against her chest. Mouth suddenly dry, she dropped her half-eaten lunch back into the canister and spun the lid shut.

One of them—the leader?—cawed at her.

This can't be happening.

Oh yes it can, another inner voice sneered. *Weren't ravens Ryan's totem animal?*

It felt as if someone jammed a knife into her guts and twisted it. Cold flooded her, followed by prickles of unnatural heat. Ravens *were* Ryan's totem. Just like they'd been his father's and grandfather's before him. She'd seen Singing Bear playing a Native flute and leading flocks of ravens, like some sort of Pied Piper of Hamelin.

Christ, had Ryan pulled some Native American shaman trick and sent the birds to harass her for leaving him?

She worked on modulating her breathing. Animals could smell fear. She wasn't certain if that applied to birds, but it was best to be on the safe side. Taking care to move slowly so they didn't mob her and try to peck out her eyes or something, she got to her feet and stuffed everything into her pack.

As soon as Ryan's possible link to the birds hit home, she'd started to shiver uncontrollably. Even her teeth were chattering. She fished gloves and a hat out of her pack and put them on.

The birds didn't move. For a moment, she decided she had to be wrong about Ryan. It seemed way too far-fetched. She wondered if the ravens might have some type of bird flu or, God forbid, rabies.

Do birds even get rabies?

She racked her mind, willing a return of rational thought. There had to be a logical explanation for the weirdest avian behavior she'd even seen. It was like they were part of a hive mind, acting as a unit. Birds didn't do that. Insects did. Setting her jaw in a firm line, Moira swung her pack onto her back. Almost as if they knew what she was up to, the ravens half hopped and half flew around her, blocking the trail below. Another mournful caw split the still air.

She heard something else: the sound of boots coming down from the pass. At least two people—maybe more. Aw shit! Was it Ryan?

Can't be. He hates the backcountry. My imagination truly is working overtime.

She watched the birds. Their beady eyes weren't looking at her anymore, but above her. It made sense. They could hear the footsteps too. In a whoosh of black feathers, they took to the air and surrounded her. Wings scraped against her face. Something sharp dug into her cheek. Another beak pecked just above one eye.

Always sensitive to animals and their right to the wilderness, Moira tried to restrain herself, but couldn't. She batted at the ravens with both hands, intent on protecting her head and face.

"Go away. Leave me alone," she screamed.

Twirling away from the mass of feathers, she pulled her gun from its holster and fired blindly into the air, hoping to intimidate them.

The footsteps she'd heard broke into a run. "Moira. Is that you?" a man shouted. "Are you all right?"

Tim.

The person heading right for her was Tim.

The ravens cartwheeled away from her, formed a pattern, and headed for the valley. Moira sucked air like a bellows. Adrenaline made her feel sick and light-headed. She swiped at her face, not surprised when her fingers came away bloody.

"Moira?" Tim's cries had taken on a frantic quality, almost as if he were expecting to burst around a switchback and fall over her dead body—or get shot.

"Fine," she called shakily. "I'm fine." She squared her shoulders and settled her gun on her hip. It wasn't entirely comfortable with the pack's waistband buckled over the upper part of its holster.

Ambivalence roiled through her. She wanted to see Tim. But she was angry he hadn't paid any attention when she said not to follow her.

She stared after the flock of birds. They'd all but disappeared in clouds floating above Baxter Lakes. "I'd feel better if they flew the other way," she muttered, turning to face the sound of rock fall as Tim dislodged chunks of granite in his haste.

"No need to break your neck," she called, cupping her hands around her mouth. "I really am okay."

"But you were screaming. I heard you. And a gunshot!" He pelted around a switchback, still running hard right at her. White-blond hair streamed behind him, and his blue eyes were filled with concern—and worry.

She took in his khaki pants, blue-and-green patterned fuzzy jacket, and lightweight leather boots popular with fast packers. Groaning inwardly at how inadequate his clothing was, she glanced at his backpack. It was one of those barely there things that didn't hold much. They worked fine so long as the weather didn't turn. If it did, the lack of more substantial equipment and warm clothing could be deadly.

Breathing hard, he threw his arms around her and pulled her close, his body vibrating with alarm.

"You need to put on more clothes." She hugged him back before stepping away.

"What the hell were you screaming about?" He looked closely at her. "Christ! What happened to your face? Who'd you shoot at? I heard the gun." He peered at her wounds. "That one might need a stitch."

"Maybe not. The cold should close it up." It was easier to talk about her injuries than what happened.

"Once we get to where your trail crew is, I at least want to rinse those places with antiseptic."

Moira blew out a breath, not sure what to say next. Before the conversation turned to her wounds, he'd asked questions she didn't want to answer. She didn't see how she could possibly tell him that her husband might've sent a raven hit squad to hassle her. It sounded so fantastic, Tim might pull some doctor thing and send her off to the loony bin. After all, he had her boss's phone number.

She glanced behind him. Something didn't compute. "Who were you traveling with?"

"Huh?"

"I heard more than one of you coming down the trail."

Tim looked genuinely confused. "Nope. Just me. You're the first person I've seen since I left the trailhead."

Okay, then...

Had she been so overwrought from the ravens, she imagined more than one set of footsteps? To avoid wandering still farther down the metaphorical slope of her sanity, Moira edged toward more neutral territory. "Guess you decided to follow me anyway."

He offered her a crooked smile. "Yup. Didn't want to let opportunity escape me twice. Besides, I just got great news. I wanted to find you so I could share it."

A warm glow started deep inside, but she forced herself to refocus. "Did you bring warmer stuff than what you have on?"

He looked sheepish. "Uh-uh. Didn't think it would be this cold. The forecast was for clear weather. And the pass took longer than I thought it would."

"It's six thousand feet of climbing."

He shrugged. "I've run Western States and a few Iron Mans. I'm used to elevation gain. When my pack is light, I can cover five or six miles an hour—sometimes more. It's how I caught up with you. By moving faster."

Moira didn't bother to tell him a sponsored ultrarace with rest stations every few miles and volunteers pacing the runners, bore very little resemblance to solo backcountry travel. Speed wasn't nearly as critical in the wilderness as having enough equipment to see you through an emergency.

"What kind of sleeping bag do you have in there?" She pointed to his small backpack.

Color stained his tanned face. "Um, just a bivy sack and my down jacket and pants." He reached for her. "I thought, er hoped, we could keep each other warm."

She shook her head and crooked a finger at him. "Come on. We can talk about that later. Not much privacy in a trail crew camp for more than talking, though. We need to get moving. It's too cold to stand around chewing the fat."

A smile transformed his face into something classically handsome. Clean lines of cheek and jaw blended into one another. "I'd follow you anywhere, *mo ghrá*. Lead on."

Moira scampered down the trail, elated Tim cared enough to come after her. But she felt wary too. If Ryan truly had sent the birds, Tim's presence would only make things worse. The sky, which had backed off momentarily, was getting darker again, heavy clouds blotting out what was left of light from the day.

She was shocked by how little Tim had brought with him. If the weather turned truly hideous, his best bet would be to retrace his steps and retreat over Baxter. But that option was looking less likely by the moment.

He made a choice without consulting me, and now I'm responsible for him and me both.

Her earlier delight faded. Another involuntary shiver ripped through her. She had a feeling—irrational though it might be— that the birds would be waiting for her near the lakes. What would she do then?

Unfortunately, no answers came.

"Somehow I thought you'd be happier to see me."

Moira turned to glance at Tim, keeping pace right behind her. "Just thinking. Sorry."

"Are you angry because I came after you told me not to?"

"Maybe, a little. There's a trail crew down below that I'm supervising. This isn't like a regular backpacking trip where we'd have time to reconnect."

"Isn't it a little late in the year for trail maintenance?" He sounded mildly curious.

"Yeah, but we didn't get funding approved for deadfall removal until a couple of weeks ago." She shrugged. "Your government at its finest."

He laughed. "You're telling me! I work for them too. Public Health Service."

"I wondered how you ended up at the clinic in Bishop." Moira retreated behind small talk. It beat perseverating about Ryan and his pet birds.

"It was the only way I could afford medical school."

"Government service to pay off your student loans?" She turned to look at him.

He nodded. Laugh lines crinkled in the corners of his eyes when he smiled, and he had a deep cleft in his chin.

Moira studied his walking stick. "That's a beautiful staff. Maybe if there's time later, I could take a closer look at the carving."

"Sure. It was a gift from Liam."

"The Druid, Liam?"

He quirked a brow at her. "Did you ever meet him?"

She shook her head. "I don't think so. Grannie told me about him. To listen to her talk, I think she was half in love with him."

Tim laughed. "She might have been. He was quite the Lothario."

A snowflake hit her cheek, followed by another. The wind howled dolefully.

"Boy, that came up fast. Wasn't so bad when I was going uphill, but now I'm cold." Tim's breath whistled through his teeth. He zipped his inadequate jacket all the way closed and started jogging in place.

Moira clicked through a few buttons on her altimeter watch and groaned. The barometer was definitely falling, which probably meant they were in for it—at least for the next few hours. She dove in without preamble. "We have to step up the pace. I'd send you back over the pass, but you don't have enough clothes. Hopefully there are some at camp that will fit you. How cold did you think it would be anyway?"

"Thirty?"

"You wish." She spun to face him. "If you're lucky, it will bottom out at ten degrees. And that's only if it snows. If it clears, zero is a distinct possibility."

"Oh." He sounded subdued.

Since he was a doctor, she could spare them both the lecture about how fast hypothermia could kill.

"Don't you think you're being a bit draconian?" His smile faltered once the words were out.

"No. Following protocols and planning ahead are what's kept me alive in the backcountry all these years."

"What are you suggesting?"

"That you stay in one of the trail crew's tents until tomorrow. If the weather clears, you should go back over Baxter and let me do my job here."

And if it keeps snowing, we'll be in a world of hurt.

His set his jaw in a stubborn line. "Goddammit, Moira. You sound like my mother. Not that it's necessarily a bad thing—"

"I've been part of too many search and rescue missions with bad outcomes. Look, Tim, if this storm keeps rolling, the only way out of here will be by chopper, either directly, or by a bird dropping skis or snowshoes for us. It's not June. We're headed into winter."

As if to underscore her words, it began snowing in earnest while they talked.

He twisted his head from side to side, looking around him. Then he yanked his hood over his head. "Gee, you have a direct pipeline to the weather gods or something?"

"You never know, I just might. We need to hurry. It's coming down pretty fast. On second thought," she unbuckled her pack, dropped it and pulled her weatherproof parka and pants out, sliding into them, "no point in getting soaked." She yanked the hood over her head and zipped the garment—Park Service brown, just like all her gear—all the way up.

He stood watching her. "I'm sorry."

"Huh?"

"All I could think about was surprising you and getting to explain all the things I never could before. I didn't plan this very well."

A place deep in her damaged heart started to melt. "It's not that I don't appreciate seeing you, but this might've been easier if we weren't staring down the maw of what's starting to look like a survival marathon."

"Like you said, we need to get moving."

Moira looked at him incredulously. "Oh brother, don't tell me you don't have storm gear."

"Uh, no. Didn't think I'd need it." He cleared his throat, sounding uncomfortable. "Even I know my down garments will become less than worthless if they get wet."

"Crap. Here." She dug back in her pack and handed him a stretchy top. "At least put this on under your jacket. It's not much, but it's one more layer." She waited for him before hefting her pack and taking off down the trail at a trot. Worry for Tim's safety ate at her. "Keep up," she called over one shoulder. Moving's a good hedge against the cold. The trail's not obvious once we hit the lake basin."

"Yes, Mother."

"You need a mother," she shot back, "if you come into the mountains unprepared."

She led the way around the lakes to where she was sure she'd find the collection of mules and tents the trail crew used. She had to correct her course a couple of times. It was snowing even harder than she anticipated, obscuring her vision. Finally, she pulled her GPS out of its case on her gun belt and started clicking keys.

"What are you doing?" Tim sounded as if he were trying to keep his teeth from chattering.

"Putting in the coordinates for the camp."

"Thank God you have them." He wrapped his arms around himself, rubbing his hands up and down his arms.

"Don't you have gloves?"

"Just liners. They'd soak through pretty fast."

Moira peered closely at him. His face had white patches that could be the beginnings of frostbite. His fingers didn't look any better. "Put your hands in your jacket pockets and follow me. It's only another half mile." She tried to infuse a confidence she wasn't feeling into her voice. It was conceivable winter could show up right now and not leave until the following May. She'd seen autumns like that in the high country. She hoped some of the crew had extra clothes for Tim. And a warm sleeping bag. The temperature had already dropped into the mid-twenties. Even if she shared her sleeping bag, she didn't think his bivy sack, down jacket, and pants were going to cut it.

She heard mules bray before she actually saw the camp. Moira wasn't certain, but she thought she heard Tim mutter something about *stupid* and *fucking freezing to death*. Even underdressed to face the weather, there was something strikingly elegant about him. And he smelled wonderful. She'd never forgotten that scent.

Something musky and spicy clung to him. Most people just smelled like sweat after a few hours on the trail.

A bird cawed somewhere in the clouds, and her heart sank. The birds. The goddamned, fucking birds. She'd all but forgotten about them.

Great. It's snowing to beat hell. Marauding birds are out to get me. Tim's looking hypothermic. What the fuck else could possibly go wrong?

CHAPTER 4

"Hey," a voice called out. "That you, Ma?"

"Yeah, so you'd better shape up. Hide the booze and dope. Tell the girls to put their clothes back on." Moira laughed hollowly. She was glad to see the collection of cabin tents, pitched in a careful row. The wind had picked up, blasting at a good clip. Between that and the snow, visibility was less than twenty feet. Without her GPS, she wasn't at all certain she'd have found the camp.

"Guess I'm not the only one who tagged you that way," Tim joked. His voice sounded thin, like he was nearly at the end of his reserves. Cold could do that to a person. It sapped everything out of you shockingly fast.

She reached for his arm and dragged him into one of the canvas tents. Smaller versions of the ones Yosemite used for their high country camps, they were substantial: ten by fifteen feet and tall enough to stand in at the center. Extremely heavy-duty, they were plumbed for woodstoves, but she was nearly certain the crew hadn't packed any stoves in on the mules. No one expected this freak storm.

"Who all's here?" She took off her pack and propped it in a

corner, pulling her headlamp out. It was dim inside the tent, and she couldn't see very well. It was also a whole lot warmer out of the wind.

"Mitch and me."

"That you, Jake?" she asked, adjusting her light. "Oh, never mind. I can see now."

She focused the beam on a barrel-chested, dark-haired man with a full beard sitting on a three-legged stool. Dressed in his usual grease-stained down and Gore-Tex, he looked as rumpled as ever. She'd worked with him several times before. Jake liked his dope, but he was also a dependable operative—at least most of the time.

"Thought you'd recognize my voice." Hamming it up, Jake sounded wounded. "After everything we've shared—"

"Can it," she said brusquely, unsure if Tim would realize Jake was joking. "Who else?"

"We're the only ones here. Everyone else is spread between camp and the Muir Trail. Tons of deadfall there. Trail's completely blocked a bunch of places. They were going to start with the closest snarl. It's only a couple miles away."

A chilly tongue of fear bit deep. The crew should've aborted operations when the weather turned. If they had, they'd be getting back right about now. "When did they leave?"

Jake looked at his watch and mumbled. "About nine."

"How come you and Mitch didn't get on the mules and go round them up when you saw the barometer was dropping? Or did you even bother to check it?" Irritation made it hard to keep her voice cordial.

"You know the answer to that."

She blew out an impatient breath. "Yeah. You wanted to save your own sorry hide."

"I could help if there are injured," Tim said through chattering teeth.

Shit. Nearly forgot he needs more clothes.

"You won't be able to do anything until you get warm. Jake, could you round up something to fit Tim?"

"Where'd you find him?" Something ran beneath Jake's words—maybe disapproval she'd brought an outsider into the fold.

"On the trail. He doesn't have enough with him. You be nice. He's an old friend of mine. And he's a doctor. The way things are looking, we might need one."

"Oh." Jake shuffled to his feet and headed for the door. "Be right back. I think Brandon has spare clothes. Kid brought enough to practically sink the mule. Should be about the right size too."

"How many people are out in the storm?" Tim asked. Reflected in the light from her headlamp, his expression was serious—and worried.

"Seven men and two women." Moira reached for her pack, unzipped a compartment and pulled out the roster. "Crap. I suppose this means I have to go look for them."

"Not by yourself you aren't."

She bristled, and then bit down on a sharp retort. "I hate to admit it, but you're right. No point in getting lost myself. The mules are sure-footed, but I shouldn't risk any more of them, either."

Jake scuttled back through the door with a sleepy-looking Mitch right behind him. Mitch, all emaciated six feet of him, reeked of marijuana.

Something in Moira snapped. She stomped up to him. "No drugs. What part of that don't you get? And certainly not during the day when you're supposed to be working."

"What makes you think—?"

"I'm your superior here. And the law. Don't insult both of us by lying to me. Go get the dope. All of it. And bring it here."

"Oh." A sly look lit his close-set green eyes. He shoved a shock of red hair out of his face. "Wanting a hit yourself are you?"

"Just go get it. And I swear, Mitchell, if you don't bring every bit of it to me, I'll see you go to jail for violating federal law and the Drug Free Workplace Act."

Mitch looked like he wanted to say something, but he clapped his jaws shut, turned, and left.

She tugged the armload of clothing out of Jake's hands and gave it to Tim. "Go put more clothes on."

He faded into the shadows toward the back of the tent without protest. She could only imagine how chilled he must be.

"Any extra sleeping bags?" she asked Jake.

He shook his head. "Nope. We were one short as it was. Not sure how that happened. Maybe it fell out of one of the mule packs on the way in."

"Are there woodstoves for any of the tents?"

Jake shook his head again.

"Okay." She pinched the bridge of her nose between thumb and forefinger, trying to decide the best course of action. "There are eleven of you and five or six tents, so you've been sleeping two together?"

"Basically."

She knew what that meant. The dopers were all in one tent. "These tents will sleep ten. We'll put six in one and seven in another. We need warmth."

"What if the others don't come back?"

"Then whoever's left will bunk down in here." She thought about her satellite phone and wondered if she should call in an emergency. Moira looked at her watch. Three o'clock. "If the storm's still kicking ass an hour from now and the rest of the crew's not back, I'll call headquarters."

Tim came forward bundled in a puffy jacket, wool hat, and thick overpants. Gloves covered his hands. Some of the color had come back into his face. He sank into one of the camp chairs and motioned toward an iso-butane cook stove. "Mind if I heat some water?"

"Probably a good idea." She was ashamed she hadn't thought of it first. Warm clothes and hot liquids were the first line of defense against cold.

"Jake, go see what happened to Mitch. I'll make hot water for tea and coffee."

"Heh. Didn't think he'd come back." Jake smirked.

"What did you think he'd do?" Alarmed, she stared at Jake's bearded face.

"Oh, probably take one of the mules and head up and over Baxter. With his stash."

"What? He can't do that. Those mules are federal property. And the storm could kill both of them." She sprang for the tent door, but Jake beat her to it.

"You stay here. I'll go look. No point both of us getting lost out there."

Tim had located the gallon water jugs and a pot. The water he'd put on the stove was already steaming. "There enough air in here to support this?" He pointed at the iso-butane burner.

"Probably not. Stove vent hole's not big enough even if it were open. Here." She tacked the tent's door open on a hook.

"That water's all going to freeze."

"True, but we can melt snow."

A raven flew into the tent, followed by another. Tim jumped to his feet, ducking as one flew right at him, latched its talons into his shoulder, and started pecking at his head. Moira grabbed the closest thing she could find. She swung the shovel hard at the bird and felt gratified when it connected. A mass of black feathers fell to the tent floor where the raven twitched spasmodically.

"What the fuck?" Tim sputtered.

What the fuck, indeed. I thought they wanted me.

Breath rattled in her throat. Fear threatened to paralyze her. She remembered how insanely jealous Ryan could be, growling at any man who so much as told her good morning.

"Oomph!" Tim shook himself from stem to stern. "Glad you got the bird, but you nearly took my head out along with it."

"Sorry if I scared you. Remember? I used to play semipro softball. You weren't in any danger."

Tim rolled his eyes. "I'd actually forgotten that little tidbit. Did you kill it?"

"Don't know. Probably not, since it's moving," she answered, still brandishing the shovel. The other raven kept its distance.

Tim stared at her through narrowed eyes. "That's what you were yelling about up on the trail. Those wounds on your face look like beak marks. And that's what you used your gun for. You shot at them so they'd leave you alone."

"Smart man." She winced at the rancor in her tone. "Shit. I am so sorry I got you into this. Look, I'll explain later, but we've got to shoo that other bird out of here." She took off for the back of the tent, using her arms and the shovel to herd the bird forward.

"Moira, he'll leave on his own." Tim's voice was gentle, as if he thought she'd lost her mind. He picked up the still-twitching raven and chucked it out the door.

"Normal birds would," she said through gritted teeth. "But these aren't normal. Now help me before any more get in here."

As if responding to an invitation, two more flew inside.

"Grab your stuff," she panted. Ice chips skittered down her spine.

"What? Why?"

"We've got to go to one of the other tents. We'll never get them out of here."

"That's ridiculous. Of course we will."

For just a moment, she thought he was going to refuse. She didn't know what she'd do then, but Tim got his pack and the rest of the small pile of clothes Jake had brought for him. He tucked his staff under one arm and turned off the stove. Clapping a lid on the hot water, he said, "Okay. Ready."

She thought about shutting the tent door, but she didn't want to lock the birds inside the main tent. There were things they'd need in there. Besides, Moira was pretty sure the ravens would leave as soon as she was gone, so long as the door was open. Pack on her back and gun belt in hand, she squinted against the blizzard in progress and led the way to the next tent.

"The trick," she yelled to make herself heard over the wind, "will be to get us inside without any birds."

"That should be easy." Hot breath brushed against her cheek and she realized he'd placed his mouth right next to the side of her head. A shiver ran up her back that didn't have anything to do with being afraid. "They didn't follow us. Open the door. My hands are full."

She fumbled with the latch, her gloved fingers clumsy. Moira was careful not to open the door very far. As soon as the opening was wide enough, they slid inside. She slammed the canvas in place, hooking it against wind and birds. Tim set the things in his arms down. He took a hefty swig of warm water from the cook pot and walked over to her, laying gentle hands on her shoulders. "Do you want to tell me what this is all about?"

"Not really."

He nodded. "Yes, but I think you have to." He looked around the tent, twin to the one they'd just vacated. "We may end up the only two people here, since it doesn't appear Jake's coming back."

Anxiety—and guilt—clanged like discordant notes. "I—uh—I ought to go look for both of them."

"In that?" He gestured toward the door. "You couldn't find your own arm out there, let alone two potheads who want to be left alone with their dope."

"I suppose you're right." She moved away from him and set her pack down, but kept hold of her gun. Shooting the birds was an option, but killing wildlife went against the grain. She respected animals. As a ranger, she was sworn to protect them. Besides her large bore revolver would put major holes in the tent. She might even kill Mitch or Jake inadvertently if they showed up at the wrong time.

Tim settled himself on a canvas stool. "Grab a seat—" he pulled up another one and pointed to it "—and tell me why those birds attacked us."

"It's a long story—"

"Just hit the high points." He sounded deadly serious. When she didn't move toward the other stool, he stood, went to her, and pulled her into his arms. He kneaded the tense muscles in her neck and shoulders. "You're shaking. Whatever this is, *mo ghrá*, we can get through it."

Maybe it was the Gaelic endearment, but to her horror, Moira felt a sob rake its way through her chest, followed by another. It had been so long since she'd felt any tenderness from anyone that it undid her. She tried to pull away, ashamed of being weak and needy, but Tim held fast.

"Ssht. Hush. Take a few deep breaths. The birds can't get to us here."

Moira raised her head from his shoulder long enough to stare at the canvas-walled tent. She wasn't certain a raven's beak couldn't breach the stout fabric. "Not so sure about that," she murmured.

"Well, they're not in here yet. I love you, *mo ghrá*. I always have. Let me help." His voice was steady, and logic permeated his words. She wanted to believe him, but it had been a long time since she'd had faith in anyone.

"Okay," she said through a hiccuppy sob. "The short version is my husband—"

He drew back so he could look at her face. "I thought you told me yesterday you'd divorced him."

"Uh, yes. Well, no, not exactly… At least not quite yet." Her words trailed off. Heat rose to her cheeks. This tent had two plastic inserts that let at least some light in. Moira wished for the relative darkness of the main supply tent. It would've hidden her discomfiture better.

"Which is it?" He tightened his fingers on her shoulders, so her answer was important to him.

"Technically, I'm still married. But I caught him cheating and left a few weeks back. I hired a lawyer, and he's working on divorce papers."

Tim cocked his head to one side, still watching her intently, but not saying anything. He had the most incredible eyes. Like a clear sea with gold flecks where sunlight bounced off the surface.

"Ryan is Native American. Shamans for his tribe come from his bloodline. The raven is their totem."

"I think I'm beginning to understand what this has to do with the birds." Comprehension smoothed the lines that had creased Tim's forehead. "Working with Paiutes from the reservation in Bishop taught me how enmeshed Native Americans are in Earth Magic." He took a deep breath and locked gazes with her. "You think Ryan—or his kin—sicced the birds on you."

She nodded, her emotional storm under partial control. It meant a lot that Tim was actually listening to her. And taking her seriously.

"You do know how fantastic this would sound—to anyone but a Druid." The corners of his mouth turned downward.

"Yeah, I do." She gripped his jacket sleeves. "And I may be absolutely wrong, but I can't think of any other reason the ravens would've attacked first me, then you." She hesitated. "Ryan's one jealous son of a bitch."

"How'd you end up with him?"

Color didn't merely creep, it flooded her face this time.

Tim nodded curtly, but his eyes looked sad. "Understood. You found someone to sleep with and got sucked in." He reached a gloved hand and tilted her chin so she had to look at him. "Would you have stayed with me if I'd been free to make love with you? To marry you when we were twenty-two, instead of years downstream."

"How can you even ask that? Unless I'm missing something, you never asked me to marry you at all." Her voice shook from remembered hurt. "And you never told me anything. Nothing at all. You occasionally said you loved me, but your actions didn't back up the words."

"I didn't tell you anything because I couldn't. Not because I didn't want to. I didn't do a very good job of explaining myself." His voice was gentle.

"No, you didn't." A wellspring of love shoved against the lid of the vault where she'd stuffed it ten years ago. Moira struggled to keep it contained. There were a lot of things she needed to understand. "We ended up fighting all the time over whatever you were hiding and sort of lost sight of each other."

"Yeah," he agreed. "It was pretty awful. Especially those last few months. I'd try so hard to just enjoy being with you, but we always ended up blaming each other for things we couldn't change."

"You could have done *something*. You just let me walk away."

He flinched at the accusatory undertone in her words. "I'm not sure what I could have done. I felt stuck. Your grandmother already told you I had to remain celibate. Arch Druids need to keep their magic pure until their investiture.

"The worst part, though, was I was sworn to silence. If I'd broken that oath, I would've put every Druid in the world at risk. Not just those in this country. Organized churches are frightened by what we represent—threatened enough to try to wipe us out. That night I left you crying in my apartment, I ran all the way to the priory to beg Liam to reconsider. He wouldn't. Even though I couldn't see it then, now I know it was the right decision." Tim blew out a sad-sounding breath, his gaze never leaving hers.

"If I'd walked out on my Druid vows, I would've left a big chunk of myself behind. Niggling things like honor and respect. *Mo ghrá*, the man you loved had principles. I would've turned into someone different if I'd rejected them to move our life forward."

She winced, embarrassed. Tim pretty much nailed it. She'd wanted him to put her before everything else. Demanded it, without a thought as to how it would impact the rest of his life. "Guess I was pretty egocentric. I'm finally starting to understand.

Maybe I was too young, but I wish we could've had this conversation—"

"Just be grateful to the goddess we're having it now." His voice held a husky rasp that had always driven her crazy.

Moira couldn't tear her gaze away, even if his fingers hadn't been under her chin. She was losing herself in the miracle of his eyes.

"I never even looked at another woman, *mo ghrá*. No flirting, no dates, nothing. Never could get you out of my mind. I knew I had four years in medical school and another three as a resident to wade through. Got an MPH first, while I was waffling about whether I really wanted to be a doctor, so that added another year. I always told myself I'd find you—"

"Why didn't you ever call me back? Or answer any of my letters?"

"Because nothing had really changed, and I was too much of a traditionalist to tell the Arch Druid to go to hell. Liam's been like a dad to me. Not sure if you remember, but the Druids pretty much raised me after my parents were killed. I don't know if they would've done it if I hadn't had such a strong aptitude for magic— or been slated to be the next Arch Druid—but that part doesn't matter. Liam's been expecting me back ever since I left." That same crooked grin lit his features.

She took a deep breath, hoping for a miracle. "You said nothing's changed—"

"Ah, but that was before yesterday."

He pulled her against him again and settled his lips over hers, light as butterfly wings. The kiss was soft, tender, and not demanding at all. It was a test-the-waters kiss, and she knew it. With a mind of their own, her arms wound around him. She opened her mouth to him, sucking his tongue and nibbling his lips.

Tim slid his hands ever so slowly down her back and placed them on the curves of her ass. He snugged her body against his, and she felt the jut of him pressing into the junction between her thigh and stomach. His breathing quickened. He thrust his hips against her and made a sound like a big jungle cat on the prowl. She'd always loved that sound—it was predatory and hungry and possessive all rolled into one. Except before, he'd always pulled away from her right after making it.

She shoved feebly at his chest. "But the birds. And the storm. And I'm supposed to be working."

"We can't do anything about the storm. Now that I'm looking for them with my power, I don't feel the birds, not nearby anyway. And there's not much work you can actually do right now." He tightened his hands on her butt. "We won't take too many clothes off. Please, darling. I've dreamed of doing more than kissing you since I was fifteen."

Heat raced through her. Breath caught in her throat. Her nipples hardened where they pressed against his chest. All the moisture in her body headed straight for her nether regions because her mouth was suddenly dry with anticipation. She heard herself moan low in the back of her throat. He rocked his pelvis against her. Sandwiched between them, his cock twitched with what could only be need. She couldn't wait. She wanted Tim with a desperation borne of years of denied need. Wanted to see all of him, touch him, taste him, and draw him into the empty, aching place deep inside her.

"I know you want me. I feel it in the energy dancing around you." His voice was husky with passion. A hint of an Irish lilt had crept into it, making her feel as if she'd come home. Moira knew all about Irish brogues. Both her parents spoke the Irish version of Gaelic. And it had been her grandmother's preferred language.

"Of course I want you. How could I not?" She cupped his face between her hands and ran her fingers down the stubbled lines of his cheeks and chin.

Understanding slammed her between the eyes. She'd always loved Tim beyond grace or reason. Something in him sang to her soul. She'd felt it since they were children. It hadn't dimmed with the passage of time. If anything, the light within him that called to her burned even brighter than it ever had before.

He led her to one of the low cots lined against the sloping tent walls, sat, and wrapped his arms around her waist. The warmth of his breath seared her even through her clothing. He pulled off his gloves. They made a small, swishing noise as they hit the floor. Then he unfastened the belt, snaps, and zipper on her pants and storm pants. He closed his mouth over her belly button and lingered over it before working lower. She pushed at her clothing, eager to have it out of his way, but he made a grab for the fabric layers once they hit the tops of her thighs.

Tim stopped kissing her long enough to murmur, "This is all I need for now. It's colder in here than you think."

You couldn't have proven that by her. Fire sprinted along her nerve endings. The swollen nub between her legs throbbed. All she could think about was pushing herself against his mouth and the fingers that had insinuated themselves into her pussy.

He licked and sucked, sending sparks of desire arcing through her. When he slid his fingers farther into her, Moira felt a climax spool deep in her core. He had to feel it too, from the tension in her muscles gripping his fingers. He shoved into her faster, and sucked hard on her clitoris. Spasms shook her. She heard herself screaming for him not to stop. To never stop.

Moira wasn't sure if she collapsed on top of him on the narrow cot or if he drew her down next to him. Her legs were shaking, and there wasn't enough air in the room. Snaking a hand between them, she curled it around his erection. It felt wonderful, thick and full of promise. He groaned and drove himself against her. She tugged off her gloves and fumbled with the zippers on his inner and outer pants.

Finally, his cock was in her hand, flesh against flesh. He thrust against her, breath coming fast. Even though she wanted him inside her as much as she'd ever wanted anything, Moira understood the wisdom of not getting undressed. If something happened and they had to move quickly, being half-naked could be lethal. She pumped her hand up and down his shaft and his cock swelled, on the verge of coming.

"Look at me," he gasped. "I want to look into your eyes, into your soul, when I come."

She met his gaze, shaken by the intimacy of the moment.

"Now, *mo ghrá*. Harder. Hold me harder."

She tightened her fingers, and he exploded against her, crying her name again and again. Except it was the Gaelic pronunciation. His body heaved against hers one last time, then lay still.

The only sound in the tent was their ragged breathing as they clung to one another.

"Just think what we could do if we had a proper bed," he murmured, his gaze still locked on hers.

She started to giggle.

The sound of ripping canvas froze the laughter in her throat and drove her to her feet, her heart beating furiously. Still fuzzy from her orgasm, she tugged at the zippers of her pants so they wouldn't fall down. Then Tim was standing next to her, doing the same thing. He put an arm around her to stabilize her.

A raven's head poked through a hole in the tent.

"Shit." Moira dove for her gun and clicked the hammer back.

"I suppose we should count ourselves lucky it took them some time to break in here." Tim glanced at her .357 magnum revolver. "What are you planning to do with that? Decimate the tent?"

"If I have to."

Tim grabbed his staff. She did a double take. The intricately carved walking stick glowed with a bright, white light. Tim's jaw was set in a hard line. Head high, he turned in a full circle, staff extended before him.

"Lying, cheating whore," someone shouted from outside the tent. "You're doing the same thing you're divorcing me for."

Tim looked at her. "Is that—?"

"Sounds like it, but I don't have any idea how. He hates the backcountry. Wouldn't have a clue how to get himself back here—or what to bring. The storm would've finished him off if he tried to follow me."

"Ha! I did follow you. Wasn't all that hard. That big pack of yours slows you down."

I'm not losing my mind. That was the other set of footsteps I heard.

"If it was so easy, why didn't you catch up?"

"Once I realized you weren't alone, I got smart. There are many ways to travel."

"I thought you were descended from all those generations of Indian scouts—the ones who braved ten feet of snow to hunt."

"Shut up, bitch."

Moira heard a tinny, discordant note in Ryan's voice. Something clicked. Her ex wasn't really out there, except as some sort of magical projection. And she'd bet her last buck his father was helping him.

"Did you tell Singing Bear what really happened?" she snarled.

Silence.

A different voice sounded in her mind. *"Maybe not. Why don't you tell me? You don't need words, daughter. Images will do."*

Tim tightened his arm around her. "Be careful. That one has real magic."

"Yes, but he always liked me. Give me a minute." She sent one image to her father-in-law. The one that had dogged her ever since she walked in on Ryan and his bimbo.

"Thank you. That is all I needed. You cannot lie when you send mind-pictures, and that one came from your soul." A hesitation, then, *"I am sorry, daughter."*

Muted squawks rose from outside the tent, barely distinguishable above the howl of the wind. She heard Ryan tell his father that she was a scheming, lying slut. Here she was fucking some man in the wilderness like he figured she'd done every other time she left on Park Service assignments...

Moira listened, horrified. How could she have spent ten minutes with the bitter, angry man spewing malicious crap about her—let alone almost a year?

"None of that could possibly be true." Still holding his staff, Tim turned her toward him. His face held a drawn look, as if hearing Ryan's accusations hurt him as much as it did her.

She shook her head. "No. Ryan was the only one in my bed for the few months we spent together. Actually, he's the only man I've ever had sex with. Until what we just did."

Tim closed his arms around her. She felt the staff, warm where it rested against her back.

"Thanks for believing in me." Her voice was muffled against his shoulder. Incredulity vied with joy. Ryan had never believed anything she ever told him.

"Of course I believe in you, *mo ghrá*. I love you."

She shook her head. "It's just—"

"Hush. That part of your life is over. Let's concentrate on getting ourselves out of here, so we can see what the next part looks like."

"Why was your walking stick glowing?"

"It's a magic staff. I didn't understand why it wanted me to bring it along last night, but I do now."

She let herself rest against him for just a moment, shutting out the reality of their predicament. Too much snow had fallen for them to just walk back over the pass, and the blizzard didn't show any sign of letting up.

oira reluctantly, disentangled herself from the comfort of Tim's arms. She went to the tent door and peeked through it. The storm hadn't abated one whit, but the birds seemed to be gone, along with whatever projection Ryan had managed. She looked at her watch. Just past four.

"I need to radio headquarters."

"I agree." Tim gestured at the storm. "You've got eleven people out there. Some of them probably aren't going to make it since they're not back yet."

No one would make it, including them, if it didn't stop snowing, but Moira kept that thought to herself. There was no way a rescue chopper could fly in this weather.

"While I try to raise headquarters, could you check on the mules? They're probably in a paddock just beyond the tents. Follow the line of tents. They're pitched right next to one another. When you reach the end, you should find the mules. If you don't, come back and we'll look for them together."

He nodded, finished refastening his clothing, put on his gloves, and slipped out the door. "I'll check the other tents for Mitch and Jake while I'm at it," floated back to her, garbled by the wind.

She pulled her satellite phone out of her pack. Despite her worries about her boss hounding her, she'd made a point of charging it before leaving home yesterday morning.

Something made her shiver. The sensation was so intense she looked over her shoulder, wondering if one of the birds had somehow gotten in without her noticing. She didn't find any of the ravens, but invisible strands of hopelessness dragged at her. It reminded Moira of when her superstitious mother used to natter on about evil spirits discovering your gravesite—and desecrating it.

She closed her eyes, knowing what the bleak premonition meant. Ryan hadn't given up. His father wouldn't help him anymore, but that didn't mean he couldn't cast his own warped spells.

Moira forced herself to take a deep breath. And then another. She and Tim were probably safe for a while. It would take time for Ryan's magic to recharge. At least she knew that much about how shamanistic castings worked.

Will we manage to get out of here before he tries to kill us again?

Because she didn't have any answers, Moira concentrated on setting up her phone's antenna to get a signal. She dialed as soon as she could.

"National Park Headquarters. Kings Canyon-Sequoia."

The cheery sound of Betty's voice almost brought tears to Moira's eyes. "Betty. Moira, here. I'm at Baxter Lakes. Cannot locate any of the trail crew. Repeat. Cannot locate any of my crew. More than a foot of fresh snow has fallen, and it's still snowing heavily. Visibility deteriorating, currently at ten feet or less. Requesting rescue operation."

"Oh my God." Betty's gasp was so loud, Moira had to hold the phone away from her ear. She could picture the plump blonde with her long, red fingernails, her mouth curved into an *oh* of horror. "Right away, hon. I'll get it called in right away. We were all worried about you. This freak storm just came out of nowhere. None of us were expecting it."

"I have the solar charger, but it's worthless without sun. I'm signing off to preserve my battery. And turning off the phone. Will turn it on from five minutes before six until five minutes after if someone needs to talk with me."

"Roger. Understood."

The line went dead. Moira didn't know if the satellites had dropped the call—which they did with annoying frequency—or if Betty was so freaked out, she'd been in a rush to call Search and Rescue. Moira took care to turn off the phone and return it to its case. She tucked the whole mess deep in her pack where it might stay a little warmer. Cold was hell on battery life.

Wind rushed through the door as Tim came back inside. He looked rattled. "Didn't find any people. There are four mules in the paddock. Five if you count the dead one."

"What?" She shook her head hard. "It couldn't have frozen to death. Not yet, anyway."

"Looks like the birds pecked it to death. Opened up either the jugular or carotid. I didn't get close enough to tell which. Not that familiar with equine physiology."

She brushed past him, heading toward the door, but he caught her arm. "Uh-uh. Not a good idea. It's pretty gory."

She yanked her arm away and bent to pick up her gloves. "We need to free the other mules. The blood will draw every predator within a ten-mile radius. Mules are pretty resourceful, but they're sitting ducks in that paddock. And I need to see if there's more ammo for my gun in the supply tent. Looks like we're going to need it."

Tim set his mouth into a grim line. "Any chance there might be another weapon?"

"How long since you've shot one?"

"A long time, but I'm sure it will come back to me."

"Can't you use magic or something?" She pointed at the staff.

No longer glowing, it just looked like polished hardwood, with something that might've been runic writing circling its girth.

He shrugged noncommittally. "I could, but the destructive side of power is so vast, it scares the crap out of me. That's part of my problem with taking Liam's place."

Despite the desperation of their situation, something like a small sun bloomed in her heart. Tim was finally talking with her. He wasn't hiding behind a wall anymore. "Thanks for trusting me."

"You're welcome. It's long overdue."

She bit on her lower lip, chewing on chapped skin. "Back to your question about other weapons, you probably know they're not legal in national parks. Rangers are the only ones allowed to carry them. Every once in a while, though, one of the crew sneaks something in."

"Okay, I can look through the tents more thoroughly later."

"Let's get moving." Her gaze zeroed in on him. "Actually, I'm glad to have something to do. It's better than waiting around until six to turn the phone back on."

"Know what you mean." He reached for her, catching a shoulder as she moved past him. "I know we have work to do. And we might not get out of here alive, but I want to tell you something important."

She swung around to face him. Something about his tone brought her emotions close to the surface. "What?"

He smiled. "Ach, *mo ghrá*, mellow out a bit. Let a fellow make a proclamation of love without feeling it's an imposition.

"I fell in love with you when we were just kids. Even then you looked like one of those ancient Valkyries, with all that blonde hair and your golden eyes. I've never seen eyes like that on anyone." Color rose in his face, but he kept talking. "It's not just your beauty, though. You're strong and self-sufficient. Not afraid to tackle anything on your own terms. It's why we butted heads so often. That, and our Irish tempers and my Druid vows." The rosy hue deepened, bringing a golden tone to his tanned face. "I want to marry you, *mo ghrá*. As soon as we can. I'm not making the same mistakes I made ten years ago."

Moira felt the corners of her mouth twitch into a smile. Joy whooshed through her. She reached out a gloved hand to stroke his face. "I'd like that too," she murmured. "It'll be a few months, though, until the divorce is final."

"Not a problem. After all the years I've already waited, a few months are nothing." He closed a hand over hers. "We can leave now. After you."

She led the way outside, then stopped abruptly. "I probably should tell you we haven't seen the last of Ryan."

"I didn't think we had." Tim laughed, but it held a bitter edge. "If I'd had a woman like you and fucked up as badly as he did, I'd want to do something about it too."

A lone coyote howl filled the air. Answering wails rose from all directions. Moira knew the wind could deceive, but it was clear the local cleanup crew were on their way. They had to get the other mules out of Death Corral. And damned fast. "We need to hurry."

He moved in front of her, leading the way along a trail he'd already made through calf-deep snow. "Do you think they'll be okay on their own?"

"We'll turn them loose. They ought to be fine. Mules are way stronger than horses."

"What about all those feed sacks?"

"Not a problem. Coyotes won't eat them. But we ought to move them into one of the tents so they don't get buried."

IT WAS NEARLY time to turn the sat phone on again. Skittish from what happened to one of their own, the mules had been reluctant to do anything. It took a great deal of coaxing, cajoling, and handfuls of grain to get them to step over their fallen comrade and out of the enclosure. Despite the cold, sweat ran down Moira's sides. She had hold of one end of an eighty-pound feed sack, the last one they needed to move under shelter, when she heard voices. Jake, Mitch, and another mule stumbled out of the whiteout.

"Never mind," Tim grunted, hefting the sack to one shoulder. "I can get this. Do what you need to."

Moira stomped over to the two AWOLs. "Get the packs off that animal and his halter, then turn him loose. When you're done, help us move sleeping bags and clothes into the supply tent."

"What happened to the corral?" Jake sounded wiped. He had an arm around Mitch, supporting him.

"One of the mules is dead. It's pretty bloody." She didn't have to say anything else. Jake had been a miner before he'd opted for the relatively softer life of going on Park Service work details. Even though they didn't pay him much, they fed him. He'd told her once that three squares counted for quite a bit when you'd spent a lot of your life hungry.

She shone her headlight on her watch. "I need to turn the phone on. Talk with you later."

The sat phone rang nearly as soon as she powered it on. It didn't surprise her. Nor did the sound of John's voice. "Report," he said brusquely.

"Two trail crew accounted for. Nine missing."

"Mules?"

"Did we start with twelve?"

"Yes."

"Okay, we have five here. Six if you count the dead one. So that means six are missing."

"One of the mules is dead?" John sounded shocked. "What happened?"

"Long story, John. And it doesn't matter. We freed the others."

He cleared his throat. "I'll expect a full report once you're back in the office. As you've probably figured out, storm's too bad to send a chopper. Soon as it quits snowing, we'll come for you."

"Any idea when the weather's supposed to clear?" She tried to keep her voice from wavering. It wouldn't do to let her boss know how frightened she was.

"Not for another couple of days. Frankly, I don't get it. This weather was *not* in the forecast." Concern—and worry—permeated his words. "You have plenty of food and fuel. Just pay attention to protocols, and you should be fine."

She sucked in a breath. Two days could be a long time with her soon-to-be ex-husband on the prowl. "When would you like me to turn the phone on again, sir?"

"No point in running down the batteries. Tomorrow night at this time should be fine. Oh, and Moira, if you can get a fire going, by all means do so."

"Thanks," she murmured. John really was trying. It was a major concession for him to give her permission to have an open fire above ten thousand feet, where they were normally forbidden.

"You're welcome. Take care of yourself. I already lost two rangers this season. Don't wim to lose another."

The empty hum of satellites buzzed against her ear. She powered down the phone and buried it in her pack. Moira looked around the tent where she and Tim had kissed and snuggled. A tender glow started in her belly, radiating outward. He was such a wonderful man, kindhearted and sensitive. She wondered if she could possibly be lucky enough for the love between them to take root and grow this time, without all the pain and hurt and endless arguments.

Hope I live long enough to find out.

She grabbed the sleeping bags, shouldered her pack, and moved through the storm to the supply tent. It would be a tight fit, with the four of them and most of the community gear, but until she was certain the coyotes would be satisfied with the sacrificial mule, she wasn't taking any chances.

When she got inside, battening the door against wind that had to be gusting at close to forty miles an hour, she saw Tim bent over Mitch. "What's wrong?"

"Hypothermia, frostbite. Too much booze and dope. Not enough food or water. Probably has some kind of viral hepatitis to boot. He's pretty yellow. Whichever MD cleared him for this work detail should have his license suspended." Tim sounded angry—and troubled. "I got his clothes off and wrapped two down bags around him with hot water bottles inside, but he's delirious. I need him awake enough to eat and drink since I obviously don't have any IV equipment here."

Wending her way among stacks of gear, she dropped her pack and the sleeping bags on a cot. An unpleasant odor from Mitch's unwashed body permeated the already stale air in the tent. She could only imagine what it would be like by morning. She walked over to Tim and peered down at Mitch. He thrashed weakly on a cot. His color was horrid, face a ghastly shade of gray. The whites of his eyes were lemon-colored.

"I'm surprised he made it back here," she said.

"Yeah. Me too."

"There should be either a full EMT or paramedic pack in with the supplies. Do you want it?"

Something painfully close to hope flared in Tim's eyes. "That would be great. Any medical supplies are better than what I have, which is nothing."

Turning up the beam of her headlamp, Moira rummaged through boxes stacked along one side of the tent. It took her a few minutes, but she located the crate of medical supplies and carried it over to Tim. "Where's Jake?"

"Bringing stuff from the other tents. Did you talk to the Park Service?"

"Uh-huh." She stopped, trying to figure out which piece of bad news to deliver first.

"And? Come on, Moira, don't make me work to get information. I'm having a hard enough time."

She felt instantly contrite. "Sorry. No chopper till after the storm, and that's at least two days—"

"What?" Blue eyes flashing, he got to his feet, took her arm, and pulled her away from Mitch's cot. "Barring a miracle, he'll be dead long before then."

"Him and the others out on the trail," she muttered.

Tim raked his hands through his hair. "I feel goddamned helpless."

She put her hands on his shoulders and met his gaze. "We aren't helpless. This is what happens when you leave civilization. You have to rely on your wits. If you'd somehow missed meeting up with me, you'd be in a world of hurt. Not dead, but headed in that direction."

"That's not helping."

"Maybe not, but you need to hear it anyway. Modern life has lulled us into a sense of complacency…" She felt like she was being patronizing, so she shook her head and started over. "Things are more…real out here. More immediate. But more dangerous too. You realize what a slender margin separates being alive from falling prey to something that can kill you. It puts a finer edge on things—"

Jake shoved his way into the tent, his arms full of clothing and sleeping bags. "Whew. Stinks in here. How's Mitch, Doc?"

"Not good."

Jake dropped his things onto a pile of clothing. "Shit. I was afraid of that. He was pretty far gone when I found him. But he sort of rallied. And he knew who I was. Damn." He hunkered next to his friend. Tugging an arm out of the sleeping bag, he took Mitch's hand and stroked it.

It was such an oddly tender gesture from the burly mountain man that Moira felt the quick bite of tears. She swallowed hard. She couldn't afford to be emotional. The stakes were too high.

Jake tucked Mitch's arm back into the bag, straightened, and started out the door. She called him back. "We have plenty of warm things in here. HQ said we could have a fire—"

Jake's braying laughter drowned out the rest of her words. "Damn straight of them," he sputtered after he could talk again. "Jesus Christ himself couldn't get anything to burn out there. 'Sides, even if the snow let up, wind's brutal."

A chortle bubbled up from somewhere deep in Moira, followed by another. She tried to hold them in, but failed. Soon she was howling just like Jake had been. The whole situation was black humor at its finest. The storm, the birds, the lost trail crew. Permission to light a fire under impossible conditions.

"I'll be fine, really I will. Got to get some air," she managed. Moira stepped outside. Snow blew in her face, effectively blinding her. She raised her hands to wipe it away and realized she'd left her gloves in the tent.

Christ! I'm really losing it.

Feeling disgusted actually had a salutary effect. The craziness left as quickly as it had come. She inhaled deeply, letting the chilly air clear her mind.

Just before she let herself back inside, she heard a raven caw, and her blood congealed in her veins.

CHAPTER 6

im dug through the EMT kit, a nearby candle lantern providing a thin beam of light. "Who the fuck packed this? An extra from Catch 22?" He held up a steri-pack that contained an intravenous needle and another with tubing. "What good are these without saline?"

"I think they only pack that when they expect to have a paramedic along."

"What are you? Doesn't the Park Service require you to have some medical training?" Judging from the bitten-off tone of his words, he was having a hard time controlling his frustration.

"Yes, but I'm only an EMT with a Wilderness First Responder certification."

"Oh." He sucked in a breath. "Sorry I was short with you. I might be able to save this man, if I had what I needed."

Turning away from her, he extracted a tube and squeezed it into Mitch's mouth. It was probably the glucose paste they used for diabetics. The stove was going, so she pinned the door flap open a few inches for better airflow. Hopefully, the raven she'd heard wouldn't take it as an invitation. Tim pulled poly bottles out of Mitch's sleeping bag, refilled them with hot water, and tucked them back next to the comatose man.

Now that she had time to think, Moira couldn't figure out what had happened to the rest of the trail crew. Only some of them were newbies. Everyone else would've known to turn tail and run once it started snowing hard. Which meant they should have been back hours ago. It was only about six miles to the Muir Trail Junction. If what Jake told her was accurate, the crew had been working just a couple of miles from camp. For an ugly moment, she pictured the dead mule and wondered if Ryan was deranged enough to send his bird hit squad after her people. It made sense, in a sick sort of way, for him to pick off anyone who might help her protect herself.

She swallowed hard, fury battling with horror. If he'd really done something like that, she'd see him hung from the nearest yardarm.

"Goddammit. No, you don't," Tim yelled. Moira twirled to look at him. Tim pounded on Mitch's thin chest. He tilted his chin, fished a plastic protector out of the EMT kit, and started rescue breathing.

"Need help?" Jake was by the cot in an instant.

Tim eyed the other man. "Do you know how to do this?"

Jake shrugged. "Sort of. We all had to take a basic first aid course to be Park Service workers."

"Okay. You do the breathing. I'll do chest compressions. He looks like he has osteoporosis. Got to be careful. If I hit him too hard, I'll break a bone."

Moira bit her lower lip until she tasted blood. Mitch had been close to worthless on two other crews she'd overseen, but that didn't mean she wanted him to die. Needing to do something to distract herself from the thumping and wheezing coming from Mitch's cot, she organized the boxes and piles of gear, sorted finger food for dinner, and hauled out the big pot to start melting snow for drinking water, since the gallon jugs were well on their way to being frozen.

Time dripped past, punctuated by a wet, gurgling that didn't sound good.

"It's no good. He's gone."

She turned in time to see Tim straighten.

"You sure?" Jake's eyes looked haunted. Moira knew the feeling.

"Yeah. CPR hardly ever works outside of a hospital, and we had too many things going against us. Thanks for helping, though. It meant we could keep trying longer."

"I'll move him to one of the other tents." Jake hoisted Mitch, sleeping bag and all, over one shoulder and lumbered out the door. "Probably won't be back for a while. Need to say goodbye, proper like."

"I'm sorry." Moira went to Tim and laid a hand on his arm.

"I knew he didn't have a chance after I first examined him—"

"But you tried anyway. And I love you for it." The minute the words were out, she clapped a hand to her mouth, not believing she'd actually said them. "Ah, what I meant was—"

"Don't ruin it, *mo ghrá*. I know you didn't feel safe, or loved, last time around, but I plan to change all that. It's just going to take us some time." He drew her into his arms. "It's okay about Mitch. I learned I couldn't save them all early on in med school. Death doesn't bother me as long as I know I did everything I could."

She felt the beat of his heart against her ear. And something else too: a sense of the rightness of being with him. Long-buried knowledge that she belonged with Tim, now and forever, clamored for recognition. She let it run free. The time for pretending it didn't exist was over.

"Okay. I won't try to take back what I said. Besides, I really did mean it. I fell in love with you when you helped me pick up my books after those bullies taunted me about being Irish and tried to run my bike off the road."

A soft smile lit his face. "I remember that. We were about fourteen at the time." He snugged his arms around her. "*Mo croi.* My heart. I'll keep right on protecting you for the rest of your life if you'll let me."

She leaned into him. He felt solid and comfortable. When she tilted her face up, he settled his lips on hers, gentle at first, then firm and more demanding. His tongue sank into her mouth. She felt her body respond, melting into his, and twined her arms around him.

"Ah, whoops. Sorry. Didn't mean to interrupt."

"It's okay, Jake." She moved out of the circle of Tim's arms. "Both of you. There are things you need to know. Mind you, I'm not certain of any of them, but still… You remember Ryan?" She eyed Jake.

He made a face and spat on the floor. "Unfortunately. Never liked that man. Never could understand why you didn't see what a shady bastard he was."

Wonder why it was so obvious to everyone else?

She cleared her throat. "He used some sort of Native American magic to command a bunch of ravens. They're what killed that mule. And it's why they've been flying into the tents. For all I know, they attacked the rest of the crew." She blew out a tense breath. "It's the only reason I can think of that none of them came back here."

"Mules would've come back on their own—" Jake began, apparently not fazed at all by her statement.

"Unless they'd been hobbled," she broke in, "and there was no one left to untie them." It was Park Service policy to secure stock at worksites when they weren't being used.

"Do you want me to try to look for them?" In a departure from his normally laid-back manner, Jake finally sounded worried.

She shook her head. "Definitely not. That would be suicide."

"Wait." Tim cocked his head to one side. "What was that?"

She started to say *wind*, but the word died on her lips. "Mules," she said, excitement thrumming through her. "That's mules braying."

"Could be the ones you turned loose," Jake reminded her.

"Might be the others too." She grabbed her hat and gloves from a cot near the door. "I'm going to find out."

"Not alone." Both men spoke in unison.

The wind seemed a little better when she went outside. Still brisk, but she didn't have to fight against it to stand upright. It was almost totally dark. Between that and the snow, it was disorienting. Moira clicked on her headlight and held herself still, listening.

"I think it's coming from over there." She pointed with a gloved hand and started off, wading through snow that had drifted knee-high in places.

Too bad I didn't think to bring snowshoes.

Moira made clucking noises as she walked. The mules knew those usually presaged a grain sack and sometimes came running. But sometimes not. They were far more contrary than horses, and much more independent.

"Come on, sweetie. Come to Momma." A bay-colored head materialized in the beam from her headlamp. "Yes, it's going to be all right."

"Is it one of the other ones?" Tim was right behind her.

"Uh-huh. Let's see who he brought with him. Mules don't usually travel alone."

"Moira?" A female voice rasped.

"Yes. Oh my God, yes. I'm here. Paula?"

"No, it's Christine. Paula's—" A sob cut off her next words and then a tall, thin woman bundled against the storm, hurtled out of the dark and into Moira's arms. The woman shook violently, crying and gasping as bits of what happened tore out of her.

"Only one—I'm all that's left. Me and the mules. Five of 'em anyway. Birds got the other one." More sobs. "And everyone else too. Christ! Never seen nothing like it before. Fucking ravens pecked out everybody's throat. Knew they was bad luck, but they went for us like… like…"

"Hush. You don't need to say any more. Here. Let Jake take you inside and get something hot into you. Tim and I will take care of the mules."

"Oh. I'm sorry. Truly I am." Christine raised a blotchy, tear-stained face. "Didn't pack up the saws. They're probably ruined under all this snow. I—"

"They're not important."

"But the regulations say—"

"I know what they say," Moira interrupted. "I helped write them. Now listen to me. You have to believe me when I tell you no one will blame you for leaving Park Service equipment under the circumstances. No one."

"Well, if you're sure…" She transitioned from Moira's arms to Jake's.

"More than sure. Now go. You won't do anyone any good if you die of hypothermia like—"

"What?" Christine sounded stunned. "Who else is dead? For fuck's sake—" Fresh tears started to flow. "Must be Mitch. Crap!"

Moira winced, feeling like an idiot, and an insensitive one at that.

"It'll keep." Jake's gruff voice ended the conversation. "Come on. Hot water's on the stove."

Five mules milled around them. Tim had already started removing the tack from one. "What do you want to do with this stuff?"

"We need to put it in one of the tents. Let's move the mules closer, so we don't have to carry it as far."

"Humph. Should've thought of that." He re-buckled a strap.

CHAPTER 7

By the time they came back into the supply tent, her headlamp was dimming. Moira grabbed a couple of triple-As from her pack and swapped them for the ones in the lamp. Christine was curled on her side on a cot, snoring softly. Jake sat watch over her looking like Cerberus guarding the gates of Hell.

"How is she?" Moira asked quietly.

"Frightened. Exhausted. But she'll make it. Got food into her and about a quart of tea."

"Good work." Tim laid a hand on Jake's shoulder. "Did she pee?" Jake nodded. "Even better."

"Lucky we only lost two mules," Jake muttered half to himself.

Yeah, not so lucky about the nine people.

Moira kept that thought to herself. She had no idea what she'd tell John when it was time to turn the phone back on.

Uh, you see, my ex is this deranged Native American. He called up spirit birds and they—

Moira dropped onto a three-legged stool. Supporting her head, she closed eyes that felt gritty and tired.

"You ought to eat something." Jake eyed her, seeming to

understand how shattered she was. "You laid out food, but I bet you didn't eat any of it." He clasped his hands behind his back and moved his gaze from her face to the floor. "This won't help your appetite, but before Christine fell asleep she told me there were at least fifty of those damned ravens. They tag-teamed the attack, almost as if they could communicate with each other."

"How'd she escape?" Moira opened her eyes to look at Jake.

"Brandon. Fool kid threw himself on top of her. Birds got him. Couldn't get to her."

"Don't think about it now. Nothing we can do." Tim scooped up the plastic lid where she'd put their dinner and dropped it in her lap. He pulled up a stool and started eating. "You said something about tea?" He looked hopefully at Jake.

"Yeah. Pot on the stove is full. I'll rustle up some cups."

Half an hour later, stuffed with jerky, cheese, crackers, tea, and cookies, she did feel better. "We need a plan."

"Uh-huh, like sleeping in shifts," Tim said. He shifted his gaze to Jake. "Any more guns here? Other than Moira's that is? I meant to look, but never got around to it."

The other man looked away.

"It's okay, Jake," Moira said. "I won't tell, and we may need it."

He got to his feet. "Back soon."

Tim scooted closer to her and cupped her chin in his hand, examining her face. "I never did get to those wounds, but they don't look infected, and that one did close up. You need to rest. Jake and I will flip for first watch. We'll do two hour shifts." He shone his headlamp on his watch. "It's nine now. Means I won't have to wake you till one."

She considered arguing. After all, she was supposed to be in charge and responsible, but the day had taken a toll on her. She wouldn't be much good for anything if she couldn't close her eyes for a little while. "Okay." She tried to smile, but it felt forced. She was scared. Damned scared. Something that could wipe out almost her entire trail crew could make short work of them too.

In a horror-stricken corner of her brain, she imagined Ryan somewhere close, just waiting to loose the ravens.

It was almost as if Tim had read her thoughts. "We're ready for them," he murmured. "And we won't make the mistake of underestimating how much damage they can do." He turned her face toward his. "I will not let anything happen to you. There hasn't been a day since we separated that I didn't think about you. Now that fate's finally brought us back together, I'm not going to sacrifice joining my life to yours for anything."

His jaw tightened. "If that fucker you were married to would show up in the flesh, I'd fight him like a man. This spirit mumbo jumbo is crap. He's sending the hired help to do his dirty work for him."

She snorted. "Yes, that would be Ryan. Never got his hands dirty if he could sucker someone else into—"

"You flaming, fucking slut. You never give up, do you?"

Moira stiffened. She got to her feet, staggering from weariness, and raked the darkness with her gaze as she spun in a circle. It was Ryan's voice, but where the hell was he? And what the fuck was he doing? Hiding in some sort of psychic space spying on them?

"You always were a coward," she growled. "Show yourself."

The air developed an electric quality, almost as if it were on fire. She smelled ozone. A cracking sound came from behind the iso-butane cook stove. Ryan's form gradually took shape, floating a foot above the ground.

She heard Tim suck in a breath. She didn't blame him. The whole thing was damned intimidating. She'd watched Ryan a time or two when he dabbled with magic. Once she'd even walked in on him when his face was painted with something that looked like blood.

Moira took a step toward Ryan. "This is between us," she snarled through clenched teeth. "Do not kill anyone else."

"Or?" The mocking tone of his voice made her want to

choke him, but lunging for his projection wouldn't buy her anything. Bile burned the back of her throat. Her stomach roiled.

She shifted gears. "Does Singing Bear know you came back?"

A shrug. "Yeah, I convinced him you lied."

I fucking doubt it.

Anger and adrenaline surged. Good. She needed the energy. "No. You're the one who's lying. I lived with you long enough to recognize the signs." She spat in his direction. "Pah. You lie so much, you wouldn't recognize the truth if you tripped over it."

"Cheap Irish whore. Watch who you're spitting at."

"Moira." Tim walked up beside her, staff held in one hand. He placed the other on her arm. "Don't antagonize him. Let me handle this."

"I don't want you involved," she gritted out. "Go find Jake."

I don't want you to get hurt. Couldn't stand it if you got hurt because of me...

"Noted, but not your choice." Tim didn't move.

"Got yourself another lover boy so soon? Touching he's so loyal." Ryan swung his gaze to Tim. "She's a real cock-hound. Can't do without it for even a day. I'm surprised she lasted this long—unless she's been keeping you on the side."

"I'd watch your mouth." Tim's voice was quiet, but there was steel behind his words.

"Or?" Ryan chuckled nastily. "You two don't get it. I have all the power here. You can't do shit to me."

"Where's your father?" Moira asked.

"Busy," he smirked.

Yeah, right. Wonder if Singing Bear would show up if I called?

"So," she squared her shoulders, "you seem to have us right where you want us. What do you plan to do?"

"You used to be smarter than that, wifey-dear. You're worth much more to me dead than alive. There's that accident insurance the Feds carry on you. And your savings accounts. Didn't matter while we were still married, but you got this bright idea to dump me. That, darling, was a big mistake."

His projection pulsed, radiating danger. Moira's mind raced. What could she say to buy time? She'd known Ryan had an anger problem, but she hadn't realized he was truly insane. Maybe that would give her something to work with. Psychopaths—the cold-blooded killers of the world—never bothered to explain themselves. Other varieties of crazy people wanted you to understand why they were planning to hurt you.

"Okay." She took a measured breath. "How about something like this? You and I develop an, uh, arrangement. Think of it as détente. You're free to do what you want, so am I. And we'll stay married."

He snorted derisively. "You expect me to fall for that? With Mr. Serious hanging on your arm? He'd never tolerate something like that. And," he leered at her, "I'm not crazy about sharing you, either. You're a great piece of ass, babe. Not sure I want anyone else's dick in there...

"Enough of this." Ryan interrupted himself by making a clicking sound. He wove his hands in circular patterns in front of him.

"Shit." Tim blew out a tense-sounding breath. "He's calling the birds."

"How do you know?" When she looked at his staff, it was glowing again.

Tim took a step back. She missed the warmth of him against her. A Gaelic chant filled the room. Confusion swirled through her. What was he up to? She was afraid to take her eyes off Ryan. Afraid he'd do something horrible if she wasn't looking. The sensation she'd had earlier, of being dragged down by an invisible, sucking web resurfaced, but she fought it.

It's illusion, she told herself. If Ryan could actually harm her directly, she'd be dead by now. No. He needed the birds for that. Or did he?

She stamped her feet and shook herself to sidestep bonds winding tighter about her. It didn't work. Panic rose. Could Ryan do something to cut off her breathing? A strangled gasp rose to her lips. Feeling like an idiot, she grappled with invisible pressure that felt as if it were crushing her windpipe.

Tim said something to her in Gaelic. She didn't understand and asked, "What?" her voice barely there.

But he'd resumed his earlier chant. Staff extended, his gaze was fixed on the Ryan projection. The inside of the tent took on a shimmery blue-gray hue. Spots swam before her eyes. Moira swayed on her feet, close to passing out. Her lungs burned. It was like drowning but without the water.

The tent door flapped open in a gust of wind. Jake raced past. A rifle report nearly deafened her, and the reek of gunpowder filled the air. A hole blossomed in the tent wall. Jake stood, rifle against one shoulder, his face twisted into a grimace. "You son of a bitch," he snarled.

The projection wavered, then resumed its previous form. Ryan laughed like a madman and smirked. "Don't waste your bullets."

She could breathe again. Maybe Jake's shot hadn't been a waste of ammunition after all. It was possible Ryan could only do one thing at a time in his current form. She gulped air, savoring its sweetness in her aching lungs. Because she was facing Jake, she saw his sharp gaze sweep over the tableau.

"Hit the deck and stay there," he screamed at her. "There's about to be a war in here."

"Like hell," she shot back. "If there's going to be a war, you need my help." Four ravens streamed into the tent before Jake got the door shut. Moira grabbed the first thing her hand closed over. An ice axe. She judged the distance and drove it into one of the bird's bodies. It fell with a squawk and lay still.

"You can't kill my birds, you sorry bitch." Ryan sounded wounded—and deranged. She felt like a fool for not seeing the signs sooner.

"Oh, really? Watch me." She buried the aluminum adze in another raven. Part of her recoiled from killing, but it was her or them. And maybe it would help keep Ryan off-balance.

"I'll take care of the last two," Jake yelled. "Get the fuck down, woman. You don't understand what we're up against, and I ain't got the time to explain." He swung the butt of the rifle he was holding and knocked one of the birds out of the air. The last one took off for the shadows at the back of the tent, cawing piteously.

"He's right." Tim's voice sounded like it was coming from a long way away. "Get down and stay there."

Moira glanced at him. Blackness shimmered in a circle, and it was obvious he was summoning magic of his own, but he'd told her he couldn't use magic that destroyed things.

No, what he said was it scared him.

Crap! He's doing this for me. A different inner voice was deathly calm.

Fear twisted her stomach into a knot. If anything happened to Tim— If he died protecting her, she'd never be able to forgive herself. Moira looked around for something—anything—she could do to help. She balled her hands into fists, frantic because she didn't know how to fight against magic. It went against the grain, but maybe the best way to help Tim was to stay out of the way, so he didn't have to split his attention.

The air got thicker. It smelled of mead and heather. The staff blazed so brightly, she couldn't look directly at it. She backed toward Christine's cot, amazed the woman hadn't woken with all the racket.

Tim turned then, hands raised in front of him like an old-world prophet. The staff pulsed in time to his chanting. His eyes glowed like otherworldly gemstones. A blushing nimbus surrounded him, protecting his body from the blackness, and his voice took on a compelling quality. Even though she couldn't understand everything he said, she picked up enough to realize he was calling on the Tuatha de Dannan—the fairies—to send Ryan straight into everlasting darkness.

Not knowing if it would help, she added a prayer of her own to the household goddess who'd blessed their hearth when she was a girl. Her grandmother had whispered stories to her about Brigid and the miracles she produced. They'd left offerings to her when things were rough. Moira felt the quick sting of tears.

If I ever needed a miracle, she prayed, *I need one now.*

Wind howling outside the tent intensified until it sounded like fifty freight trains bearing down on them. The canvas flapped so hard, she worried the tent would collapse. The door blew open, its latch ripped from its moorings.

When Jake started for it, a vicious gust knocked him on his ass. "Goddamned, motherfucker!" He screamed into the teeth of the storm.

As if it had been an invitation, twenty more birds flew inside. They split forces, but the ones heading for Tim gave up fast when they couldn't get their beaks into the light shield surrounding him.

"Down, Moira!" Tim and Jake shouted almost in unison.

She ignored them and swung the axe she'd never let go of at birds swarming around her. Two of them exploded in feathers and blood, but the rest closed on her, squawking in eerie harmony. She alternated protecting her head and face with dealing death to every bird within reach of her axe.

Tim's chanting escalated to a fever pitch, the light around him too bright to look at. A few tenacious birds flapped back to him, but they burst into flames. The odor of burned flesh thickened once Jake finally wrestled the door shut. He swung his rifle in an arc, knocking more birds out of the air.

Sparks shot from Tim's outstretched hands auguring into Ryan's image. Where they connected, long rents formed.

The Ryan projection wavered. "No!" He held up a hand. "I

didn't know what you were. I'll go, Druid. You don't have to go this far. The bitch isn't worth it."

"She's worth everything to me." Tim kept walking toward him, chanting, the staff ablaze with ghostly light.

A hand clutched her leg. Moira realized Christine was awake. "H-how did he get here?" Her voice shook, and she pointed at Ryan.

"I think it'll be all right," Moira murmured, not wanting to disturb whatever spell Tim was casting.

"No it won't." Christine's words took on a shrill note. "That creep got me drunk at a party at your house, and, uh, well you know. I tried to get him to stop, but he just kept telling me how much I wanted to fuck him—" She clapped a hand over her mouth and turned bright red. "Sorry. Probably too much information."

"Jesus." Breath rattled between Moira's teeth as she wondered how many other women Ryan screwed while he was married to her. She tore her gaze away from Tim. "You should've said something. That sounds a lot like rape."

"He said I'd be sorry if I opened my mouth." Her thin face twisted in disgust. "Said it weren't like I was a virgin. You probably wouldn't understand, but stuff like that happens to girls like me." Christine started to cry.

Moira bent and wrapped her arms around the distraught woman. "Hush. He's not really here. He can't hurt you." Then she remembered being half suffocated and hoped she was telling the truth.

A different note entered Tim's vocalizations, something higher, multi-tonal. The air felt even heavier, more threatening as if something cataclysmic were coming. Moira's skin crawled, and the fine hairs on the back of her neck lifted.

"No! Don't," Ryan shrieked just before his projection whooshed into flames, flared, and disappeared. The stink of ozone and sulfur was so strong, Moira felt ill.

The remaining ravens, seeming to sense their master was

gone, flapped cautiously, milling in a rough circle. Jake raced toward them, rifle slung upward like a bat.

"No!" Moira let go of Christine and rushed forward. "Open the door. They'll leave now."

"You don't know that," Jake growled.

"Yes," she said, "I'm not sure how I know, but I do." She clicked on her headlamp. The magical illumination had faded, and it was hard to see.

Tim dropped his arms. He closed his eyes and inhaled sharply, blowing out the breath before taking another. The staff clattered to the floor. He bent to retrieve it.

Keeping a wary eye on the birds, Jake pushed the tent door open. The ravens scuttled through, seeming to understand they'd been given a reprieve.

"It wasn't their fault," Moira murmured.

"No." Tim sounded like himself again. "It wasn't. Ryan forced those birds to act against their nature. The Tuatha will see he pays for that."

"If the Native American spirit guides ever catch up to him, they will too," she added.

Jake pinned the tent closed, turned slowly, and walked to Tim. When he was about a foot away, he lowered his head. "Thank you, Master." He straightened and trained his gaze on Tim. "I wasn't certain it was you when Moira dragged you out of the storm. It was a long time ago. You probably don't remember me, but I signed on as an acolyte about twelve years ago. Never had enough magic, though. They were nice enough about it, but they asked me to leave the priory."

Tim nodded. "I do remember you, but I'm no one's master. Never was, really." He made a sound partway between a snort and a grunt. "It's been so long, I'm surprised I recalled the incantation I needed."

Moira nailed both men with a stern look. "Who's going to tell me what just happened?"

"Yeah," Christine seconded, shoving tangled dark hair behind her shoulders. She struck a match and lit a candle lantern sitting next to her cot. "I'd like to know too. I wasn't really sleeping through most of that, I was just afraid to open my eyes. But when I did and saw Ryan—" She shrugged sheepishly. "I don't know, something just sort of snapped. I didn't realize how upset I still am about what he done to me."

Moira glanced first at Tim, then at Jake. "Well?"

"It's not my story to tell," Jake said. White teeth shone against his dark beard as he grinned at her. "Even though I never was really one of the, uh, order, I always honored the part about secrecy."

"Then you'll understand why this isn't your story to hear." Tim looked meaningfully at Jake.

"Yes, I do." Jake tapped Christine's shoulder. "Let's give these two a spot of privacy. There're sleeping bags in the next tent too."

"Okay. Let me get all my outdoor stuff back on." Christine stuck a leg into a pair of storm pants.

Tim waited until they left, then walked to Moira and drew her close. The staff felt warm against her back, even through her clothing.

"You already know some of this tale, *mo ghrá*. But I will start it at the beginning. I was raised by Druids to be the Arch Druid in this country. Problem was, I didn't want to be. My magic was strong enough, but it wasn't a calling for me like it was for some." He kneaded her back with strong fingers. "Never had much stomach for the destructive side of Druid power. That's what Arch Druids do, among other things. They mete out punishment. And kill enemies."

His arms tightened around her shoulders. "Druid vows are for life. Long before my birth, it was foretold I would be the next Arch Druid. I couldn't just tell Liam, 'Sorry, but I quit.' Like I said earlier, I couldn't tell you anything. That grated on me worse than the rest of it put together."

"So what changed? You never did tell me that part." She drew back so she could look at him. Her heart thudded heavily. It was tough to breathe. His answer would determine if they had a future together or not.

"Liam called to warn me I was in danger. It was the first time he'd called me since I left the priory, so I took the warning seriously. He'd had a vision and thought you were mixed up in things somehow. It was one of the reasons I set out after you on the trail." Tim stroked her hair tenderly back from her face.

"Before we hung up, he gave me permission to be honest with you and to ask you to be my wife." A corner of Tim's mouth turned down. "I think he finally figured out he'd never get me back any other way."

She laid her head in the crook between his shoulder and neck. Relief flashed through her, and her cheeks dampened with sudden tears.

"I haven't summoned magic for years." Tim's voice rumbled against her hair. "In truth, I was surprised the gods and goddesses helped when I asked. They can be pretty prickly about being ignored."

Moira threaded her arms around him. "I asked for help too," she admitted. "From Brigid."

"Well." He pushed back enough to smile at her, laugh lines crinkling around his eyes. "That explains it then, sweetheart. I had help."

TIM FELT a difference in the air. He spun away from Moira, staff extended, every sense on edge. The staff wasn't glowing, but maybe that didn't mean anything other than its magic needed to recharge.

"What?" She clutched his arm.

"You can stand down, son. Were you believing I'd not be by your side, knowing you faced such danger? Tch."

Relief made his knees weak. "It's all right." He touched Moira's hand and lowered the staff. "This spectral visitor is Liam." He started to laugh. "Those astral planes must be pretty crowded tonight."

He saw her eyes go wide, searching the tent for clues.

"You passed every test tonight, son, even without my help—though I was standing by, mind you. I was there while you called and controlled the most difficult part of our power. Strong work. 'Tis proud of you, I am. You forged a bond with your heritage, protecting the woman you love. Call on me as soon as you can. Even beyond what will pass between you two this night, I will see you are properly wed in the eyes of the world."

"Thank you." Gratitude swelled within him. Liam's praise—and support—meant the world. To have that, and Moira too, was everything he'd ever hoped for.

"Did it just get warmer in here?" Moira's gaze found his face, seeking confirmation.

Tim draped an arm around her shoulders. "Yes. But it will cool pretty quickly once Liam leaves."

The Arch Druid's laughter rang in Tim's ears. *"And I can be taking a hint."*

"Can you now?" Tim aped his accent. *"Do you not think I've waited long enough for yon maiden?"*

The laughter escalated.

"I just heard someone laughing their head off." Moira quirked a brow at Tim. "What was so funny?"

Warmth faded slowly from the room.

He turned so he faced her and pulled her close again. "Liam has quite a sense of humor. I'm looking forward to the two of you getting to know one another. But right now, I have other priorities."

CHAPTER 8

"**D**o you suppose those cots would be stable if we pushed a couple of them together?" Tim glanced at her, his eyes glittering naughtily.

When she looked closely, he appeared drawn. Liam's visitation aside, whatever Tim did tonight had obviously cost him.

"We might be better off making a nest out of foam pads and sleeping bags on the floor." She hugged him briefly and then stepped back. "I'll do that. Why don't you drink some tea? We never did get much supper."

He picked up the pot and tipped it. She saw his throat work as he drank, and bent to the task of nest building. By the time she felt his hands close around her waist from behind, she had a respectable heap of bedding piled against one wall.

Moira had been thinking as she pulled their bed together. "Do you believe Ryan's really gone?"

"Oh, yeah. More than gone."

She turned to face him. "What am I going to tell my boss?"

"What do you want to tell him?"

"The truth might be easiest, but somehow—"

"He wouldn't believe you," Tim cut in.

She snorted. "No. I can hardly believe it myself. Okay, guess I can stick with showing up here, finding Jake and Mitch, confronting Mitch about his dope—"

He laid a finger over her lips. "Ssht. We'll have lots of time to figure that out. Right now, there are more important things. Things I've waited my whole life for."

She cocked her head to one side, feeling the corners of her mouth twitch into a wide smile. "Oh, really? And what might those—"

He slashed his mouth down on hers and crushed her to him. This was nothing like the first kiss they'd shared. His lips were hard and insistent, his breathing fast. His tongue plumbed her mouth, and she sucked on it. His erection jutted against her almost immediately, and he made that incredible, possessive, growling noise deep in the back of his throat. Tim's unique, exotic scent—musk mingled with heather—filled the tent. She inhaled hungrily.

Hands on her ass, he pulled her firmly against him. His cock jumped against her belly. Sexual heat churned through her. Her core turned molten, panties soaking through with wanting him. Her nipples hardened, and high voltage current coursed along her nerve endings all the way to her toes. She tugged at his jacket, wanting to get rid of the clothing between them.

Moira was desperate to feel him skin-to-skin against her. She craved his cock—needed it to fill the empty space deep in her belly that clamored for him.

He lifted his mouth from hers. Back arched, she pushed against him, wanting his lips again. Tim settled his hands on her shoulders. "Open those gorgeous, golden eyes, *mo ghrá*."

When she did, panting, keen for more of him, she was surprised by how serious he looked. "It's okay," she managed, trying to figure out why he'd stopped, "I have an IUD."

"Nay, *mo ghrá*," was followed by a string of Gaelic.

She shook her head. "English, please. It's been three years since Grandma died. My Irish is rusty."

"I was asking if you're sure you want this."

She wondered how he could doubt that. Her hips writhed against him. "Yes."

He shut his eyes for a moment. When he opened them, his gaze augured into hers. "If we join our bodies, we'll be wed. It's an ancient Arch Druid ritual. In truth, we'll be more than wed. You will have joined your soul to mine for all eternity."

She drew away from him. Once she got enough space between their bodies so she could think, something nagged at her, and her next words came slowly. "I finally understand. That's why you'd never have sex with me." An unpleasant thought intruded. "Weren't you sure you wanted to spend eternity with me back then?"

"I was sure, *mo croi*. But the covenant said I couldn't wed—or have sex—until after my investiture as Arch Druid. And that wouldn't happen until Liam's death."

She snorted. "It took a while, but I finally think I know who he is. Never made the connection when Grannie talked about him. He has to be the one with the long white beard. He used to scare the hell out of me when I was a kid. Besides, looks like he's still very much alive."

"That he is. It's why he was willing to bend the rules. Of course, he didn't excuse me from all the work I'll have to do eventually to hone my magic." Tim chuckled. "When the Druids drew up that covenant sometime during the thirteen or fourteen hundreds, the average lifespan wasn't much more than thirty years. People who made fifty were ancient—"

"I don't care about people who lived hundreds of years ago. I care about us. You asked if I was sure. Are you?" Moira felt a trembling deep in her belly. She wanted Tim to love her more than she'd ever wanted anything.

"When Gaia answered my call and helped me deal with Ryan,

she reminded me you were my one true love. And told me not to blow it this time."

He laughed. "Even without her friendly little boot in the seat of my pants, something about you resonates in here." He tapped his breastbone. "You feel *right* in a way no one else ever has." A hesitation. He dropped his gaze, and then raised it so he could look at her full on. "Your turn. Do you feel it too, *mo ghrá?*"

She nodded, unable to look away, her throat clotted with emotion. "Yes. I've always loved you. I left because I didn't think you loved me."

"So, does this means you're sure?" he asked again. "There's no going back once we cross this bridge."

She swallowed hard. "Yes. More than sure." For the first time in her life, she felt absolutely certain she was doing the right thing. "Now can we lie down?"

"I thought you'd never ask." His smile warmed her to the depths of her soul. "I want to look at you, Moira. Can you stand the cold long enough to let me undress you?"

"Funny, but I was about to ask you the same thing."

He brought the candle lantern close and started with her jacket. As he stripped the layers off her body, he strung kisses across newly exposed flesh. When he drew her sports bra over her head and bent to take her breasts in hands and mouth, she arched against him.

He raised his lips from her breasts long enough to ask, "Did anyone ever tell you how beautiful you are?"

"You make me feel beautiful."

He started working on her pants, but she batted him aside. "Not fair. You still have everything on. This is starting to feel like a one-sided strip poker game." She heard him make that husky little passionate sound again as she unzipped his borrowed down jacket. Next came his brightly patterned fuzzy jacket, a vest, and his long john top. With hands that were trembling a little, she ran her fingers over the well-defined muscles in his chest and torso.

Golden hairs sprinkled lightly over his bare chest. Hard planes of muscle disappeared into the waistband of his pants.

Her breath stalled in her throat. Gorgeous. She'd never seen such a beautiful man before. He could have passed for one of the Greek gods.

"*Mo ghrá?* Is something wrong?"

She shook her head, incapable of speech. Bending her head, she licked one of his nipples and heard him gasp before he drew her close. His body felt extraordinary pressed against hers. His skin was alive where it touched her, hot and silky. She'd dreamed of what he'd feel like naked in her arms so many times. To finally have him in her arms was almost more than she could bear.

She raised her lips, and he brought his mouth down on hers. She felt hunger and desperation in that kiss—and love. The love she'd always craved from him, and never gotten before. She straddled one of his legs, rubbing herself against him. To know he wanted her as intensely as she wanted him stoked her lust. Every cell ached for release. A climax spooled deep inside. It wouldn't take much to unleash it.

"Let's get the rest of these clothes off." He pulled her down onto the heap of sleeping bags, tugged one on top of them for warmth, and unzipped both layers of her pants.

"Boots," she gasped. "Need one off."

He moved down and busied himself with her bootlaces. He worked one heavy, leather boot off her foot, and then started on the other.

She pulled him into her arms. "One's all I need."

He kissed her again, taking his time as he nipped and licked her lips. She yanked one leg free of her pants and tackled freeing his cock. Maybe because she'd figured out how to work her way through the layers of fabric and down before, it went faster this time. She loved the feel of him, hot and hard in her hands.

"Tell me what you want." His voice was rough with passion.

"You. Inside. Now." She spread her legs and felt him settle on top of her. The head of his cock probed for entrance. She wrapped her legs around his hips, her arms around his back, and curved her body against him, feeling him sink his full length into her.

He supported himself on his arms and gazed tenderly at her. "You are my first, and you shall be my last, my one, my only love." He waited, body quiet within her. "Now you," he urged a bit breathlessly. "It's the Druid wedding ceremony, although I'm sure Liam will do something more formal."

"You are my first, and you shall be my last, my one, my only love," she murmured, nearly overcome by the sentiment. "I love you."

"And I love you. I always have. I always will." He pulled nearly all the way out, then drove himself home inside her.

She could tell he was trying to make it last, but both of them were too hungry. They'd waited too long for each other as it was. The orgasm, dancing beneath the surface, rose closer and closer. The next time he sank inside her, she tightened her legs and ground her sensitive nub against the base of his cock.

He sensed her need and slammed into her, harsh, primal, fierce. His gaze never left hers. She felt his cock swell as her climax took her. Somewhere in the midst of her release, she felt him judder inside her. He cried out in Gaelic. Long moments passed before he let himself down on top of her, breath hot against her neck.

When she could talk again, she murmured. "That part about you being my first wasn't exactly true. Will it matter?"

He rolled off her onto one side and propped his head on an elbow. Joy etched deep into his face, making him even more striking. He reached out a hand and lovingly stroked her breasts. "No, *mo ghrá*. What matters is that now we are bound, soul to soul, through this life and all lives to come. Have you ever made love like this, drowning in your partner's eyes, in their spirit?"

"No."

"Then the most important part of you came to me as a virgin. All is well."

She cuddled against him. Peace enveloped her. She felt like a ship that had finally found port after a long and arduous journey at sea. Her hull had been breached, her sails ripped, but there was finally an opportunity to mend the rents in her soul.

Moira closed her eyes. She didn't realize she'd drifted off, but Tim's voice woke her.

"Where do you live?" he asked.

"Three Rivers and Fresno. Depends on the season. I own a home in Three Rivers. Or I think I do. Depends how the divorce comes out."

"He'll be declared dead once his body is found. As a macabre aside, it will be interesting to see where it is. Liam will marry us legally as soon as the ink's dry on the death certificate."

Tim sounded so sure about Ryan, she decided not to question him. Magic still unnerved her.

"Do you want to keep working?" he asked.

"Huh?" She wasn't sure she'd heard him right.

"You wouldn't have to," he murmured, his voice mellow against her ear.

"I-I'm not sure. Besides, after I file my report on what happened to my trail crew, I may not even have a job."

"We don't have to make any decisions right now. I'm sure I can find another medically underserved area around Fresno and transfer the last year I owe the U.S. government for paying for my schooling. Or you could move to Bishop."

Sleep tugged at her eyelids. It had to be well past midnight. "Morning—" she began sleepily, fitting her body to his. "We can figure things out in the morning and after that too."

"Sure, love, we'll talk more then." He cradled her against him and stroked her hair.

～

WHEN SHE OPENED HER EYES, it was unnaturally quiet. The soft sound of Tim's breathing filled her ears. The howl of the wind had died. She scrabbled on the floor for her watch, not wanting to disturb him.

My God!

She tapped the crystal with a grimy finger, not believing it could possibly be noon. Moira started to slip out of bed. She wanted to look outside to assess just how much more snow had fallen.

Tim stirred. He reached out a hand, closed it around her wrist, and made a sleepy, satisfied male sound.

She laughed, surprised by how happy she felt. "Let go, silly. I want to put my clothes on and take a look outside."

"Storm's over."

She looked at him. "Well, I don't hear the wind anymore, but how can you know?"

He shrugged. "Maybe it's another gift from the gods. I dreamed about several of them last night. I think they were pleased to hear from me again."

"You're feeling better about your Druid roots and vows."

He turned a brilliant smile her way. "Maybe I'm not the only one who's prescient. Liam tried to explain how everything needed an opposite, but I don't think I truly understood until I called up the side of the magic I've always hated last night."

An odd expression—sheepish and resolute at the same time—crossed his face. "I didn't just summon destruction. I embraced it with my entire being. And I'd do it again in an instant if you were threatened. One of the things I plan to do, after we get out of here, is tell Liam he was right."

"I guess you're seriously considering the Arch Druid thing." She quirked a brow his way.

He cocked his head to one side. "Yes, *mo ghrá*, I am. Once I've paid my debt to the government. Would you mind?"

She touched his face with tentative fingers, still coming to grips with the fact her one true love had dropped out of the sky and back into her life. "No. I wouldn't mind at all. I want you to do what feels right."

He closed a hand over hers. A beatific smile lit his face. "I love you. It's so wonderful to finally be free to tell you that." He reached for his clothes. "Time to get going and see what gifts this day will bring."

"I don't need any more gifts." Joy, an unfamiliar emotion, warmed her. "You were the only one I ever wanted."

"*Mo ghrá—*" He kissed her, and the warmth of his embrace lit a path all the way to her soul. Maybe it was the Druid wedding ceremony, but she felt the bond linking her to Tim as if it had a life of its own, and she reveled in the rightness of it.

She'd just fastened the last of her outer clothing and laced up the boot she hadn't slept in when she heard the whirr of chopper blades. Moira ran to the door and yanked it open. When she waded out into thigh deep snow, she was rewarded by the sight of a helicopter circling.

How the hell is the pilot going to land?

"Grab a couple shovels," she called over her shoulder. "Hurry. We have to hog out a platform for the chopper."

She and Tim were shoveling as fast as they could when Jake and Christine joined them. It didn't take long to clear a forty by forty foot square. The four of them dropped back to be out of the way of the rotor wash when the bird's skids kissed the earth.

John Musgrove, five foot ten and burly, clambered out of the helicopter as soon as it touched down. He loped through the snow and stood facing her. With his brown hair in its usual crew cut, his rigid bearing practically screamed ex-Marine. Deep worry lines were etched in his forehead and cheeks.

He muttered, "Aw, to hell with protocol," before he swept her into a bear hug. "Thank Christ you're okay," he said as he stepped away from her. "This has been a hell of a season for deaths."

His gaze strayed to Jake and Christine. He walked the few

steps to where they stood and held out a gloved hand. "We're taking you home," he said, his voice gruff. "And we're paying you double for this trip."

"Oh, you don't have to—" Jake began.

"Shut up." John punched his shoulder affectionately. "Beyond that, you've been working for us for years. Isn't it time you signed up for a real job?"

Jake's eyes widened. "Really?"

"Yes. Really. You're in. Ask Betty for the paperwork once you get back. I've already signed it. You too, Christine."

"Wow! Thanks, sir." Her face broke into a grin, then she shook her head. "Don't feel right to be happy just yet. Too many ain't comin' back from this trip at all."

"Yeah, thanks, sir. Uh, Mr. Musgrove." Jake sounded so nonplussed, Moira gave him a hug.

"It'll be all right," she said. "You'll see. Maybe they'll let both of you be my assistants on trips like this."

She turned to John. "What do you want to do about the rest of the crew? And the mules?" Even before the words were out, she wondered if she'd be able to find any of the bodies without search and rescue dogs.

John looked at her. "It's the weirdest thing. Just like it was a freak storm, we also weren't expecting this break in the weather. It's supposed to close in for at least three more days by tonight. Once it clears—and we get some meltage—I'll send a crew in from Cedar Grove with dogs to round up the bodies and the stock." He grimaced. "Probably won't be much left of the remains by then, but it can't be helped."

He clapped his hands together. "Get your things. We've got time for two or three chopper trips, tops. So hurry."

He looked at Tim and frowned. "Who are you?"

"I ran into him on the trail," Moira said. "He's a doctor who lives in Bishop. And a very old friend of mine. We grew up together."

"Not sure quite what you were doing on the trail." John eyed Tim sharply, no doubt taking in his borrowed U.S. Park Service clothing. "Judging from your duds, I'm betting this woman probably saved your life."

"Yes, sir. I give her full credit." Tim held out a hand. John clasped it warmly.

John smiled, really smiled. He was usually so serious, it took Moira by surprise. "Come on, everybody." He clapped his hands together once more. "Get moving. Need to take advantage of this weather window while we've got it. Let me know how I can help."

"Most of the expensive stuff is in here." Moira pointed to the supply tent. "And Mitch's body is wherever Jake laid him out."

"Okay." Her boss's usual dour demeanor was back in spades. "We'll start with Mitch and see that he's in the first chopper trip out of here. Lead the way."

MOIRA EYED THE SKIES. So far, luck had been with them, and the chopper was just returning from its fourth trip shuttling material back to Cedar Grove, the roar of its rotors loud in her ears.

"Clear weather's not going to last much longer." John made his way to her side burdened with two full packs.

Tim dragged one of the heavy canvas tents to their staging area. He'd broken it down and packaged it for transport. "What else?" He walked to where she and John stood.

"Probably all we'll have room for," John replied. "This next trip will be the last one. Wind's picking up, which is never a good sign. I'll do one more quick pass to make certain we didn't miss anything critical." Turning, he trotted over the tamped down snow and disappeared into one of the two tents they'd left standing.

Moira took the opportunity to give Tim a quick kiss. "Thanks." She beamed at him. "You've worked your ass off for us."

"Least I could do." He grinned back and took her hand. "What happens once we get back? I'll be on the wrong side of the Sierras."

"Guess I'll just have to grab a park vehicle and drive you home."

"Ask for a couple days off. Once we get there, I suspect you won't want to leave." He winked broadly.

"I like the way you think." Her heart swelled with love for the man by her side. She wanted to throw herself into his arms and never leave.

"Don't encourage me, *mo ghrá*. You never know where it might lead—"

John loped back to where they stood. "Nope. We're good."

The chopper touched down amid blowing snow. Once the fine, white mist settled, they each grabbed something and loaded the helicopter.

Once that was done, Moira settled into one of two back seats across a narrow aisle from Tim. The bird rose, banked, and headed west. When Tim snaked a hand across the aisle and rested in in her lap, she clasped it.

Happy. I never believed I could be this happy.

"Believe it, *mo ghrá*," sounded deep in her mind. *I'll devote my life to making certain you stay that way."*

"Will I be able to talk with you that way?" She kept her words low, but there wasn't much risk of John or the pilot hearing over the engine noise.

Tim nodded. "Probably. It's part of how we're bound." He tightened his fingers around hers and she squeezed back. "Try to get some rest."

She stroked the back of his hand with her fingertips, loving the feel of him. "Great advice, but this is a really short chopper ride. Less than half an hour."

"Let me help then."

A soothing warmth surrounded her, tinged with Tim's heather

and mead scent. It was like he was hugging her from across the aisle, and she sank into the warmth of his love.

All too soon, the bird circled, preparing to land.

"Did that help?" Tim caught her gaze and held it. At her nod, he went on. "I'm sorry about Ryan. If there'd been any other way—"

"I know," she cut in. "Now's a time for us to look forward, not back."

"Agreed, but if you ever want to talk about—well, about any of it, we can. I want you to be able to talk with me about anything."

"Same goes on my side."

"Hang on, kids." John's voice cracked through the speaker. "We're almost home."

CHAPTER 9

*T*im glanced sidelong at Moira before returning his attention to the road. They'd left Three Rivers hours ago, and she'd needed a break, so he'd taken over at the wheel. Another ninety minutes, and they'd be in Bishop. Moira sprawled in the passenger seat with her head resting on an arm propped against the window. Her wheat-colored hair spilled around her, lush with curls. He loved looking at the clean lines of her cheeks and jaw. At her full lips and up-turned nose. At the swell of breasts beneath her uniform shirt.

He still couldn't believe they were linked for now and forever, and he thanked whichever of the gods—or goddesses—had allowed him a second chance to be with the only woman he'd ever cared about. His cock rose to attention remembering the feel of her body around it. At first he ignored the sensations streaming through him and pushed his erection to a more comfortable position, the reaction second nature. After all, he'd sublimated his sexuality for years.

I don't have to do that anymore.

The revelation was startling and thrilling. His cock throbbed against his belly, clearly liking the idea too. He glanced out the window, hunting for a place to stop. It didn't matter when they got to his house. Moira had the rest of the week off. This part of Highway 395 held a million possibilities, with dirt roads leading into the mountains on both sides. He found a likely prospect and slowed the car. Turning off the pavement as gently as possible, he drove for another half mile down a rutted dirt road.

Moira stirred, and her gorgeous eyes flickered open. "Where are we?"

"Around the Tioga Pass turnoff. I thought… I mean I hoped…"

Moira's laughter chimed like temple bells. She slid a hand into his lap and curled it around his ridged flesh. "Hoped you'd get lucky?"

Tim felt his face flush. He pulled onto a spur off the dirt road and killed the engine. Holding out his arms, he quirked a brow. "Well, will I?"

"I'd say it's a strong possibility."

She fell across the console into his arms and angled her face for a kiss. He covered her mouth with his, delighted when she opened to his questing tongue. Moira closed her arms around him and splayed her hands across his back. She nipped his lower lip and kneaded his shoulders with strong, nimble fingers.

He could've kissed her for hours, exploring her face and lips and ears and neck with his mouth. She moved a hand back to curve around his cock, caressing it through his trousers. He reached between them to unbutton her blouse, and she tore her mouth from his.

"Outside."

He was so lost in wanting her, the word didn't register. He tugged her shirt out of the way and rubbed her erect nipples through her bra.

Moira cupped the side of his face. "Outside. There's a tarp in the back of the car. We can lay it on the ground and—"

Tim grinned feeling like an idiot. "Sorry, *mo ghrá*, afraid I missed lovemaking 101. You'll have to be patient."

She cast a fond smile his way. "It's not about patient. This is a totally self-serving suggestion on my part. Plus, I didn't notice any gaps in your knowledge base the other night."

"Yeah, well, you can thank med school for that. Plus I've been making love to you in my dreams forever."

"That's very sweet, 'cause you never left mine, either. Not really." She gave him one last, lingering kiss and pushed the car door open. Going around to the back, she opened the hatch of the Park Service SUV. He joined her, peering inside. "What can we use?"

"This." Moira handed him a folded tarp. "And I'll get a couple blankets. Every car has something slightly different in it. Basically, they're equipped for survival if you get stranded."

He trotted to a patch of level ground and deployed the tarp. They were far enough from the highway, he wasn't worried about being disturbed. When Moira came with the blankets, he pried them out of her arms and arranged them over the tarp. With a small mock bow, he wove a hand around her waist. "Your bower awaits, *mo ghrá*."

She came into his arms, body full against him. He pushed his hands up under her hair and cradled her head, just looking at her, drinking in her beauty. Hunger for him danced in the backs of her eyes, and she ran a finger down the side of his face. Turning, he captured it in his mouth, sucking on the tip.

"I still can't get over being able to make love with you whenever I want." A catch rode beneath her words.

He let go of her finger. "It does feel like a miracle, all in itself." One at a time, he finished undoing the buttons of her shirt, not in any hurry, enjoying undressing her. She reached behind her back to unclasp her bra, and he pushed it up so he could fill his hands with her luscious breasts. He rolled the nipples between his fingers, and she leaned into him, making a purring noise that did extraordinary things to his cock.

"We made ourselves a bed. Let's lie down," she murmured breathlessly.

Tim knelt on the blankets and eased her down next to him. He unlaced her boots and levered them off before returning to her breasts. Her fingers were busy at his waistband, and she unfastened his belt and pants, freeing his cock. Her hands on him were better than his wildest imaginings, but when she slithered out of his grip, kissed her way down his belly and took him into her mouth, he had to weave magic into the mix to keep from exploding.

She ran a hand up his shaft and laved the head of his penis with her tongue. Everywhere she touched him, a million sparks danced. He plunged a hand between her legs and met fabric. Placing a hand on either side of her head, he pulled his erection from her mouth.

"Hold that thought, darling. I got sidetracked. Let's get the rest of these clothes off you." He undid her pants and pulled them down her legs, freeing both this time. Next he stripped off her panties and socks. Starting with her feet, he ran his tongue between her toes, sucking each one before moving up her inner legs, keeping his mouth glued to her warm, pliant flesh.

She jackknifed her body around and recaptured him in her mouth, taking him deep. He thrust into the steamy heat of her and forced himself to continue his thorough exploration of her legs with his mouth, getting to know every muscle, every nuance. He wanted to plunge his tongue into her musky center, but hoped she'd be so primed for him, she'd come almost as soon as he latched onto her clit.

Moira altered his plans when she dragged his mouth upward until it was inches from her hot core. He held off, just breathing on her as her hips writhed beneath him. In a single movement, he pushed two fingers inside her and closed his mouth over her clit, sucking hard. She dissolved around him in a flood of heat, crying his name. In her passion, she worked his cock harder with mouth and hands. All the magic in the world couldn't stave off his orgasm, and it bubbled out of him in jets of white hot glory that didn't shave much off his lust.

She drank him dry, and he pulled from her mouth. "Turn over." His voice was rough with wanting her. "We're not done."

"I'll never be done with you." She grinned wantonly. "We waited too long for this."

"Over, wench. On your knees."

Her chest and face were splotched with a lovely rose color. When she flipped over, he saw that her back was too. Her sex gleamed wetly, surrounded by golden curls.

With a cry he barely recognized as his own voice, Tim surged forward, burying his still-hard cock in the scorching heat of her. Because he'd just come, he didn't have to ride an edge of control. He drove into her hard and fast, wanting to make her his forever. She met him stroke for stroke, pushing back against him until the whole world was awash in sensation.

His cock swelled inside her, harder than it had ever been. He gripped her hips like a drowning man. When he felt the contractions of her climax around him, he let himself go, juddering into her until the world shimmered with power, and he realized sex was yet one more road to his magic.

He held her against him, kneeling behind her, until his cock softened and slid from her body. Then he lay next to her and gathered her into his arms. "If I'd known how good this would be, I don't know if I'd have been able to hold off."

She cradled his face in her hands. "No looking back. I'm just happy we have a life ahead of us. I still can't quite believe it."

"Me, either." He kissed the tip of her nose and held her, glorying in the feel of her in his arms.

She shivered and pulled one end of the blanket over them. "Probably should get moving. I'd love to stay here forever and block the world out, but I'm hungry."

"You being hungry is a very good thing. We should take

advantage of it." He sat and handed her clothes to her before gathering his own and putting them on. Getting to his feet, he offered her a hand and then bent to the task of folding the blankets. Moira tackled the tarp.

The cool breeze around them shifted to a harsh wind. Bushes and trees rattled, and stones rose in small vortices, creating glowing mandalas in the air. Tim scented power, and dropped the blankets. He wrapped his arms around Moira, who'd let go of the tarp.

Her eyes widened; her body stiffened in his arms. "What the hell is that? I thought Ryan was dead."

"He is. Make no mistake about it. What you feel is magic, though. Native American, if I'm any judge." He urged her toward the car. "I can handle whatever this is, but I need you to lock yourself in the car. Metal will shield you from—"

"There's no need for that. I do not mean her harm."

Singing Bear stepped from one of the shimmering mandalas. His silver-streaked black hair was braided into two thick plaits that fell to his waist. Form-fitting leather garments hugged his tall, spare form, and homemade boots laced to his knees. Deep lines accentuated his hawk-like nose and high cheekbones. A silver bracelet set with turquoise curled around one wrist.

Tim faced the apparition with his hands raised to summon power. He didn't sense danger, but Ryan's father might well want revenge for his son's death. Tim picked his words carefully. "I recognize your energy from when I first met you. Why have you chosen to show yourself?"

"I think it's all right. He always liked me." Moira twisted away from Tim and addressed her next words to Singing Bear. "I wondered if I'd ever see you again. I'm sorry about what happened to—"

He waved her to silence. "Ryan is why I'm here. Indulge me for a moment, daughter-in-law. I owe you an apology."

Tim waited, energy at the ready in case it was a ruse.

Singing Bear inclined his head Tim's way. "Thank you for allowing me to speak. Your magic is more powerful than mine, and you could force me away."

"Why do you owe me an apology?" Moira asked. "I never blamed you for Ryan's screw-ups."

"You don't understand." Singing Bear's form wavered, and then solidified again. "Your friend will, though, since he is a magic man in his own right. Power marks you, brands you, if you will. It takes a strong vessel to hold power and not be seduced by it. Controlled by it." He cast a glance Tim's way as if asking for help.

Tim nodded. "It's the same with my order. Those who have weak characters don't do well. Power drives them mad. We try to weed those out at the front end of things. Easier for everybody that way."

"Exactly." Singing Bear made a hand sign of assent. "It pains me to admit, but Ryan was weak. I knew his spirit was too fragile to wield power, but he was my only son, so I kept hoping something would change. In truth, I never should have let him anywhere near anything magical."

He latched his dark gaze onto Moira. "That, white woman, is what I am sorry for. I hoped you might change Ryan. Give him the strength he lacked." Emotion played over his stark features. "I encouraged the marriage—even though it was outside our bloodlines. Not for you, but for my son."

Singing Bear turned away. "I knew what Ryan was. I should have warned you, but I was selfish and held my peace. I have far-seeing dreams. I ignored them all—until the one that told me your life was in danger. Then I acted. I thank the Great Ones I was not too late."

"You couldn't have known," Moira said in a pain-filled voice. "You did your best by Ryan. I saw you try to help him so many times—"

"Stop! Don't make excuses for me. I used you. I hoped your strength of character would rub off on my son and somehow save him." The old Native American bowed until his head almost touched the ground before straightening. "For that, I am most humbly sorry."

"We appreciate the effort it took for you to come to us—" Tim began, cognizant of the other man's pain, and wanting to mitigate it.

"I'm not done," Singing Bear cut in. "My next words are for you, Druid. When I understood Ryan had returned that night in the wilderness—still intent on killing Moira—I hurried back, but another Druid stopped me. Assured me you had things under control."

Tim nodded. "That would've been Liam. He was worried about me, yet knew my time to wield destructive magic had finally arrived."

Singing Bear paused, his features scrunched in embarrassment and resignation. "It was providential you were there because you finished what I didn't have the heart for. Ryan needed to move on. He was too damaged to remain in this life. Perhaps when his journey begins anew, his spirit will grow straighter."

"I hope that too," Tim said, all too aware of how broken hopes and dreams could scar a life.

"For the two of you," the shaman spread his arms wide, "I offer my blessings for a long and fruitful life together. It isn't much, but I want you to know I bear you no ill will. Quite the opposite."

Tears streaked Moira's face. "If you were here, I'd hug you."

"Thank you, daughter. You were a far better wife than my son deserved."

The air turned incandescent around them, bathing the glade where they stood with every color of the rainbow. Tim wrapped his arms around Moira from behind and held her until the colors faded.

"He's quite a man," Tim said. "To be that candid and blunt about your own blood is rare."

"He gave us a clean slate." Moira's eyes sheened with fresh tears.

Tim nodded. "That he did. To be forgiven by the one who has every right to hate me and to curse me through this world and all the ones beyond, is enormous. It truly does offer us a fresh beginning—even beyond the one we'll create for ourselves." He tightened his hold on Moira and snugged her against him. She turned in his arms and hugged him back.

"You killed for me. I'll never forget that." Her voice was muffled against his shoulder.

"That I did. And I'd do it again to keep you safe and by my side forever."

"Forever," she echoed. "I like the sound of that."

"So do I." He linked a hand beneath one of her arms and guided her back to their car. "Now let's see about that dinner."

"Yes. I'd like that." She bent and picked up the tarp, and he retrieved the blankets.

Once the things were back in the car, he tipped her chin up with an index finger. "I love you, Moira. You bless my life with your presence."

"I love you too, Tim. I always have. I should've known better than to—"

He laid a hand over her mouth. "No looking back. After Singing Bear's words, we truly don't have to."

"You got it. Can we plan our wedding over dinner?"

"Absolutely, *mo ghrá*. Absolutely. In truth, it's a good idea to have what we want firmly in hand before Liam takes off with the bit in his teeth."

"The more I hear about him, the more I can't wait to get to know him better."

Tim winked. "I'm sure he feels the same way. You were his prime competition. He thought he could wait you out—but he didn't count on what I wanted."

Her smile faded, replaced by a solemn expression. "Thanks for never giving up on us."

Love flooded him and cracked his heart wide open. "No thanks needed. Now let's see about that dinner."

"You're on." She sprinted around to her car door and got inside.

Tim stood for a moment watching the clean lines of her body as she moved. After mouthing a silent prayer to the gods for reuniting them, he joined Moira and nosed the car back to the highway.

IF YOU ENJOYED this peek into the High Sierra, keep reading for a story that will take you deep into myth, magic, and Andean mountain gods out for blood. Mountain stories cut close to home for me. I've spent many a day, week, month, and year with a pack on my back. It's why I can write stories about living in the backcountry. I've been there. Done that. And captured my very own alpha while I was at it.

BOOK DESCRIPTION: ALPINE ATTRACTION

Book Description:

Tina made a pact with the devil seven years ago. It's time to pay the piper—or die.

Independent to the nth degree, Tina meets everything in her life head-on—except love. When an almost-forgotten pact with the devil returns to haunt her, Tina throws a trip to the Andes together to face her nemesis. Better to die on her feet than wait for him to make good on his threats.

Craig never understood why Tina walked out of his life years before. He's never loved anyone like he loved her. His mountain guide service takes up all his time, but he's never forgotten her. When his back's been up against the wall, he's invited her to fill in as expedition doctor, but beyond that, he's kept his distance. Having his heart stomped on once was quite enough.

Caught between misgivings and need, Tina signs on as team doctor for one of Craig's climbing trips to the Andes. Though he was the love of her life, she pushed him away years before to keep him safe. Even if he doesn't love her anymore, there's still no one she'd rather have by her side in the mountains. And if she's going to die, she wants to make things right between them.

CHAPTER 10

A heavy weight jammed Tina McKenzie against her mattress. The pressure doubled and then tripled. Her eyes snapped open, but her bedroom was inky black, and she couldn't see a thing. Breathing became a struggle. Her physician-trained brain panicked. She writhed against an invisible mass on top of her.

It pushed back.

A burned odor with overtones of death and rot invaded her nostrils. It smelled like the cadaver lab but without formalin. Insidious cold seeped into her bones. Whatever held her down was freezing her from the inside out. Her heart stuttered. Breath clogged in her throat, unable to move past her squashed larynx. How long could she live without oxygen before she sustained brain damage? A few minutes at best. Her mind shied away from what was happening. The thing in her bedroom wasn't human. It couldn't be; it wasn't breathing.

Shit. I'm going to die here.

In full panic mode, she thrashed against her unseen assailant, but she couldn't budge it more than an inch or so. No point wasting energy screaming. She lived so remotely, no one would hear. She tried to raise her arms, but they were pinned against her sides. A flickering white haze fractured her vision.

People don't die in dreams.

Nice try. I'm not dreaming, another inner voice chimed in.

"No, you are not dreaming." A guttural voice sounded deep in her mind.

Accented, it reminded her of… Understanding slammed home and left her reeling. It wasn't possible. Shivers cascaded down her body. Her blood turned to ice.

"Good," the voice continued, silky smooth, almost like a macabre caress. *"You remember me."*

"What?" she sputtered, "You can read my thoughts?"

"Of course." He chuckled, but the sound was ominous. *"You made me a promise. I gave you seven years. They've nearly expired. Consider yourself fortunate I was kind enough to remind you."*

"Y-you tracked me down?" Her teeth chattered.

The chuckle morphed into a laugh. *"I have always known where to find you. Did you delude yourself you were invisible here in the United States? Blood for blood, doctor. You owe me."*

As quickly as it had come, the pressure squeezing the life out of her body vanished. Tina shot to a sitting position and sucked air until her oxygen-starved lungs calmed. She wanted to scream —to curl into a ball and howl—but she was afraid if she gave in to hysteria, she'd never get herself under control again.

Even though common sense told her the danger had passed, she couldn't stop shaking. Once she thought her legs might support her, she tottered to the window, grasped the light-blocking drapes, and shoved them aside. Medical school and residency had destroyed her natural sleep-wake cycle. She'd installed the room-darkening shades in an attempt to normalize it, except it hadn't worked. She still was awake until very late. Most nights she struggled to get four hours sleep.

Still numb and shaking, she gazed out the window. The glass

frosted with cold told her it must've dipped below freezing last night. The sky in the east held a pearlescent cast. Dawn. It would be a sunny autumn day in Leadville, Colorado. Too bad the sun wouldn't percolate into her soul. Tina wrapped her arms around herself. She was so cold she wondered if she'd ever get warm again.

Think, she commanded herself. *There's got to be a way out of this. Yeah, like what?*

Years had passed since she entered into what she'd always considered a pact with the devil. The farther she'd gotten from that nightmare in the Andes, the more certain she'd become that she'd never have to keep her end of the bargain. So much for that pipedream.

Tina walked to her dresser. She tugged the ragged, sweat-soaked T-shirt over her head and surveyed her bedroom. For once in her life she was unsure what to do. Gooseflesh rose, a visceral reminder of her nakedness. She pulled black sweatpants and a top out of a drawer and put them on, followed by ankle socks and her running shoes. She picked up her iPhone to consult its calendar and then dropped it back onto the top of the dresser. October 15th. In two months and ten days, her time would be up.

Adrenaline shot through her. Her stomach roiled. Bile burned the back of her throat. She strode down the hall and stopped in the kitchen long enough to pour water and beans into the coffee maker and set the timer. Knowing she'd have hot coffee waiting when she returned, she let herself out the back door and sucked in a restless breath. The vista of the Rockies, jagged against a bluebird sky, usually soothed her.

Not today.

Her jogging route was always the same: eight miles and two thousand feet of climbing. It took a little less than ninety minutes. She did it every day she was home, regardless of the weather. In winter it took longer because she used snowshoes.

Tina turned to glance at the buff-colored, turn-of-the-century, two-story farmhouse she called home. It had been in her family for ages. A few miles out of town, she'd always considered the location perfect because no one bothered her.

Wind bullied the last of the leaves off the aspen trees. She debated returning to fetch a hat, but didn't want to go back inside. Her house wasn't hers anymore. The thing—mountain spirit or shaman or whatever the fuck he was—had invaded her territory. It felt sullied. Unclean.

I'm going to have to get over that.

She didn't believe in the paranormal. She was a scientist, goddammit, trained to believe in what she could see and feel and touch, in what was illuminated under her microscope when she worked in an Emergency Room. Her experience nearly seven years before had been so surreal, she'd relegated it to high altitude hypoxia.

Tina ran hard to clear her mind, except it didn't work. Sweat slicked her sides. Her breath came fast. She'd buried the memory of what happened in Bolivia, but it came roaring back with a vengeance, almost as if it resented the hell out of the subterranean prison she'd confined it to at the very bottom of her psyche.

Seven years ago in the Andes

Tina struggled against wind. It wanted to flatten her, or worse, blow her off Illimani's long, summit ridgeline. She was by herself. Twenty-two hundred vertical feet separated her from her camp on the edge of the glacier.

"At least I can still see," she muttered. "And I got the summit."

She glanced at her watch illuminated in the beam of her headlamp. One in the morning. Normally, she would've waited until around then to start climbing, but wind shrieking like a banshee had made it impossible to sleep. She'd set up her camp at eight p.m. and headed for the mountaintop without stopping to think too hard. She wanted Illimani's summit. It was the second highest peak in Bolivia and a huge massif with five separate highpoints.

And now I've done it.

Careful, a different inner voice cautioned. *Ninety percent of climbing accidents happen on the way down.*

A vicious blast of wind buffeted her. Tina slammed one of her ice axes into the snow to anchor herself to the mountain. As if her grim thoughts were prophetic, clouds descended, obliterating what had been a clear sky in a matter of minutes.

What the fuck?

She peered through impenetrable muck and halted her descent. "Shit," she muttered. "I can't see." Surely the clouds were a momentary event. They'd pass, especially in this wind. They had to. Minutes ticked by. Visibility eroded even farther. She took a steadying breath and then another. No sat phone. No radio. No one even knew where she was.

Yeah, I broke a bunch of really important rules.

This peak was supposed to be easy.

Oh, shut up.

"Got to pull myself together." Tina spoke out loud to calm herself. She visualized where she'd been on the mile-long ridge. She'd passed the false summit, so she had to be close to the lip that dropped off a fifty-degree cliff. Her heart thudded against her ribs. She panted from more than the twenty thousand foot altitude. She swallowed, but dry throat tissue grated against itself. Stooping, she gathered some snow in a glove, made a ball out of it, and placed it in her mouth.

Another blast of wind was so intense she planted her other axe. "Get going," she instructed herself. "Now."

Moving by feel, one painstaking step at a time, Tina worked out a rhythm. She probed the snow ahead with an axe. If it held, she moved down to it and stopped. To counteract the vertigo from navigating through thick fog, she counted steps. Her first guess was it wouldn't take more than five hundred to reach the edge of the ridge. On three fifty-six, one of her axes punched through into open air. Tina threw her body backward, gasping.

This was how climbers died. By getting cocky and making bad decisions.

She got to her feet on legs that shook and shoved an axe into the snow. A chunk fell away. She moved a few degrees to the right; more snow flaked off. By the time she'd inscribed a forty-five degree arc, she knew she had to be at the end of the ridge. Tina fumbled at the hardware belt hanging from her harness and got an ice screw. She threaded it carefully into what felt like firm snow, clipped in a carabineer, and ran her rope through it. Next came a breaker bar attached to her harness so she could rappel down the steep part.

If this went well, she'd be on the glacier in minutes.

Her breath came fast. She moved more by feel than anything else. Her headlamp beam was weak, and she didn't have fresh batteries. She tossed out a silent prayer to the god who took care of climbers, children, and fools. That done, she double-checked her rope and attachments, and turned to face the slope. Her ice axes dangled from her wrists; her crampon points bit into the snow. She backed down until she felt the slope steepen and then moved the hand that would control her descent out to the side. Her other hand gripped the rope over her head to steady her descent.

The minute she put her full weight on her anchor, it ripped out of the snow. The rope, worthless since it wasn't attached to anything, flew through the breaker bar. An end whapped her in the face.

Holy Christ. I'm falling...

She flailed her axes like a wild woman. Once. Again.

One connected with something and held. Tina slammed in the

other, followed by the front points of her crampons. She screamed. Wind ripped the sound away as soon as it left her throat. Fright balled her stomach into a burning knot. One of her crampon front points slipped.

Can't stay put. Got to move down. No point in going up. Nothing solid up there.

Images of falling to her death pounded through her head. To keep from going mad, she lectured herself out loud. "Move one thing at a time. Three solid points of attachment before I move anything. Test everything. Then test it again... Okay, here we go."

Finally, the angle of the slope eased. Her rope had been nothing but a pain in the ass, dangling from the breaker bar attached to her harness. She'd stabbed her front points through it time and time again. Past the steepest part, she let herself move a little faster. The edge of the glacier was the most welcome thing she'd ever found.

She tugged the rope free and tried to coil it, but her hands shook so badly she couldn't. Tina dropped the rope onto the snow and sat on it. It was an indulgence, but she cradled her arms around her body and cried. She was a long way from safety, but the sheer relief of being off the steep face was overwhelming.

The wind hadn't let up at all. Though not as bad as it had been on the ridge, it was still gusting at forty or fifty miles an hour. She unbuckled her pack and forced herself to eat an energy bar washed down with water from the bottle stashed in her parka to keep it from freezing. Her headlamp flickered. She shut it off.

Tina shivered. She was still a thousand feet above her camp, and she had to cross a glacier riddled with crevasses. The transit would be child's play on a sunny day—or even by moonlight. A night like this one with near zero visibility turned it into a deadly game of Russian roulette. If she'd brought a sleeping bag, she would've stayed put for what was left of the night.

She wasn't totally certain exactly where her camp was. She hadn't thought to set wands to mark her route. She didn't have a

GPS with her. Tina struggled to her feet and buckled her pack into place. She'd made a series of neophyte climbing errors, beginning with assuming clear weather would last the next twenty-four hours. She'd badly underestimated Illimani.

The mountain was laughing at her.

Tina thought about laughing back, but didn't want to tempt fate. Besides, she didn't feel much like laughing. She flicked her headlamp back on and checked her compass to make sure she wouldn't descend the wrong side of the mountain. Back to counting steps, she contained her fear as best she could. The glacier wasn't particularly steep, but…

A brutal chop of wind sent her sideways. She planted both axes, but the snow beneath her gave way. Tina tumbled into blackness.

Aw shit, it's a crevasse, a crevasse, a crevasse, echoed in her mind.

She crashed through two snow bridges. The third one held. She was afraid to breathe, afraid to do anything that might threaten the fragile margin standing between her and death. In the feeble beam of her headlamp, she glanced upward.

Fifty feet. I fell fifty feet. Thank God nothing's broken.

Snow bridges were always thicker at their ends. She moved ever so cautiously until she was right next to the smooth inner ice wall of her tomb. She slung an axe into the ice. It bounced off. She tried again. Same result. She kicked with her front points. After many attempts, she was sweating and panting.

"Goddammit," she shrieked. "Fuck."

"Got to get hold of myself," she muttered. "If I don't, I'm as good as dead."

Tina shut her eyes. If she couldn't climb out with her tools, maybe she could pound in ice screws. They had threads. She wasn't certain she had enough to make it all the way out, but she could recycle them as she climbed.

No choice. Not really. She'd freeze to death if she didn't keep moving. It was very cold in the crevasse. Colder than it had been out on the glacier.

It took a long time to twist the first ice screw in. The second one was easier. Using screws, carabineers, her rope, and jumars, she made it about twenty feet from the snow bridge when her headlamp died. "Shit." She pounded impotently against the ice. "I can't believe I was this stupid. Shit. Fuck. Damn it all to hell."

I can curse all I want, I'm going to die here.

She hung limply in her harness. Her sweat-damp body shivered. The doctor part of her wondered how long it would take to die. Freezing to death was a lot like going to sleep. She wasn't certain what time it was, but it couldn't be much past four. Dawn was at least two hours away. Maybe she could hold on, but she didn't think it likely.

A putrid smell filled her nostrils. It got even colder. *"Human woman,"* sounded deep in her mind in a strangely accented voice.

"Who said that?" Tina twisted from side to side, but she couldn't see a thing in the blackness.

Aw crap, I'm hallucinating.

"I offer you a chance to live," the voice continued.

"How could you possibly do that?"

Am I losing my mind? Hypoxia? Harness cutting off my wind?

"If I bring you to the surface, you will return to me and live out your days in the Cordillera Real. You must give me your word."

"Huh? What do you mean return? I'm already here." Tina's brain felt wrapped in cotton batting. None of this made sense. Maybe she was already dying, and her mind was playing tricks on her.

"You will have seven years in your human world, doctor. Once it is over, you must return to me. Do you agree?"

Her mind raced feverishly, but she had nothing to lose by playing along. "Um, sure. If you can get me out of here, go for it."

"Unlatch the thing holding you to the wall."

Fear sluiced through her, and she tightened her hands on the rope. "Not on your life."

A macabre chuckle filled the icy hole under Illimani's glacier. *"Not my life, yours."*

She started to ask how he knew she was a doctor when a high-pitched whistle bounced off the crevasse walls. The infernal screeching stabbed ice picks into her brain. Cold air closed around her. It smelled like a charnel pit, ripe with things long left to rot.

Her ice screw popped from the wall. She made a grab for the rope and closed her arms around it. Air currents jockeyed her upward and out onto the glacier.

Tina blinked. The thick cloud cover was gone. Between an almost full moon and a sky full of stars, she could see without her lamp. She started to coil the rope, but the same insistent air pushed her. "Okay, okay." She held the mass of Perlon against her chest and staggered down the glacier. It was easy to avoid the crevasses. She could see where they were now.

Her mind rebelled at what had just happened. Maybe she'd died in the crevasse or maybe she hadn't fallen into one at all. Maybe she'd hit her head when she plummeted off the ridge, had a seizure on the glacier, and this was a postictal state. She shook her head sharply, willing a return of rational thought.

"We are not done, doctor. Stop there."

Tina couldn't move. Her feet were mired in place. A glowing form took shape next to her. She stared up at it and gasped, surprised she had any adrenaline left to react to anything. This wasn't possible. It couldn't be happening. The thing was over seven feet tall, and it shimmered so brightly she couldn't look directly at it.

An unseen force yanked one of her arms away from her body. The rope fell in a pile at her feet. Bright light descended. It cut through her jacket and the clothing beneath. She tried to twist her body away, but couldn't. Blood welled and dripped onto the snow.

Clear white light enveloped her, and something thick and golden oozed into the open cut on her arm.

"What are you doing?" Terror skittered along her nerves, and she shook uncontrollably. She tried to move, but was still frozen in place.

"You made me a promise, doctor. I am sealing your word with a blood bond. Seven years. If you break your vow, our shared blood gives me the right to kill you."

Tina opened her mouth to protest, to tell the thing it hadn't told her everything before she agreed, but the pulsating light vanished. She turned in a circle to make certain she was alone. Blood dripped from her arm, staining the snow crimson. Her tent shone pale yellow in the moonlight not a hundred yards away. She staggered toward it.

What the hell had just happened?

Stop! I can't think about this now. If I do, it'll drive me into a place I don't want to go.

Inside her tent, she stripped off her jackets and long underwear. She flicked on a lighter and took a look at her arm. At least there wasn't any evidence of the golden goo. Maybe she'd imagined that part. She needed stitches, but they'd have to wait. She was just too tired. As a stopgap, she doused her arm with Betadine, wrapped it with a pressure bandage, and fell into an exhausted sleep.

Tina glanced around her. Still lost in the past, it took a moment to orient herself. She was about a mile-and-a-half from home. Colorado sunshine shone warmly on her, but she was chilled to her bones.

After leaving Bolivia, she'd returned to the rental house she shared with her climbing partner and lover, Craig Robson. He'd been guiding clients in Antarctica, so she had the house to herself.

At first, she'd thought her solitude was a boon, but the harder she tried to make sense out of what happened to her on Illimani, the more tangled things became. She wondered if she were having a late schizophrenic break, or if she'd truly traded away her humanity in a pact with the devil.

Craig blew through their front door one day in mid-January with a huge smile on his face and a ring in his pocket.

Tina grimaced and forced herself to run faster. It was hard to think about the day Craig asked her to marry him. There was no way she could be his wife. She had no idea what she'd gotten herself into in Bolivia, no inkling of what the ramifications would be. The whole thing was too weird to even try to explain, and she was frightened she'd put Craig at risk if she told him anything.

Even without Bolivia, she'd had other reservations. In truth, she hadn't been ready to marry anyone—not then, and not in the years since. The look on his face when she turned him down still haunted her.

She slammed into her house, blowing hard. Usually, she cooled down. Today she was too edgy, her nerves jangling with tension. Tina poured coffee into an oversized mug and slugged some back. It burned, but its bitterness tasted good. She savored it and waited for the blast of caffeine to hit.

Cup gripped in her hand, she forced herself into her study. No more running today. She had things to do. Reaching down, she booted up her computer. No getting around it. She had to go back to Bolivia. If she didn't, the next supernatural visit would mean her death. Better to die on her feet in a direct confrontation than pinned to her mattress.

The Microsoft menu scrolled across the screen. She brought up the Internet and typed in the URL for Craig's guide service. If she got lucky, he'd have a trip to Bolivia planned in the next couple of months. She wanted to see Craig one last time before she faced whatever had hauled her out of the crevasse and threatened her this morning in her bedroom.

She'd signed on as team doctor for his expeditions a few times, but they'd never talked about anything personal. This time she'd gather her courage and apologize. If she was going to die, she wanted to leave with a clear conscience, and she'd never felt right about how they parted.

CHAPTER 11

Four weeks later in the Bolivian Andes
"Hey, Tina. Hold up."

She ground to a halt. The air at fifteen thousand feet was thin enough she didn't mind stopping. "Yeah, Craig. What is it?" She turned to face him.

"Everyone else is at least half an hour behind. The countryside is riddled with banditos, so we need to wait for the clients." He chugged up beside her, panting. "Shit, had to run to catch you." He bent forward, hands on his knees, and sucked at the high altitude air.

She swiped at sweat dripping down her forehead. "I haven't seen anyone since we passed that bunch of would-be revolutionaries burning tires in the middle of a donkey track a couple hours ago. You know how these South American countries are. There's always civil unrest. Besides," she laughed, "if they kill off the tourists, they fuck themselves."

Craig Robson straightened his six-foot-four-inch frame. Broad shouldered and slim-hipped, he wore a tattered pair of black Patagonia climbing pants, heavy glacier boots, and a green-striped Polartec jacket, topped by a black down vest. He'd stopped panting, his breathing under control. At the mercy of a stiff breeze, shoulder-length blond hair wafted around his high cheek-boned face.

He moved his dark glasses to the top of his head and narrowed his green eyes. "I wish you wouldn't make light of things. It's dangerous—"

She waved him to silence. Wind plastered red strands across her eyes, so she tucked her hair under her jacket hood. "The real danger in these mountains is what you can't see."

"What's gotten into you, Tina? This part of the Andes doesn't have anything particularly technical. Shit. You've climbed in the Himalaya and Alaska and Antarctica. Canada too. Now those are some gnarly peaks." He rolled his eyes. "These are almost a joke."

She winced. Seven years ago, she'd thought the same thing and look where it led her.

Can't tell him that.

"Uh, the snowpack isn't as good as it was when I was here last. Global warming, or something, has had a hell of an impact. We'll be lucky if falling ice blocks don't knock the lot of us into oblivion."

He cocked his head to one side and eyed her speculatively. Craig knew her. They'd lived together for a few years. Both hard-headed, they'd butted opinions often, even before his marriage proposal sent her running out the door.

No matter what, climbing was her first love. She'd seethed all the way through medical school and her residency in emergency medicine, impatient for the time she'd be free to sign on as team doctor for big mountain expeditions. In the meantime, she'd done all the climbing she could in her native Rocky Mountains and in the Sierras, Cascades, and Alaska. Climbing was the life she wanted. Marriage—especially to a climber—would only complicate things. Climbers' wives ended up sitting home raising children.

She and Craig climbed together long before they became

romantically involved, as perfectly attuned to one another roped up as they were in bed. The worst part about ending their relationship was losing her favorite climbing partner.

While she'd been honing her medical skills, he built a reputation as an ace guide, eventually starting his own company. She hadn't seen him for at least five years, then one day he called out of the blue and invited her to the Karakoram. Their team doc had gotten sick, and the expedition was leaving in a week. Could she fill in?

Tina loved the Himalaya. Its vastness and eight thousand meter peaks were like a magnet, drawing her back again and again. She'd expected him to hit on her on that trip, but he never had. He'd called her a few more times to join trips, but he'd always been unfailingly proper: sociable, but cool. His lack of interest disappointed her—never mind, she'd been the one to leave him—but she'd matched his nonchalance.

The current trip to the Andes was a last minute request as well, but with a twist. She'd been the one doing the asking.

He was still looking at her, his brows drawn together. "You were pretty vague about why you wanted to come on this expedition. You've already climbed Sajama and Illimani."

Uh-oh. Dangerous territory.

"Is there some rule that says I can't climb something twice?"

"Well, there are a lot of mountains. Eventually, we run out of time. What are you now? Thirty-seven?"

"Thirty-six," she mumbled. "My pack's heavy. Do you mind if we get moving again? Base camp's at least another couple miles. It will take a while at this altitude."

"Hang on." He keyed his radio and held a brief conversation with Gunter, his co-leader for the expedition, who was herding the clients along the rocky, uphill trail. Craig dropped the radio back into a pocket and nodded at her.

"Yeah, we can get moving. The others aren't far behind

anymore. I was hot moving uphill, but the breeze has a bite to it now that I'm standing still." He fell into step next to her.

"So what's with the rest of the team? How'd they get so far behind?" Tina thought about the six Americans who'd hired Craig for this Andean climbing junket. All males, none of them had known one another before meeting in La Paz four days before. She'd started dosing three with Diamox since even the thirteen thousand foot elevation of the airport gave them a raging headache. One was already coughing. Not a good sign. Illimani was over twenty-one thousand feet. Half the clients didn't have a chance in hell of making the summit.

Craig shrugged. "Gunter's shepherding them along. I know the two of you didn't hit it off, but he's a good assistant guide. I've taken him on at least ten trips, maybe eleven. I've lost count."

Tina thought about the intense young German with short, dark hair and dark eyes. Medium height, with elegant mannerisms and a lithe build, he looked like an escapee from an elite boarding school. Top of the line climbing gear too. She wondered where he got the money. Most climbing guides were poor as dirt. His command of English was so meager, she'd given up trying to talk with him. It struck her as unusual, since most Europeans spoke English quite well.

She shook her head. "I don't mean Gunter. Although, since you brought him up, what if something happens? He can't speak English, which means he won't be able to communicate with the clients."

"He knows enough." Craig sounded defensive.

"Mmph." She recognized the protective note in his voice and changed subjects. "What's with the clients? They seem incredibly inept. When you had them practice with their harnesses and jumars, it looked as if half of them had never seen a rope before."

"They all told me they'd been to at least fourteen thousand feet. I figured they'd manage. The climbing's not especially technical. Peaks here are high-altitude walkups."

Tina clamped her jaw shut, thinking she needed to keep her opinions to herself.

"What?"

"Nothing."

"I know that look. Whatever's running through your head isn't *nothing*."

"Okay. Fine." She ignored the rich baritone of his voice and lengthened her stride. Her almost six-foot height and long legs meant she could out-walk and out-climb most men. Let him keep up if he wanted to hear her next words.

"There are crevasses on all the snowfields. The snowpack is thin. When I was last here there was a snow bridge before that fifty degree pitch just below the summit plateau. I'll bet it's gone now. It will be tough getting around that crevasse and the one butted up against the face. Especially with this group."

She stopped and spun to face him, hands on her hips. "You used to screen clients. What the hell happened?"

An uncomfortable look flitted across his face. "Not so many clients, what with the recession and all. I can't be as picky as I used to be. Besides," he glared at her, "the Andes are the easiest high altitude peaks in the world."

"People still die here," she said through gritted teeth. "Just look at all the crosses at the mountain huts."

"Let's not fight." He flashed a grin. "I haven't lost too many clients over the years. Not planning to add to the tally here. Lighten up, doc."

She turned from him and began walking again. Even if he were worried, he'd never talk with her about it. He'd been a guide for too long. They kept their fears locked deep inside. Almost as if giving voice to them would tempt fate.

In an attempt to divert herself, she swept her gaze across her surroundings. The countryside was beautiful, rolling alpine meadows with streams cutting through them. Llamas grazed in small groups. They'd left trees behind before they passed through

Estancia Una. At twelve thousand feet, it was the last real settlement before Illimani base camp. Pinaya was a little higher, but it wasn't much more than a collection of dirt-floored huts with thatched roofs.

They'd also left the few horses, pigs, and chickens belonging to the villagers behind as they ascended the steep track winding upward. She breathed in the thin air. It was clean and bracing. Living in ten thousand foot Leadville gave her a definite edge. It was why most mountaineers lived high if they could. Acclimatization to altitude was much easier if your body was already used to eight or ten thousand feet.

She thought about Craig. His energy pulsed behind her, warming her back. He wasn't wearing a wedding ring, but many climbers didn't. The metal bands had a nasty habit of snagging on rocks. She opened her mouth to ask if he had a wife stashed away somewhere, but shut it with a snap before the words could escape. It was none of her business.

Craig was incredibly good looking, like one of the ancient Vikings. The years had chiseled his features and made him even more handsome than he'd been in his twenties. A stubble of blond beard covered the sculpted bones of his cheeks and chin. He had the straightest, whitest teeth she'd ever seen and a sensual smile that promised as much as it gave.

Sex between them had been dynamic. A demanding lover, he'd always known what she craved, sometimes before she did. Tina's cheeks heated. She instructed herself not to go there. The last thing she needed was to crawl into Craig's sleeping bag. It would bring back so many fond memories, she wasn't certain she'd be able to resist him this time round.

Oh, stop.

He probably doesn't even want me anymore. It's not as if he's as much as kissed my cheek since we met at the airport in Los Angeles. The other trips we've been on, he only spoke to me when he had team doctor stuff to discuss. For all I know, he has a wife and half a dozen children in Flagstaff.

She'd had a string of relationships since him. None had lasted more than a few months. Once the initial rush of sex with a new man wore off, she lost interest. None of them had appreciated her for who she was. They either wanted to be with her because she was a doctor, or because she was an accomplished mountaineer. No one ever made her feel special just for being her like Craig had.

Tina quested about for a neutral topic. "The mules?"

"Gunter has them."

"Good, they're carrying my medical supplies."

"And most of our food. Don't worry."

Good advice. Too bad I can't take it.

They walked until dirt changed to snow that crunched under her boots. Tina checked her altimeter and frowned. She turned to face Craig. "We should wait here for the others. We'll never make Nido de Condores at this point. It's a thousand feet above us."

"Condor's Nest." He grinned. "I've always liked that name. I was just about to say the same thing. Looks like we'll be walking on snow for the duration. We should stay together. We'll rope up once we hit the glacier."

"We're at sixteen-five." She shot him a worried look.

He glanced at his multiple-function watch. "About what I'm reading. So?"

"Last time I was here, I hit continuous snow just past fourteen thousand feet. And it was close to the same time of year."

He shucked his pack, turned it backside down, moved his ice axes off to one side, and sat on it. "I see what you're getting at. Here." He patted the ground next to him. "Take a load off. It may be a while."

She unbuckled her waist belt and sternum strap, catching the heavy pack by its haul loop as it slid off her shoulders. Once it was off, she rooted through an outside pocket for her down jacket, took off her shell, zipped into the down, and replaced the outer jacket over it. She pulled both hoods over her head and buried her hands in her sleeves.

"Brrr." She glanced at her watch and clicked a few buttons. "No wonder. Eleven degrees. Guess I'll dig my heavier gloves out next time I stand up."

In the meantime, Craig had done much the same, bundling against the cold. He handed her a water bottle. "Has Gatorade in it."

"Thanks." She tipped it back, crunching ice chunks. They flowed into her mouth along with the liquid. "Guess it's time to put the water in my parka." She handed his bottle back, tugged hers out of a side pocket of her pack, and dropped it into an inner jacket pocket.

He held out some cheese and a couple slices of salami. "How many years since you were here?"

"Seven." She took the food, munching gratefully. "You?"

He pursed his lips together. "Three. No, make that four. But you're right we did hit snow much lower." He shook his head. "I'm trying to remember if the glacier had any particular issues. If the snowpack's shrunk, it should be easier to see the crevasses."

Yeah, on a normal mountain. This one's anything but.

She kept her thoughts to herself. Silence stretched between them. "We've been here for twenty minutes. How long do you think we should wait before we go back for your charges?"

"They'll show up."

"But if they don't, shouldn't we go look for them?"

He held up a hand and pulled his two way radio from a parka pocket. "Gunter. Where are you?"

A volley of German crackled from the speaker.

She looked at Craig. "Can you understand him?"

He shrugged. "Sort of."

"Well, what did he say?"

"I think he said they're in the last hanging valley we passed through."

Tina felt her eyes widen. "But that's seven hundred feet below us." She dropped her head into a hand and massaged her temples to get her anger under better control. This bunch of clients had no business on Illimani. None. They weren't strong or fit enough.

"I know what you're thinking."

"Oh, really." She tried to rein in her sarcasm, but it bled through anyway. "What?"

"It was foolhardy of me to accept clients like these to climb anything."

She looked up, and the corners of her mouth twitched into a frown. "That about nails it. Why did you?"

His face took on a guarded expression. "I already told you. Times are harder than they used to be." He blew out a breath. It plumed white in the chill air. "I don't have a trade like you. I can't just drop into the neighborhood ER and pick up a thousand bucks an hour."

She snorted. "Try three or four hundred, depending on the shift."

"Still."

"Point taken." She shifted her body so she could look at him. "Have you considered going back to school?"

He threw his head back and laughed, but it held a bitter edge.

"I don't get it." She snaked out a gloved hand to stroke his arm, but pulled it back before she actually touched him. "What's so funny?"

"Who's going to support me while I go to college?" He met her gaze. "Don't take this wrong, but my life isn't anything like yours. I didn't have a family homestead to move into. I have a mortgage. The business has debts. Mountaineering equipment isn't cheap. Neither are the permits when I go to the Himalaya. I have to buy them before I know if I'll have clients. Lost my shirt last season. I'd planned for fifteen on Everest and ended up guiding five. The

Nepalese government doesn't reimburse you for unused permits. They're about fifteen grand a pop. I sold some of them, but I was still out for five."

"I can see where they wouldn't pay you back. The permits reserve space on the mountain. It's not like Nepal can resell them."

"Exactly. A lot of the guide services were in the same boat. I was lucky to sell those few I did. If I'd gotten stuck with all ten unused permits, I'd have had to declare bankruptcy." A bitten-off quality in his tone made it clear he was sorry he'd been so open with her.

"I'm sorry. I had no idea things were so tough in the climbing world." She took a measured breath. "I think we should set up camp here. It'll be dark before the group gets to us, and they'll probably be too tired to push on, anyway."

Most clients could make the fifty-four hundred foot elevation gain from Estancia Una to Nido de Condores in a long day. Not these.

"I suppose you're right, but the mules have most of the tents. I'm only carrying one."

"We can set it up plus the one in my pack. And we can start water heating. There's an open creek about twenty yards down the valley." She pointed. "It will save fuel if we don't have to melt snow tonight."

Craig got to his feet. "Thanks for listening." In the fading light, she saw his face flush from more than the cold. "Didn't mean to unload on you."

"It's okay." She stood too. "How about over there?" She pointed. "It's nice and flat, and there should be room for all the tents."

They worked in a companionable silence. Tina was amazed how easily they fell into their old pattern of teamwork, positioning the two tents, hauling water, and starting soup and tea. It felt good to be setting up camp with Craig. Too good. The trips she'd gone on with him since he'd invited her to the

Karakoram two years before, had porters who took care of those things.

Bells from the mules' harnesses jangled an hour past full dark. They hadn't gotten any radio calls from Gunter, but concern for the clients nagged at her just the same. She and Craig sat on foam pads in the snow, sharing mugs of soup.

"Thank God." She tapped the beam of her headlamp down so she wouldn't blind Craig and looked at him.

"Yeah. I was starting to get worried too. I'll go greet them and show them where we are."

Tina watched him walk briskly toward the track and turn downhill. An uneasy feeling soured her stomach. She'd been relieved once she knew they wouldn't spend tonight on the glacier. Whatever had suckered her into that bargain was waiting for her up there. She felt its malevolent presence and shivered.

I need more of a plan before I face it again.

CHAPTER 12

Craig strode through shallow snow toward the trail. Rocks and gravel crunched under his boots. It was a clear night, and the sky was riddled with millions of stars. Long years of guiding taught him to mask his feelings, but he'd been ecstatic to hear the bells. Gunter would've called him on the radio if anything had gone truly wrong, but the young German's assessment of situations wasn't always accurate. For one thing, he tended to use himself as a measuring rod. If Gunter wasn't tired, he assumed the clients weren't, either. Craig had gotten more than one complaint about his assistant guide, but they hadn't been serious and the price was right. Gunter was more interested in earning his chops as a guide than in money. Besides, judging from his clothing and equipment, he had plenty from somewhere.

Craig blew out a breath. Money. It had turned into a perennial problem. There was never enough. He loved the high mountains of the world. Adored them. They were the only place he felt truly at home. He'd been so enamored with climbing as a teenager, he would've done anything to ensure he had as much time cragging and peak-bagging as possible.

Decisions he'd made years before rose to mock him. Tina had

suggested going back to school. Craig snorted and turned downhill to meet his clients. He wished he'd gone to graduate school. A bachelor's degree in history wasn't worth much. Couldn't even use it to teach at a junior college. He'd been set to get his masters, but Alpine Attack, one of the pre-eminent guide services, offered him a job. Getting paid—even if it wasn't enough to live on—to spend time in his favorite places had proven too seductive to refuse.

The glow from seven headlamps lit up the night as his little group topped a ridge. Craig hastened his steps. He hoped the clients weren't in as bad a shape as he feared. Calling a trip was never a popular decision, particularly since clients understood it didn't mean a refund. All that was laid out in the client contract each had signed.

"That you, Craig?" a raspy voice called out, followed by a chest-wrenching cough.

Who the hell else would it be?

"Yes, Joe. It's me. Sounds like you're still feeling a bit rough."

"Nah, nothing—" The next words were obliterated by coughing.

Crap. Hope Tina has something for him that doesn't involve going down.

One of the problems with only having one assistant guide was if Gunter had to escort a client back to La Paz, Craig would have to manage the remaining ones on his own. With more competent climbers, it wouldn't have been a problem, but with this bunch… Tina had been right to be shocked by their lack of skill. He was too, but he couldn't let it show.

Tina could help as a guide. He'd have to pay her more, but it would be chicken feed compared with what she got as their doctor.

"Gunter." He clapped the German on the back. "Nearly gave up on you."

The other man avoided his gaze, dark eyes hooded. "Why you not come down? Zwei, er two men sind krank."

"Yes, I can hear they're sick. Why didn't you call me on the radio?"

Gunter shrugged. "Maybe get better?" A crooked grin lit his features. "Never go down."

Yeah, the mountaineer's creed.

"We'll let Tina take a look and see what she thinks. If she says they need to descend, you'll take them."

Gunter stepped back, shock mirrored in his face. "Ich habe nicht vor diesem Berg erklommen."

"I don't care if you haven't climbed Illimani before. You're a guide. The clients are our first concern."

Gunter turned away, muttering under his breath in German. Meanwhile, the six clients had caught up. "Hey, I understood that. I speak German." Ted sounded winded, but at least he wasn't hacking.

"Yes, well, so did I." Craig tried to sound affable. "I'm certain he didn't mean it. Shall we? We're close to camp for the night."

"Thank God," Ted muttered. "Longest six miles I've ever walked."

Craig fell into step beside him. "You haven't come six miles. That was the distance to high camp. We're still a thousand feet below it. You told me you'd climbed all the fourteeners in Colorado."

"Uh, well, that might've been a slight exaggeration."

Craig pressed his tongue against his teeth and fought back annoyance. Damned clients, anyway. What did they gain by lying about their climbing pedigrees? He winced, knowing the answer to his rhetorical question. They gained entrance to trips where they didn't belong—where they put their teammates at risk. Never mind their guides, if they had to haul their sorry asses out of a dicey situation.

Guiding was a word of mouth endeavor. Happy clients were

clients who stood on top of something, took a bunch of photos, and got home in one piece. They were the best advertisement Craig could hope for. Many days, he felt more like a nanny than a mountaineer. Clients like these ruined his alpine experience with their bitching, moaning, and lies.

I've got to stop feeling sorry for myself. I accepted Ted and Joe and the rest of them. They're my responsibility until we get back to La Paz.

"So how many did you climb?" Craig tried not to sound as if his teeth were gritted together.

"Don't recall exactly. How far is camp? I'm about done in."

Craig took hold of Ted's arm. "Let the rest of them go on by. Camp's close."

"What? Let go!" The other man tried to shake his hand off, but Craig held tight.

When the last of the five mules had clomped past, he said, "I'm trying to give you some privacy." Craig inhaled sharply, the thin cold air bracing. "I need the truth about how much actual mountain climbing you've done. From the look of things, this is the first mountain you've ever been on. Am I close?"

Ted, all overweight five-foot-ten of him, jerked his arm away. His short, black hair was hidden by a wool cap. "Why is it important?"

Craig rounded on him, any semblance of hanging on to his temper gone. "Because I'm responsible for your life up here. If you give me bogus information about what you can do in the mountains, it's the same as lying to your doctor about your medical history. It puts your life at risk. Unfortunately, it puts mine on the line too. And everyone else on this trip. I'm giving you an opportunity to tell me the truth."

Ted turned his head away. "You're pretty close to right. I've never really climbed anything."

Damn, damn, damn! Fuck!

"Why'd you want to come on this expedition?" Craig forced the words out.

"It said on the Internet these mountains were easy."

Craig's jaw clenched. "They are—compared with the Himalaya or Alaska. Try again. Why'd you decide to begin climbing mountains on peaks that are over twenty thousand feet?"

"Midlife crisis?" Ted laughed, but it came out more like a squawk.

"Come on." Craig started walking. "We'll sort this out in the morning. I think Joe has the beginnings of pulmonary edema. If Tina agrees, he'll be going back to La Paz with Gunter, and you'll be going down with them."

"You can't force me—"

Craig balled his hands into fists inside his mitts. He wanted to land a punch right in the middle of Ted's overfed face, but he swallowed his anger. "It says on page four of the contract you signed that I can. Now, are you coming?"

Ted stomped along the trail beaten into the snow.

Craig was grateful the other man didn't try to talk. It would've been a struggle to be cordial.

"Craig." Tina met him a few feet from camp. "I need to talk with you." He noticed the men had started setting up the other tents, including the larger mess tent. Good.

"Thanks for getting them moving setting up camp. Or did Gunter do that?" He followed her behind a group of good-sized boulders which would shield their conversation.

"Not a problem. Someone needed to. Gunter blew through here muttering in German. I haven't seen him since."

"Shit! I told him he'd probably have to escort some clients down. He got mad. Bet he's gone off halfcocked to climb the mountain by himself." Craig grappled in his pocket for the radio, keyed it, and called Gunter's name.

Static crackled. The German didn't answer. "Damn it!"

Tina grunted. "Well, it's what you or I would've done at his age. To be this close to the second highest peak in Bolivia and have it snapped out from under—"

"Not the point. I'm paying him to do a job," Craig growled. He rubbed his jaw to ease the tension in his facial muscles. "What did you need me for?"

"Joe has pulmonary edema. He's got to go down. Brice may have the beginnings of cerebral edema. His headache is worse, and he's not tracking well."

"I figured as much when I heard Joe hacking. Bummer about Brice. Can we wait until morning, or do I need to radio for a chopper?"

She cocked her head to one side. "I shot both of them up with Dex. Joe's propped up in his bag with a warm drink. Robert's in the tent with him. I described specific things to watch for. Brice is sitting up wrapped in a sleeping bag. He got an opiate along with the Dex. Give me an hour, and I'll let you know."

Craig tried not to stare at her. Tina was one of the most striking women he'd ever met with her long, red hair, dark blue eyes, and lithe, six-foot frame. It had been the saddest day of his life when she refused his marriage proposal.

She turned to go.

"Wait."

"Yes?" She looked over one shoulder without actually turning around.

What he wanted to do was sweep her into his arms and feel the press of her body against him.

Don't be a fool. She doesn't want me.

"Just wondering if you'd help with guiding after I send Gunter down. Assuming the clients can wait until morning, that is."

Tina spun to face him, the movement so rapid it caught him by surprise. "Sure. Be glad to help, but I'm afraid you may be facing bigger problems. For one thing, I'm not all that certain Gunter will be back."

"Why wouldn't he be? Even if he's sneaking in a summit bid, it's only another five thousand feet or so. He's young and strong. He'll be back before we get up tomorrow."

She looked away. Watching her in the flickering light from his headlamp, Craig sensed she wanted to say something. He considered prodding her, but kept his mouth shut. Tina could be stubborn. He gave her lots of space.

The line of her jaw tightened. She looked up. "There's something wrong with this mountain."

"Huh?"

"You heard me. Something…strange happened last time I was here." She laughed. It sounded hollow—and haunted.

Craig reached for her, but she shook her head. "I haven't lost my mind. And I can't tell you anything else. I'm afraid if I do, I'll put you at risk. Shouldn't have said what I did. Uh, I really need to get back to my patients." She turned on her heel, her boots making a squeaky sound in the snow, and strode toward camp.

He stared after her retreating back. What the hell? Tina was the most level-headed person he'd ever known. Quick and sure, her decision-making was impeccable in life and death situations. It was what made her a good doctor. The Tina he knew would never have made a blanket statement that something was wrong with the mountain.

They'd met when they were twenty and undergraduates at Colorado State, drawn together by a mutual love for the outdoor life. Their love for one another sort of crept up on them. She'd started medical school two years later, and he'd thrown his full energies into building credibility as a guide.

He still wasn't certain what went wrong between them. He'd been so sure she wanted to spend her life with him…

A familiar sadness washed over him. He'd married on the rebound after Tina dumped him. Predictably, it hadn't even lasted a year. He winced. He still remembered Jessica screaming at him, "I'm not Tina, goddammit," just before she slammed out the door for the last time. Since then, he'd kept his heart to himself. It wasn't fair to offer such a damaged item to another woman. He'd had his share of one-night stands, but they'd been sex, pure and simple. And only when his balls ached so badly he had to have the feel of a woman around him again.

Craig kicked at the snow. He needed to get his head out of his ass. Emotions had no place in the mountains. He'd always prided himself on being cool and calm when things were going to hell. Gunter's unauthorized solo trip nagged him. He'd never hire the German again. Craig only gave assistants one chance. If they proved untrustworthy, that was it. He blew out a breath, and then another, seeking a calm center as he jogged back to camp.

Once there, he made the rounds, chatting with the six men, or trying to. Ted had very little to say. Brice seemed better, but he said he wanted to go down. The specter of cerebral edema had scared the crap out of him. Craig found Tina in the larger mess tent. "Joe and Brice seem well enough to wait until daylight. Do you agree?"

She nodded. "Yeah. I'm thinking Brice just had a really severe headache, exacerbated by altitude. He lives in Seattle—sea level. Joe's lungs are sounding a little clearer. I gave him some more Dex. He should be able to walk out of here tomorrow. Speaking of which—"

Craig held up a hand. "Hold on to that thought. I need to see to the mules. Gunter usually does that. Wouldn't do to have one wander off and get stolen by the locals. Keep some water hot for me."

She smiled. "Sure. Not sleepy, anyway."

"You still don't sleep well?"

Tina shook her head. "Nope. Collateral damage." She made shooing motions with her hands. "Doesn't matter. You probably still sleep like a stone. Better get moving so you can get some rest. Stove's going, so leave the door cracked."

He stepped back into the night and went to hunt down the mules. Like horses, they'd scratch through snow to get to the grass beneath. But they also carried a couple days' worth of feed for themselves in their packs. Normally, that's all it would take to climb Illimani. One day to get to high camp, five or six hours to summit and then back to Estancia Una the same day.

Craig thought about the conversations he'd just had with his clients. Only two, Robert and Peter, felt strongly about going on. Red-haired twin brothers from Colorado Springs, they were fit and well-acclimatized. Both admitted they'd stayed with the other four because they didn't trust Gunter to take care of them. Craig hobbled another mule and did a nose count. Yup, all five present and accounted for.

He considered what to do. If Gunter returned, it was simple. He'd send the German back to La Paz with Ted, Joe, Brice, and maybe Sam, depending on what the retired attorney decided in the morning. If Gunter didn't come back, his options thinned dramatically. He'd have to escort the clients to Estancia Una, radio for transportation for them, and then go back up the mountain to find out what happened to Gunter.

Craig walked slowly back to camp. Tina was waiting. For a moment, his spirits lifted, then reality took over. "Yeah, she may be waiting," he muttered, "but not that way."

Watch it. I have enough problems on this trip. I don't need to add to them by pretending we could make a life together after all this time.

"Craig?" Tina's voice carried through the still night air.

"Coming." He hastened his steps and ducked into the mess tent. She had a lantern lit, so he doused his headlamp.

"I was getting worried about you. Thought you might need some help with the mules."

His heart did a small flip flop. "Nope, just thinking."

"You always were a planner."

He snorted. "Me? You should talk, Miss Don't-Let-Anything-Get-in-the-Way-of-My-Career."

Tina laughed. "Guess I was pretty intense."

He looked at her, surprised to see her blue gaze right on him. "I'm thinking *was* isn't the proper verb tense."

"Maybe not. I've been doing some thinking of my own. If

Gunter doesn't show up, you need to take everyone down."

"I'd come to the same conclusion." His lips twitched into a smile. He and Tina had always been on the same page when it came to mountain safety. "The twins can come back up the mountain with us if they want to try for the summit. You could take them while I see if Gunter had some sort of accident."

His smile faded. "Not feeling terribly kindly disposed toward him at this point, but if he doesn't come back, I have to try to help him if I can."

"You don't need me to take the group down the hill."

"What? You're going to stay here?"

She shook her head, looking grim. "No. I have business up there." She gestured toward Illimani's summit, hidden by darkness and the tent wall. "I suspect I'll run across Gunter, so there's no need for you to come back."

He kicked a three-legged stool open with his boot and sat heavily. "You're talking in riddles."

"Here." She handed him a mug of instant soup and a handful of crackers. Craig drank and ate. He was hungry and held out the mug for seconds.

"You could probably close the door if you're done cooking. It will stay warmer in here. Anything sweet handy?"

She dug out a package of Mother's Taffy cookies. "Your favorites." At least the dour expression on her face softened a bit.

For a time, the only sound in the mess tent was his chewing. Something was wrong, and if he knew Tina, there was a whole lot she wasn't saying. He looked right at her. "You used to trust me. Please tell me enough so I understand. I'm guessing you would've come here even if I hadn't had an expedition on the books."

She nodded and bit her lower lip. After a while, she seemed to come to an internal decision. He recognized it in the defiant tilt of her chin.

"Okay. I suppose someone ought to know since it's not likely I'll ever leave this mountain." A hesitation. "I'm worried." She blew out a tense breath. "More than worried. Scared shitless. If I tell you about him—or it—you might be in the same kettle of fish I'm in." She stared hard at him through narrowed eyes. "Believe me, you do not want this kind of trouble."

He came to his feet and held out his arms. To his amazement, she dove into them. Her body trembled. More than anything, her distress gave him pause. The Tina he knew wasn't afraid of anything.

He tightened his hold on her. "I've been cheating death for years. Whatever's eating at you, let me help. We made good partners once."

He felt her nod against him where her head nestled in the hollow between his shoulder and neck. Her scent, something uniquely Tina, with hints of cinnamon and vanilla, enveloped him. His cock hardened where their bodies pressed close. She must've felt it, because her hips pushed against him, and she threaded her arms around his back.

Craig moved away a little so he could look at her. Tina's face was turned up, her lips parted.

"If I'm going to die here," she murmured, "I'd like to make love one last time." A half-smile flitted across her face. "We were always good together."

A warm spark ignited in his belly and moved outward. "The best. But now's not the time." Reluctantly, he disentangled her arms from around him. He needed a clear head, not a sex-fuzzed brain. "Tell me what happened last time you were here. Between us, we'll be able to beat whatever it is. I know we can." He placed a gloved finger under her chin and tipped her head up to meet his gaze. "Once we're safe, we can make love all you want."

If she's still interested then. He pushed back hope flaring painfully in his heart.

"It's a deal." Her blue eyes glowed tenderly. "Give me a few seconds. I need to think how to tell you this, so it doesn't sound crazy and disjointed."

CHAPTER 13

Tina cracked the door and busied herself with the small, white gas stove. Tea would go well with what she had to say. She wanted to burrow back into Craig's arms. He felt so damned good against her, like coming home. He was right, though, to be strong enough to say no. They both needed to focus. Deep in her breast a stubborn burst of hope caught, blazing bright. Maybe there was still a chance for them after all—if she lived through the next forty-eight hours.

She glanced over a shoulder. "Do you still carry single malt scotch on these trips?"

"Um-hum. I'll go get my flask. We can spike the tea you're brewing."

She listened to his footsteps fade, muffled by an inch of new snow. It had begun snowing lightly about an hour ago. Wind had picked up too. The canvas sides of the tent rattled, making a hell of a racket. Craig ducked back through the door and held out a flat, silver flask.

"Nah. Hang on to it. We'll pour the scotch in once the tea's done." She quirked a brow. "Wouldn't want to burn off any of its wonderful alcohol content."

"Guess not." He returned to his camp stool. "Weather seems to be turning to shit out there. I don't get it. Forecast indicated clear for at least a week."

She handed him a titanium mug, pulled her own camp stool close, and retrieved her mug from next to the stove. "Do we need anything else before I sit?"

He shook his head and poured a jot of liquor into his cup before holding it out to her.

Tina velcroed the door shut, settled herself, and took a sip of the steaming beverage. The scotch burned all the way to her stomach. One of life's small pleasures, it felt lovely: rich and smooth. She took off her gloves and curled her fingers around the warm metal cup. "What do you know about Andean mythology?"

"Almost nothing. I know something about the Himalayan mountain gods, but I don't suppose they count for much here." He shot her a crooked smile. It lit his face from the inside out, and her heart skipped a beat.

"Well, I didn't either. Know anything, that is. I studied up on it after the thing showed up…" She shook her head. "No. I need to tell this in some sort of order. Let me start with a local legend."

He took a sip of tea and motioned with a hand for her to begin.

"Viracocha is sort of a god. He had four sons, each lords in their own right. Guess they fought like cats and dogs. I don't think it's accidental their names are local peaks." She shut her eyes for a moment, opened them, and forged ahead. "Illampu was Lord of Light. Illimani, Lord of Water. Huayna Petosi, Lord of Stone. And Mururata was Lord of Air. Viracocha was sick of their perennial arguments, so he sent his deputy, Tunupa, to see what could be done. Long story short, Mururata was punished by beheading and isolation. His head became Sajama—"

"Which stands alone," Craig finished for her. "So there's the isolation part. How does this fit in with you feeling threatened? Sajama's a long way from here."

"Yes, but Mururata's right next to Illimani. Nothing I could find in the library mentioned it, but I don't think the Lord of Air ever gave up. Remember when I spent six weeks in the Andes during my second year of residency? We were still together then."

"Of course. I was guiding in Antarctica while you were here."

Tina took two large gulps of tea and then held her hand out for the scotch. She poured more into her cup and lifted it in a mock toast. "Here's to liquid courage. I spent a couple of weeks in the small settlements between La Paz and the Cordillera Real. Every chance I got, I ran off and tackled a peak. Sort of like what Gunter just did."

Craig nodded. "I can see where it could work. These are easy mountains."

She grunted. "Yeah, I thought so too. Christmas day seven years ago, I finished with my patients in Estancia Una around the middle of the afternoon and took off at a jog for Nido de Condores. Figured I'd sleep for a couple of hours, start for the summit at one in the morning, and be back in Estancia by noon the next day."

He dug into the cookies, dipped one into his tea, and waited.

She'd always appreciated Craig's patience and was grateful he wasn't pushing her now, mining for details before she was ready to spill them.

She started talking again. "I made Nido de Condores just fine and set up my tent. The wind was ripping." She gestured toward the tent door. "Sort of like it is now, only worse. Figured I'd never get any sleep."

Tina looked away. She hated to admit the next part because it had been foolhardy, but Craig would understand. Any mountaineer would.

He crossed one long leg over the other, set his cup down, and steepled his fingers together. "Let me guess," he murmured, his lips twisted into a wry smile. "You said what the hell and went for the summit."

"Yes, I did. I was well-acclimatized—"

He held up a hand. "Spare me your rationale. We've all made summit bids when common sense would've dictated otherwise."

She smiled back. "I actually did fairly well. Wind was bad, but visibility didn't really sock in until I was on my way down. I've never seen it drop so fast. One minute I could see. The next, it was like pea soup. I was close to that lip at the edge of the summit plateau right above the steep section, and believe me, I was barely crawling along. Tested every step with my axe to make certain I wasn't going to step through the cornice."

He offered the flask. She drank from it. Despite the liquor, her muscles felt tight. She'd avoided even thinking about that night since shortly after it happened. The impromptu rerun while out for her daily jog in Leadville had been damned unsettling. Talking about what happened—even with Craig who would never judge her—was hard. Tina stood and paced from one end of the very small space to the other. It took about three steps before she had to turn around.

More of her story unfolded. The words felt like bits of glass; they cut deep leaving the safety of her mouth.

"You must've been petrified." Craig's voice was warm and soothing. She'd just told him about falling from Illimani's ridge.

She flashed him a grateful smile. "Only another climber would understand. I was scared and alone and fighting feeling hopeless. Once hopeless happens, we may as well cash in our chips. I wasn't sure how far I'd fallen. It didn't matter, really. I wasn't climbing back up."

A look of admiration crossed his face. "God, but you're gutsy."

Tina felt her face heat at the unexpected compliment. She kept pacing while she talked. Movement made things easier somehow. "Once I got off the cliffy part, I just sort of sank into the snow, put my head in my hands, and cried."

"Was it dawn yet?"

She shook her head. "Nope. Not even close. Still dark as pitch—"

"I'm trying to picture the glacier," he broke in. "You were at what, about nineteen thousand feet?"

She nodded. "Something like that. Anyway, I started to pick my way down. The tracks in the snow I'd followed on the way up had been obliterated by the wind, and I hadn't set wands. Didn't even bring any." Tina rolled her eyes. "Sometimes I don't understand why every young mountain climber doesn't end up dead."

"You and me both," he seconded. "But go on."

"I'd just sidestepped a mother of a crevasse when a huge gust of wind knocked me to one side. My crampons skittered on ice and all hell broke loose. The snowfield disintegrated under my feet. It's not the first crevasse I've fallen into, but it was the worst by a good big bunch."

She looked at Craig. His forehead was creased; his hands had balled into fists. She'd just described a series of events, any one of which would've made the top ten hit parade in climbers' worst nightmares.

"I figured I was as good as dead."

"You tried to climb out, didn't you?" Craig's voice was terse, as if the words had been torn out of him. He leaned toward her.

"Of course. I tried until I was so winded I could barely breathe. It didn't do any good. When I knew I'd never get my crampon points or axe into the ice, I started drilling in ice screws. Made it about twenty feet and my headlamp died."

Craig's breath rattled from between clenched teeth. "Shit!"

"Funny. Same thing I said, followed by fuck and a whole bunch of other useless cursing. I knew I'd have to wait until dawn. It was so cold, I was afraid I'd freeze to death if I wasn't moving…"

Tina steeled herself. The next part was going to be hard. She lurched into a halting description of the thing that had visited her in the crevasse, led her to safety, and bound her with blood, ending with saying she thought it was likely Mururata.

She dragged her gaze upward to meet Craig's. He shook his head and looked away. "Aw, come on, Tina. That's not possible. You must've been hypoxic. I've had high altitude hallucinations before—"

"It wasn't a hallucination," she hissed. "Look." She shucked both jackets and rolled up her left sleeve. A jagged scar ran six inches up the inside of her forearm. "A normal cut wouldn't look like this." She traced white, ridged edges that resembled out of control scar tissue. "I doused it with disinfectant and bound it that first night. Didn't have energy for much else, and I had to stop the bleeding. I tried to put stitches in the next morning but the edges were too tough for my suture needle. It wouldn't puncture the skin." A corner of her mouth turned down. "Made it harder to delude myself the whole thing hadn't happened."

Craig's green gaze zeroed in on her. "It's right out of mythology. I saved you, so you belong to me now."

Her chest was tight. Her skin crawled. She shrugged to loosen things up. "Yeah, not so different."

He nodded. A muscle twitched in the set line of his jaw. Craig pushed to his feet and placed his arms around her. He kissed her forehead and moved away. Handing her jackets to her, he helped her into them. "I believe you, but it sure stretches the edges of credibility." He poured more water from the pot into his cup, followed it with scotch, and sat back down. "What happened then?"

"Next day I went back to Estancia Una and tried not to think about any of it." Tina snorted. "Did a pretty good job until a month ago when my supernatural buddy showed up in my bedroom and almost suffocated me to remind me of my debt."

A whistling intake of breath told her more than words. "Is there anything else?"

"Isn't what I've told you enough?"

"Probably. But you know me, I like to be thorough."

"One of your more stellar traits, actually." She glanced at him. He had the beginnings of circles under his eyes. "You need to get some rest."

"I will. Once we come up with a plan."

"Well, we can't very well make one until we see if Gunter shows up."

"Sure we can. We can come up with Plan A and Plan B. What happens if you just go back to Colorado?"

"He'll show up like he did the other morning, except next time he'll kill me." Heat rose to her face. "I mentioned suffocate, but I didn't elaborate about him pinning me to the mattress and cutting off my oxygen."

"No, you didn't. Any other small, insignificant details you left out?"

She winced. "I deserved that. No. You know everything now."

"What do you suppose he does with his captives? And how about those other lords you mentioned? Wasn't Illimani one of them?"

She nodded. "Yeah, Lord of Water."

"Well, do you think he'd be willing to help? Or Illampu. What was he lord of? Light?"

"Good memory." She shrugged and drained the rest of the liquid in her cup. It was stone cold and beginning to freeze. "How the hell do you ask a mountain spirit for help?" She slipped her gloves back on.

"We're brainstorming here, Tina. Let's get all our ideas out on the table. Surely we can come up with something better than you offering yourself up to Mururata, or whatever his name is, like a sacrificial goose. If that's your best plan, you could've stayed in Colorado and let him kill you there. It would have been easier and much less expensive."

She snorted. "Expensive for whom? Remember, you're paying me."

He furled his brows. "Didn't you offer to come along pro bono if I'd already hired another doc?"

"Yes, but—"

"Tina. I'm teasing you. Listening to what happened to you seven years ago was painful. It probably wasn't any easier for you to tell than it was for me to hear, but we need to move beyond feeling shell-shocked, if we're going to be effective strategizing solutions."

Tina dropped back onto her stool. "You always had a way of cutting right to the heart of things."

"My pleasure." He inclined his head. "What were you thinking you'd do once you got here?"

She rolled her eyes. "I don't know. Engage him in hand-to-hand combat? Spit in his face? Tell him to find some other patsy?"

"That's my girl. You weren't going down without a fight."

"Would you?"

"Hell no. Help me think here. Maybe there's some way to beat him at his own game. If he were any good at this, the mountain would be littered with corpses."

"Maybe it is, and they're all hidden in crevasses."

"Now there's a cheery thought." He snapped his fingers; they didn't make any sound since he had gloves on. "I have an idea. What if he targeted you because you're female?"

"What if he did?"

"If you could lure one of them, sweetie, maybe you could enlist one of the others to help." His gaze tracked the length of her body. "You've never appreciated how stunning you are."

"Oh, bosh." She waved a hand in the air.

"Humor me. There're still a few hours of dark left. Come back behind the boulder pile where we talked earlier. I'll go with you. Take off enough outer layers so your, um, assets are visible, and ask Illimani and Illampu for help."

"Christ, Craig, I thought—"

"Do you have a better idea?" he countered. Getting to his feet, he held out both hands to her. "We have to stop thinking like twenty-first century humans. If the thing that has you in its gunsights in as ancient as you believe, we need to think more like him."

"Got it." She stood, sucked in a weary breath, and walked out of the mess tent with Craig right behind her. She was willing to try just about anything if it would free her from Mururata's clutches.

CHAPTER 14

Craig's brain raced a million miles an hour. He'd kept a neutral expression, but Tina's story made his guts clench in horror. Not much had that effect on him. For a fleeting moment, he considered offering himself to the hostile mountain god, but Tina would never accept his sacrifice.

He could hear her say, "Got myself into this mess. It's not your problem." Besides, if his theory about gender held water, he was the wrong sex.

They all took risks when they went to the high places of the world. From what it sounded like, Tina would be dead if it weren't for whatever had intervened, and all because she hadn't stocked extra headlamp batteries. As he followed her another idea took shape.

He angled his body into the wind. Spindrift blew into his face, the small pieces sharp as shrapnel against his bare skin. He pulled up the hood of his parka and zipped it so his chin was covered.

"Only for you would I do this." Tina's voice drifted back to him. "Weather's a real bitch."

He caught up with her. Fortunately, the large boulders provided a windbreak. "Yeah. No one will climb anything until it clears. And maybe not then, if it dumps enough snow to avalanche. I'll hold those." He extended a hand for her jackets and held both close. Next came her down vest. He added it to the pile in his arms. The clothing smelled like her. A wave of longing so intense it startled him hit him in the solar plexus.

"Do you think this is enough?"

He looked at her with a critical eye. The full curves of her breasts were visible beneath her form-fitting long john top. She wasn't wearing a sports bra. His hands itched to curve around those wonderful breasts again, but he restrained himself.

"How about if you take off your hat and let your hair down."

She pulled off her wool cap. Long, red hair cascaded around her torso. "Now what? Can't stay like this long. I'm freezing."

"Call for Illimani and Illampu to help you. Beg them. I won't be listening, so don't worry about sounding like a fool."

"Last thing on my mind," she muttered through chattering teeth.

The drone of her voice—seductive but laced with desperation—rose and fell around him. She even raised her hands like a supplicant. Her hair twisted like a live thing in gusts of wind that made their way around the boulders. Dear God if she didn't look like the statues he'd seen in Greece and Rome, timeless and gorgeous. His groin tingled, and he realized a full-blown erection pressed against the front of his climbing pants. What an incredibly sexy woman she was.

He told his body to stand down. He still didn't know why she'd dumped him. They'd never talked about it. All she'd said was she couldn't live in anyone else's shadow. He'd protested he wasn't asking her to, but she'd said she couldn't take a chance.

Tina covered the few feet separating them and held out her hands for her clothes. "Can't think of anything else to say. Brrrr." She shrugged into her things. "Thanks for holding them next to your body. There's still some warmth in the down."

"Best get into your sleeping bag." He heard the raspy undertone of desire in his voice.

She heard it too. "Want to join me?"

He sucked in a breath. "I'd love to, but no."

She turned to face him. "You made me a promise. All the sex I can tolerate."

"It's one I intend to keep. I—" He bit back the words. He'd almost told her he still loved her. This wasn't the time. "Let's get out of this mess first." Bending toward her, he kissed her ever-so-gently. "I hope we did some good out here tonight."

Craig walked her to her tent. The rest of them were doubled up for warmth. If there'd been another female on the expedition, Tina would've shared her tent. As it was, she had a two-man tent to herself. "Will you be warm enough? I bought a couple extra bags."

"I'll be okay. I've got the minus forty one with me. Thought it was overkill when I packed it. Now I'm glad I did. Thanks for asking. See you in the morning." She leaned against him for a moment and then ducked to unzip the tent fly so she could crawl inside. "Whoops." She straightened.

"What?"

"I'm going to check on Brice and Joe one last time."

"I could do that for you."

She tapped his arm as she walked past. "Nah. If something didn't look right, you'd come get me, anyway. Once I'm in my bag, I want to stay there."

Craig knew what she meant. Pulling cold boots on was a hassle. Easier to only do it once—in the morning. He detoured off to one side of the camp to relieve himself and then let himself into his tent. Gunter would have shared it, but the German had taken all his gear with him, adding fuel to Craig's suspicion the German was headed toward Illimani's summit.

He heard Tina's footsteps crunch through the snow and the

screech of a frozen zipper as she got into her tent. He smiled, glad she was safe—at least for tonight.

Since he'd been unsure about when Gunter would return, Craig had tossed the extra sleeping bags into his tent. He was glad to have them. He layered one over his foam pad and tucked his own bag into the other extra one. It still took a while to get warm. He shut his eyes and willed his breathing into the slow pattern that let him drift into sleep. It didn't work. A vision of Tina, naked and straddling him, danced behind his lids. All her amazing hair hung over his chest like a curtain of living flame. His cock throbbed, hot and hard where it lay against his stomach.

He wanted Tina. Ached for her. Maybe he should've taken her up on her invitation, but it hadn't felt right. People in life and death situations fucked to remind themselves they were still alive. He knew all about that because he'd done it a time or two. Nameless bodies swathed in layers against the cold on peaks he could barely remember. Only two body parts were required to get the deed done. It was easy enough to finesse. Craig winced. He didn't want it to be like that between him and Tina. He needed her to choose him for himself, not as a hedge against the void.

His cock twitched. It didn't care about philosophy. It wanted release. Craig clicked on his headlamp and grappled in his pack for a towel. He lay back down, doused his light, and made a neat package of his cock wrapped in the towel. Dipping beneath its soft layers, he wrapped a hand around himself. He wouldn't be able to sleep until he took the edge off his lust for Tina.

He closed his eyes and visualized her taut breasts pushing against the thin fabric of her long underwear. Pebbled against the cold and wind, her nipples had been fully visible. He'd never forgotten what they looked like, strawberry circles tipped by wonderfully sensitive points. He'd made her come just by suckling her many a time.

He pumped his shaft, moving fast and sure. His breathing quickened, and his heart hammered against his chest. Her pussy with its red curls filled his mind. He pretended he was pushing into her, feeling the heat of her close around him, inhaling the musk of her arousal... His cock pulsed hard in his hand. Craig imagined her muscles clenched tight around him and stroked himself until the last jets erupted.

He lay against the down and nylon of his bag, panting. The towel had caught the worst of the mess. He tossed it out of his sleeping bag. The damp parts would be frozen long before morning, but it didn't matter. This time when he closed his eyes, he slept.

WIND WOKE HIM. No longer satisfied with just howling, it had risen to a screech, which would've roused the dead. The light filtering through the yellow tent fabric was gray. He tilted his wrist to look at his watch. Six. Time to see how everyone had survived the night. It was pretty clear they weren't going anywhere but down today. He was grateful they weren't far from Estancia Una. Much closer than they would've been if the clients had been more like normal ones and able to make the usual location for high camp.

Gunter.

The thought crashed into him. It was obvious the German hadn't returned during the night. Craig grabbed the two-way radio and called him again. All he got was static.

Nothing I can do about that right now. He tossed the dice and wasn't very lucky...

He struggled into his clothes, keeping as much of himself in his nest of sleeping bags as he could. It was bitterly cold. Well below zero.

"Hey, you decent?" Tina's voice sounded from just outside his tent.

"Yeah. Have you checked on everyone? I was just about to do that."

"They're all fine. Brice still has a headache, but it's manageable. Joe's lung sounds aren't any worse. The weather's sort of like it was last time I was here. Can't see five feet in front of me."

"I'll talk with the twins. Maybe I can offer them free passage on another trip in exchange for this one not working out. Or maybe we could still pick up Sajama after you and I are done, uh, hunting for Gunter." Craig was all too aware the others could probably hear their conversation. The wind had a strange way of magnifying things.

"That would be nice. They're the only two mountaineers in the group. They understand we need to retreat. Both of them said as much not five minutes ago."

"Did anything, uh, unusual happen after you went to bed last night?"

He heard her snort. "If that's a roundabout way of asking if I had any unexpected visitors, the answer is no."

"I had another idea. We'll have time to talk about it after I'm up."

"Okay. I'm going to boil water for oatmeal. Want some?"

"Sure." Craig smiled. Oatmeal and coffee had been their staple breakfast in the mountains all the years they'd climbed together. It felt right somehow. Just like being with Tina felt right. She was still a part of him. He'd forced himself to keep going without her, but there'd always been an empty place.

Craig scrambled into the rest of his clothes. He wore all his layers, but he'd still be cold until he got moving. He cursed as he shoved his feet into his frozen glacier boots. He'd considered bringing boot heaters, but even if he had them, he'd never have bothered with them on a rinky-dink climb like this one. No, they would've been with the gear he left in La Paz. He blew into his mitts to warm them, slipped his hands in, and unzipped the tent and fly.

Wind hit him full in the face, along with a mouthful of blowing snow as he fought to close the partially-frozen tent zipper. *Crap!* Tina hadn't been kidding. He reached into a pocket and pulled out goggles, settling them around his head. The lenses were orange to improve visibility in low light conditions.

If I were superstitious, I'd believe this trip was cursed.

He stopped by each of the tents and told his charges to put on everything they owned. He also told them they'd be returning to Estancia Una where he'd either see them settled on a bus or in taxis to make the drive to La Paz. He explained he wouldn't be returning with them because he needed to try to find Gunter. To his relief, no one seemed upset.

"How about breakfast?" Ted asked.

"Hot water's in the mess tent. You can have hot cereal, dried fruit, and tea or coffee."

"No pancakes?"

"If you want to try to cook them, go for it. I think we should clear out of here before things get any worse." Craig made an effort to sound cordial. What he wanted to tell Ted was it wouldn't hurt him to miss a meal or two.

Don't antagonize the clients. One of his Alpine Attack teachers told him to pretend it was a logo stenciled on his soul.

"I have to check on the mules. Best thing you can do is to finish dressing, eat something, and get your personal gear packed."

Without waiting to see if Ted came back with a snarky rejoinder, Craig turned toward the area he'd hobbled the mules. They brayed reproachfully at him, and he dug oats and their nose bags out of their partially buried pack frames. He couldn't finesse what he needed to do with his thick alpine mitts, so he pulled them off. By the time he was done, and the braying had mutated into contented crunching, his hands were numb. He stuffed them down his pants and stifled a shriek as they came in contact with his stomach. Blood returning to his fingers created a small agony of its own. Once it was manageable, he put his mitts back on and headed for the mess tent.

"There you are." Tina glanced at him. "Your oatmeal was freezing solid, so I gave it to one of the clients. Let me mix you up another bowl."

"Thanks."

"Sheesh. You look like the abominable snowman. Your face has rime ice on it."

"Good thing most of it's covered by my beard, otherwise I'd be truly cold." He tugged off his goggles and pushed his hood back. "Mules seem okay. Has everyone gotten something to eat? We need to get them out of the tents and everything packed and back onto the mules. It won't be easy in this wind."

She stopped stirring and handed him a bowl. "Eat quick, while it's hot. Yeah, all the clients have stopped by for food. I think we should leave a couple of tents pitched here. For one thing, if Gunter manages to stumble off the mountain, he'll be trashed. For another, we're coming right back. Doesn't make sense to break camp only to set it up again a few hours later."

He spooned oatmeal into his mouth. It was good: warm and creamy. Tina had added sugar and powdered milk. "Thanks." He gestured at the bowl with his spoon. "I suppose it would make sense to leave your tent and mine here and some of the food and supplies. The mess tent too. I'd planned to send it all to La Paz. A tour outfit I work with there would store it for me, and not steal too much."

"We can keep my drugs and medical supplies here. They don't weigh much since I didn't bring oxygen." She pursed her lips. "Even if things go well, I don't imagine we'll be back much before dark—"

"Which means we won't be heading uphill until tomorrow," he finished for her. "Not a problem. I'll mark this site with the GPS. It may be the only way we can find it again. It's starting to snow more. By the time we come back, there won't be any tracks to follow."

"It will be a problem for Gunter," she murmured. "If he's still alive."

Craig put his bowl down, walked up behind her, and put his hands on her shoulders. "I've tried to raise him on the radio a dozen times, starting last night after I got to camp and realized what he'd done. He hasn't answered. What do you think the odds are?"

"Not good."

He grunted. "And getting worse by the moment. I want to talk about something else, though. Have you run tests on your blood since your, um, experience on this mountain?"

She ducked from under his hands and spun to face him. "Uh, what kind of tests?"

"You're prevaricating. You know, blood count, blood chemistry, whatever you guys call it."

Her usually direct gaze scooted away. "Why?"

He lowered his voice and spoke close to her ear. "I thought maybe the mountain spirit might've shared some of his power with you when he completed the blood bond ritual."

Two spots of color bloomed high on her cheeks. "I should've called you seven years ago. Maybe we could have stymied him if we'd had time to dissect things." She captured her lower lip in her teeth. "My blood's not the same," she admitted, her voice soft enough he had to strain to hear. "I won't bore you with the details, and I never bothered to run the DNA, but looking at my chem panel, I'm not all that human anymore. It's bad enough, I do my own labs and destroy them once they're run." She hesitated and then whispered the next words in his ear. "There are elements I don't recognize."

He shut his eyes for a moment, not understanding why he wasn't more surprised by her revelation. Craig's instincts had always been good. They'd kept him alive all these years in a sport where over thirty percent died. He ran with the first suggestion his inner voice came up with. "Before we leave," he said, keeping his voice soft, "I want you to make a cut big enough to bleed at least a couple of tablespoons. Let it run into the ground. I'll scrape the snow down for you."

"I don't understand."

He shook his head. "Neither do I, not really. But I trust my intuition. These spirits are ancient. The one thought he needed blood to bind you. Maybe you need blood to call him back. It's better to meet him on our turf, Tina. That would be here, not out on the glacier with a crevasse field to trap us. Most of the openings will have filled in with the new snow, so we won't be able to tell where they are."

"We have to look for Gunter. That means the glacier."

"Not if it's not safe for us," he countered. "Rule number one is—"

"I know." She held up a hand. "If we do something stupid and die, we can't rescue anyone. I suppose if he were still alive, he'd have radioed for help."

"Not necessarily. He knows what he did was wrong. He's probably too ashamed to use the radio. He knows it would put me in a tough position of having to choose between him or the clients."

A thoughtful look creased her forehead. "Your blood theory makes sense in a macabre sort of way. After all, why would the bond force me to his bidding, but not the other way round?"

He shrugged. "Afraid I don't have an answer. The other thing your blood might do is make the other ones—Illimani and Illampu—more, um, sensitive to your attempts to communicate with them."

He picked up his bowl, scraped the rest of the semi-frozen oatmeal out of the bottom with a titanium spoon, and ate it. Then he moved around Tina, grabbed a mug, and made himself a cup of instant coffee liberally laced with sugar.

She pounded a gloved fist into her other hand. "You're shooting in the dark."

A corner of his mouth turned down. "I am. If we come up with enough ideas, though, one is bound to pan out."

"Wish I knew more about the native people here. I looked up their legends, but didn't study them because most of the source materials were written in native languages, and I couldn't find anyone to translate."

"It might not have helped." He polished off the tepid coffee in a couple gulps. "If you're done in here, help me break camp. We'll need to batten down the tents we're leaving."

"You aren't kidding. I don't want this to be another Mount McKinley where we staggered back to our camp on Denali Pass only to discover it had blown away. It's a miracle we didn't die that night. The ice was like glass and close to vertical. One slip would have done it."

"Well, we didn't." He quirked a brow before repositioning his hood and goggles. "I like to think we've learned something since then."

Tina snorted. "Yeah, me too." She held out her arms.

Craig fought with himself, but the battle was brief. He stepped into her embrace and hugged her back. "It'll be all right," he murmured.

"Wish I was as certain as you sound."

He stepped away. "We can talk more about this later, but there's got to be a reason he gave you seven years instead of shanghaiing you on the spot. Maybe his blood needed time to do its work in your body. Hell, Tina, maybe you have some sort of power to rival his. For all we know, he did something to make you worthy of being his consort."

Her face twisted into an unpleasant expression, as if she'd bitten into something sour. She shuddered. "Let's get the blood thing over with. You dig down to earth and I'll meet you outside with a scalpel."

"How about behind those boulders?"

"Sure. I'll be right behind you." She snorted grimly. "It's beginning to feel like my second home.

He headed out the door without bothering to answer.

Her footsteps crunched through the snow. Craig straightened. He'd used an ice axe to scrape through a thin coating of rime ice between two boulders. It was a protected spot, and there hadn't been much snow to clear.

"Here." She took off her gloves, thrust her coat at him, and rolled one sleeve up a couple of inches. A deft cut in the meaty part of her thumb and blood flowed into the place he'd cleared. "Damn."

"What?"

"It's so fucking cold my blood wants to clot." She squeezed the edges of the wound and shook her head. "That's going to have to do it. I'm not chopping into myself again." She wound a bandage around the base of her thumb and secured it with tape. He helped her into her jacket.

Tina dropped her medical supplies into a pocket and slid her gloves back on. "Glad that's over with. Thanks for helping me." An uncomfortable expression crossed her face.

"You're welcome. What's wrong?"

She shrugged. "If I let myself think about it, this feels too woo-woo for words. Doesn't matter. It's done now. Let's take the rest of this one step at a time. I'll roust the troops and make sure they have everything. You batten down our two tents and this one."

He gave her a mock salute. "As you say, my lady doctor. I'll make it so."

She laughed. "Whoops! Wasn't trying to steal your thunder, Jean-Luc."

"Don't worry about it. Let's get going. Sooner we get this show on the road, the sooner we'll be back here."

CHAPTER 15

Tina slogged uphill. Her initial estimate of how long it would take to sort things out and escort the clients back to civilization had been wildly optimistic. They might have another fifteen minutes of daylight. It would be well past dark before they reached the tents. They'd left all the mules but Xavier in Estancia Una. The bells from his harness tinkled in her ears. He'd been pretty frisky since his pack frame was empty.

"I know how you feel, buddy." She patted the side of his neck. "My pack feels a whole lot better with twenty pounds in it than sixty."

Footsteps pelted toward her as Craig caught up. He'd sent her and the mule ahead while he finalized last minute arrangements with the taxi drivers. Tina made Joe promise he'd stop by the main hospital in La Paz before leaving Bolivia. He'd improved after descending four thousand plus feet, so she wasn't particularly worried about him anymore, but it never hurt to have an extra set of eyes take a look.

"Sorry," Craig said. "Took quite a bit longer than I thought it would."

"No kidding. Everything did. The foot of fresh snow when we left camp didn't help, but it didn't last long. Good thing too since I've never seen a group move quite so slow."

"Know what you mean. I'll make a point of trying to meet clients before accepting them from now on. Or at least do a better job of checking their climbing résumés. Too risky, otherwise."

She lapsed into silence, her emotions in turmoil. One of her inner voices chided her for not telling Craig to go back. This was her battle, not his. She'd spurned him years before. It wasn't fair for her to take advantage of his goodwill—and whatever feelings he might still have for her—if it put his life on the line.

She'd heard the telltale signs of him masturbating last night. Their tents were right next to one another. The hitch in his breathing when he got close to orgasm was unmistakable. If he'd been that aroused, why hadn't he taken her up on her offer and joined her in her tent? She blew out a sad breath. Craig was a decent guy. She should've married him when she had the chance. Plus, he was still sexier than hell. Knowing he was stroking himself to a climax not ten feet from her made her so hot, she'd rubbed herself to her own peak with a jacket stuffed into her mouth so she wouldn't give herself away. Her face heated at the memory.

"Penny for your thoughts."

"Nothing, really." She turned away so he wouldn't see how flushed she was. "We should hatch up a plan, though." She gestured toward the westering sun. "It'll be down in a couple minutes. Did you try to raise Gunter again?"

"No point. The radios have a stated five mile range, but they don't work very well in the mountains until you're much closer."

"Since you're the blood guru, what do you think we should do after we get back to the tents? Besides dinner and bed, that is."

"I'm not sure. It wouldn't hurt for you to spend the time between now and then asking Illimani and Illampu for help."

"Not Huayna Potosi?"

He shook his head. "Not sure we need the Lord of Stone. Besides that peak's quite a way from here."

It felt like a fool's errand, but she didn't have any better ideas, so Tina threw her mind wide open. The weather had cleared as they'd descended, but it was going to hell again, almost as if some mountain god were warning them away. She latched on to that as a starting point and told Illimani about her dilemma.

"Tina."

"Huh?" She'd been so deep in thought, Craig's voice came as a surprise.

"It's snowing harder and it'll be completely dark soon. Stop, put on warmer clothes, get your clear goggles out. And your headlamp."

"Yes, Daddy."

He snorted. "I kept thinking you'd do it on your own. Let me help with your pack."

A rush of love so intense it nearly undid her, threaded outward from her belly. She opened her mouth to tell him she'd been a fool, that she'd never stopped loving him, but snared the words before they could escape from her throat. Craig was just being Craig. Doing the right thing was as natural to him as breathing.

"Thanks," she murmured and rooted in her pack for her storm gear. She had to be careful. The wind wanted to rip her things right out of her hands. Snow pelted her in the face. She squinted against the developing storm, wondering why she hadn't noticed how bad it had gotten.

Once they were underway again, he asked, "Any luck communing with the mountain gods?"

She started to say no and then set her mind to analyzing what had happened. "I'm not sure," she replied at last. "I was in a trance state. A pretty damned deep one since I didn't even think to stop and layer up until you told me."

"Did anyone tell you anything?" he persisted.

She shook her head. "It wasn't like when Mururata spoke into my mind. It's possible someone was listening to me. Christ! How could I know something like that for sure? My scientifically-trained brain is tripping me up. I need to suspend that part, and it's not easy."

"Do you know for certain the one dogging you is Mururata?"

"No. It's just conjecture since he was the miscreant who was beheaded. Back to reality, do you think you should fire up the GPS? We have to be close."

"If we don't stumble across the tents in the next few minutes I will."

Xavier tugged on his lead rope. "Hey. He wants us to bear left."

"Go for it. He'll know where we were last night. He's probably hoping there are oats left."

"Are there?"

"He could eat himself sick if I gave him all of them." Craig laughed. The sound was welcome. The closer they got to the upper mountain, the more apprehensive she felt.

"Maybe he can smell them." She let go of the rope and trotted after the mule. "Home," she called over a shoulder. "We're here."

"Great. I'll take care of Xavier. Want to get something going for dinner?"

She headed for the mess tent, checking the other two were still where they'd staked them and hadn't been disturbed. Tina breathed a sigh of relief. She hadn't expected the weather to sabotage their tents, but the campesinos—Bolivian peasants—were so poor, they often broke into climbers' camps in the Andes and took whatever wasn't nailed down. Because their camp was so low, it was close enough to Estancia Una and Pinaya to be easy pickings.

Likely the rotten weather had saved them from thieves.

The snow wasn't much deeper than when they'd left, but it

wouldn't stay like that for long the way it was coming down. Tina stamped snow from her boots and stepped into the mess tent. She shucked her pack, set it in a corner, and got a candle lantern going. She grabbed a large pot and debated walking to the stream she'd gotten water from the night before. Not wanting to deal with the worsening weather any longer than she had to, she went outside, filled the pot with snow, and set it on the white gas stove, keeping the door pinned open for ventilation. While the snow melted, she rustled through their freeze-dried options.

By the time Craig came in, she had an approximation of fettuccini alfredo bubbling on the stove. "Mmmm," he murmured appreciatively. "Smells wonderful. What are we having with it?"

"Here's soup." She pressed a mug into his hands. "And I was thinking maybe rice pudding for dessert."

He pulled up a camp stool and dropped onto it. "I checked the other tents. All our stuff's still here."

"Heh! I did the same thing. On a more serious note, did you try Gunter?"

He shook his head. The sharp sound of static filled the small space. Craig's eyes widened. He pulled his radio from a pocket and depressed the send button. "Yes?"

"Thank God," was followed by a torrent of German.

"Slow down," Craig said. "Try English."

"Lady doctor. She is still there?"

"Yes. Tina's still here. Why?"

"I am near Nido de Condores. Leg broken. Cold."

Craig's forehead creased with worry. "I've tried you lots of times with the radio. Why didn't you answer?"

"Fell. Knocked out."

Tina exhaled sharply. Great. With a head injury and a broken leg, he'd be hard to evacuate. She tapped Craig's arm and mouthed, "We should call a chopper."

He shook his head. "They can't fly in this weather."

"Was sagten Sie?"

"Never mind. Wasn't talking to you."

The radio cracked again. "Sorry, I am—"

"We'll figure something out. Do you have your GPS?"

"Nein. Lost much when falling."

Tina made chopping motions with her hands and pulled out her avalanche transceiver.

Craig nodded his understanding. "Gunter. Turn your avalanche beacon to send. We can track the signal. Turn your radio off. We may need to communicate with you and we won't be able to if you run it out of power, talking. Turn it back on at the top of every hour for five minutes. Put on everything you have with you and try to find a sheltered spot."

"Ja. Danke."

Craig set the radio handset on the table. "Shit. As if we didn't have enough problems."

Tina walked around him and looked out the open tent door. She shone her headlamp on the ground. "An inch has fallen since I came in here." She ducked back inside and velcroed the door shut.

"May as well eat. We won't do him any good by not being well-fed."

She plunked the cook pot onto the folding metal dining table and handed him a titanium fork. "Want tea with it? Water's still hot."

"Sure." He grabbed his soup mug from where he'd set it and handed it to her.

She settled next to him. For a time they ate in silence, sharing the cook pot between them. Food that got cold froze. "If we don't go after him tonight, he'll probably be dead by morning," she murmured.

"He may die, anyway. Concussions at altitude are usually serious."

She snorted. "Where'd you go to medical school?"

He slammed a fist down on the table, startling her. "We are not going after him unless we can see. Which means this storm has to die down. I don't mind night rescues, but I'm not going to negotiate my way up the glacier if I can't see my hand in front of my face. We'd end up at the bottom of a crevasse."

She held up gloved hands. "I'm not the enemy. What you say makes sense, but I have a patient up there who may be dying—"

"Tina, stop. Think basic triage. If we can't do anything for him without taking on an unacceptable level of risk for ourselves, we could die. If that happens, Gunter won't have any chance at all. Let's concentrate on talking through your problems with the renegade god." He pushed to his feet and picked up the empty noodle pan. "I'll get dessert going."

"Crack the door before you turn on the stove."

"Yes, doctor."

She propped her head on her hand, feeling tired. Gunter was a complication they didn't need. Yet they couldn't ignore him. That ranked up there with climbers on Everest who marched right past dying comrades, choosing the summit over compassion. Something nagged at her. The wind. She couldn't hear it anymore. Tina stood and went to the tent door. She peered outside, and a shiver went up her back. It was impossible, but the night sky had cleared. A half-moon and millions of stars winked against its blackness.

It felt as if someone had socked her in the gut. Weather didn't act like this on any other mountain. It took time, goddammit, for storms to move in, and for them to leave. She didn't hear the hiss of the stove anymore, so she closed the tent and turned to face Craig.

He'd just put the cook pot back on the table with their pudding in it. "What?" He raised his brows in twin question marks. "You look like someone just walked over your grave."

"They did. This whole thing with Gunter is nothing but a setup."

"Huh? Sit back down and finish your dinner. You're not making sense."

She didn't feel like sitting. "The weather," she grunted through clenched teeth. "It's clear as a bell out there. I can even see the stars. Doesn't it strike you as a tad too convenient it went from storming like a sonfabitch to clear right after we get a distress call from Gunter?"

He met her gaze, his green eyes troubled. "Sure. But I don't get why you're so outraged. You figured out the weather here was unnatural seven years ago."

She paced in a tight circle. "It's a trap. Mururata set it for me."

"Well, he's getting both of us."

A knife pierced her soul. Tears pricked, hot and bitter behind her lids. "I don't want you to come with me."

"Noted, but you don't have any control over my choices." He spooned pudding into his mouth. "Come get your half of this before I eat it all."

"Not hungry."

"Doesn't matter. I'm not usually hungry at altitude, but I eat, anyway. You know the drill, Tina. Sit your ass down here and eat. It's going to be a long night. You need all the calories you can stuff into yourself."

She picked up her spoon, stood over the pot, and shoveled the rest of the pudding into her mouth. "There," she said. "Satisfied?"

He turned, grabbed his pack, and rummaged through it.

"What are you doing?" she asked.

"Getting the sat phone. I'm going to see if I can call in a rescue for Gunter. It would solve at least one problem."

She listened while he spoke in fractured Spanish, cursing her near-inability to learn any language but English. After a sharp exchange, he punched the end call button so viciously she thought the phone would fly out of his hand.

"I'm guessing whatever it was isn't good."

He made a rude sound and shook his head. "It's worse than not good. The dispatcher accused me of lying about conditions. Seems it's storming everywhere but here."

A small animal with sharp claws crawled up her spine. She started to shake. For a minute, she was afraid she'd puke up her dinner. How the hell could something be powerful enough to control the weather? Worse, what hope did she have against it?

"Whoa." He stood and pulled her against him. "I'm pretty blown away by it too. It's like facing something impossible, something that flies in the face of everything I've ever believed, and having someone say, 'Tough shit, it's real.'"

"I'm scared. Scratch that, I'm terrified." Her voice was muffled against his jacket. "But no matter how I feel, this is my battle. If something happened to you—" She choked back a sob.

"Ssht." He tightened his hold on her. "We're partners, remember? Climbing partners who have each other's backs. I'm not bugging out when the going gets tough. I'm staying to see things through."

"But—"

"Uh-uh. No buts. Do you honestly think I could live with myself if I sent you out to do battle alone with some esoteric monster?"

"I-I never should've involved you in this. I just thought I'd piggyback onto your trip and stay here once it was over."

His arms tensed around her. "Why my trip? There are other operators who run expeditions to Bolivia this time of year." She was silent so long, he prodded, "Well?"

She wanted to scream *because I never stopped loving you*. Her throat thickened with suppressed emotion.

I can't answer him. It will just complicate things.

To her horror, a whimpering moan ripped out of her chest, followed by another. She jerked away to pull herself together. "I don't know what's wrong with me." She sucked in a steadying breath. "We need to get moving. Tears are an indulgence. I'm just feeling sorry for myself."

He had an odd look on his face, almost as if he could see into her soul. "Okay. We do need to get moving, but we're not going until we're clear how we're going to do this. I started a list in my head of what we'll need. We're making certain we've got each and every piece of equipment between us."

Tina made over a dozen trips back and forth to the other tents, gathering ropes, ice screws, travois materials, food, and medical supplies, while Craig fashioned wands out of three foot pieces of bamboo topped with colored ribbon. Being on the move had a salutary effect. She didn't feel as lost and desperate as she had when the night shifted from stormy to clear and the helicopter dispatcher corroborated they were trapped in the *Twilight Zone*.

"There." She dropped a final armload of gear into the mess tent. "I think that's all of it."

Craig grunted, got to his feet, and picked through the piled goods. He snapped up his climbing harness and stepped into it. "You too. We're going to rope up before we leave camp."

"Why? The glacier's not for a couple of miles." She snugged into her harness and pulled the straps tight.

His mouth turned up in a grim approximation of a smile. "Because I want to keep track of you. I don't trust the weather to stay benign. I had time to think while I was making enough wands to get us to where I believe Gunter is. I expect whoever's running the show will throw everything but the kitchen sink at us as soon as we get clear of camp. I aim to be ready."

He looked so determined, it made her heart ache. She picked her words with care. "I'm hoping we'll find Gunter alive. Once I've done what I can to stabilize him and you're safely away, I—"

"Not on your life, sister. We face this together. All of it. End of discussion. Let's split the gear down the middle, pack up, and get this choo-choo moving."

Tina recognized the stubborn set of his chin, and the light dancing in the back of his eyes radiated danger. "What would you do if I said no?"

"Deck you. Sit watch over you until the bastard who wants you shows up, and take him on."

She squared her shoulders and faced him. "Thanks."

"You'd do the same for me."

A slow smile spread over her face. "Yes—" she nodded "—I would."

Craig tied himself into his end of the rope. On one hand, it felt ridiculous. The night was clear and cold. A three-quarter moon shed enough light he didn't even need his headlamp. It had taken less than fifteen minutes to load their packs and get moving. He glanced behind him. "You good?"

"Yup. Lead out. I let Xavier run loose. At least that way if things don't go well—"

"They'll be fine," he broke in. Giving voice to negative thoughts was never a good idea, and the mule had a scrappy temperament. He'd probably make his way back to his owners in Estancia Una.

"We should come across Gunter in an hour. Did you radio him?"

"Uh-huh."

"How'd he sound?"

"Weak, but not disoriented. Maybe his head injury's not all that bad." Craig looped the rope through a gloved hand and started uphill. She muttered something. "What?" he called over a shoulder. "I didn't catch what you said."

"We deserve a break."

He started to tell her things didn't work like that. Not in the mountains where surprises were mostly of the negative variety, but he bit his tongue. Craig forced himself to glance at the high alpine vista bathed in moonlight.

He'd always loved the pristine quality of endless snowfields at night. He felt more comfortable here than in his living room. All significant climbs began between ten at night and one in the morning. Snow was much more stable when it was cold. Less likely to avalanche or send boulders tumbling down steep slopes. The Himalaya were an exception. It was so cold on eight thousand meter peaks, climbers often didn't start uphill until closer to dawn.

He listened to Tina's boots crunching along behind him, separated by fifty feet of rope. He'd brought nearly four hundred feet with them, the hundred-ninety-eight foot length linking him to Tina plus one more just like it. One would be used to fashion part of the travois to move Gunter down the mountain.

Craig stopped, tapped in a wand, and activated the GPS to mark its placement. Tina knew to stop when the rope between them went slack. In moments, he was on the move again. With each step, he checked off an item in his head. Best be sure about what they had before they were so far from the tents going back was less of an option. He set his mouth into a grim line. His obsessiveness had saved his ass on more than one occasion.

Once he was satisfied they had everything on his list, he relaxed the iron grip on his thoughts. They immediately turned to Tina. It felt so good to hold her in his arms again. More than good —incredible. The years hadn't changed her a bit. If anything, she was more beautiful than she'd been long ago. Her eyes were such a dark blue, they reminded him of a Rocky Mountain sky at sunset.

She hadn't answered when he asked why she'd chosen to come to Bolivia with him, but he thought he knew the answer. Tina had come to South America convinced she was going to die on the slopes of Illimani. They'd been close once. Maybe she hadn't found anyone else she felt as safe with in the years they'd been apart. She didn't wear a ring, so he was pretty certain she wasn't married. He'd itched to ask if she had a husband or a lover, but hadn't. It wasn't any of his business. Even if she did, she'd chosen to spend what she feared might be her last hours with him, not a mythical husband, lover, or boyfriend.

He was certain she'd loved him once. Maybe she could feel that way again. The attraction between them still burned bright.

I don't know that, his common sense voice butted in.

Not on her side, anyway. For all I know, her invitation to have sex was just because she thought it would be the last time.

He breathed deep and urged the cold, thin air to quiet his thoughts. He needed the calm, rational objectivity that brought him home unscathed. He'd always been a lucky climber. He didn't talk about those things, though. Mountaineers risked their necks over and over. They understood luck was part of the game. And a pretty large one at that.

Tina's voice sounded from behind. "We should put on crampons. It's steepening and I just slipped sideways on some ice."

He stopped walking and turned toward her, careful to keep the rope out from under his feet. "Sure." He glanced at the altimeter on his multi-function watch. "About two hundred more feet to Nido de Condores." He tapped in another wand and marked its placement with the GPS. So long as his electronics didn't crap out, he didn't need the wands. They were a backup system. What he'd used before the advent of the fancy GPS devices.

She came up beside him, coiling rope as she moved close. "I know. We're making good time." She barked a short laugh. "Funny, I didn't expect the clear weather to hold this long."

"Me, either. Let's make hay while we can." He shucked his pack and pulled his crampons from one of the outer pockets. Buckling them with mitts on was nearly impossible. He sat on his pack, fitted the steel spikes to his boots, and attached them as fast as he could. "Brrrrr" He shoved his hands back into his mitts, sighing when their residual warmth soothed his aching fingers.

"Cold and clear. Doesn't get much better than that for climbing." Tina bent to put on her crampons. "I got this newer kind with snap buckles. Don't have to take off my gloves."

"I looked at those. Then I went home and counted how many pairs I already own. It was hard to justify a couple hundred bucks for what would have made the twenty-fifth set. They never wear out."

She laughed. He loved how she tossed her head and the musical quality of her laughter. "Are you still sharpening them yourself?"

"You bet. Still making my own climbing hardware too."

"Chomoly pitons?"

He grinned. "Yup. I still have the set I made for you."

"You always reminded me of a Renaissance man. So self-sufficient…" Her voice trailed off. "Someone's been trying to talk with me."

His pulse sped up. He batted down apprehension—and hope—flaring in his chest. "For how long?"

"Since we were just a few minutes out of camp. I'm not certain who, but I don't think it's Mururata. I know what he sounds like. These voices are different."

"Can you understand them?"

"No. They're speaking something that sounds like a cross between Aymara and Spanish. Though it's hard to be sure, it seems like they're pissed because I'm using English to communicate."

Craig slitted his eyes. "Makes sense. If it's Illimani or Illampu, they'd speak whatever the native tongue used to be here." He jumped to his feet, unable to sit still. "Those legends you read came from somewhere. There must've been a time when the spirits and human inhabitants of these parts were able to communicate." He took two steps to where she sat and clapped her on the shoulder. "Maybe leaving your blood back there was a better idea than I thought."

She twisted her lips into a tight smile. "I hope so. I don't want to die. Or turn into some warped paramour for Mururata. Some things are worse than dying. That's one of them."

He hunkered next to her and took her hands in his. "I will not let that happen."

She gazed at him through the clear lenses of her goggles. "Let's play this one again from the top. If you're thinking of bargaining with him and offering yourself in my place, forget it."

"Tina. I will do whatever I think needs doing. I won't know what it is until we're in the thick of things. This is a lot like climbing. Spontaneity and flexibility, eh?"

She rolled her eyes. "Ach, you're impossible."

"Watch it. Your Scottish roots are bleeding through. Come on." He stood and held out a hand to help her up.

She shouldered her pack and turned to face him, running the rope between her hands to straighten it. "You asked me why I chose your trip. It's because if these are going to be my last hours on earth—or my last as a human before that monster gets hold of me—I wanted to spend them with you."

His heart leapt. He wound his arms around her, clumsy because of her backpack. "Tina. Darling. My love," he whispered against the hood covering her hair. Joy swooshed through him, so bright it could've lit a small town. There was still hope for them.

"Hey, you're tangling the rope."

"My ever-practical doctor."

"Yep, that would be me." She leaned into him and kissed him gently before pushing away. "We need to get moving. I just thought I ought to tell you in case— Well, in case something happens and I don't get another chance."

He looped the rope around an arm and walked close beside her. "When did you— Uh, I mean, how long have you—"

She laughed. "I knew I made a mistake not marrying you the first time I went climbing without you. It just felt so empty and lonely without you next to me. I've done mostly solo climbing since we split up. Never found anyone who fit with me anywhere near as well as you. They were too slow, or too inept, or too arrogant. Part of staying alive up here is just what you said. Being flexible and not clinging to a plan that isn't working anymore."

"Why didn't you hunt me down?"

She shrugged. "Pride, mainly. I kept myself too busy to think about it most of the time."

Sudden understanding blossomed, but he needed to hear her say it. "That's not all."

"What? Is everybody on this mountain psychic?"

"You're hedging. You'd only been back from South America for a few weeks when I asked you to marry me. I thought about it a lot when I was climbing in the Vinson Range in Antarctica. Came back convinced you were the only woman for me and there was no reason to wait."

She nodded. "I am hedging. Truth is I was still reeling from what happened here. It was so off-the-wall I didn't know where to compartmentalize it. And I was in the middle of my second year of residency. Not sure if you remember, but I was assigned to an inner city hospital, and it was tough. Who would've thought Denver had gang wars? Whoops. Sorry." She bent to pull the rope out of a crampon point.

"Here." He did a better job of coiling the nylon loops around his arm. "This is why you don't walk side by side. I'm bending the rules, though. I've waited a long time for this conversation."

"Better watch it, Robson. You're slipping. Break one rule, next thing you know—"

He swatted her on the rump. "Not interested in rules right now. Hell, you didn't tell me anything seven years ago. Just said you couldn't marry me and walked out of my life."

"What happened to me here was so bizarre, I couldn't find words for it. Part of me thought I might be having a late schizophrenic break. Maybe I'd hallucinated the whole thing, including my time in the crevasse." She blew out an exasperated breath. "Regardless, whether I was going nuts or my life was on the line, I didn't want to involve you. Didn't seem fair."

"It would've been better if you'd let me make that choice for myself." He tried not to sound reproachful, but it leaked out, anyway.

"There was also my ambivalence about anything—marriage and children, for instance—getting between me and the mountains."

"You still should've talked with me."

"What can I say? It's the whole caretaker thing. I make decisions for other people all the time. Most of my patients are too sick to be active participants—"

"Tina." He latched a hand around her arm. "I wasn't your patient. I was your lover."

"I'm sorry." Her voice was low. "It doesn't make it any better, but I've suffered from my choices as much as you."

His head snapped up. "Wind. Can't feel it yet, but I hear it."

"Me too. It's just a faint drone, but it'll be on us in no time. Let's hurry. I'll drop behind. We're faster when one's in front. Lay into those afterburners. I won't have trouble keeping up."

The terrain steepened. Wind swirled yesterday's snow into patterns. They looked surreal, glittering in the moonlight. If it didn't get any worse, they'd be fine. Right now it was less than a minor annoyance. Craig checked his bearing from time to time using the GPS function in his watch. It wasn't as accurate as the standalone GPS, but it was good enough.

He stopped to tap in another wand, but most of his energy was focused on Tina.

He couldn't believe his good fortune. The only woman he'd ever wanted as part of his life wasn't lost to him. Energy pulsed with every step. Tonight, he could've climbed Everest without supplemental oxygen and had strength to spare.

"The voices are back. What should I do?"

"Be open to them. Thank them. Ask for their help."

He clicked on his avalanche transceiver. Nothing. It wouldn't pick up Gunter's signal until they were within a hundred feet or so. Craig checked his altimeter. He figured they'd find the German somewhere between seventeen-five and eighteen thousand feet. They were already at seventeen-seven. He pulled the radio out and keyed it. No answer. He tried again. "Gunter!"

"What's going on?" It was hard to hear Tina over the wind. "He's not responding?"

"No." Craig slipped the radio back into his pocket. "But it's not the top of the hour. His radio is probably off." He cupped his hands around his mouth and cried, "Gunter!" The wind ripped the word away and made it echo strangely.

Tina climbed up next to him and slammed an axe into the slope to stabilize herself. "Nido de Condores has to be close. My memory is it's the flat area at the top of this stretch."

"Let's go." He powered up the last hundred feet and came out on a flattened shoulder. The upper mountain rose before him like a prehistoric beast. It was stunningly beautiful, with three of its five summits clearly illuminated by the moon.

"I've got a signal!" Tina's voice held a note of excitement. She raced up behind him. "Angle left about twenty degrees. Transceiver says he's a hundred and twenty feet from us."

Craig moved quickly. Ever-present wind had scraped snow off the rocks. His crampon points skittered over uneven blocks of talus. He tilted his transceiver so he could see its display.

Yes!

He held the device flat in his hand and followed the arrow. Digitizing avalanche beacons had been a huge step forward. With the older analog ones, you had to walk a grid to find someone. The DTS Tracker in his hand would lead him right to…

"There he is." Tina moved around him and bent into wind that was worsening by the minute. She fell to her knees in the snow beneath a huge boulder and turned her headlamp on high. Next she pulled her gloves off and tucked them under one knee, her hands busy at Gunter's neck before they moved down his body.

"How is he?" Craig asked as he moved up from behind.

"Unconscious. Probably a blessing. Could you help me with more light?"

Craig angled his own headlamp to provide extra light. Once he saw Gunter's gray face, he opened his mouth to tell Tina not to bother. Before he could say anything, she said, "Move a little farther right. Your light helps a lot." She slid her pack off and retrieved her medical kit, extracting a syringe with a long needle. Climbers used them to inject medications through their clothes. She pulled three vials out of an inner pocket of her parka and loaded the syringe from them before jamming it into Gunter's upper thigh.

"What'd you give him?"

"Dex, a broad spectrum antibiotic, and a small dose of a non-steroidal anti-inflammatory. His heartbeat's weak and thready. Left femur's broken, so he's lost a lot of blood. It's why his skin is so gray. We'll need to reduce it—pull the bone back into place—before we try to move him."

"I know you're an MD and I'm just a dirtbag climber, but I think he's dying."

"He is dying," she snapped. "But maybe I can alter the odds. I don't think he has neurological damage. His pupils are equal and reactive to light. His core temperature is low, but that one's a mixed bag. It's probably the only reason he's still alive. His femur's bled like a stuck pig, and I'm pretty sure an edge of the broken bone clipped a minor vein when it came through the skin. It's why his pants are soaked with blood."

"Are you going to give him something for pain?"

"Why? He's unconscious. Plus, I don't want to depress his respiratory function any further."

The wind blew harder. Craig's instincts, the ones that had kept him alive in many dicey situations, went on high alert. Clouds appeared out of nowhere. The clear sky vanished. Thick snow fell blanketing them. Tina stuffed her hands back into her gloves and jammed them over her ears.

He knelt in the snow next to her and pulled her hands away from the sides of her head. "Talk to me, Tina."

"They're shouting at each other in my head. Christ! I finally know how it feels to be mentally ill."

"Who?"

She tilted the beam of her headlamp out of the way and turned toward him. "Not Mururata, the other two." She grappled for her medical kit and slid it back into her pack.

"Humph. Seems like a positive development."

Gunter's eyes snapped open as if pulled by an unseen puppeteer. They gleamed silver in the beam from his lamp.

"Holy crap!" Running on nerves and intuition, Craig shot to his feet, placed his hands under Tina's arms, and pulled her against his body.

"What the fuck?" she sputtered, thrashing against him.

"Hush. Look." He angled his headlamp beam toward Gunter.

"Shit! If I didn't know better, I'd think—"

Still looking like a marionette, Gunter jerked upright. He took a step toward Tina, mouth contorted in agony. And then another.

"No!" Tina reached for the young German. "Don't try to—" Her words were drowned out by an unholy shriek.

Craig yanked her back a few more feet. Adrenaline thrummed along his nerves, driving them into high gear. "Your first guess was right," he ground out. "It's not Gunter. Wouldn't surprise me if he was dead before we got here. That's why you haven't seen Mururata. He's been busy reanimating a corpse."

"No. Gunter had a heartbeat when I examined him," Tina insisted. "Mururata doesn't."

Gunter's body took another step toward them. He extended a claw-like hand. "Your companion is clever. I thought I might be more palatable to you if I took on human form. It is time, doctor. Leave his arms and come to mine."

"Never," she shouted over the wind.

In one fluid motion, Craig shoved her behind him. "Head down the mountain, Tina. Do not look back. Go as fast as you can, but don't take any chances." He thrust the GPS at her. "The wands are programmed into it."

"Nice try." She stomped to his side and stood shoulder to shoulder with him. "We're doing this together. Climbing buddies, remember? We don't bug out when the going gets tough."

Despite the desperateness of their situation, Craig grinned. What a hell of a woman. He eyed Gunter. He'd brought a cylinder of white gas with him. If he got lucky, he could douse the corpse and set it on fire before Mururata could disengage. He reached into his parka for the gas and a lighter.

"Illimani! Illampu!" Tina shouted into the howl of the wind. "I left you my blood. Help us."

CHAPTER 17

ina screamed for the mountain gods again. She heard Craig mutter something. He took a few fast steps forward and threw something at Gunter. Her nose twitched. White gas.

"No." She made a lunge for Craig's arm, but it was too late. His windproof lighter was already flaring like a blowtorch. He chucked it at Gunter. The German's body flashed into an inferno. The smell of burning flesh rose, thick and cloying, along with the stench of scorched cloth and plastic.

Laughter, malevolent and fey, filled the air. "I feed on heat. It strengthens me. I should thank you, human. Instead I shall kill you. There is ample fire. Come."

Craig took a jerky step forward. "No!" Tina shrieked. "What are you doing?"

As if he couldn't hear, Craig took another step.

She pushed between him and the tower of flame that had been Gunter. "Leave him alone," she snarled at Mururata. "I'm the one you tricked into that bargain. Wouldn't surprise me if you shoved me into the crevasse. I'm pretty sure-footed. Never did understand how I stumbled and fell that night."

Craig dropped heavy hands on her shoulders. He was breathing hard. "Thanks. Don't know what I was thinking." He pulled her against his body. "We're stronger together, and we're not going down without a hell of a fight."

"Close your mind to his suggestions," she muttered. "They're deadly."

"No shit."

The fire advanced toward them. Flames sliced between their bodies. Craig jumped away. "Run, Tina. I'll try to hold him."

"Like hell." She scooped snow and smothered a place where his jacket was smoldering. Wind tugged her. She fought it, but her axes were in the snow next to where Gunter had been. It was all she could do to remain upright.

Craig latched on to her arm. Fire crashed down on his hand. He plunged his glove into the snow before it incinerated. His body arched as if something had hit him.

He rose a few feet in the air, spun, and fell, crashing against the snow.

"What have you done to him?" Tina shrieked. She tried to throw her body over Craig's. Wind pulled her away. She dropped to her knees, slithered to Craig on her belly, and wrapped her arms around him.

"I grow weary of your games. You promised yourself to me. Must I kill your companion to get you to leave his side?" The fire advanced toward her.

"Leave him alone."

The wind came alive, whipping around her body. No surprise since Mururata was Lord of Air. Heat from the fire made it hard to hold her ground. She clung to Craig, but flames pushed under her gloves, burning her fingers. She wanted to do something, anything, but how could she fight what she couldn't get close to?

"I will kill him where he lays, human woman. Leave him now."

Craig's body writhed and bucked beneath hers. A moan tore from him. She crawled backward. This was her fight, not his.

Maybe Mururata would spare him if she played her cards right. "All right," she gritted. "Let him go. I'm the one who was deranged enough to fall for your bargain."

Tina staggered to her feet. Her mind churned, and the metallic taste of fear flooded her mouth. There had to be something she could do. Mururata beckoned with a burning arm. Wind gathered behind her. It shoved her hard. She took a step forward because she had no choice. Heat seared her. "If you burn me, I'll die."

"You have my blood. You will never die. You must be punished for your hostility toward me. I am your master. It would amuse me if you were to suffer endlessly."

"You've lost your mind."

"Tina." Craig's voice was gravelly. "Run, goddammit."

"Not without you."

"How touching," Mururata snarled. Flames zipped past her. Craig's jacket caught fire. He rolled in the snow.

Got to get him away from Craig.

Breath clotted in her throat. She grabbed one of Craig's axes and backed away, fighting against the wind. At least she had a weapon now.

The air shimmered and grew brighter. The glare intensified and separated into two figures. Like Mururata seven years before, they were impossibly tall and draped in luminous robes that shaded through a rainbow of colors. One had blond hair hanging loose to his waist. The other's was dark. Their eyes were whirling pools of golden light. High cheekbones and sharp noses blended into the most arresting faces she'd ever seen.

Tina wrenched her gaze from Mururata and stared. "Illimani and Illampu?" She bowed her head in a sign of respect.

They ignored her. Both were focused on Mururata. One raised an arm and barked a command. A third figure rose from Gunter's burning body. Without the god to animate him, the German's form crashed into the snow and howled piteously.

Good god. How could he still be alive? Tina stared in horror at the burning body. She screamed at Gunter to roll in the snow. Either he didn't understand or he was beyond being able to help himself.

Craig groaned, rolled over, and staggered to his feet. "Nothing you can do for him," he croaked. "White gas and nylon is a lethal combination."

The god who'd raised his arm shifted his attention. Tina felt it as a command deep in her mind. She gazed at the pulsating light and shielded her eyes. "Illimani?"

"Nay. I am Illampu. Mururata told us you wished to become his queen."

"Never. He tricked me."

"She was willing to accept my help when her life hung in the balance," Mururata growled. His voice was tinny. He sounded different than Illampu. "All assistance comes with a price."

"Is it true you welcomed his aid?" Illampu asked.

Tina squared her shoulders, grateful Illampu was using English. It was accented and archaic, but at least she could understand him. She considered what to say. Not much point in lying. As impossible as it seemed, these were gods. "Yes, I accepted his help. I was even grateful for it. I was trapped in a crevasse. Would have died there if he hadn't interceded. I agreed to his terms because—"

A piteous cry rose from Gunter. "Please." Tina held out both hands. "Could you put out the fire? He's suffering."

Illimani shifted slightly from his stance near Illampu. Snow gathered itself from the mountainside and crashed atop Gunter. Tina raced to his side. Craig followed. Together, they pulled the German's smoking body out from under a foot of powdery snow. He moaned. His eyes flickered open, their normal dark brown again.

"Please." His gaze sought hers. "Hurts," he moaned.

She grappled with her pack, got a syringe, and filled it with morphine. "Craig. Can you cut through what's left of his jacket and the clothing beneath so I can find a vein?" Tina held the syringe in her mouth and stripped off her gloves.

"Yeah. I'm not hurt. More dazed than anything." Craig dug for a pocket knife. Charred bits scattered when he cut the burned fabric away. Some of it had bonded with Gunter's skin. "Good enough?" He glanced at her.

She jimmied what was left of the sleeve up another couple inches, looped a tourniquet around Gunter's arm, and hunted for a vein. "Okay," she breathed. "Got one." Tina threaded the needle home and loosed the tourniquet. "Hush," she murmured. "Relax. It will be like going to sleep."

Tears filled her eyes. She'd helped more than one terminally-ill patient cross the veil when their life became untenable. It was never easy. It felt too much like playing God. Between burns, exposure, and blood loss, Gunter would die, anyway. The least she could do was see he didn't suffer more than he already had. He'd been in the wrong place at the wrong time. If Mururata hadn't been lying in wait for her, Gunter would probably still be alive.

Tina rocked back on her heels. It was done. The young German's body relaxed. He'd finally moved beyond pain. Not dead yet, but soon. She glanced over at the mountain gods. What would happen next?

"We conferred while you eased the human man to the place beyond," Illampu said. "Since you did give our brother your word, we believe it binds you."

"Ha!" Mururata moved closer. "Leave off your worthless ministrations. The man was as good as dead when I came across him. Prepare to leave. You are mine now."

Tina's stomach clenched. "Like hell I am," she snarled. She pulled the syringe from Gunter's arm and clutched it in a hand. "Just try to take me." She withdrew more morphine from the vial in her pocket. "I'll kill myself before I let that happen."

Craig yanked the syringe from her and chucked it into the snow a few feet away. His green eyes blazed. "I will not let you throw your life away. You're everything that's strong and beautiful and good." He sprang to his feet and faced the three gods. "I love this woman. She's agreed to be my wife. Her bargain with Mururata must be severed."

"You had no right," Mururata screeched at Tina. "You promised yourself to me."

"No." Tina sat in the snow, holding Gunter's hand, her fingers on his pulse. It was weaker now and slowing. "You forced my hand. You never asked if I was willing."

"Why did you return to these mountains," Illampu asked, "if not to join your life to my brother's?"

"Because Mururata paid me a visit a month ago and damn near killed me. It was either wait in Colorado for him to return and finish the job or meet him here and fight for my freedom."

"We have heard enough," Illampu said. He floated to Mururata and wrapped long fingers around his arm. "We do not force humans to our will. They must agree because they want to, not because they fear for their lives. You told us she asked to become your queen after you rescued her."

Tina snorted. "I did no such thing. He made it clear he'd leave me to rot and die in the crevasse if I didn't agree to his terms."

"It is past time for us to leave," Illimani said. "We do not often involve ourselves in human affairs."

"What about me?" Mururata pushed his shimmery form closer to the other two. Now Tina could see him more clearly, her eyes widened. He was headless, just like in the legend. No wonder his voice sounded so odd. "You were amenable to me taking a human wife so long as I added my blood to hers and made her one of us."

"That was before we knew the truth of things." Illampu spoke sternly.

"We never gave you permission to trap or force a human into accepting you," Illimani added.

"Who would take me otherwise?" Mururata's tone was bitter. "You beheaded me, turned me into an abomination."

"You would question the will of our father and ruler, Vinococha?" Illimani's voice was dangerously smooth.

"Yes, I would—"

"You will accompany us," Illampu broke in. "Vinococha will be most interested in this latest development."

"No!" Mururata edged away, but one of the others grabbed him before he got far. The glittering brightness dimmed.

"Wait." Craig pushed to his feet. "What about the blood Mururata shared with Tina? What will it mean for her?"

The light brightened again. Illimani, blond hair floating around him, moved close to Tina. "Human woman." She looked up. "I would have you stand."

"This man is dying. If I leave his side, he will die alone."

Craig took two long strides and hunkered next to her. "I'll take over. Go on."

Tina laid Gunter's hands in Craig's, tugged on her gloves, and got to her feet. She stood facing the god. A frisson of apprehension ran down her back. What did he want with her?

He raised an arm and drew it downward. A mild electric current traveled the length of her body. "Have you noticed anything different since my brother shared his blood with you?"

Tina tried to look away but couldn't. The god held her in thrall. Fright sharpened her nerves to a fine edge. Her hands fisted at her sides. She tried to say *nothing*, but the word wouldn't leave her mouth because it wasn't true. She straightened her spine. "I know who will live and who will die. It's been useful in my work."

"You have the gift of prescience. You also have the gift of long life."

"How long?"

Illimani shrugged. "Perhaps double a normal lifespan. Had you joined yourself to Mururata, you would have become immortal."

Her mind raced. She did not want to live an extra eighty years if it meant being alone. "Can you do the same thing for Craig?"

Pealing bells sounded. It took her a moment to realize Illimani was laughing. "Presumptuous of you, human woman."

"I love him. We lost a lot of time we could have been together because of my stubbornness."

The god was silent so long, Tina was certain he'd refuse. After all, he didn't owe them a thing. For all she knew, he'd smite her to a cinder for having the temerity to even ask.

Something in the whirling depths of his eyes shifted. "Climb to Pico Sur, highest of my five summits. I shall meet you there at dawn and marry you. Blessings from me shall yield your heart's desire and wipe the slate clean of my brother's misdeeds."

Light flashed so bright, it left an afterimage behind her closed lids. When she opened them, the gods were gone. She blew out a shaky breath and hurried to where Craig sat in the snow. "Is he—?"

Craig nodded. "Yes. He stopped breathing when the gods left. Look." He pointed. Gunter's face was relaxed. A faint smile took the place of the rictus his mouth had been.

"Maybe they took his spirit with them."

"Who knows?" Craig smiled at her. "Maybe they did." He got to his feet. "Take a look at my jacket. How badly is the fabric burned?"

She walked behind him and shone the beam of her lamp on his back. "I think it will be okay. There's a good sized hole with rents running out from it, but your pack will cover the damage."

"Good enough. I'll ditch it when we get back to La Paz. I have an extra outer shell in the things we left there. Lucky my gloves are still intact."

"Gear be damned," she snorted. "We're lucky we're *intact.*"

"Isn't that the truth?" He shouldered his pack. "I want to pile rocks over Gunter, or commit his body to a crevasse, but we can do that on the way down. I heard your conversation. Sounds like we have a date on the mountaintop."

She glanced at her watch and gathered her scattered things. It was two in the morning. They had about four hours until dawn. "Hope we make it in time. It's still over three thousand feet."

"I have a feeling he'll wait for us."

She dropped her pack over her shoulders and tightened the straps. "Let's make sure he doesn't have to. It's been a long time since we climbed a peak together. I'm looking forward to it."

"Me too. You always were my favorite partner. Here." He handed her the rope and coiled the excess.

She clipped into it and started up Illimani's steep, exposed ridge. It felt good knowing Craig was behind her at the other end of the rope. In that moment, she knew she'd always trusted him beyond measure. He'd held her life in his hands on every mountain they'd ever tackled. She'd been there for him too. Some people smirked and said roped climbing was a suicide pact. It could be if you picked the wrong partner.

A smile tugged at her mouth. Craig had stood up to three gods for her. She had no doubt he would've done battle if it came to that. What a man. She was damned lucky to have a second chance with him.

Tina settled into a rhythm, planting her axes and crampon points again and again. She said a small prayer for Gunter. She'd known he had no chance at all when she first found him, but she'd tried anyway because she didn't like losing. When she was still in training, she'd sometimes felt she was engaged in a contest with death. It had taken maturity for her to learn death was a kindness when balanced against a life of constant pain and dysfunction.

She was surprised how quickly the steepest part of the climb ended. The only thing separating them from the summit was a long, airy, low angle ridge—and another thousand feet of climbing. She stopped to wait for Craig. "That was a whole lot easier than last time I descended it."

He grinned at her and pulled her into his arms. "I just bet it was." His bent his head and covered her mouth with his. He tasted wonderful, like sweet, new-mown hay and wildflowers. She opened her mouth to him. Her nipples hardened where they pressed against his chest. Her breathing, already fast at over twenty thousand feet, quickened some more.

"Hey." She pulled away, panting lightly. "You're supposed to wait until after the ceremony to kiss the bride."

"Just practicing up."

Tina laughed. She felt light and giddy and happy, lost in the rightness of the moment with the only man she'd ever loved. "Guess we ought to shake a leg here. It's still an hour if I remember right. This ridge is deceptive. It goes for a long way. We have to go up and over the false summit."

"Yeah, but there's not much more climbing. We'll be fine. I can't believe how beautiful it is up here."

"That's because you're beautiful, Craig Robson. And because we're sharing a place that's sacred to us both. I love you." She hugged him again and then started uphill.

His footsteps sounded close behind her. "I've got the rope. Don't worry. Terrain's not bad so I thought I'd get close enough to talk."

"I like having you right next to me."

He laughed and patted her ass. "The feeling's mutual. Does it seem odd to you the weather's so perfect? There's not a scrap of wind. It's not even all that cold. Zero by my watch."

"Maybe we have divine intervention. The only other time I was here, the wind was hideous."

"I've climbed this mountain half a dozen times. It was always windy on this ridge, usually so much so it was hard to stand upright."

"I'll have to remember to thank Illimani. Won't be hard. There are lots of things I'm grateful for."

"Can you stay in South America for a while?"

She considered it. "I suppose I could. I didn't schedule any shifts at the hospital because I didn't think I'd be back." Tina thought about the shuttered house with her will sitting atop her roll top desk. She'd left the house to one of her cousins and parceled out the rest of her things in that will. Relief surged. She stopped walking and turned to Craig. "I'm damn grateful I still have a life ahead of me. I was so certain—"

"Ssht." He pulled her close. "We have lots of living to do. I love you, Tina. God but it feels good to say it."

"It's pretty danged good to hear too." A warm glow started in her belly and spread outward. "Why'd you ask about staying in South America?"

"The twins are at a climber's pension in La Paz. Told me they'd wait a week. They still want Sajama."

"I'm game. Hell, we could even bring them back up Illimani. They move fast enough, and we left all that gear in Estancia."

"I was hoping you'd be agreeable. It's too risky guiding without a doctor on board. It's in their contract with me."

"Come on." She grasped his hand. "This isn't about guiding or doctoring. Today is about us. Hurry. I can see the summit cairn."

The eastern skyline was lightening when they reached the top. Tina checked her watch. Six on the money. "We made excellent time. Thirty-five hundred feet in four hours at this altitude should qualify us for a gold medal."

"All I want it to qualify me for is a life with you next to me, sharing each day as it happens." He unbuckled his pack, set it in the snow, and sat on it. He patted his lap. "Come sit. Illimani should be along soon."

She'd just gotten her pack off when the air brightened. Craig scrambled to his feet and stood by her side with an arm draped about her.

The god became more visible. "Stand there." He pointed to a spot a few feet away. "It is auspicious. Are you both certain of this?"

Craig gripped her gloved hand in his. "Yes."

"I am too," Tina said.

"Good. This is not like a human wedding. Once I join you,

your souls will belong to one another through this life and all lives to come. If you are not firm in your commitment, one to the other, you must speak now."

The same electric warmth she'd felt from the god when she was standing next to Gunter began at the crown of her head and moved to her feet. She smiled. "If you were going to check, why bother to ask?"

He didn't answer. "Do you, human woman, take this man as your consort from now through all lives to come?"

"I do."

"Do you promise to be faithful to him in all things? To love him with every fiber of your being? To support him through good times and bad? To care for him if he falls ill? To sit by his grave and mourn for him if he should die before you?"

"I do."

Illimani turned to Craig. "Do you, human man, take this woman as your consort from now through all lives to come?"

"I do." Craig's baritone thrummed with emotion. His grip on her hand tightened almost to the point of pain.

"Do you promise to be faithful…"

All too soon the ceremony was over. "Stand very still and receive my blessings," Illimani intoned.

The air danced with multicolored light. Tina blinked, but it didn't go away. A comforting tide swept over her. She leaned into Craig, wondering if he sensed the same thing.

"Thank you for blessing my mountaintop with your love." Illimani smiled at them.

"Thank you for everything you've done for us." Craig put out a hand and then drew it back. "Sorry, human custom."

Illimani laughed. "You would not like it if I touched you. My skin is very warm, warm enough to dissolve yours. I wish you both well. If you were to climb to my summit again, I would visit with you."

"We'll be back," Tina said. "This is one of the most beautiful mountains I've ever climbed. Thank you for the clear weather."

"You are most welcome. It would have been self-defeating for me to allow the God of Air to blow you off my ridge this day. Besides Mururata is otherwise occupied just now. Until we meet again, human friends."

This time she was ready for the flash of light and shielded her eyes. She dropped her gloved hands. Tina felt changed, complete in a way she hadn't been before. She melted into Craig's arms.

"Do you feel…different?" he asked.

She nodded against his chest. "The world shifted. I don't know if it makes sense, but I feel whole, perfect. Like something was missing before, but it's been made right. What about you?"

"You did better putting words to it than I could have. But yes, something is definitely different and much better for the change." He crushed her to him.

She reveled in the feel of his body against hers and his arms holding her. There wasn't anywhere in the world she'd rather be. "Funny, but I hated this mountain. Now it's our special place. I was telling the truth when I told Illimani how stunning the summit is. It's like a crown with five uniquely crafted points."

"Yes," he murmured. "Illimani has a beauty all its own. Maybe we could climb it every year on our anniversary." He pushed back so he could meet her gaze. "I want to hold you in my arms forever, love, but we should start down. It will take a while to pay our final respects to Gunter's body. He's too close to high camp, we have to move him."

She tilted her face up. "One more kiss and then we'll get moving. I can't believe you'll be here to kiss and touch and hold whenever I want."

"I'm still getting used to the idea myself." He laughed, dipped his head, and kissed her. She wrapped her arms around him and clasped the back of his jacket. His cock swelled where it was sandwiched between their bodies. Her nipples pebbled into points of desire and sent lust arcing through her. Moisture flooded her nether regions. Tina couldn't help herself. She moved a hand and closed it around his erection.

He broke their kiss and grinned. "That, you shameless hussy, is for later."

"Not much later I hope."

"Since we're married, I guess I can't say no anymore."

She grinned back. "Nope, you can't."

"Come on. The sooner we get back to camp, the sooner I can lick and kiss every inch of your amazing body."

"Eww. I'm all dirty and sweaty."

He quirked a brow. "Do you want to wait until we get to a hotel in La Paz?" She shook her head. "Well, I don't either. We'll melt some snow for wash water and make do. Let me help you with your pack."

CHAPTER 18

Craig was surprised his feet connected to the snow. He felt light enough to fly. Of course they'd have to have some sort of civil ceremony once they returned home, but their spiritual binding atop Illimani was the real deal. Married by a god. He shook his head, still not believing it had truly happened. Sun peeked over the massif of the Cordillera Real, turning the snowcapped peaks a lush shade of pink. Shaded by the Cordillera, Illimani's west ridge never got sun until eight or nine in the morning. He glanced at his watch. Right on time.

He blew a kiss to the mountain god. "Thanks," he called out. "For everything."

When he'd jumped to his feet and confronted the three gods, he had no idea things would turn out so well. He'd been prepared to die if it meant saving Tina from the twisted, headless monster who'd suckered her. Now he'd met him, Craig suspected Mururata had shoved Tina into the crevasse that almost killed her.

"Off belay. I'm down."

Good. Tina was off the steep part. "Belay off," he called. Craig drew the rope up and coiled it. He glanced at the fifty degree slope and tested the snow with his crampon points. Still plenty firm, but best to be safe. He threaded in an ice screw, ran the rope through a carabineer and the breaker bar attached to his harness, and turned to face the slope. With a combination of rappelling and his front points, he was by her side in minutes. A sharp tug on the rope and it slithered down, forming a mass of coils at their feet.

"The sun followed you." Her eyes were wide. "For a minute there you looked like one of the mountain gods."

"You should've seen the ridge in the rising sun. It looked pretty ethereal too." He bent to the rope, coiling it automatically. Once it was straight, he handed her one end to clip in to just until they were off the glacier. "Come on. Let's get this next part over with."

She turned and started off at a lope. The roaring blizzard from a few hours before had cleared the glacier, scouring the top layer of snow off it, and its crevasses were easy to avoid. Her crampons kicked up snow as she went. He raced after her long-legged form, enjoying the easy way her body moved. Tina had a natural grace and athleticism that put most people to shame. She wasn't even aware what a thing of beauty she was. Poetry in motion, just like the song by...but he couldn't think who'd written it.

Time passed as they moved down the mountain. The sun rose higher in the sky. A few more minutes and he'd have to deal with Gunter. Craig swallowed hard. Dead bodies weren't his favorite thing. He'd seen enough of them, but he'd never gotten used to their grim reminder. No matter how much he might try to delude himself that he could beat the odds with solid preparation, the line between life and death in the mountains was thin.

"Craig." Her voice held a sharp note.

He hurried toward her. "What?"

"Gunter. He's not here."

"But that's impossible." Craig trotted up beside her. He took in the juxtaposition of the rocks, the bits of charcoal staining the snow black, and their tracks. "I think we're in the right place. Let me check the GPS."

"I already did. You handed it to me, just before you told me to get the hell out of here last night. Besides, despite how windy it was when we got here, you can see demarcations in the snow from where we walked to this spot."

"Do you think Illimani, uh, did something?"

She nodded. "Yes." She cocked her head to one side. "Maybe he doesn't like corpses in plain sight, littering his slopes."

"We'll never know." Craig held out his hands. "Come here. We'll say a prayer for his soul. Christ, Tina. He was only twenty-three." A surge of guilt left a bitter taste in Craig's mouth. "This is partially my fault. I knew how young and inexperienced he was, and I still—"

"Stop." Instead of placing her hands in his, she laid one over his mouth. "He was the same age you were when you started working at Alpine Attack. He knew what he was getting into. The mountains are great levelers. They don't play favorites."

He raised a brow. "Oh, so Lady Luck doesn't really ride on my shoulder?"

"She'd better not. I'm not into threesomes." Tina tilted her goggles back and then pulled them off. Her blue eyes twinkled. "Let's each say good-bye and Godspeed in our own way. Then we can start down."

She slipped her hands into his. He shut his eyes and murmured a silent prayer, hoping Gunter had found peace. "Ready?"

"Um-hum, could you dig around in the outer compartment of my pack for my dark glasses?"

"Sure." He gave them to her. "If you hand over your goggles, I'll tuck them in your pack. Also, I don't think we need the rope anymore."

"Agreed." She fed it to him to get the kinks out. He coiled it and draped it around his torso.

As they moved downhill, his groin tightened in anticipation.

Soon, very soon, he'd sink himself full length inside Tina's body. Her warmth would close around him and… He rolled his eyes and pushed his more-than-erect cock to a less cramped position, grateful she was ahead of him in case his tired body got the better of him, and he came just from thinking about her. The way things were looking, it was a distinct possibility.

It was close to two in the afternoon when they got to their tents. The day had shaped up to be sun-drenched and warm enough he was sweating under all his layers. They'd been awake for thirty-two hours, most of that moving. Only the thought of holding Tina again, of making love with her, kept him from falling on his face.

Tina beat him back. She'd lengthened her sensuous, long-legged stride after telling him she had things to attend to. He bent to unbuckle the straps holding his crampons to his boots and placed them next to Tina's on a canvas mat outside the mess tent. He hadn't needed the metal spikes once they got off the steep section right below Nido de Condores, but hadn't wanted to stop to take them off, either. So long as there was snow to walk on, crampons weren't a problem.

Tina had snow melting in the big pot over the white gas stove. She grinned when he ducked into the mess tent. "Glad you didn't take all the fuel. I worried about that while I was walking back. It's been days since I've had a bath. I can smell myself."

He dropped his pack by the door. "Guess you'll want me to clean up too?"

She clapped her hands together. Her blue eyes sparked with mischief—and lust. "I have a splendid idea. How about if we wash each other? It can be sort of like foreplay."

Craig threw his head back and laughed. "Good God, woman. You're still just as warped as ever."

"That's a good thing. Right? Water's close to tepid, and the stove's made it warm enough in here, it's almost bearable." She ran her tongue over her lips. "I'd love to watch you undress. I'll turn off the stove so you can close the door. Oh yeah. Shocked the crap out of me, but Xavier was still here. I bedded him down with a full sack of feed."

"Great. Means we can actually pack up everything and move it back to Estancia in one trip tomorrow."

Tina snapped her fingers. "You're stalling. Clothes. Off. Now."

"Hey! You're the one who brought up the mule." Suddenly self-conscious, Craig felt heat rise to his face. Tina had always had a frank, open sexuality that probably scared a lot of men away. *Good thing,* an inner voice piped up. *Means she didn't get snapped up by someone else.*

"Um, sure. Let me get my boots off first."

He perched on one of the three-legged camp stools and peeled off his mitts. He undid the Velcro strips holding his gaiters together and started on the buckles of his plastic glacier boots. The inner boot layer had laces so it took a while. He levered first one and then the other off followed by two layers of socks. He wriggled his toes. "Mmm...feels heavenly to get those clodhoppers off." He glanced at Tina and smiled.

She made hurry-up motions with both hands. "Surely you're not going to stop there. I may be taken by your raw sexuality, but feet were never my thing." Tina carried the steaming kettle closer, along with some cloths, and set both on the mess table. "Here, sweetie, let me help." She bent her head and kissed him. The kiss was sweet and sensual—lips and teeth teasing him—and much too brief. He made a grab for her, but she sidestepped him. "Uh-uh. That was just a pre-appetizer."

"Umm." A sound like a big cat on the prowl rose from his throat, surprising him. "When do I get the main course?"

"After you get those clothes off." She crinkled her nose. "I'm still waiting to see more than your toes."

Craig laughed. It felt wonderful to be with Tina again. Practical, pushy, sexy as hell. What a combination. "Towels?" He winked at her. "It's not bad temperature-wise in here, but we won't want to stay wet for long."

"I found a couple of them, plus fresh long johns for us both and our camp slippers. They're all in a pile over there." She pointed to a mounded heap on the only other table in the tent.

"Sheesh. You put me to shame. Is there ever anything you don't see to?"

Tina knelt in front of him and wrapped her arms around his waist. She laid her head in his lap. "I figure I owe you since it was me who cheated us out of seven years we could have been together."

Love surged through him. It set a small sun blazing in his chest. He laid his hands on her head and massaged it through her thick hair. "You don't owe me a thing, sweetheart. I'm just glad—" His throat thickened, making the words hard to get out. "—you're here with me now."

"Me too." She snuggled into his hands and then pushed to her feet. "This is delightful and romantic, but I need to see more skin."

He snorted. "It's the whole doctor thing. I always suspected you guys went to medical school because—"

"Hush." She swatted him and then unzipped his shell jacket and tugged it off his shoulders. Next came the down inner jacket and vest and the straps holding his avalanche transceiver to his body. Tina fingered a small hole in his wool long john top. "Never did sew much, did you? I can take care of things like this now."

She drew her fingers down his torso. Her touch sent tongues of exquisite sensation pinging against his skin.

"I don't want you for your domestic skills," he growled, grabbing the bottom of his long underwear top and yanking it over his head.

Tina took a step back and gasped.

"What?" He grinned ruefully. "Do I smell that bad?"

She shook her head. "I'd forgotten how gorgeous you are. Most blonds have fair skin, but yours is like sun-kissed copper."

She reached a hand and moved it from his neck down the muscled lines of his arm. A trail of fire followed her movement. Next she ran her fingertips from his chest over his flat stomach. Her breathing quickened right along with his.

She fumbled at the catches holding his over pants in place. "Stand up." Her voice was husky with desire. He remembered how she sounded when she wanted him, and wouldn't take no for an answer.

He pushed to his feet. Tina had his pants in a puddle on the floor in record time—all three layers. He stepped out of them, all too aware of the raging hard-on curved against his stomach.

She started with his balls and traced a delicate path the length of his cock with her index finger. "Not fair," he gasped. "You still have all your clothes on."

"You have the most incredible penis." She ran her finger up him again and licked her lips. Her gaze never left him. Desire and love blazed in the depths of her eyes. "I swear it's even bigger than I remember. Most men would sell their soul to be hung like you."

His cock throbbed. If it swelled any more, it would burst. He wanted to rip her clothes off and take her right there, up against the wall of the mess tent. His heart beat hard against his chest. He reached for her, but she ducked out of the way again.

"Wash first. Rinse really, since there's no soap. Even that will be an improvement." She dipped one of the small cloths into the hot water, wrung it out, and swiped it gently down his face. "Clean your hands," she said, wiping the rag over her own face. "We'll get our hands and faces before we contaminate the water with our bodies."

A laugh pushed its way up from his belly. "Do you ever stop being a doctor?"

She shrugged and laughed too. "Probably not. Better get used to it."

She ran the cloth under the water. "Turn around. I'll start with your back."

"Hey," he protested. "If we're going to wash each other, how about getting your clothes off first? I want to see you naked too."

"Sure. In a minute." Warmth laved its way down his back. Her hands felt so good on his skin, it was all he could do not to say to hell with the bath. She squeezed his butt cheeks as she rubbed the warm rag over them, and his cock throbbed. God, he wanted her. The cloth worked its way between his buttocks and down his upper thighs. Water dripped on the canvas floor of the tent. Something warm settled in the small of his back. Her mouth.

"No fair." He spun around and grabbed her just as she straightened.

"Sorry." She threw him a coquettish look. "Couldn't resist. You have the most perfect—"

He crushed her against him, dipped his head, and kissed her. Her arms wove around him and held on tight. She opened her mouth, and he plumbed it with his tongue. She'd always had a spicy, exotic scent. It intrigued him and made him hotter than hell. Cinnamon, vanilla, and something unique to her that he didn't have a name for.

He pulled away. "Got to get these clothes off you," he muttered thickly. He unzipped her outer jacket and tugged it off. She wore her avalanche transceiver atop her down inner garments. He unsnapped the straps. It joined her jacket on the floor. The soft curves of her breasts came into view once he'd unzipped her down jacket and pushed it off her shoulders. Her nipples were already peaked. He yanked her long john top out of the way, bent, and settled his mouth atop a breast. She moaned. He sucked harder. Her hips bucked against him just before she twirled out of his embrace.

"There's still your front to wash," she admonished, breathing hard. "And all of me." She slid her top off and dropped it onto the heap of her other clothes.

He reached forward with both hands, filling them with her

breasts. "Your body is incredible," he murmured. "A goddess would be jealous of it."

His cock was on fire. It wanted her, had to have her. His balls ached, desperate for release. Reluctantly, he let go of her breasts. He jimmied the washcloth out of her hand, rinsed it, and ran it over her back and shoulders and breasts. He stood closer than he had to so his cock could brush against her. He followed the line of the cloth with his mouth, lingering over her sensitive nipples. She pushed against his touch and moaned.

"Hurry."

He glanced at her feet. Good. Her boots and gaiters were already off. He dropped the washcloth into the cooling water and undid her pants. Her breathing had a hitch in it. She put her hands atop his and helped him push her bottom layers down her hips. She stepped out of the tangle of fabric, made a grab for the cloth, and ran it down the front of his body. When she wrapped it around his cock, he felt as if the top of both his heads were about to explode.

"Careful. It's been a long time." He was so crazed by lust, it was hard to get the words out.

"Here." She thrust the cloth at him. "Do me."

He rinsed the cloth in water that had developed a grayish tinge and ran it down her hips and between her legs. She writhed against his touch. Craig couldn't help himself. He switched the cloth to his other hand and plunged his fingers inside her. She was hot and wet and oh-so-ready. He met her gaze. Her eyes had darkened to a midnight blue. Her cheeks were flushed, and her lips parted.

"If you keep doing that," she panted, "I'll come."

Craig gazed around the mess tent to see how they could keep their bodies off the floor. He moved the pot of water and scooped an armful of clothes, scattering them on the table. "Your bower awaits, my love. We can get fancier later on in the tent."

Tina's mouth split into a wicked grin. "Looks great!" She

wrapped her arms around him and pressed the full length of her magnificent nakedness against his body. She turned her face up, and he kissed her, burying his tongue in her mouth. His hands gripped her ass, and he pulled her hard against him. Her full breasts flattened against his chest. She moaned and rubbed her nipples back and forth, her fingers tightening on his shoulders.

He thrust his cock between her legs. She writhed to bring her clit in contact with him. Wet curls and the feel of her, hot against his hardness, sent shivers up his spine. They'd fucked standing up before—in closets and in theaters. A heat haze from lust descended, enveloping him. He couldn't wait any longer.

He repositioned himself to slip inside her. She rubbed her pussy against him and then disentangled her limbs and pushed by him. "My legs are too shaky to stand," she murmured. He thought she'd lie on the table, but she bent over it. The rounded globes of her ass separated tantalizingly. Her gleaming wet pussy shone through its tangle of red curls.

He groaned and wrapped a hand around himself to guide his cock inside. As her body closed round him, he gasped with pleasure. He couldn't believe how good she felt, all heat and liquid snug around him. He took a breast in each hand, tweaking the nipples the way he knew she liked. She thrust her hips back against him. Not subtle, his Tina. She wanted him to fuck her hard and fast.

He let go of her breasts, settled his hands around her waist, and drove himself into her. She cried out. The sharp flare of her pelvis pressed against his hands, and she met him stroke for stroke. Her muscles clenched and clenched again. He wanted to make it last, but he was too keyed up from not having had her for so long.

The climax started in his balls. They tightened against his body, and semen arced out of him. The ecstasy was so intense, it was almost painful. It had been over a year since he'd made love.

Her muscles milked him, and he realized she was coming too. He thrust over and over until her body quieted.

His legs trembled. He didn't understand why he was still hard.

She squirmed beneath him and butted her ass into his belly. "Let's finish this in bed."

He stepped back and pulled himself out of her body. It wasn't easy since his cock wanted to take up residence and never leave.

He glanced muzzily around the tent. Light was fading from the day. "How about if we have a quick meal first? We've scarcely eaten anything since we left here yesterday."

She straightened and turned to face him. Her skin was flushed. Her eyes aglow. "Good idea. It will give us fuel for another few rounds. Brrr. For now, I'm going to get dressed."

He opened his arms. "Naked hug first?"

She snuggled into his arms. They were a perfect fit. Always had been. Her nipples pressed against his chest, feeling like polished stones. She straddled one of his legs and wiggled against him. "Mmm...I could come a million times. You feel so good."

"So do you. I never did feel complete without you. Promise me you'll never go away again." His breath caught in his throat. Her answer meant everything to him.

She backed away enough to tilt her head, and her gaze locked with his. "Silly. I'm not going anywhere. Illimani bound us forever. Even if he hadn't, I'm not into repeating my mistakes." She laughed. "Too many new ones to make to keep stumbling over the old ones."

He pulled her close. "My wonderful Tina. I love you so much."

"Not as much as I love you." She turned her face up for a kiss.

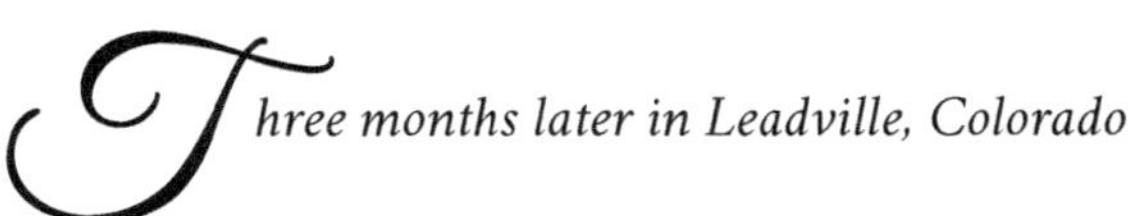

hree months later in Leadville, Colorado

TINA TOOK one last critical look at herself in her bedroom mirror. She straightened the spray of roses pinned to her emerald-green suit jacket and patted her unruly locks into better order. "Are you certain I look okay?"

Craig rolled his eyes. Dressed in a cream-colored raw silk sports coat, pale green silk shirt, and black linen pants, he looked elegant. The soft colors set off the blond sheen of his hair. "I think you're gorgeous when you're wearing a climbing harness and goggles. Yes, you look fine."

"Well, it's not every day a girl gets married."

"We're already married," he reminded her.

She waved her hands in the air. "You know what I mean. Married in the sense our friends and relatives will recognize it." She winced. "I didn't tell anyone about our mountaintop adventure. They might have pulled my medical license and carted me off to the loony bin."

He chuckled. "Know what you mean. I've been pretty quiet about it myself." He walked to her and put his hands on her waist. "The important thing, though, is we know we belong to one another irrespective of any piece of paper."

She turned her face up for a kiss. "Careful, don't muss my makeup."

"Humph. What happened to kiss the bride?" He kissed his fingertip and laid it lightly on her glossed lips.

"You can muss it then, once everyone's had a chance to see us in all our sartorial splendor." She glanced at her watch. "We still have a few minutes before we need to leave. Come into the front room. We'll drink a toast to a long and happy life for ourselves and chat."

She stopped by the built-in wine rack and selected a bottle of twenty-year-old Cabernet. She'd been saving it for something special, and it didn't get much more special than today.

He snagged the bottle and went to the kitchen, presumably in search of a corkscrew.

She pulled two of her grandmother's cut crystal wineglasses from the china cabinet and carried them to the coffee table. While she waited, Tina gazed about the familiar room. Carved wooden wainscoting covered the walls halfway up. A floor-to-ceiling stone fireplace occupied most of one end of the room. Scarred oak furniture that had been in the family for over a hundred years was scattered about, replete with plump, colorful cushions. She settled onto a loveseat her grandfather had carved.

Craig bent and poured wine into each glass and then handed her one. "To us."

"Yes." She smiled. "To us." Tina drank deep and patted the cushion next to her. "Sit."

He took a long sip of his wine, savoring it. "My but that's good. We should buy a few more bottles."

"Can't. I'm sure this vintage isn't available anymore." She

cocked her head to one side. "Are you certain about moving to Leadville?"

"Absolutely. It's three thousand feet higher than Flagstaff. Better for conditioning. Plus, I already put my house on the market. I forgot to tell you, but the real estate agent called me yesterday to say we had an offer coming in early next week."

She set her wineglass down and clapped her hands together. "Oh, Craig! Wonderful news!"

He glanced around the cozy room. "Hope you still think so after I move all my stuff in here. We may need to build an addition on the garage."

Tina placed a hand on his arm. "We'll make it work."

"Yes." He smiled, making her feel al melty inside. "We will. We live in a tent together for weeks on end when we climb without tearing one another's hair out. If we can do that, we can do anything."

There was something infectious about his good humor. She grinned back, and he laid a hand over hers. "Think we should kill the wine and get moving?" she asked.

"Well, we can finish what's in our glasses. I'll cork the rest. We can celebrate after we get home."

Lightness filled her. "I like the sound of home when you say it. This has always been my home, but there's been something missing since you stopped coming here—"

"You mean since you walked out of our Denver apartment. The invitations to Leadville weren't exactly forthcoming after that."

"Don't quibble." She poked him in the ribs.

"You're right." He got to his feet and drained his glass. A rakish edge to the angle of his brows lent him a naughty aspect. "I do believe I'll save the quibbling until after you've signed on the dotted line and can't escape."

She joined him, stumbling slightly. He reached a hand to steady her. "Damned high heels," she sputtered. "It's why I hardly ever wear them." She picked up her glass and tipped it back, draining its contents. "Ready?"

"Never been readier." He held out a hand. She took it. Together, they walked out the front door.

Happiness radiated from the center of her being, warming her soul. "Thanks," she murmured.

"For?" He held the car door and helped her in.

She waited until he was behind the steering wheel and buckled her seatbelt. "Being you. You're the best gift of all."

THE NEXT MOUNTAIN tale came to me after I'd climbed Mount Darwin. I know the Evolution area in the High Sierras well, and it's one of my favorites. Read on, and join me for one more story set in the best playground of all.

A RUN FOR HER MONEY

A SCIENCE FICTION ROMANCE NOVELLA

By
Ann Gimpel

Tumble off reality's edge into an alien invasion and unexpected love

Sara's day begins like any other. A routine extraction in tandem with a local Search and Rescue team. *Routine* crashes to a halt when she ends up trapped in a hut, high atop Muir Pass in the Sierras. Four days later, running out of food for herself and her dog, she makes a bold dash for safety.

Jared's walking the Muir Trail when all hell breaks loose. After hunkering beneath a boulder pile for days, he dares a difficult cross-country route, hoping it'll put him into position to approach a backcountry ranger station. Surely one of the rangers will know what happened, because he sure as hell doesn't.

Jared locates the cabin, but it's locked tight. He's getting ready to leave the next morning when a helicopter lands, with Sara at the helm. There's no time to trade war stories. It takes a leap of faith, but they throw in their lot together. Can they face the impossible and come out the other side unscathed?

CHAPTER 19

My name is Sara Holcomb and I'm a Ranger for the U.S. Park Service, a post I've held for better than twenty years. There are those who say I should've transitioned to a desk job long ago, but somehow I don't think I'd like that nearly as much. See, I've loved the backcountry ever since I was a little girl, probably because my daddy was a Park Ranger too. He used to tell me stories about the forest creatures from the saddle we shared while he patrolled Yosemite Valley. I'm sure you couldn't get away with dragging your daughter along on horse patrol now, but things were different back then. Another thing is I don't really like people all that much, so wandering the trails in the national parks is about as perfect a job as I'm likely to get...

Her forehead furrowed in thought, Sara read over what she'd written as she absent-mindedly swept a strand of greasy hair out of her eyes with grime-crusted fingers. It didn't stay put, though, and she found herself looking through the lank, black strands again almost immediately.

"Well," she muttered, "this doesn't have to be a literary masterpiece. I'm just writing it so people will know what happened to me if they find my body."

She cleared her throat to flush the thought of her possible

death out of her mind and picked up her pen again. That was one of the good things about the Muir Hut, there were lots of pens and paper as well. Too bad some desperate traveler had chopped up the only table and burned it for firewood years before. The Park Service debated replacing it, but in the end they decided not to. If one table could burn, a replacement might meet the same fate. Besides, it wasn't easy to get supplies to the beehive shaped stone hut sitting atop twelve thousand foot Muir Pass.

Blowing air out through her pursed lips, Sara frowned as she considered what to write next. She'd planned to dive right into the meat of things, but whoever read her journal really needed to know how she'd ended up trapped in the Muir Hut, so they could understand all the rest.

...I'm getting ahead of myself here. I've been stationed at the McClure Meadows Ranger Station for the past few summers. Sometimes there's another Ranger with me, but usually there's not. The Park Service has had some cutbacks in recent years. McClure Meadows is in Evolution Valley, and it's my favorite of all the backcountry stations. It even has a geothermal spring so I don't have to heat water for baths. At ninety-six hundred feet, it's below timberline, so there are lots of trees around it— not just granite and shale. Incredible wildflowers dot the meadows all summer.

About six days ago, I got a radio call for help late in the day. A climber was stranded on Mount Darwin, and things weren't looking good. I put in a call for the rescue chopper, packed up what Jake and I would need, and started on the five mile trek to Evolution Lake. Jake is my coal black, search-and-rescue German Shepherd the Park Service finally agreed to let me keep in the backcountry.

It was pretty much a mess when we got there. Suzy, the missing climber's wife or girlfriend, was hysterical and it took me over an hour to get anything useful out of her, like which route her significant other had taken. By then the chopper was circling to land. There are some flat areas at the south end of the lake that are perfect for that...

A chill seeped into Sara from the cold, stone floor, so she

changed positions. As she rubbed feeling back into her butt cheeks, she wished again for the missing table. She could've sat on it. A stone bench leaned against the wall of the hut outside in bright sunshine, but it was safer if she didn't go out there. Benches lined the hut's walls inside too, but they probably wouldn't be much warmer than the floor. Stone was a real heat-sink unless it had a chance for the sun to warm it. She gazed back over what she'd written and shrugged. Pushing to her feet, she stretched, rotating her torso first in one direction, then in the other.

Fingers pressed against the ceiling, she blessed her height and her strength, shaped by years of grueling, manual labor. She could do anything a man could, and she was proud of that. Though frequently the object of admiring glances, she'd been very selective in that regard. The occasional co-worker had possibilities but, while the Park Service said *relationships are fine so long as you're not in a direct line of command* on paper, Sara didn't think they were especially open-minded in that regard, so she kept her dalliances brief and private.

Sometimes it was a lonely life, but it was the one she'd chosen. Her hours and time away from home wouldn't have played well with most men, anyway. Children were out of the question. Not if they ever wanted to see their mother.

"Crap, my thoughts are really wandering," she said wryly as she reached over to stroke Jake's soft head. When she'd come to her feet, the Shepherd did as well. "Not much point in telling whoever might read this about the rescue," she went on, talking to her dog. "The climber was dead when I got to him, so the main problem was figuring out how to get the poor son-of-a-bitch out of there."

Jake whined as if he understood exactly what she was saying.

The actual extraction had taken hours. The SAR volunteers—God only knew where they'd been trained—had been less-than-useful. They were competent enough as climbers, but one began puking at the sight of the dead guy's mangled remains, and the other had a hell of a time forcing himself to actually touch the corpse. Since she ended up doing most of the packaging-up of the body herself, Sara was exhausted when she slithered down the last steep talus slope above the southern end of Evolution Lake. Nearly twenty-four hours had passed since she'd started on the rescue mission, and she was surprised she was still capable of sentient thought.

One thing that still bothered her was an unusual amount of rock fall during her descent. Not that she could see anything, but explosions boomed around her. Usually if you heard rock avalanches, you could see them, but not this time. One of the SAR dudes had asked what the fuck all the noise was, but she'd been too tired to have much of an answer.

It had been a relief when the chopper left, and she and Jake were alone again.

In the few hours she'd been high on Mount Darwin, autumn had attacked the aspens around Evolution Lake with a vengeance, and fall colors blazed from every hillside. That was the way things happened above ten thousand feet. Winter lasted a really long time, while the other seasons came and went in the blink of an eye.

After feeding Jake, she'd keyed her radio to report in, finding a small pleasure in hearing Lonnie's cheerful voice. He was her boss, and he ran the dispatch service from Park Headquarters.

"How's it going, pumpkin?" he'd asked. In his sixties, Lonnie didn't pay much attention to the latest governmental directives about not using words that might be construed as sexual harassment.

"Not bad," she replied. "But I'm tired. I'll camp here tonight and head back to McClure tomorrow."

"Now that you mention it," he drawled, "think you might have enough energy to run up to the pass?"

Sara didn't feel like *running up to the pass*. It was another four miles and fifteen hundred feet of climbing. "Uh, not really," she murmured. "At least not tonight."

"Come on, Sara," he'd urged. "We've been getting odd reports from that area. I'd like some firsthand data. You move fast. You could be there in well under two hours." There was a pause, then Lonnie added, "It won't even be dark by then, princess."

Maybe it was the *princess* that did it—her father used to call her that. Sara gathered what she thought she and Jake would need for a few days, stashing all her extraction gear behind a boulder pile. Then she shouldered her pack and struck out for Muir Pass. Lonnie was right, she did move quickly over the trails, her long-legged stride capable of eating up over three miles an hour uphill, more if she was coming down.

Distracted as she replayed the tragedy on Mount Darwin, Sara was surprised how quickly she reached the hut. It was still twilight. Plenty of time to get herself situated.

She dragged herself back to the present, settled on her spot on the floor, and picked up her pen again.

...The extraction was long, but uneventful. No point in describing it here. Once it was over, my boss sent me to Muir Pass to check on reports he'd been getting of unusual activity. While I wasn't anxious to do more traveling that day, I do know how to follow orders. Jake and I reached the hut around six-thirty. I pushed the door open and, as always, was greeted by whichever of the resident rodents chose to take a stand. Jake made short work of them while I shoveled last season's snow into poly bags so we could melt drinking water. Dredging my tent out of my pack, I smiled at the small, satisfying clicking sounds the segmented poles made as they nested into one another.

I didn't know then it might be one of my last smiles ever.

So much of setting up camp is automatic, I'm surprised I even noticed. What did grab my attention, though, was Jake. While he sleeps next to me after I turn in, he usually prefers roaming about when I'm getting our camp set up. Not that night, though. Oh, he started wandering all right, but before I was even done with the tent, he was back by my side whining, with his ears back and his tail tucked low.

"What's the matter, boy?" I asked, but of course I didn't get an answer.

Some of you reading this might wonder why I didn't just bed down in the hut. Well, huts are always, always cold. It's actually far warmer in my down bag and my double walled tent than in a stone hut. In a winter snow storm, I might use one of the widely-spaced huts that dot the Sierras, but never in the summertime or autumn.

Just as I was settling in to melt some of the snow I'd gathered for water and dinner, the light—or what was left of it—began to look really odd, all flickery with iridescent fingers reaching down out of the sky. Searching for a reason, I glanced up and froze. Right above Jake and me was this really large thing that could only have been a spaceship. It was oblong with blue and green lights lining the long sides, and white lights at either end. It was huge, maybe over two hundred feet, though it's hard to measure things when they're in the sky. Jake clung to my side like a shadow as I stared upward in utter and absolute disbelief. He head-butted me toward the open door of the hut, so I told him he could go inside if he wanted. Pretty silly to tell a German Shepherd that. They're trained to die by your side, so, naturally, he didn't go anywhere.

The ship altered course. It had been heading pretty much due east, but it began circling and getting lower and lower. In the meantime, I'd grabbed my radio but, for some odd reason, I couldn't get anything out of it. Usually, high places like the pass have great reception. I checked the battery indicator, and it said eighty percent, so that wasn't the problem.

At first, the ship looked exotic and, well, fascinating. I majored in ecology and wildlife management eons ago. As I studied the ship, I tried to tap into some of that scientific training to figure out how something that non-aerodynamic could fly.

I should probably tell you I'm—or, I used to be—a helicopter pilot. I got my training during a brief stint in the military right after college. I'm pretty sure that's why the Park Service hired me in the first place since they were short of Rangers who could fly back then. Anyhow, I'm getting off track here. I'm not sure how long I spent gawking at the thing in the sky. It was mesmerizing in a weird sort of way.

As it got lower and lower though, I began to get scared. Really scared. At one point I crooked my fingers into a sign against evil I haven't used since I was a child. Then one of those unnatural light beams sweeping the ground found a pica and vaporized it. One minute the little guy was there, looking hopefully at me as I pulled dried food packets out for dinner. The next he was gone in a poof of smoke, leaving this icky, burned smell.

Well, that certainly mobilized me. I dove through the door of the hut and huddled next to Jake on one of the benches. I did leave the door open a crack, though, so I could still see. As soon as I was inside the hut, the damned thing altered course again. It stopped circling and resumed its easterly trajectory, despite being, probably, a thousand feet lower—too low to clear the passes next to either Wallace or Echo Cols. Even though I willed it to crash, I'm sure it didn't. I would've heard something...

Sara skimmed over what she'd written. She wanted to make sure she hadn't missed anything important, at least up until when the ship appeared. Laying the paper aside, she shivered. It was nearly as bad reading as it had been to live through. It also shed a whole new light on what she'd labeled as rock fall when she was descending from Mount Darwin. Maybe it had really been some kind of detonation.

She bit her lower lip. No point dancing around the issue. Not *detonation*, a dry rather clinical term, but bombs. The noise on Mount Darwin sounded like bombs, and maybe that's what they'd really been.

"Crap. Crap. Crap. What the hell is going on?"

Jake whined sympathetically and moved closer to her. She arranged her sleeping bag, laying it out on a foam pad on the hut's floor, before leaning into the dog's warmth. Things had only gotten creepier since her retreat into the hut. Another shudder racked her, and she got inside the bag, trying to regroup.

She'd been in tough situations before. Hell, backcountry life was one tough situation after another, but she'd never felt so out of control.

Right after the ship left her line of sight, she'd retrieved her mostly-erected tent and shoved it sideways through the door of the hut. Once it was upright on the stone floor, she'd gone back outside and tossed her other belongings—scattered on the dirt, snow and rocks—after the tent. It didn't take a genius IQ to understand there was something about the stones of the hut that masked her presence from whatever was in that ship.

The next day, Sara packed up at first light and headed anxiously down the trail with Jake at her heels. She hadn't gotten a quarter of a mile, though, before the dog began to whine. Scanning the surrounding mountains, she didn't see a thing— until she glanced upward. The ship, the fucking abomination of a ship, was on its way back. With the memory of the vaporized pica fresh in her mind, Sara sprinted up the switchbacks toward the hut. Fear clawed at her, making her stomach ache. As she ran, she fought against a helplessness that threatened to immobilize her. Once she and Jake got back to the hut, she sat inside it for a long time, trembling.

They'd beaten the ship to Muir Pass by the narrowest of margins, not an experience she was anxious to repeat.

Days passed.

Four long days, where it required every ounce of Sara's willpower not to simply take her chances and make a dash for freedom. Despite trying the radio regularly, it never came back to life. There were other things that worried her too. Like no other hikers on the Muir Trail. It was only mid-September and there should've been at least twenty to thirty backpackers on that part of the trail each day. She remembered the wilderness permit rosters transmitted via satellite to McClure Meadows daily. Yes, there certainly should have been hikers. There weren't any airplanes, either. This part of the Sierra was on an east-west flight trajectory across the country. Normally, planes passed over regularly.

Sara experimented. The longest she was able to stay outside, before the ship reappeared on the horizon, was sixty-five minutes. Sixty-five minutes wouldn't even get her back to Evolution Lake. She needed at least two hours to make the nine-and-a-half miles to McClure, and that would have to be running, not walking.

Lying in her sleeping bag at night, she wondered if it was the same ship. If there were more than one of them, what did that mean? Had the United States been attacked by alien life forms? Was that why there were no other hikers and nothing else in the sky?

...I tried to leave, but the ship chivvied me back. I don't mind telling whoever may be reading this, I've never been so frightened—ever. And I don't scare easy. If it hadn't been for Jake, I would've really lost it. By the fourth day, I was running out of food and fuel for my stove. No fuel meant no water. Jake was out of kibbles. He was pretty handy at catching rodents, but I had to do something. And that something meant leaving the hut. I didn't know if I'd be smarter making a run for my cabin at McClure, or if I should head for the LeConte Ranger Station, two-and-a-half miles closer. If I got lucky, I just might be able to make the seven miles downhill to LeConte in ninety minutes. My other option was to climb out over Echo Col and head for Lake Sabrina where there was a paved road and, maybe, people.

I thought about it a lot that night. The next morning thunderhead clouds brewed on the western horizon. I didn't know if the alien craft could see though cloud cover, but I packed up everything to be ready and, for the first time since I was a child, I prayed. Not to any sort of organized type of deity, just to whatever might be out there listening to a forty-something woman, who desperately needed help.

By ten, the clouds were thick, and it started to snow. This weather might give us our only chance to escape. We'll be heading toward LeConte since it's closest, and likely to have food. I'll bring these pages with me and add to them as I can...

CHAPTER 20

ondering if she'd ever see the Muir Hut again, Sara pelted down the trail, careful not to twist an ankle on the slick, wet rocks. She scanned the skies anxiously, but the clouds were so dense she had trouble seeing the trail at times, let alone what was above her. Keeping a close eye on her watch, she was grateful when she passed the small string of no-name lakes below Wanda Lake in forty minutes and got herself below timberline shortly thereafter. She figured it would be much harder for the ship to find her and Jake as the protective canopy of the forest thickened.

Panting, and dripping with sour-smelling sweat, Sara followed the winding side trail to the LeConte station and banged peremptorily on the door. She wasn't surprised no one answered, but she was taken aback to find the door locked. LeConte should still be manned. While a station was manned, it was always left open, unless the Ranger left a note telling travelers where to find him. The board by the door, magic marker dangling by its string, was blank. Heart thrumming like a trip hammer; she yanked her pack off her back and dug into the recesses of the top compartment for the master key that unlocked all the stations. As soon as she got the door open, she called for Jake, who'd gone off to hike his leg against a tree.

What she found inside shocked her. Sara knew Stuart Palmer. He'd spent just about as many years at LeConte as she had at McClure. Of an evening, they often spoke on the radio. A wiry, mousy character, Stuart—with his bald head and sharp, dark eyes—was always neat as the proverbial pin, yet his station looked as if a tornado had blown through it. Papers, dishes, clothing, and park paraphernalia mingled together on the rough, wooden floor. Sara's tolerance for clutter was pretty high, but the stark departure from normalcy in that small cabin made the mess appalling.

"What the fuck happened here?" she blurted, casting about for something, anything, to explain the chaos. Jake bounded into the hut then stopped cold as he, too, seemed to sense the wrongness troubling his mistress.

Sara pushed her pack inside. Drawing the door shut to keep the snow-rain mix out, she stepped gingerly through the mess and stripped off her parka, shaking it briskly over the stone hearth. When it was as dry as she thought it could get, she hung it on a hook near the cold stove. Next she laid and lit a fire. Thank God there was kindling and wood near the stove. At least that part of Stuart's tidiness was intact. She pulled Jake's pack off, pumped some water for him from the kitchen sink, and culled through Stuart's debris for clues, staring with the corner where the radio was.

Without much hope, she tried to raise headquarters, but all she got for her efforts was static. When she began reading the dispatches, though, her heart fluttered oddly and her knees buckled, depositing her unceremoniously on the floor.

There *had* been an attack, a major one. Alien ships—squadrons of them—had bombed both the east and west coasts. Pandemonium reigned.

As best as she could tell from thumbing through dispatches

that had begun right about the time Lonnie ordered her to check out Muir Pass, millions were dead. Everyone who wouldn't surrender to the aliens and adopt their lifestyle—whatever that meant—had been killed. Apparently Earth's world leaders had reneged on some sort of ultra-secret intergalactic trade agreement. But the dispatches stopped right after mentioning it, so she couldn't figure out what the aliens were so upset about.

Sara's fingers trembled as she clutched the flimsy pieces of paper. Tears formed in the corners of her eyes. No wonder her radio hadn't worked atop the pass.

"Aw, shit," she groaned, wiping her eyes. "Are Jake and I the only ones left?"

Stumbling to her feet, she dropped the radio transmissions in an untidy heap. It felt as if she were choking as she moved to the rear of the cabin and pried open the door to the subterranean cellar that was part of every ranger station. Realizing she'd need light, she retreated to scrabble through her pack, extracting her headlamp. Reassured somewhat by its warm, yellow glow, she let herself down the ladder to take stock of what Stuart had left.

It turned out he left pretty much everything. Sara let out a breath she wasn't even aware she'd been holding as she shined her light over tidy rows of canned goods and dried, backpacking foods. In another corner of the cellar was a regulation chain saw and two five-gallon cans of fuel. Hefting first one, then the other, she was relieved to find them mostly full. Stuart likely hadn't had too many fires this summer as it had been pretty warm.

Lucky for me, she thought, realizing she was planning to stay at LeConte…at least for now. What choice did she have?

Sara checked the ammo shelf. "Damn," she muttered under her breath. Her luck, which had been running pretty strong that day all-in-all, had just petered out. Stuart had taken his service revolver and virtually all the ammunition. She had her gun and about twenty shells, but it wouldn't be worth much after she ran out of bullets. Scanning the floor for strays that might've fallen off the shelf, she lectured herself grimly about making every shot count when she went hunting.

She needed to eat before she could figure much more out, so she snagged two cans of pork and beans—one for her and one for Jake—some freeze-dried fruit, and a box of tapioca before heading back up the ladder.

Once her belly was full, really full for the first time in days, she dragged the big pot from the back of the woodstove over to the pump and filled it. As water heated on the stove, she stripped off her clothes, determined to clean nearly a week's worth of sweat and grit off her body. Dumping her clothes into the pot once she was done bathing, she searched for a comb to untangle her hair. Stuart had one, along with a small hand mirror.

The face that stared back at her was disturbing. Familiar, yet not. The blue-gray eyes were the same, but her cheeks were sunken. Lots more lines radiated out from her eyes than before she'd left her cozy lair at McClure. Where had the fine gray streaks in her dark hair come from?

"Damn!" she sputtered. "I look five years older than I did a week ago."

And that, sister, is the least of my problems.

"Thanks," she told her inner voice. "You can keep your opinions to yourself."

She hauled a change of clothes out of her pack, layered one of Stuart's jackets over her long john top, and went to wring out her laundry. She'd spent enough of her life in situations where survival was iffy to know she needed to focus on the present. She had food and shelter for herself and her dog. It was more than she'd had that morning and, since she was flat out of other options, it would have to be enough.

...It's been a week since Jake and I ended up here, and I haven't been keeping this journal up like I meant to. I've been pretty busy. If winter

comes early—and it could—I need meat for Jake and me and firewood. So far, I've cut and split about four cords of wood. I haven't done as well with the meat side of things. I never was much of a shot at a moving object. It's a bit late in the game for target practice, so I guess I just need to do better at finding animals that are standing still. I did set some traps I found in the back of the station. That netted us a few marmots. And I caught and salted some fish. If I could just get a couple deer, that would likely last us through the cold season.

I still try the radio once a day. It recharges via solar panels, so no worries about running out of juice. No one ever answers. Some days I've had to remind myself to do the radio. It would be a shame if someone was there, and I missed them because I got lazy. Still no backcountry travelers, but as the season grows later, I'm less and less hopeful. From time to time, I've tried to tell myself this whole attack thing was bogus, but I know that's just a fairy tale to make myself feel better.

It took several hours to get things in order here at LeConte. I read through all the radio dispatches, then arranged them chronologically by the date and time they came in. I picked up everything, and the place is clean enough Stuart wouldn't find fault with me if he came back.

I wish he would—come back that is. I always thought I didn't like people very well, but when I let myself think about, maybe, being one of the only humans left on earth, it makes me crushingly sad...

TOWARD THE END of their second week at LeConte, Sara took stock of the fact that she and Jake had been out-of-doors for hours nearly every day. There hadn't been even one ship in the sky. She hadn't seen any since leaving Muir Pass, and she'd certainly looked. The first few days she'd been so focused on the sky, it had been difficult to get anything accomplished.

She wondered if being well below timberline in a thick, evergreen forest might be the reason, and decided to try the radio once again. This time, to her amazement, it crackled to life, and Lonnie's voice came over loud and clear.

"Sara, that you, sweetie? We were all wondering what happened to you. I sent someone to McClure, but they came back and told us it looked as if you never returned there. Where are you, anyway? We need to clear out the forest before winter."

"Lonnie? Oh, Lonnie," she managed, before dissolving into tears.

"Sara, what's happened to you?" Lonnie's gruff voice was filled with concern. "I've never heard you cry before, pumpkin."

"I…I…" She didn't know where to begin, so she started with the simple questions. "What happened to Stuart?"

"Uh, his wife was in an automobile accident. He raced out of there in a godawful hurry since the doctors weren't sure she was going to make it." A long silence, then, "Is that where you are? LeConte?"

She stiffened. An accident wouldn't have been a reason for Stuart to take all the ammunition. Rangers used their guns so infrequently, she'd been known to leave McClure without a weapon. A hard, cold edge of suspicion bit deep.

Divulging just where she was seemed like a bad idea. A very bad idea.

"Sara?"

"Yes, I'm still on the air."

"So, where are you?"

"I—I'm not sure I want you, or anyone else, to know." Silence sat heavy between them for so long, she checked the bars on her radio to make sure they were still connected.

"Okay-ay," Lonnie said finally in a probing, single, drawn-out word Sara didn't like much.

"I, uh, I'm going to sign off for now," she said, severing the connection and turning off the set. It had an emergency override. She stared hard at the radio, half expecting Lonnie to engage the emergency frequency to call her back. But the only thing she heard was the sound of her own ragged breathing. Even though she hadn't told Lonnie where she was calling from, she was sure he could figure it out. It had been incredibly stupid of her to ask about Stuart. Nothing like a dead giveaway.

Riding on intuition, she gathered up Jake, a jacket, and her gun, then went to a tree she was using for a hunting blind about a hundred yards away.

Sure enough, within half an hour she heard the *whump* of helicopter blades. Resisting an urge to just shoot the chopper out of the sky when it got low enough, she forced herself to wait. What if she was mistaken? What if there was something wrong with her, and this past month had been some bizarre mental breakdown on her part?

Nope. That doesn't explain the radio transmissions, or Stuart's precipitous departure with all the ammo.

The helicopter banked, hovered, and then finally landed. What came out of it made her breath catch in her throat and almost stopped her heart. Pulling Jake close, she motioned the big dog to silence. Lonnie and Stuart stood in the yard in front of the LeConte station looking about. Lonnie even called out, "Princess?" When she didn't answer, the two bent close, talking with one another.

There was something grotesquely wrong with them. Their faces were the same, but those familiar heads were attached to reptilian bodies with short, squat rear legs and long tails. Sharp red-tipped talons glistened on dinosaurish forelegs, and the pale autumn sun shone off copper-colored scales covering their trunks and extremities. How the hell had they managed to fly the chopper? She swallowed down bile. The low hum of their voices was so chilling, she fought an almost irresistible urge to run.

Finally understanding the reality of what she was facing, Sara gave Jake the hand sign that meant stay. Jaws clenched so her teeth wouldn't rattle and give her away, she scooted silently closer to the two men—or whatever they were. It was easy because they faced away from her. Taking two deep breaths, she raised her Colt, clasped in both hands to shooting stance, and aimed for their heads. She'd have to be fast and sure. Whoever she didn't shoot first was sure to rush her.

As first Lonnie's, then Stuart's, heads dissolved in twin sprays of gore, Sara shut her eyes against the horror of what she'd just done. Gulping down air, she strode to the helicopter, with Jake hard at her heels, growling. Thank God he'd stayed put while she was shooting. Unsure whether the two abominations had been the sole occupants of the chopper, she kept her gun up, ready to annihilate anything that moved.

It only took a few seconds to determine Lonnie and Stuart had been alone. Relief that she wasn't going to die—at least not today—spilled through her as she walked toward the bodies. Pushing at one of the strange corpses with a booted foot, she muttered, "Here's food for us, if I can find something to cut through those hides."

As if to test her assumption about the bodies being edible, Jake was already licking up blood and nibbling at a thread of something that turned her stomach if she looked too close.

Spinning abruptly in the other direction, so she wouldn't have to watch her dog eating what had once been her friends, her gaze landed on the Park Service helicopter. A wobbly grin split her face. She was rusty, but she remembered how to fly. The chopper meant freedom. Not to leave LeConte, because she'd decided to remain there just as long as she could. But it sure enhanced her ability to gather things she'd need to survive...and to move on if she had to.

Sara focused her thoughts as she stood in the sun-drenched clearing next to the ranger cabin, gun still clutched in her hand. She had to do something about the bodies, so they wouldn't draw every predator in the area. After that, she'd fly back to McClure where there was a stash of aviation fuel and plenty of dried meat, not to mention all her things and kibbles for Jake. She could fly really low, only a hundred feet or so above the ground, pick up what she needed, and fly back to LeConte. It'd take less than ten minutes to cover the sixteen trail miles between the stations. Surely that small amount of time wouldn't alert one of the alien ships.

Besides, they seemed to have moved on. Or was that wishful thinking?

Whistling a chirpy tune to calm her jangled nerves, Sara went into the cabin, raised her gun, and then lowered it. Engaging the safety, she set it aside. No point in wasting a bullet, even though she had lots more at McClure. Picking up an axe off the hearth, she hefted it and brought it down hard on the radio. As her link to the outside world dissolved in a spray of glass and wires, she began to cry.

Alone. I really am all alone.

No doubt drawn by the crash of the axe, Jake padded into the ranger cabin, his ears pricked forward, snout red with gore. Hunkering next to him, Sara draped an arm around his thick neck. "The bastards may get us eventually," she snuffled, pulling the dog close to her, "but we'll give them a helluva run for their money."

He licked her, smearing her with blood. Sara wiped her face. Before she lost her nerve about testing the skies, she straightened. "Come on, Jake." She clucked to him. "We're going for a ride."

Sara strode outside and almost tripped over the bodies. She didn't want to take the time to butcher them. The scaly hide looked like it would be a bitch to cut through. Nowhere to secure them, either. The thought of tossing them in the cellar beneath the cabin didn't play well.

"Shit." She chewed her lower lip, and finally settled for dragging them a hundred yards from the cabin. If predators got to them first, she couldn't do much about it. Her main priority was making a run for McClure—before something happened, and she couldn't.

Jared Donovan's foot slipped on an ice covered piece of granite, shooting his heart into hyper drive.

"Gotta stop and pull myself together," he muttered, casting about for somewhere out of the wind. He was close to the top of Glacier Divide. Supposedly, the other side, the western one, was easier. He hoped it was true. More of a backpacker than a mountaineer, he felt woefully out of his element.

Two more dicey steps put him in the lee of a huge boulder, and he hunkered in its shadow, shaking from more than the chill breeze. He scanned the sky, watching clouds close in. At least he hadn't seen another of the ominous ships since day before yesterday. He drew a long, shuddering breath and crossed his arms around his body, shoving his hands into his armpits to warm them.

He'd tried this ascent with gloves on, but didn't have the grip he needed. Consequently, his fingers were white from cold. Because he'd stopped, he dragged his cell from an inner pocket and thumbed it on. Still no signal, which was weird. He should have line of sight to somewhere from as high as he was. He double-checked the solar charger hookup and tucked the phone back into his clothing to keep it warm.

Not that anyone in particular was waiting for him back in San Francisco. He'd taken several weeks off from his biomedical engineering firm to tackle the two hundred mile plus Muir Trail. It was late season, but he moved fast, and he figured he'd be done well before winter set in. The solitude had been a welcome break from his usual urban craziness—until a couple weeks ago.

He'd been returning from a resupply stop for food he'd packaged and left in a bear box at the North Lake trailhead when things had gotten truly weird. Airships—dozens of them—darkened the sky until they blotted out daylight. Explosions nearly deafened him, and he'd taken refuge in a primitive stone cave. It was the best he could find on short notice, but it shielded him from debris hurtling from the skies. He'd waited the ships out, but it meant he'd made one more trip to the trailhead and scouted through all the bear boxes, finding oodles of unclaimed food—and only a few cars in the parking lot.

Feeling like a sneak and a thief, he'd helped himself shamelessly to the food in the boxes, cramming everything he could carry into his pack.

He'd been considering thumbing a ride to Bishop, a small town in the Eastern Sierra Nevada Mountains, but the lack of any people put the kibosh on that plan. Besides, the deserted campground and trailhead held an eerie feel. One that activated the small hairs on the back of his neck. In truth, he could've walked the eighteen miles into Bishop, but Jared had faith in his instincts, and they screamed at him to bury himself in the backcountry until he knew more.

No text messages or news on his phone compounded his worries. Because he'd felt exposed on the open trail—and didn't trust the ships wouldn't return—he'd studied his maps and opted for a shortcut over Glacier Divide. If he played the navigational card well, his route should plunk him down not far from the McClure Meadows Ranger Station. Surely there'd be a backcountry ranger in residence who could clear up what happened, and advise him whether it was safe to complete his planned itinerary, or if he should backtrack and bail out at Lake Edison.

Retrieving his car from the other side of the Sierras would be somewhat of an inconvenience, but certainly doable. If returning to civilization were even possible, his car was the least of his worries.

He glanced at the rocks above him and worked out a rough plan. If he could just make it another fifty feet or so, it appeared the harsh terrain would ease. Tugging out his map, he studied it, running a grimy finger over its worn folds. He'd picked what he hoped was the easiest route to cross the divide. Lucky for him, there'd been a few low snow years, so the perpetual glaciation had retreated. Finding a route over broken talus blocks was possible, minus all that ice. If conditions were more normal, he'd have been shit out of luck without crampons and an ice axe. A snort bubbled past his lips. Not that he knew how to use either of those items.

Jared eyed his chosen path once more. The longer he looked at it, the closer he came to imagining he could see a way through.

Damn good thing it's not getting worse.

It was barely past dawn. He'd gotten a zero dark thirty start today because this was his second attempt to find a way across the divide. Yesterday's effort had been stymied by near vertical cliffs. At least he didn't see anything that impenetrable above him. If it weren't for his heavy pack, he'd be home free, but climbing with forty pounds hanging off his six-foot-two frame challenged his normally spot-on balance.

He shifted his gaze from the craggy heights above him. Once he left where he sat, there'd be no more breaks until he crested the divide. Shoring up his energy was a good plan, so he slugged down Gatorade-laden water and scrabbled for a protein bar. The back of one hand scraped over ten days' worth of stubble dotting his face, and he laughed wryly.

No one at his firm understood what he saw in his trips to the world's wild places. They didn't get it that he only truly felt alive in the outdoors where survival depended on his wits, not trips to the local grocery store.

Always a loner, he was often tongue-tied and uncomfortable in social situations. At thirty-eight, that wasn't likely to change. At least he'd pried himself out of the pathology lab where he'd spent all day, every day, examining bits of human bodies for evidence of disease. All those hours had given him ideas, though. And those ideas landed him enough venture capital to launch his own biomedical research firm a few years ago.

Donovan Enterprises had done well, so well he could take extended trips like this one, trusting his staff to hold down the fort in his absences. He'd hired two M.D.s in addition to himself, and half a dozen Ph.D. scientists. They made a solid team.

"Need to get moving." He spoke aloud, knowing he was stalling. The next hour would be the crux of things, and he'd do well to get it behind him.

He pushed to his feet and cinched his waist belt and shoulder straps to minimize the pack's lateral motion. A few centering breaths, courtesy of years of martial arts training, and he started upward. His long, lanky limbs served him well as he gripped the cold granite with his lugged boot soles and fingers that had warmed fractionally.

A gust of wind grappled with his pack, and he pushed his body into the rock until it passed. So far, so good. Another few feet and he'd have this puppy nailed. He skirted a large talus block, scraping his pack on sharp granite, but when he hunted for his next move, what he saw stopped him dead.

He hadn't seen the chasm that loomed before him from below,

which made sense because it opened downward, mocking him. Too wide to jump across by a good big bunch.

"Crap." He doubled up a fist, but stopped shy of slamming it into the rocks. Injuries wouldn't help his predicament. No cliffs like yesterday, but the chasm was almost as bad. He'd have to down climb at least seventy-five feet into a pit lined with spiky rocks, and regaining the lost elevation on the other side didn't appear straightforward.

He took a breath and glanced around, hunting for other options. Sometimes different perspectives helped. A jagged ridge stretched from where he stood to a rounded low point that looked as if it led through the escarpment. It would be fast—if it worked and he didn't end up falling off the sheer drops on either side. Maybe only half a dozen steps.

Wind whistled, and he settled his hat more firmly on his head. Clouds closed in, enveloping him in a white world with small ice chunks that tore at his exposed flesh. Numb before this latest assault, his hands at least quit complaining—because his body had rerouted blood away from them. He hoped to hell the damage wouldn't be permanent. Frostbite led to necrotic tissue and amputations, but he needed his hands, skin against rock. Gloves wouldn't offer the control he required.

No help for his hands. Not until he crossed the divide and moved a whole lot lower.

He peered at the ridge once more. Maybe it would be safer if he took his pack off...

Jared discarded the thought before it finished forming. The items in his pack were his lifeline. Backcountry travelers who became separated from their gear died.

The thought galvanized him. No matter what else happened today, death wasn't on his personal menu. He stared harder the ridge through slitted eyes, then pulled off his dark glasses until they dangled around his neck by their safety strap. He'd hoped for clearer vision without the shades, but the whiteout was worsening by the minute.

He had to move and move right now.

"Don't think, just do," he muttered.

Extending his hands to his sides to improve his balance, he waited. Timing would be crucial. Those few moments between wind gusts were his friends. If a gust hit him on the exposed knife-edge, he'd be done for.

"Now," he shrieked to push himself past inertia. "Go, now!"

He narrowed his focus to his next step. One down. Five to go.

Two down. Goddammit, but he had to move faster. The next burst of wind howled in the distance, amplified by the peaks surrounding him.

Three down.

His boot slipped, sloughing sideways, but he was ready for it and had the fourth step in place. Breath steamed through clenched teeth and adrenaline surged, leaving a metallic taste on his tongue. Rancid sweat dripped down his sides.

Five down.

The next step was longer than he expected, but he had to do it. Wind made a grab for him. He pivoted to use it to his advantage and leapt across the seven foot gap. His pack dragged at him, and he pushed his torso forward to counteract it.

Another gust of wind slammed against his back and he fell to his knees, but he was safely across. Bruised kneecaps didn't matter a fuck. A feral shriek tore from him, followed by another. He didn't realize how terrified he'd been until he made it. A quick glance across what he'd just crossed didn't help. If he'd seen the ridge from this side, he'd never have attempted it.

"Go," he urged, still talking out loud, and staggered upright.

He couldn't see a foot in front of him. Not good. What if the other side of Glacier Divide was as rugged as what he'd just conquered?

"I'll figure it out," he muttered. "Got this far."

He climbed the last few feet to the crest by feel over flattened talus blocks. Because visibility—and the ever-present, shrieking, goddamned wind—did nothing but get worse, he turned and faced toward the slope. Backing down was safer.

Something wet landed on his face. Snow. Shit. Shit. Shit. Could things get any worse?

"Stop it. Get off this ridge. Get to somewhere protected, and take a break. Eat something, drink something, put gloves on."

Jared smirked. He was talking like someone who had a future. Maybe he needed to match actions to his words. A centering breath. One more, and he started down. If the topo map was correct—and if he was where he thought he was—the slope's angle would ease after he'd descended a couple hundred feet.

He should've fired up his GPS when he stopped for Gatorade and food on the other side, but he hadn't.

He made his way through the murk so slowly he ground his teeth together, but he couldn't move faster. He couldn't see his next step until he was on top of it. He did keep an eye on his GPS, though. Two hundred feet didn't make much difference. Two hundred fifty did, the terrain finally easing off.

Panting and sweating despite the temperature, which hovered around twenty degrees according to his watch, he finally faced outward and made slightly better time. A thousand feet below the crest, visibility cleared a little, and he hunted for somewhere he could shelter. He was worried about his hands. They felt as if they belonged to someone else.

He needed to fire up his stove and melt snow for a hot drink. His hands had progressed beyond simply warming them up in gloves. They'd hurt like a son of a bitch when blood returned to them.

He hunted, but didn't see any possible stopping places until he passed the first gnarled trees at timberline. By then, he'd descended nearly two thousand feet. Despite his hands and the weather, excitement filled him. He'd cheated death and was going to win this one.

Don't get cocky. I'm not down yet.

He threaded his way into the heart of a grove of stubby aspens and glanced at his watch. Three in the afternoon. For the first time since four that morning, he unbuckled his pack and let it slip from his shoulders. He was tired, wanted to curl up next to his pack and sleep, but knew better. The day hadn't warmed much, and it was still snowing off and on.

No. He needed to set up his tent and make himself a meal. If there was still some daylight left after that, he'd drag out his GPS and determine just where McClure Meadows was—and how far from his current location.

Going on autopilot, he put his tent together, pulled his sleeping bag out of its dry sack, and inflated his foam pad. That done, he sat on the bag so at least part of his body was sheltered and started his stove, keeping it cradled between his knees. He made soup from melted snow and instant packets, forcing himself to drink an entire quart. He needed liquids. Midway through the soup, the agony in his hands began. He'd known it would be bad, but he was lucky to get the soup pot on the ground before the worst pain hit.

Howls tore from him. He tried to hold them back, but gave it up for a lost cause. No one could hear, but they hurt his pride. Gritting his teeth against the hot knives sensation chopping through his nerves, he flexed his fingers over and over, forcing a return of circulation. When it was finally over, he checked his hands with clinical precision, pleased to only find two whitened patches.

Frostnip, not frostbite. He'd heal, so long as he didn't require an extended time period without gloves again anytime soon. Relief sluiced through him, and he reached for cheese and crackers to chase his soup. Losing fingers, as he'd feared might happen, would put a big crimp in his research work. He needed dexterity to prep slides, never mind his interminable hours on the computer.

While he ate, he fished the GPS out of his pack and turned it on. It took its sweet time latching onto the satellites, but it finally moved off the "searching" screen. He dragged the map back out and took a few readings, triangulating as he went.

A smile split his cracked lips. He'd done better than he hoped. He was in almost a direct line with McClure. All he needed to do was lose another two thousand vertical feet over relatively easy terrain. Jared glanced at his watch. Just past four. It was tempting to stay where he was since he already had camp set up, but he really wanted to know what the deal was with all those UFOs.

Had it been some kind of Hollywood stunt? Were they filming a movie here in the Sierras? Surely the ranger would have all the relevant info on anything like that happening in his area. Daylight savings time still reigned, so even a leisurely pace would bring him to the ranger station before full dark.

He shook his head. Jared was deluding himself about Hollywood or stunts, and he knew it. Something hideous had happened, and he hoped to hell the ranger could fill in the blank spots.

Decided, he began packing up. One advantage of all his time on the trail was it didn't take long. Fifteen minutes later, he hefted his pack and started downhill, with his hands firmly tucked into thick mitts. They still stung a little, but they'd be fine, and so would he.

His mind drifted as he made his way down talus strewn slopes, with increasingly thick tree cover. Maybe he'd get that dog he'd been considering. A companion would be welcome on at least some of his outdoor adventures. Of course, he wouldn't be able to bring a pet into any of the national parks, but there was lots of forest service land where there weren't any prohibitions. Thinking about a dog was much easier than picking through what might have happened that cleared out the North Lake campground.

The GPS kept him on track, and he wasn't surprised when he broke out of timber into a clearing with a well-constructed stone and wood cabin.

"Hello." He raised his voice in greeting.

When he didn't get a reply, he tried again. Still nothing.

Jared made his way past a bubbling creek to the front of the cabin. On a white board secured to the building someone had written in a scrawling hand.

Tuesday 12th. Went to Evolution Lake for a SAR mission. Back Wednesday or Thursday. If you need me before then, Evolution is five miles south along the Muir Trail.

Tuesday the twelfth? He peeked at his watch. Today was Sunday, two weeks later. What exactly did that mean? Had the ranger stumbled into something that held him up? He frowned and turned toward the stout front door, testing the latch. He didn't expect it to be open, and it wasn't.

Something tightened unpleasantly in his gut. Anxiety. Fear. Foreboding. He'd hoped against hope for another human being, but the ranger was just as absent as campers at North Lake.

He really was tired. Too tired to knock off five more miles hunting for a ranger who probably wouldn't be at Evolution Lake, either. No. His best bet would be to pitch his tent in the trees behind the station, make himself something more to eat, and grab some rest. He wasn't much more than ten or twelve miles from Vermillion Valley Resort, located on Lake Edison to the west. Tomorrow, he'd do the prudent thing and make his way back to civilization. He'd let his fears get the better of him. Remaining in the Sierras for a protracted period of time wasn't rational.

I don't know that.

Too weary to think about it, Jared retraced his steps around the ranger cabin. As he hunted for a sheltered campsite, he found a pebbled path leading to a natural hot spring.

"Hey! Son of a bitch." He grinned. Things were looking up. He'd not only get food and rest. He could also take a bath, a true luxury. Not that the ranger would give a shit, but at least if he showed up—which wasn't likely—Jared wouldn't smell quite so bad when he accosted him for information.

$\mathcal{J}$ared opened his eyes to full daylight. Tugging his arm out of the sleeping bag, he tilted it to peer at his watch. "Shit! Eleven. How could I have slept so long?" he muttered.

He bolted upright in his sleeping bag and rubbed grit from his eyes. The hot water had felt so good, he'd lingered in the hot spring for a long time after he'd eaten. The combination of a full belly, physical exhaustion, and a warm body sent him right to sleep.

He'd obviously needed the rest, but it was well past time to be up and moving. He unzipped the tent and glanced out at a fairly sunny day. Not especially warm, but at least the wind had died down, and the snow from yesterday was well on its way to melting. He could still make Vermillion Valley Resort with no trouble. Surely there'd be someone there who knew something. It was a busy resort on the Sierra's western slopes. This time of year, it played host to hunters as well as other backcountry travelers.

Before he'd turned in for the night, he'd played his options carefully through his mind. He'd have to leave the backcountry in a few weeks anyway since he lacked winter survival gear. May as well face whatever was waiting back in civilization now.

It couldn't possibly be as bad as he feared.

He dressed and packed up while heating coffee water on his stove. Once it was hot, he mixed in instant crystals, along with powdered milk and sugar. That and an energy bar would be breakfast. He needed to get moving. He was just putting his cook kit in his pack when an unexpected noise froze him in his tracks.

The characteristic *thump-thump-thump* of a helicopter's rotors sounded unnaturally loud in an environment that had been devoid of any noise since that day when he'd taken shelter from the explosions.

A reluctant smile formed. He'd been overreacting after all. Nothing was particularly amiss, and the chopper overhead proved it. Leaving the protective circle of trees where he'd pitched his tent, he hurried to where he could get a clear view of the sky. Not only did a helicopter—and one flying damned low—come into view, it was obviously heading right for the ranger cabin.

Maybe the ranger was returning after all.

Jared's mouth filled with the metallic taste he associated with adrenaline. Now that it came down to it, he wasn't all that certain he wanted anything corroborated. Not his fears. Or someone casting a patronizing glance his way if he admitted his concerns. He stayed back, well out of the rotor wash, until the bird was settled on the ground, and the pilot cut the engine.

The door opened, and an enormous black German Shepherd bounded out of the chopper and headed right for him, barking ominously.

Jared knew better than to move, so he stood quietly, hands by his sides. The dog stopped five feet away, growling.

"Jake!" a woman's voice cried. "Stand down."

The dog spared a glance over one shoulder before he quit snarling, but he didn't move, either. His intent canine stare bored into Jared, daring him to make a wrong move.

A woman, who looked about thirty-five, strode briskly toward them. She was tall and broad-shouldered. Long, dark hair fell halfway to her waist. Sharp cheekbones and a defined chin lent her an arresting air. Dressed in Park Service brown except for a fluffy, dark green parka and stout, black boots, she examined him closely. When she got closer, she pushed her dark glasses to rest atop her head, and narrowed her blue-gray eyes.

At a hand sign from the woman, the dog retreated to her side.

"Are you the ranger?" Jared asked, then kicked himself. It was obvious from her garb she was a ranger. Maybe not the one who lived here, but it didn't matter.

She nodded. "Sara Holcomb." Walking closer, she held out a hand.

Jared clasped it. God, it felt good to touch another human being. "Jared Donovan. I'm glad to see you," he blurted and released her hand. "Came over the divide last night aiming for this station. Since no one was here, thought I'd head for VVR today, except I got a late start..." He rolled his eyes. "Sorry. I'm babbling. Haven't seen anyone since— Well, since whatever happened with the ships and explosions. Do you know exactly what that was?"

He held his breath, aware of tension thrumming through his body. Here it was. Either she'd confirm his worst fears—or lay them to rest. He waited, but she just stood there looking at him, the oddest expression on her face. Maybe resignation mixed with compassion.

"Guess you don't know anything, either," he said after several long minutes ticked by. "Nice to meet you, but I need to get moving if I'm going to make VVR before dark."

"Probably not a good idea."

Jared frowned. "Why not. There'll be people there, and I can figure out how to retrieve my car. It's parked in Yosemite Valley—"

She shook her head and made a chopping motion with one

hand. "Sorry, I know I haven't said much, but the last thing I was expecting was to find someone here. Someone human, that is."

He focused intently. Maybe something was wrong with the woman, like a mental illness. "What do you mean?" he asked, keeping his voice tones neutral. "What would you find that wasn't human? Are you talking about animals?"

She closed her teeth over her full lower lip. "Explaining will take time. It's something I don't have much of right now. I got lucky flying here from LeConte—"

"That's the next ranger station to the south, right?" he cut in. "Past the Evolution area."

"Yeah. Anyway, my plan was to come here, pack up a bunch of stuff, and fly right back. Who knows if it'll still be safe if I wait."

Tension settled between his shoulder blades and twisted his stomach into a hard knot. Sara sounded serious—and worried—but not crazy. "If it's not safe for me to go to Vermillion, then where—?"

A bitter laugh shot from the woman, and she looked away. Color stained her high cheekbones as if her outburst embarrassed her.

Annoyance ratcheted his tension upward a notch or two. "Look. Aren't you supposed to help backcountry travelers?" he demanded, stopping shy of a reminder just whose tax dollars supported her job.

She pinched the bridge of her nose between her thumb and forefinger before squaring her shoulders. "Yes. I am. The only way I can help you is if you come with me." She laughed again. This time something hopeless mingled with the bitterness. "I don't expect you to join up with me. It's quite a leap of faith, and I don't have time to explain things right now."

She gestured with both hands. "Like I said, I need to stock LeConte, which is why I came here."

Intuition drove his next question. He didn't want the answer, but needed to know, so he asked anyway. "Stock LeConte for how long?"

Her gaze skittered away. "Maybe forever. However long that ends up being."

Jared fell back a pace. "Shit! Aw, shit. So it's true. You guys have radios, so you'd know. Something horrendous happened, and there's nothing to go back to. At least you can tell me that much."

Sara nodded. Something suspiciously like tears sheened her eyes. "I thought Jake," she jerked her chin toward the dog, "and I were the only ones left."

He'd harbored the same fear—about himself being one of a select group of survivors. It was one of the reasons he'd been so focused first on McClure and then on VVR. To figure things out.

Jared inhaled and blew it out. Then he did it again. His options had narrowed considerably, and he made up his mind. He and Sara were stronger together than individually. "I could help you get things in the chopper," he offered.

The mask her face had become crumpled, and something akin to hope lit her features. "Does that mean you want to come with me?" She paused a beat. "I wanted to push, but it didn't feel right."

"I kind of have to." He grinned crookedly. "It's the only way I'll get you to tell me anything. Is everybody else really dead?"

"Lots are. Others have…changed, but don't ask me more about that right now. No time, and I can't stand to talk about it." All business again, Sara loped to the cabin's front porch and pushed a key into the lock. "Follow me."

He ducked into the cabin. Sara stood in a corner unlocking yet a second door that looked like it led into a cellar. "Do you have a headlamp?" she asked.

"Sure. In my pack. I'll run and get it," he offered.

"In a minute." She turned and faced him, pocketing the key. "What I need from down there is ammunition, dog food, and food for us. Cart everything you find outside."

"Doesn't the helicopter have weight limits?"

"Of course, but we shouldn't be anywhere near them. There're also fuel cans down there. Gasoline for my chain saws. While you're doing that, I'll be gathering clothes and gear." She glanced at her watch. "If we could be gone in half an hour, it would be a plus."

"Why? Do you have some sort of inside information?"

Sara snorted. "Yeah, right. Wish I did. The sad truth is I don't know much at all. Just enough to be scared out of my wits." She turned away.

He hurried outside to where he'd left his pack leaning on a tree. Hefting it, he hauled it in front of the cabin and snapped up his headlamp. Sara didn't look like a woman who scared easy. To have her admit she was terrified gave him pause. His elation at finding someone to share whatever they faced as a team faded, replaced by grim determination.

No matter what was out there, he'd be damned if he'd let it get them.

Sara's estimate of how long it would take to load what she needed into the chopper turned out to be wildly inaccurate. Even with both of them working, ninety minutes elapsed before they were ready to leave.

She'd been shocked to see the man in the clearing next to her cabin. At first, she hadn't believed it, thought he had to be one of the aliens masquerading in human form to trip her up. Once he'd clasped her hand, though, and she felt the all-too-human warmth of him, it took everything in her not to collapse in sobs of relief. Long years of discipline to shield her reactions were all that saved her.

She'd watched the play of emotion cascade over his face at her news nowhere was safe, and that she was planning for an indeterminate time at LeConte. Even with that, his offer to help surprised her. He looked to be an independent sort. Tall and rangy, he was built like a climber, slender with long arms and legs. Coppery hair fell about his face almost to shoulder length, and a weeks' worth of stubble dotted sculpted cheekbones and a square chin. His eyes were brown, a deep, dark, liquid color that warmed when he smiled. Patched clothing, scuffed boots, and a well-used pack spoke to many miles in the backcountry. She pegged him in his late thirties, but he could be as much as ten years older.

"Is that it?" His voice, a rich, mellow baritone, broke into her reverie.

"Think so." Sara locked her cabin. She considered putting the storm shields over the windows, but didn't want to take the time. "I need to top off the chopper's tank. Then we can leave."

"You have aviation fuel here?" Surprise flowed beneath his question.

"Sure." She looked away. Jesus, he was good looking. "This was my station, and I made sure I was ready for damn near anything. This way." She trotted to where fuel cylinders were stacked and hefted one. He did the same.

"Funny, but I was certain the ranger would be a guy."

Sara glanced sidelong at him. "Yeah. Most people make the same mistake. We're actually about fifty-fifty in terms of who lives in the backcountry these days."

"You said this was your station." He helped her position the fuel over a funnel, waiting while it poured into the chopper's tank. "Why are you moving everything to LeConte? Wouldn't it be easier to just stay here?"

It was a good question. She gave him points for it. "LeConte is over a thousand feet lower. Better hunting. Milder weather. Year round stream." She paused. "And farther from civilization. It's thirteen miles up and over Bishop Pass, and then you're only at South Lake, and it's another seventeen to a town."

"Does LeConte have a hot spring?"

"Nope. One amenity that's lacking." She glanced his way. "I guess that means you found the one here."

"Indeed. It felt amazing."

"Good memory to hang onto when we're heating water over the woodstove." She quirked a brow. Lowering the empty fuel container, she picked up the second one, and he helped her tilt it so its contents ran through the funnel.

"Sounds like it's almost full," he noted.

She'd thought the same thing and capped off the cylinder, carting it back to the stack a few yards from the cabin. Sara whistled for Jake, who'd vanished once it was apparent the strange man wasn't a threat to her.

He came at a run, an unrecognizable, mangled animal clamped between his strong jaws.

Jared grinned. "Nice dog. I thought they weren't allowed in national parks."

"They're not. It took me years to talk my way into keeping my own SAR dog with me. Let's get moving." She stood aside so Jake and Jared could get in. The dog, sensing he'd been booted out of the ramrod seat, slithered to the back of the bird. He arranged himself over stacks of goods and Jared's pack, crammed atop everything else.

Jared buckled up. She got in, shut the door, and did the same, firing the engine.

"What are the odds of us making it back to LeConte?" he asked without preamble. "What exactly is it we're avoiding?"

"Do you know about the ships?"

"If you're asking if I saw them, the answer is yes. It's when I thought hiding out in the backcountry was a better bet than trying to hitch a ride to town."

She glanced at him and nudged the craft skyward. "Were there any cars?"

"No. That was part of the problem." He paused a beat. "You didn't answer me."

"It's because I don't know. I'll be flying as low as I can without clipping trees or mountains. Worst case, one of the ships will spot us. If we see them first, I'll do my damnedest to land."

"What happens if there's nowhere to set down?"

"I suspect they'll vaporize us." She hurried on. "Look. I need to concentrate for two reasons. It's been years since I've flown one of these things, and I'm breaking FAA minimums, which means a vicious downdraft could pull us into a mountainside."

He reached across the few inches between their seats and laid a hand on the side of her thigh. "Tell me how I can help."

His kindness almost undid her. She'd been strung tight ever since that horrible night the pica went up in smoke. Today's confrontation with Lonnie and Stuart hadn't helped.

"I meant it," he urged. "I'm here, and I'm not doing anything."

"Just keep watch. You know what the ships look like. This is a short trip. Only another five minutes, and we'll be there."

She rested her hand on the cyclic. Light and steady did the trick. Gripping it made the craft do weird shit. Familiar landmarks shot past her field of vision, and she breathed a sigh once they passed the Muir Hut where she'd been trapped for so many days.

"Look." He angled his head.

Her blood congealed to ice. Another chopper—another Park Service chopper—appeared on the horizon. Had it seen them? She was low, in the shadow of thickening timber. Other pilots wouldn't look quite so low. And she was far enough away, they might not look at all.

"Should we land?" he asked. "There's a spot over there that might work."

Sara bit her lip until she tasted blood and kept her focus trained on the other bird. It kept right on flying, maybe a mile to the west of them. "I don't think it saw us," she said.

"Don't these things have radar in them?" He glanced at the instrument cluster. "Guess not." He answered his own question.

"The newer, fancier ones do, but not these models," she replied and set them up to land at LeConte. Her breath came fast, and she felt like she wanted to puke. They'd had way too close a call for her taste. How many Lonnies and Stuarts were cruising around in Park Service property, pretending to still be human?

"I need to know what's going on," he said as she hovered right before setting them down.

"Yeah, I know you do. We need to get the bird unloaded, and then we have an unpleasant task. I wouldn't blame you if you didn't want to help with it."

He followed her and Jake out of the chopper. "What kind of unpleasant task."

"Butchering aliens." Before he could ask her anything, she added, "We need meat, and I figure they're as good as anything else." It was a good lead in, so she started at the beginning and told him everything she knew as they unloaded the chopper.

CHAPTER 23

Jared didn't say much. He'd asked a question or two for clarification, but he mostly listened as Sara's story spilled out of her. Any tendency to not believe her vanished in the face of the aliens' bodies.

He'd kept a stoic front, a skill honed through his years as a doctor, until she led him to where she'd stashed the two bodies. Jake beat them there and he'd made a significant incursion into one of the corpses.

"Humph. Guess it's better than kibbles." Jared tried to make a joke to lighten the grisly aspect of the dog feeding on the bodies. It wasn't that dead things bothered him. He'd earned a living examining tissues and organs, but that was in a controlled environment. The hybrid aliens laying in the dirt took it to a whole other level.

"Shoo!" Sara batted her hands at the dog. For the barest moment, it looked as if he might disobey, but the moment passed, and he hopped out of the way, sprinting back through the forest.

Jared hunkered next to the nearest body and ran his fingertips over its scales. "What I wouldn't give to have my microscopes and lab equipment."

"What do you do? Or what did you do?" Sara stood behind him, arms crossed over her chest.

"I'm a doctor, but I don't see patients. Not live ones, anyway. I run a biomedical research firm. I'd love to study the DNA that made these."

"I don't have your background, but I'll bet the science behind this transformation doesn't work like anything you've ever seen before. These men were my friends." Her voice ran down and she started over. "In a matter of a couple weeks they turned from human to that." Sara extended a hand, pointing at the corpses.

He considered it. Recombinant DNA could work fast, but to blend humans into a whole other form in mere days defied credibility. Jared pushed to his feet. "Are they how the chopper got here?"

Sara nodded. "I hadn't gotten around to telling you that part, except you knew I arrived on foot, so I guess you put two and two together."

He narrowed his eyes. "Yeah. It's part of what made me a decent researcher. Do you think someone will come looking for these guys?"

"I have no idea." She shrugged. "The little bit I saw of Lonnie and Stuart before I—" she faltered before going on "—killed them, they seemed to still think like humans."

Jared eyed her. "You okay?"

"Truth?"

He wanted to hold out his arms and cradle her against him, but knew at an instinctual level it would be a mistake. "Of course, truth." He infused as much compassion as he could into his words, in lieu of the hug he wanted to give her.

Her expression altered, became less guarded. "I don't think I'll ever be okay again, but that doesn't excuse me from doing the best I can to stay alive."

The words, resolute, determined, jarred him. He swept his earlier decision to keep his distance aside and opened his arms.

"That's one of the bravest speeches I've ever heard. Now come here, just for a minute. It doesn't mean you're weak. We all need someone." Jared hesitated. "It's been one of my problems. An uber-independent streak that chases support right out the window."

"Takes one to know one." She fastened her amazing eyes on him, but didn't come any closer.

"It does, doesn't it? If a hug feels too risky, how about this?" He moved to her side and draped an arm around her shoulder, squeezing lightly.

She leaned into him for all of five seconds before disentangling his arm. "We have work to do." Her tone shifted back to brusque. "Stuart kept a smokehouse down by the river. Guess I figured we'd preserve the meat that way."

Sara's voice held a broken note, as if she'd rather face a firing squad than deal with the bodies.

"Look." He exhaled softly. "We brought back a lot of food from McClure, and boxes of ammunition. Another gun too, beyond the one in that belt holster around your waist. Surely we can hunt. Even if we went to all the trouble to butcher these bodies, could you bear to eat the result?"

She favored him with a wry smile. "I worried how I'd manage. Guess I figured worst case scenario, they'd feed Jake."

"He seems pretty handy hunting up his own game." Jared spread his hands in front of him. "If you think I'm being pushy or overbearing, say something, but I'm good with burning these two. We could douse them with a splash of fuel, so it would be over faster."

She folded her arms beneath her breasts and was quiet so long, he worried he'd offended her. This was her turf. He was the guest, the interloper.

"Yeah," she finally muttered. "Let's do it. Probably should drag them closer to the river first. So we don't set the forest on fire."

"I'll take care of that part. How about if you scare up some gasoline?"

She turned and sprinted back toward the cabin.

Jared slung one of the bodies over his shoulders, staggering under its weight as he made his way downhill to where he heard running water. Once there, he moved another hundred feet downstream to a flat, sandy area.

Sara trotted up carting a red fuel can. "I'll sit with him," she said. "Or I can go get the other one."

"How about if you finish putting things away." He kept his voice gentle. "I can take care of this."

"You don't have to do that. I can fight my own—"

He pried the gas can out of her hands and set it down, then he faced her squarely. "I know you're strong. Tough as nails, as dried shoe leather, but you have help now. Their bodies may not be human anymore, but do you really want to watch their faces burn? Can you separate who they used to be from what they turned into?"

"Not entirely." She swallowed visibly.

If he knew women, she was doing her level best not to cry.

"How about this?" A tear spilled down one cheek, but she ignored it. "I'll go get Stuart, er, the other body. You can get a pyre together while I'm gone…"

"Sure, Sara. That's fine, but once Stuart is here, you can leave. I'll find you once it's over."

"You don't have to—"

"I know that. We partners. Even though we didn't say it in so many words, we made that decision back at McClure. It means we help one another. This is one small way I can help you."

Sara didn't say anything. She didn't have to. He recognized relief in the set of her shoulders and the softening of her expression before she turned away from him. He watched her move up the sand bar until she disappeared into the trees. Her arms and legs swung with an easy grace. She was probably a lot like him. More at home here in the wilds than anywhere else. Why else would she be a backcountry ranger. She'd told him about her twenty years with the Park Service. Surely after all that time, she could've snapped up a desk job—if she wanted one.

IT WAS WELL past dark by the time Jared made his way back to the cabin, working by feel since he hadn't thought to bring his headlamp. The light from the pyres masked just how dark it had grown, but the deed was done. Unlike human remains, something in the scaled skin made the bodies burn quickly. He'd wanted to do a cursory autopsy to determine just how much of the parts beneath the scales weren't human anymore, but he hadn't.

For one thing, all he had was a pocket knife. For another, it felt disrespectful to chop into men who'd been Sara's friends. One had manned LeConte. The other had been her boss. Surely the loss added to her grief and horror about aliens commandeering Earth. She'd mentioned humans reneging on some kind of intergalactic trade agreement, and he was looking forward to hearing whatever she had by way of information to shed light on the incidents that had blown into full-fledged war.

He saw LeConte's lights long before he came to the cabin, and the sight warmed him. In a very real way, it felt like coming home. Not home to his old life, but home to a new one. One he was just beginning to explore. Sara was someone he wanted to get to know better. Not because she was tall and striking, but because she was bright and resourceful and loved the backcountry.

He'd had his share of women, but a few nights in a tent sent them running for the hills. None of them could tolerate leaving civilization behind for very long. Even the ones who'd enjoyed his body and his mind drew the line at multiple days in the same clothes with only cold creek water to wash in. Balanced against no Internet, no one appreciated the wonder and the glory of sun-dappled meadows and alpenglow that lasted for hours, turning the world a stunning golden pink.

He had a feeling Sara nurtured a self-sufficiency to rival his own, and the thought excited him. He wanted to get to know her a whole lot better. To see those wonderful eyes warm when she looked his way. He snorted laughter. Nothing like getting a wee bit ahead of himself. He'd just met her. For all he knew, she had a husband somewhere, or a partner. Maybe that added to the sadness mirrored in her eyes.

A shadow detached itself from the darker places and ran to his side *whuffing* softly.

Jake.

"Hey, boy."

The dog, apparently past his earlier ambivalence, nuzzled Jared's hand and together they covered the final distance to the cabin.

SARA STOOD over the woodstove mixing ingredients into a pot. Since she had time, she opted for rice and beans over freeze dried food. It had been exceptionally kind of Jared to offer to do her job for her. Something he'd said stuck in her mind. They were partners, which meant she didn't have to do everything. Just because she didn't have to, though, didn't mean she wouldn't try. Old habits truly died hard.

With it all, the simple fact of not being alone anymore soothed her, which was odd since she'd never minded her isolation in the backcountry. Not having any front country left altered that. No Park Headquarters. No Lonnie.

Sadness welled. He'd been the one who'd hired her, and he'd been like a father all the years she'd worked for him. She'd never had another boss, and she'd miss him terribly. Knowing he was as close as her radio had bailed her out of many a situation. Not that she'd called—at least not often—but knowing she could made a lot of difference.

"Maybe I'm not as independent as I figured," she muttered and stirred salt into her stew.

Her thoughts shifted to Jared. What had he left behind? He'd mostly listened to her story. She had no idea about him, beyond his research firm. Maybe she could get him to share a little bit about his life over dinner. He was damned attractive, but maybe he had a wife or girlfriend. Hell, he probably had kids. He was plenty old enough to have that part of his life in hand.

As if her thoughts had drawn him, she heard Jared's footsteps and Jake's whine that meant he wanted inside. She hurried to the door, and then felt foolish. It wasn't locked. She wanted to see Jared, and the knowledge made her uncomfortable. She'd carved an independent life. No reason to alter that.

It's logical to want to see him. We're the only ones left.

I don't know that, the other side of her mind argued. *Where there are two, there are likely more.*

Beyond logic, her heart gave a funny little flip as she laid her hand on the doorknob and pulled it open.

"Hey there!" He grinned and moved aside so Jake could bound into the cabin.

The dog sat by his empty dishes and barked, tail thumping the floor.

"You have water," Sara told him.

"Aw, we could give him some kibbles. He might not have found anything after you shooed him away from..." Jared hesitated.

"It's okay." Sara picked up the dog's dish and scooped kibbles out of a sack she'd opened earlier when she was arranging things in the cabin. It was a small space, and she'd filled the cellar until it would be a challenge to locate things. What didn't fit spilled over into the main living space.

She dumped the food into Jake's dish, and he bent his head, chomping noisily.

Jared unzipped his jacket and hung it on a hook. He checked the woodstove and tossed a couple chunks of wood into it. "Anything I can do to help with dinner? It smells great, by the way. Thanks for taking care of it."

"Least I could do." She smiled because she couldn't stop herself. "Only thing I didn't rustle through was your pack. You must have food."

"Oh, that I do. I probably broke a bunch of laws riffling through the bear boxes at the North Lake campground. Took as much as I could carry."

"I'll never tell. Sit." She gestured at the small table. "I'll dish us up."

He tugged a water bottle out of one of the side pockets in his pack that she'd propped against one wall and drank deep before pointing at the pump. "Water okay to drink?"

"It comes from the creek. Probably. All the horses left this station a couple weeks before the attack."

He moved to the pump and refilled his water bottle. "Since you mentioned the attack, you said you had dispatches. You could tell me what's in them, or I could look through them over dinner."

"I don't mind sharing what's in them, but…" Heat rose to her face. "I was hoping you'd tell me about yourself. You found out a lot about me, but all I know about you is what you do for a living."

A smile began in his eyes and spread to his mouth. "Sure. So long as you do the same. All you really described was how you ended up trapped in the Muir Hut and making a run for this station. I can look at the dispatches anytime."

"Fair enough. We can play you show me yours, and I'll show you mine." Her face grew warmer. "Crap! I didn't mean it to come out quite like that."

His grin broadened. "It sounded fine by me." He stopped by the stove and peeked into the pot. "Is it ready? I'm hungry."

"Yeah. Told you I'd dish up."

"I know you did, but I don't need you to wait on me." He

picked up one of the bowls she'd laid out and ladled stew into it. Then he did the same with the other bowl and held it out to her. "Come on, Sara. Let's eat."

They settled at the table and tucked in. She was hungry too, and didn't pepper him with questions until they'd begun on their second bowlfuls.

She caught his gaze. "Where do you live? And what do you do when you're not working or in the backcountry?"

"Would you like me to start at the beginning so you don't have to feed me questions?"

"Sure. That would be great." She took a drink from her water bottle, waiting.

"I live in San Francisco. Moved there to go to medical school and never left. My residency was in internal medicine and pathology, and I worked in the path lab at City General for six years, most of that for the government. They paid for my med school, and I owed them service.

"Got a few ideas about how to address some of the worst diseases. Also brainstormed a bunch of fertile possibilities to stave off the aging process. On a whim, I floated them past some venture capital firms, and no one was more surprised than me when offers for funding began rolling in." He shrugged.

"The rest is history. I opened Donovan Enterprises, and it's done well enough for me to employ several people. We have—or had—some boutique cures in the FDA's pipeline. If even one of them panned out, it would've made us all rich. We were actually planning an Initial Public Offering for our company in the next few months."

"So you would've been on one of the stock exchanges?"

"Exactly." He cocked his head to one side. "You know. Give John Q. Investor a chance to share in the spoils."

Sara pushed back enough from the table to cross one leg over the other. "Where'd you grow up? Do you have family?"

"Oh." He rolled his eyes. "Funny how I always leave out the personal stuff. Long habit."

"Know what you mean. You don't have to answer—"

"No. I want to. I grew up in Portland. Both my parents died quite young from cancer, which was why I was so interested in studying it on a cellular level. I have one brother. He's a dentist and practices in Seattle." He angled his head until his gaze met hers. "Never been married. No kids. No dogs, but I was contemplating changing that."

"So you have a fiancée?" She forced the words out. Wanting to know, but not.

He threw his head back and laughed. "No. What I was considering changing was getting a dog. I've always been way too much of a loner. Not that I didn't have girlfriends, but no one ever shared my obsession with the backcountry." He winked at her. "That was always one of my make-or-break requirements."

He got to his feet and carried their bowls over to the stove. "Do you want more?"

Sara shook her head. She was outrageously pleased by his answer about no fiancée, and trying her damnedest to hide it.

"Me, either." He pumped water into their dishes and left them on the roughhewn counter next to the pump.

She started to get up.

"Hold up there, sister."

"What? Why?"

"Well." A slow lazy grin made him heartbreakingly gorgeous. "We got the *me showing you mine* part over with. I'm waiting for the quid pro quo."

CHAPTER 24

*H*e stood by the pump watching her. Did she have any idea how striking she was? Now that her body wasn't covered with layers of cold-weather clothing, the lines of her full breasts were outlined beneath her stretchy top. Her uniform pants fit snugly over a trim waist and slender hips. He'd bet her legs were shapely with muscle.

His cock stirred to life. He moved back to his chair to hide the errant part of his anatomy.

A lovely rose color crept up Sara's face. Thank God her gaze was above his waist. "Um, okay."

"Not used to talking about yourself, either, huh?"

"Uh-uh. Goes against the grain."

"I'm a patient man. Take your time. Too bad we don't have snifters of brandy. We've got the roaring fire and the dog." He angled his chin at Jake, curled up between his dishes and the woodstove and twitching in his sleep.

"Not sure about brandy, but there is booze here." She cast a sidelong look his way. "Are you picky about what kind?"

Jared snorted. "Once upon a time, yeah, but I'll take whatever's available."

287

Sara got to her feet and plucked a headlamp from where it hung on a nail next to the cellar door. "Give me a minute. Stuart liked his liquor. Said it helped him pass the time."

The sounds of her rooting about beneath the cabin's floorboards were interrupted by the *clink* of glass as she set bottles on the floor in front of the opening. He stood and moved to the growing pile of liquor bottles.

"Hey, Sara. That's plenty."

"There are other varieties down here."

"Doesn't matter. I'd rather have your company. There's more hooch here than we could drink in a month."

"Good." Her head appeared as she climbed up the ladder. "Guess it's one thing we won't run out of."

"It's a good disinfectant too." He offered his hand to help her up the last few steps. She clasped it briefly before turning to close the cellar door.

"Yeah, I've heard that." She glanced at the collection of bottles. "Pick your poison."

"Scotch okay?"

She shrugged. "Sure. Not much of a drinker."

"Neither am I, but I do appreciate brandy of an evening. Are there cups?"

Sara walked to the cupboard on the wall cattycorner from the stove and opened it. Cups, bowls, a first aid kit, and tools came into view. She handed him a cup and took one for herself before shutting the cupboard.

Armed with the scotch bottle, he joined her at the table. A cot was pushed against one wall. He'd already decided to offer to sleep on the floor. No way he'd take her bed, even if she offered it. Once they were settled, he poured a couple fingers of amber liquid into each of their glasses. "Your turn." He repeated his earlier words.

She took a contemplative sip from her mug and made a face. "Geez but that shit burns going down."

"You're stalling." He drank from his own mug.

"Probably so, but there isn't all that much to tell. My dad was a Park Ranger in Yosemite. Mom died when I was about ten, so it was just the two of us. I always wanted to follow in his footsteps, so I majored in a field that was likely to get me a job—"

"What field was that?" he cut in.

"Ecology and wildlife management. Ranger jobs were scarce, so I did a stint in the military, mostly to learn to fly helicopters. Once I got out, the Park Service hired me, and it's where I've been ever since."

He waited, but she didn't say anything further. "Well?" he urged.

She took another drink. "Well, what?"

"Same questions you asked me. Is your dad still alive? Are you married? You don't wear a ring, but that doesn't always mean anything."

She glanced at her hands as if to corroborate the absence of a wedding ring. Color stained her face again, and she blew out a breath. "Dad is alive, but he has Alzheimer's and is in a home in Fresno. No husbands. No kids." She glanced away from him. "I'm gone too much for relationships. No one would put up with it."

He almost blurted, *Hey! That's really good news*, but managed to keep the words inside.

"Nothing more to tell," she went on. "Not really. I own a house in Three Rivers and Dad's house in Fresno is deeded to me. It's worth a lot, and I don't guess I really need to keep working, but I love it back here." She spread her arms expansively. "To get paid to do something I love is such a plus. I figured I'd hold onto my post until they tossed me out."

He reached across the small space between them and captured one of her hands with his. "I understand that part because I love the wilds too." He paused, thinking. "Not that I don't appreciate my state-of-the-art lab, but out here is where I feel truly alive. Connected to something bigger than myself."

She raised her gaze to his and smiled warmly. "I feel the same, and that might be a good note to turn in on. While you were taking care of Lonnie and Stuart, I pitched my tent out back, and my bag and pad are there. You take the cot, and I'll see you in the morning."

"Oh, hell no." He sprang to his feet. "I'll bring your bag back inside. I can sleep in your tent, but it's better if I lay my foam mat on the floor in here."

"I already decided—" she began, also on her feet and moving toward the door.

He didn't consider his next move. He just closed the distance between them and wrapped his arms around her from behind. "So did I."

He expected her to pull away from him. Instead, she turned in his arms and laid a hand on each side of his face. "You're a pretty man, Jared. Too pretty. We need to get to know each other a whole lot better before—"

He closed his mouth over hers, cutting off her words. He had no idea where his sudden burst of courage came from. He wasn't generally forward with women, usually waiting to be damned sure they were interested before he made a move.

She tightened her fingers on the sides of his face and opened her mouth beneath his. She tasted of the liquor they'd shared as she teased his tongue with her own. He ran his hands down her back and snugged her against his growing erection. Though his cock had subsided earlier, arousal returned with a vengeance. Her nipples pebbled where they pressed into his chest, and her breath quickened.

Evidence of her arousal stoked his own, and he explored the hard, muscled planes of her back and buttocks with his fingers.

Time dribbled past. He drew away, stroking strands of dark hair away from her face. "You're beautiful."

"So are you." She smiled softly. "But this is enough for now. I really am going outside to my bed now."

"No. You're not." He stepped back, aiming for a return of rational thought. "It's not safe. What if someone comes looking for Lonnie and Stuart?"

"They're not going to show up in the middle of the night," she protested.

"How do you know? We have no idea how their physiology operates. For all we know, they could have exceptional night vision."

"How?" she countered. "Reptiles are cold blooded. They go into a kind of stasis at night. The other half—or whatever percentage it is—is human. How do you get sharp night vision out of that combination?"

He bit back a laugh. "I thought I was the scientist."

"Then think like one."

"I am. I'm also going outside to retrieve your sleeping bag." At the look on her face, he stopped and moved his hands to her shoulders. "I promise to behave, and we truly are safer inside."

From his place near the hearth, Jake *whuffed* as if he agreed.

"What if I don't trust myself not to behave?" She ducked from beneath his hands and shot an impish grin his way.

"We can take turns being strong." He blew out a breath. "And we can talk about what we're doing next. The alien invasion is as good a libido dampener as we're likely to come across."

Sara snorted. "No kidding. Okay. I suppose it would make sense for us to be together, along with a couple of loaded weapons. I'll go outside and collect my stuff. You can get your bag and pad out."

He watched her walk out the door, captivated by the swing of her hips. He tried to focus on what he'd told her. They had bigger problems than the attraction growing between them. He hoped there'd be a time to draw Sara into his arms and make love to her, but that time wasn't tonight.

Pushing his cock to a more comfortable position, he bent to

his backpack and opened the lower compartment to extract his sleeping bag and inflatable foam pad.

∾

SARA WELCOMED the chilly night air on her overheated cheeks. She hadn't meant to let him kiss her, or to kiss him back. It just sort of happened, and it had felt so good, so right, in his arms, she'd gone with the flow. She hadn't made love with anyone for over a year, and her body clamored for more of what she'd just walked away from. Her panties were damp with wanting him, and her breasts felt heavy, their nipples puckered with need.

Ignoring all of it, she unzipped her tent and grabbed her bag and mat. They were the only things she'd put in the tent, so there wasn't anything more to clear. She thought about taking the tent down, but figured morning was soon enough. Still feeling warm from Jared's embrace, she let herself back inside and latched the door. It wasn't much of a lock, but it would buy them time.

Jake would alert them if anyone was outside.

Jared had laid out his things near the stove, so she dropped her bag on the cot and rolled her sleeping pad. She wouldn't need it since the cot had a thin mattress.

"I didn't notice before." His voice caught her by surprise. "But there's a hell of a mess in the far corner that looks like it used to be a radio." He rattled a sheaf of papers. "Are these the dispatches?"

"Yeah. I figured out something was fishy before Lonnie and Stuart showed up with the bird. Jake and I traded the cabin for a vantage point where we could keep an eye on it, but not be seen. I wasn't certain, but I suspected if I waited, something would happen."

"Good instincts." He nodded approvingly.

"Thanks." The unexpected compliment pleased her. "Back to what happened to the radio. After I shot Lonnie and Stuart, I didn't want anyone else trying to contact me, so I took the axe and decimated it. Did you get a chance to look at the dispatches?" She sat on the cot and drew her legs beneath her.

"I skimmed them, but I'd like to do more than that. Thought I'd take them to bed with me. Not quite as scintillating as a novel, but knowledge is our friend. The more we can glean from the information we have, the better we can plan."

"All true, but reading them now isn't a good idea if you want to get any sleep." Sara screwed her face into a moue remembering the tears she'd shed reading those same pages.

"Noted. If I have nightmares, I'll move closer to the dog."

She laughed and bent to unlace her boots, wondering just how much she'd take off. Normally, she slept in her long underwear and down booties. She was already down to her long john top, so all she needed to do was remove her trousers.

For chrissakes, what am I fussing about?

Mentally rolling her eyes at her misplaced modesty—after all, she'd been locked in his arms not half an hour ago—she slithered out of her pants and got into her sleeping bag. The cabin was plenty warm, so she didn't zip it.

"Nice." His dark eyes twinkled. "I was wondering if you'd undress."

"Well, now you know." She was having a hell of a time not beckoning him to her cot for a goodnight hug. To reduce the temptation, she shifted to her side and slitted her eyes watching him unobtrusively. "Good night."

"Night, Sara." He crossed the cabin to her side and bent to kiss the tip of her nose. The gesture was so sweet and spontaneous, it touched her. "If my light bothers you, let me know."

Before she could say anything, he moved to the far side of the cabin. He fiddled with the stove, damping it for the night and stripped to his long underwear before crawling into his bag, using folded clothing for a pillow. Settling his headlamp in place, he flicked it on before turning his attention to the dispatch sheets.

She let her eyes close. She'd watched him almost as closely as he watched her when he removed his shirt and climbing pants and boots. He had exactly the type of body she expected with broad, muscular shoulders and slender hips. His long legs probably ate up trail miles.

He'd mentioned coming over Glacier Divide. She wondered if he was a climber as well as a backpacker. There weren't any easy routes over the divide. They all required guts and skill.

Her eyes felt heavy, gritty. It had been a hell of a day. She almost couldn't believe it was the same one when she'd killed Lonnie and Stuart, but it was.

Yeah, but it's also the day I met Jared and found out it wasn't just me and Jake against the aliens.

Jake made little noises in his sleep, the ones that meant he might be dreaming about killing small rodents. She fell asleep between the dog's yips and the gentle bob of Jared's headlamp.

A GROWL PUNCTUATED by one short, sharp bark slammed her awake, heart beating fast. Sara bolted upright, feeling for her headlamp.

Jake nosed her arm, still growling low in his throat.

"Hush. Quiet." She kept her voice low. Jake quit snarling, but he stood right next to her, tension pouring off his furred form.

"No lights." Jared was by her side in an instant. He whispered the words near her ear before moving away.

Probably a good move to keep things dark. Lights would alert whoever was out there, make them cautious. She pulled on clothes by feel. Rustling from across the room told her Jared was doing the same.

It was still black as pitch outside. She held a hand over her watch to shield the luminosity and clicked a button to check the time. Four in the morning. What was out there? Had Jake overreacted?

Not likely. He's trained as a guard dog.

She hadn't heard rotors, but maybe she wouldn't have since she'd been asleep.

Jared settled next to her on the cot and placed an arm around her, positioning his mouth near her ear. "I'm going out there. I didn't hear anything until the dog barked, and I wasn't asleep, so that means whoever's here came on foot."

Sara gripped his upper leg. "No." She whispered back. "We go together."

"Too dangerous. I'm bringing a gun. It's dark. I don't want to shoot you by mistake. Keep Jake inside too."

She squeezed his leg harder. "Jake is trained for shit like this. He and I are used to working as a team—"

"You are not going out there without me." Even in a whisper, his voice thrummed with determination.

Sara rotated her shoulder blades, trying to move the iron bar of tension that had dropped between them. What the hell had alerted Jake? "Okay. We'll both go." She got to her feet and walked to the door, pulling the latch as quietly as she could. The dog hugged her side like a shadow.

The minute the door was open, he shoved his muzzle through scenting the air. He'd chase whatever he scented if she gave the command, but she didn't. God only knew what he'd run into, and she wanted to keep him safe. She held perfectly still, listening intently, but didn't hear a thing.

Jake wasn't pulling against the hand she had around his collar. "It's odd," she murmured, "but I don't think anyone's out here."

"I was going to say the same thing. Call it a sixth sense or something. Let's just check around the cabin, though. Maybe we'll see footprints that don't belong to us—or some evidence of something."

"Think the headlamps are okay?"

"Yeah, I do."

She glanced at his boots and clicked on her lamp to see better. "Asolo. Maybe elevens?"

"Close. Twelves. Good eyes."

"I've done a lot of tracking. Need to sort out which prints belong to you." She turned her attention to the dog. "Track but stay close."

Tail pluming, Jake bounded off the porch and down half a dozen steps into the yard. Sara followed him, rounding the corner of the cabin. At first, it didn't register, but when she saw the dog circling, she froze.

Her tent was gone.

"Jared."

He came at a dead run. "What?"

She pointed. "Someone was here. They took my tent. This is where I had it pitched." She bent, examining the ground. "Look." She extended a hand. "Here. And here. Two sets of boot prints. No. One of them are tennis shoes."

"What the hell?" He bent to examine the areas she indicated. "Should we follow them? They have to be human. Those things I burned walked upright on hind feet that looked like they belonged on a small dinosaur."

Sara considered it. "Whoever it is, they're scared, or they would've just knocked on the door. Maybe they've been watching the cabin. Backcountry travelers do that sometimes. They hang around and wait for the ranger to come back—except whoever it is, is probably scared shitless because of what happened."

"And keeping a very low profile."

Jake barked softly, probably hoping she'd loose him to track whoever had stolen her tent.

"How about a compromise?" she suggested. "Let's go back to bed. Once it's light and we've had some breakfast, we'll let Jake follow their tracks."

"Good enough for me. At least it's not the fucking aliens. I've been worried they'd come hunting for two of their own."

Sara exhaled sharply. "They still might. It's been less than twenty-four hours since Lonnie and Stuart showed up here." She led the way back inside, clucking to the dog. Jake followed her in, but the set of his tail told her he'd rather be on the prowl.

She pulled her gun from its holster and thumbed on the safety. Jared did the same, but with far less ease. "How long since you're fired one of these?" she asked.

He shrugged. "Maybe fifteen years, but it's like riding a bicycle—"

She slugged him in the arm. "Shit too. If I wasn't worried about burning through shells, I'd stand you some target practice. As it is, I just hope you have a steady hand."

He glanced at her, humor dancing in the depths of his eyes. "The hand that wields the scalpel rules the world."

Sara burst out laughing. "Cradle. That was cradle. And rocks, not wields."

"Whatever. Night." He headed for his sleeping bag.

She was still chortling when she crawled into hers.

CHAPTER 25

*J*ared woke to a gray dawn. Sometime during the last part of the night, Jake had moved next to Sara and was curled on the floor by her cot. The dog flicked an ear his way, but didn't get up. Sara slept on her side, her head cradled on an arm, her hair spilled around her like a dark, shimmering flood.

He took advantage of the moment to study her, enjoying the view. He wanted to cross the cabin and sink his fingers into all her glorious hair just before he kissed her, but they had work to do. He'd read everything that had come through on the radio about the alien invasion. As he read, something about the intergalactic trade agreement rang distant bells in his memory.

The U.S. space program had unearthed about six planets with intelligent life. He'd studied some of them as an undergraduate. While items from Earth traveled to other planets with some level of regularity, the reverse didn't seem to apply. Reading between the lines, Earth had stopped sending goods, which led to a particular planet declaring war. Even though the dispatches stopped shy of saying it, he figured the aliens needed to bond with humans to survive in

Earth's atmosphere. It was the only explanation that made sense. Otherwise, why go to the trouble of grabbing up people to merge with, when killing them would be faster and easier.

Sara's eyes fluttered open. "Morning. How long have you been up?" She stretched her arms over her head. The movement pushed the upper part of her breasts out of her sleeping bag. She still wore her long underwear top, but it didn't leave much to the imagination.

"Not long." His resolve to be all business this morning evaporated, and he left the warmth of his bag and crossed to the cot.

She patted the place next to her, and he perched on the cot's wooden frame. "Did anyone ever tell you what amazing hair you have?" He wound a curl around his fingers.

"Not lately." Sara opened her arms. "Come here, but only for a minute. We need to get moving."

"I know." He wrapped his arms around her and felt hers close behind his back. Her breath was warm against his face before he kissed her. Arousal raged through him, shocking in its intensity. He held her more tightly, enjoying the press of her breasts against his chest as he teased her mouth with his lips.

She splayed her hands across his back, strong fingers holding on tight. He wanted to lay next to her, but if he did that, they'd both be lost, so he kept his feet on the floor. She made a small moaning sound. Her nipples felt like polished stones through the thin fabric of her shirt, and her lips clung to his while she buried her tongue in his mouth.

His cock was bent at an uncomfortable angle, but it just grew harder and harder, perilously close to spontaneous release. He moved a hand to her breast and twirled the nipple between his thumb and forefinger. He hadn't meant to, but his hand developed a mind of its own.

Sara pressed into him, hips writhing with wanting the same

thing he wanted. She tore her mouth from his. "Please. Maybe it's wrong and too soon and all those things, but—"

"Sara, darling." He swung his legs onto the bed and pressed the length of his body against hers. She tugged the unzipped sleeping bag out of the way and wrapped her legs around one of his, pressing the heat of her core against him.

He reached down and straightened his cock. Even the brush of his hands against his ridged flesh almost made him come. He focused on her breast beneath his hands and then moved down to take her nipple in his mouth, pushing her shirt up and out of the way first. She gasped, and buried her fingers in his hair while her hips bucked hard against his thigh.

The scent of her arousal filled him with need, sharp, urgent. He pushed a hand between her legs under her long johns, rubbing the swollen nubbin slick with her juices. He didn't realize she'd moved her hand until it closed around his erection, warm, tight, sure. He thrust against her grip, not recognizing the feral sounds emerging from his throat as belonging to him.

Because they were so new, he didn't know exactly what she needed, so he experimented with how he touched her, alternating rolling her clit between his fingers with rubbing it in hard little circles. Her breath came fast, and color splotched across her face. He pushed two fingers inside her, while still pressing on her nubbin with his palm, wanting to feel when she came. Concentrating on her pleasure helped keep his in check.

Her pussy dissolved around his hand in a flood of liquid heat. He kept on rubbing until the spasms of her release slowed. When he finally let go of her breast and raised his gaze to her face, she gifted him with a lazy smile.

"Your turn." She slithered around and licked the head of his cock, while still pumping the shaft with her hand.

Jared gave himself up to sensation. Between her mouth and tongue swirling around the tip of his cock and her hands on the shaft, his balls tightened against his body. Semen boiled out so hard, the jets were almost painful. She licked and sucked until he was dry and then curled against his belly, fingers stroking his legs, stomach, and deflating cock.

"That was lovely, but we should get moving," she said and let go of him, moving back up his body until they were face to face.

"Taskmaster." He kissed her. Tasting himself on her tongue made him swell again.

She wriggled away. "Someone needs to be. I know how this goes. We're like kids with a new toy, and we could stay here and fuck each other senseless for days." A solemn expression crossed her face. "Given what we're facing, that's not a good idea."

"You're right." He tucked hair behind one of her ears. "Before we move into today, I want to say a couple things." Jared hurried on before he lost his nerve. "I love what we just did together. I don't make love often. It's been a long time since I've had a woman in my life—or in my bed."

A pleased look crossed her face. "Even if you're just saying that—"

"I'm not," he broke in. "What would the percentage be? You may not like some of what you hear from me, but what I say is the truth. Win, lose, or draw."

"Haven't heard that expression for a long time. It's the same for me. It's been a long time since I made love. Now let's get moving. If we're going to track whoever stole my tent, they've had a hell of a head start."

He kissed her one more time, and rolled to his feet. A peek in the stove told him enough coals remained to start a new fire, so he shaved wood off a block with a small axe and fed them into the stove until they kindled.

Sara moved past him, fully dressed, and opened the door. "Be right back," she said.

Jared grinned at her. "Coffee and energy bars okay for breakfast?"

"Better than okay, since we need to turn Jake loose tracking."

The dog woofed softly on hearing his name and followed Sara out the door.

Jared tossed bigger pieces of wood into the stove and then got dressed. The warm glow in his belly from the wonder of Sara in his arms pulsed brightly. The feel of her beneath his fingers when she came made him hard again, and he rolled his eyes. He hadn't been this horny in years. Maybe part of it was their situation, but a much bigger part was Sara. It wouldn't take much for him to fall head over heels down the well in love.

SARA TOSSED BACK the remains of her coffee and threw things into her empty backpack. A first aid kit, extra clothes, a water bottle, and snacks. They'd had a quick bite. Oatmeal along with energy bars, and hadn't been able to keep their eyes—or hands—off one another. Happiness surged. Jared was different from other men in her life. Sure of himself, not put off by her independence. Maybe, just maybe if they got out of this in one piece, something solid could grow between them.

"I can carry some stuff." Jared walked to her side. "My pack is mostly empty."

"It's all good. I don't have much. Compared with an overnight bag, this is nothing. Let's take a better look at where my tent was before we leave. We should be able to determine which direction they came from and where they headed."

"Regardless." He opened the door for her. "We should be able to get your tent back."

Jake nosed past him and trotted to Sara's side, tail pluming, breath steamy in the chill air of early morning.

She stopped at the bottom of the steps and turned to him. "Oh, I don't care about the tent. It's regulation Park Service. There are two more just like it in the cellar, and another two or three back at McClure—if we ever go back there. I'm much more interested in other survivors."

"My thoughts, exactly."

She walked around the cabin and hunkered to get a closer look at the ground. "They came from the south, and not on the beaten track off the Muir Trail, either. Look there." She extended a hand.

"So maybe they're keeping clear of the trail."

"Could be. You did."

"True. Caught me dead to rights." He strode to a few stones and bent to examine them.

"What'd you find?" She joined him.

He fingered darker places on the granite. "Blood. It might belong to an animal, but my bet is one of our nightly visitors is hurt." He straightened. "Do you have a paramedic pack in the cabin?"

Sara frowned, thinking. "Maybe. If we do, it'd be in the cellar. Why do we need one? I have a first aid kit. I'm an EMT, and my kit usually has everything I'm comfortable using."

"Because the paramedic packs have a lot more in them. If someone is injured, I might need things beyond two-by-two squares and bandage tape."

"I thought you didn't treat people."

"I don't. Not anymore, but there was a time when I did." He mock slugged her in the arm. "It's kind of like with the gun. You never truly forget."

"Here." She held out a key. "We never did lock up. It's the same one that opens the cellar."

He dropped his pack near her with an easy grace and sprinted back around the building. She watched the play of his muscles as he moved, and her belly clenched with sudden fierce need. What they'd done an hour before barely whetted her appetite. She wanted the cock she'd held in her hand. Wanted it buried deep in her body. He had a wonderful penis. Long and thick and proud, springing from a mat of tawny hair. She'd loved how he felt in her mouth, and the untamed noises when he came, pumping salty, tangy semen into her mouth.

She wriggled, her pussy awash in moisture again.

"Got it." He rounded the corner of the cabin, a red and white bag clasped in one hand. He gave her the key and dropped the medical supplies into his pack. That done, he swung the pack onto his back and buckled it into place.

Sara dropped a hand to Jake's shoulder and said, "Track."

The big dog moved at an easy pace. He knew from all his training he needed to wait for his human team. Outrunning them didn't serve any purpose. He kept his nose low to the ground, lifting it from time to time to scent the air as well as the ground. Sara had done this with him many, many times, and she trusted him implicitly.

"They may have come from the south," Jared said, "but they're moving northwest now."

"Keep your eyes open for more blood."

"Good idea. Ashamed I didn't think of it." He paused. "Maybe because I'd rather look at you."

"Flattery will get you everywhere." She flashed a grin. "Wish the dog could talk."

"What would he be able to tell us?"

"Lots of things. How cold the trail is. About how long since they walked this way. How many there were. What sex." She tugged her GPS out of its belt holster and set it to backtrack.

"Smart. It'll make getting back easier."

Sara shrugged. "The ground is mostly soft enough, we could follow our tracks. I'm just being lazy." They walked in a companionable silence for a while, moving ever deeper into difficult terrain dotted with large talus blocks and tangles of manzanita and willow bushes.

Jared lifted his head, squinting at the cloud cover. "It's cold enough to snow again. If it does, tracking our route using footprints could get challenging. Never mind we've been boulder hopping these past few minutes."

"You noticed." She grinned. "This is child's play compared with Glacier Divide."

He made a noise between a snort and a grunt. "Yeah. Almost bit off more than I could chew up there. The last part required a heaping dose of confidence on my part."

"And a few leaps from your legs as well?" she inquired archly.

"Yeah, that too."

Jake ran ahead. He barked once and stopped, his ears pricked forward, clearly waiting for her. She squatted next to him and asked, "Is this it?" Another quick, short woof.

"What—?" Jared began, but she waved him to silence and straightened, still next to her dog.

"Sara Holcomb." She raised her voice. "U.S. Park Service. Do you require assistance?"

Silence met her words, so she repeated them. Still nothing.

"Dr. Jared Donovan," he called. "Someone is injured. I've seen the blood. I can help." He turned to Sara and lowered his voice. "Why'd Jake stop tracking? He could've led us right to where they are."

"Because we're close," she murmured back. "He's trained not to run right into people, so he won't scare them, and maybe get himself shot if someone's the least bit trigger happy."

"Guess you're not the only gunslinger in the park."

She snorted. "You'd be surprised what rules people break."

"I know you're here," she called again. "My dog tracked you. I'm human. I won't hurt you."

Jared moved closer to her and spoke near her ear. "What do we do if they don't show themselves?"

Sara blew out a tightly held breath. "They will. I know how scared I was up in the Muir Hut, and I don't scare easy. I'm guessing this is just a couple of backpackers who got stuck—kind of like you did."

"Not exactly." A slightly built man with dirty blond dreadlocks sidled from the cover of a nearby grove of trees. Nondescript clothing was torn and smeared with dirt.

Jake, who'd been standing at attention, stiffened further. Hackles rose along his spine, and he growled softly.

"How many are with you?" Sara narrowed her eyes. Just because she'd only identified two sets of prints didn't mean anything.

"A few," the man said evasively.

"You'll have to say more than that." Jared took a step forward. "We offered to help you, despite the fact you stole Federal property."

"Hush." Sara shushed him and focused on the stranger. "I'm guessing you needed shelter."

"We did. Still do, actually, since that was only a two-man tent."

His words registered. "So there are more than two of you, and you came into the backcountry without shelter this late in the year." Sara stated it as fact, because she was almost certain it was true.

"Yes, there are more than two of us. And yes, we didn't bring what we'd need. This wasn't exactly a planned expedition. We were lucky to escape with our hides intact." A corner of the man's mouth twisted wryly, and his blue eyes held a haunted edge.

"Who are you, exactly?" Jared asked. "We know what you're running from, but how'd you end up here?"

"It's all right, Kevin." A plump, redhead joined the man. Her clothing was as dirty as his, and she wore an ancient pair of tennis shoes. One arm was wrapped in a blood-soaked bandage.

"What happened to your arm?" Jared trotted to the woman's side.

Sara winced. As gun shy as these people were, he probably should've waited before moving closer, but she understood he wanted to help.

The woman leaned into Kevin and gazed at Jared through

worried-looking green eyes. "You must be the one who said you were an MD."

"That's right." Jared nodded. "What happened to your arm?" he repeated.

"A big rock fell on it getting in here. It's broken, and the bone's poking out. Hurts like a bitch if I move it wrong."

Jared slipped his pack off his shoulders and rooted around, coming up with the paramedic supplies he'd had the foresight to bring. He stood next to the woman. "Do I have your permission to look at your arm and fix it if I can?"

She nodded, clearly miserable. "I'm probably a goner, anyway. I'm sure I have an infection from the compound fracture, and we didn't have any antibiotics." Shrugging, she winced. "Even if we did, this is way bigger than something like penicillin could address."

"Are you a doctor too?" Jared asked. Reaching out, he began unwinding the bandage. After a muted yelp, the woman quieted, but strain showed in lines around her eyes and the tense set of her shoulders.

"No. An electrical engineer with a biomedical background. My name is Christine."

Jared pulled a syringe from the bag and filled it from a bottle Sara couldn't see clearly. "Okay, Christine. I'm going to give you an injection of something to deaden the pain, so I can work on your arm."

"Fine." She nodded tersely. "Do it."

Sara turned away from Jared. He clearly didn't need anything from her. Facing Kevin, she asked "Who are you? How many in your party, and how'd you end up out here? Do you have enough food?"

"Lot of questions," Kevin countered.

"Yeah, and so far you haven't even ponied up one answer. I'm as close to the law as you'll find out here, and I need to know more about you."

He drew his blond brows together and seemed to come to a conclusion. Turning, he whistled a high clear note, followed by two short bursts. People walked into the clearing from several directions.

Sara waited, counting as they came. Not counting herself and Jared, twenty-one men and women stood in the small clearing. Kevin and the broken-arm woman, plus nineteen others. They all had the same end-of-the-world-survivor patina with tattered, dirt-smeared clothing. Only a few had jackets.

"Wow!" Sara let her gaze drift over the group. "We never write wilderness permits for more than fifteen."

"Like I said," Kevin cut in, "this wasn't exactly a well-planned trip. We didn't have much notice, and we sure as hell didn't stop to get a wilderness permit—"

"You're talking in circles." Sara interrupted him, not in the mood for a game of twenty questions. "Why are you in the backcountry? More pertinently, how'd you escape annihilation from the ships?"

"You're still here." Kevin stared her down.

"Yes, but I work here, and from the looks of things, I know a shitload more than you do about how to survive out-of-doors."

"You may as well tell her," a dark-haired man called.

"Yeah," a woman chimed in. "What the hell can she do to us?"

Sara gritted her teeth in frustration. She felt like tugging her service revolver from its holster and firing a few shots in the air to drag words from them. "Tell me what?" she demanded. "You snuck up on my cabin like thieves last night. You stole my tent."

"You weren't using it," another man pointed out.

"Not pertinent. Part of the backcountry creed is you never, never take what doesn't belong to you. You have no idea why that tent was left there. What if someone was counting on it being there for them? What if it meant the difference between survival and death? My ranger cabin is locked when I'm not in it." Fueled by frustration, anger got the better of her, and she balled her hands into fists.

Still by her side, Jake growled.

When she glanced over to Jared and the woman, she saw he'd gotten the bandage off. Christine's arm was a mangled mess with what looked like the beginnings of gangrene, and it held the sticky-sweet stench of rotting flesh. She hadn't been far off when she diagnosed herself as being done for.

"We're the reason you're in this predicament," Kevin said.

"Huh?" She stared at him. "You have to say more because I don't understand."

A woman with short, dark hair stepped away from the group and squared her shoulders. "We're the original group of NASA scientists who crafted the intergalactic trade agreements. And also the same ones who exited out of those agreements when it became clear the aliens planned to strip Earth of all its resources."

Sara shook her head. "But that's what they're doing now, and killing everyone in their path. How'd you save us from anything?"

"It's a long story," Kevin said. "Turned out we didn't know a bunch of important things. If we'd pulled the plug six months earlier, things would've been fine."

"We don't know that," the dark-haired woman cut in. "A year would've been safer."

"Whatever," Kevin snapped. "We had a small amount of advance warning, which is how we ended up here."

"Enough warning to flee, not enough to equip yourselves." Sara filled in details.

"That's about right," the woman replied.

Sara narrowed her eyes to slits. "Did you warn anyone? Like the government, for example? Or did you just try to save yourselves?"

"We told the Pentagon." Kevin made a sour face. "They didn't believe us. Or they didn't want to risk offending the aliens. Net effect was the same."

Sara ran her practiced eyes over the group. They looked like they'd walked through Hell. "It's been cold at night. Any injuries or fatalities beyond the broken arm over there?"

"Three of us didn't make it," Kevin said. "One probably had a heart attack. Another didn't wake up one morning, and the third was attacked by a mountain lion. By the time we got to her, she was already dead."

"Cougars don't frequent the high country," Sara protested. "That's very unusual."

"We weren't in the high country," the dark-haired woman said. "We walked in from Wishon Reservoir. Knew we were running out of time, and we were afraid if we took the time to drive to one of the high trailheads, they'd nab us."

"We're the ones who fucked them over," Kevin muttered. "They know who we are."

"Okay." Sara walked to Jared. Jake shadowed her, not leaving her side. "You hearing all this?" she asked.

"Every word," Jared replied and continued his ministrations. The bone no longer protruded through flesh, but that was the only positive as far as she could see. The redhead's face had turned a pasty color, and blood showed where she'd bitten her lower lip. She sat on the ground with Jared beside her.

"Had you planned how to feed yourselves?" Sara addressed Kevin and the dark-haired woman.

"Not exactly." Kevin seemed to be picking his words again.

"Humph. Unless we get lucky and shoot something really big, there's no way I have provisions for all of you." Sara shook her head. Maybe burning Lonnie and Stuart had been a tactical error after all.

"It's all right." The dark-haired woman patted Kevin's arm, then turned to face Sara. "We didn't expect to be back here all that long. There's a good reason the aliens want to kill us. We're the only ones who know how to send them back to where they came from."

CHAPTER 26

"Yes," the redhead croaked from where she sat next to Jared. "Problem is we've been on the move ever since we left the cars at Wishon, and we need twenty-four hours in one place to put our plan into action. Maybe as much as thirty-six. So far we've been on the move every six to eight hours."

"So that means they're after you," Jared said. "You didn't fake them out by running into the wilderness."

"That's exactly what it means," the woman replied, making a sour face.

"How can you tell when they're getting close?" Sara asked. Curiosity lined her question.

Jared poured disinfectant over the gangrened arm in front of him. It wouldn't do much good, but lacking an intravenous antibiotic, it was the best the woman would get.

"Electronics tuned to their particular frequency," Kevin spoke up. "We designed a tracking device once we became concerned they weren't happy with the amount of minerals they purchased from us."

"It would be best if we could leave this open to drain," Jared told the woman. "Can you tolerate it that way?"

She gave a sad, little shrug. "I know enough to understand I'm dying, and it won't be pretty. What difference does it make?"

"The odds aren't in your favor," he agreed, "but it's not one hundred percent hopeless. Your body could fight off the infection."

"We can leave it open." She met his gaze for the first time. "Thank you."

"You're welcome." He shouldered his pack and made his way to a small creek where he rinsed his hands before joining Sara and Jake. "Don't know about you," he said, "but I'd like to hear more about that electronic tracking system."

A high, thin wail blared from somewhere behind him, and he twisted his head. "What the hell was that?"

"Our electronics." Christine struggled to her feet, grunting with the effort. "I'm the systems engineer who designed them. Before you ask," she walked slowly toward the noise, "it alerts us before they're close enough to get a bead on us. It's the only reason any of us are still alive."

"So basically you've relocated every time your alarm system went off?" Jared asked.

"That's about the size of it," Kevin said.

Jared turned to Sara. "Didn't you say the Muir Hut made you invisible to the ships?" When she nodded, he went on. "I found the same thing. I hunkered under two overlapping boulders the first few days after the attack."

"Good piece of intel," Kevin said. "Now all we need to do is find a place made of stone where several of us could stay long enough to fix this mess."

"But no one's left," Sara protested. "What good will fixing anything do now?"

"There are people left." The dark-haired woman stepped forward. "I'm Vivian, by the way." She grimaced. "If you got hold of official-looking dispatches, they were fake. Lots of people are dead, but nothing like what they want you to believe. It was part of their strategy to demoralize everyone, so they'd play along."

"I need more information," Jared muttered. "Lots more."

The siren blared louder, and Christine walked forward cradling something in her good arm. She stared intently at it and made a few adjustments. "Need to move that way." She pointed back the direction they'd come.

"I want to know more too," Sara said. "One of you needs to come up with at least an annotated version of what's going on while we're walking. Do you have things to gather?"

Vivian nodded. "Yeah, but we'll be ready to roll in less than five."

Jared watched her and the others walk away. "What do you think?" he asked Sara, keeping his voice too low to be overheard.

She squinched her forehead in thought. "I don't know. Either they're on the up-and-up, or they're nuts."

"It's unlikely so many would share a delusion," he said. "Plus, there'd be no percentage in them lying to us."

"Same conclusion I came to." She shook her head. "If stone will do the trick, maybe I could chopper them up to the hut. That alert device of theirs might make the trip less dangerous."

"Let's see what they have to say, first."

Instead of answering, she leaned into him for the briefest moment. Her action warmed him, made it feel like they were truly a couple. He wrapped an arm around her and held her close before letting go.

The NASA group gathered in twos and threes. When everyone was accounted for, they set off, using Christine's device as a guide for which way to go. Jared and Sara flanked Kevin and Vivian, with Jake by Sara's side.

"Go ahead," Sara urged. "Fill us in."

"I've been thinking about how to do that," Kevin replied.

"Don't think too hard." Jared couldn't keep suspicion out of his voice. "Just plunge right in and tell us."

"The background doesn't matter much," Vivian said. "What does is the aliens are dependent on a harmonic from their ships."

"They have trouble with the atmosphere here," Kevin broke in. "Too much carbon dioxide for their physiology. It's why they've merged with humans."

"Even doing that," Vivian picked up the recitation, "they still require a particular frequency that their ships generate. Without it, they'll lose their ability to breathe."

"We have a generator that should interrupt the harmonic," Kevin said. "But it needs to run continuously for a minimum of twenty-four hours. Thirty-six would be even better. After that, any aliens left here would certainly be dead."

"What's to stop more of them from arriving?" Sara asked.

"Fear?" Kevin laughed hollowly. "Their only chance was to strike fast and hard."

"We never actually thought they would," Vivian said. "But they have an inexhaustible appetite for trace minerals that they used up on their world. It's why they approached us in the first place about a trade."

"What was in it for us?" Jared asked.

"Money. Learning more about another race." Kevin shrugged. "At first it seemed like an ideal match, but that was over five years ago. Over time, their requirements escalated until we couldn't meet their needs."

"Are you sure this harmonic deal will work?" Sara demanded.

Kevin nodded. "Absolutely. I created it with Vivian and a couple of the others. We worked offline, since our funding doesn't encompass developing destructive technology."

"Has it been tested?" Jared asked.

"Not outside our lab," Vivian admitted, "but I have confidence in it." She paused a beat. "More importantly, the aliens believe we hold the key to their destruction. It's the only reason they'd have come after us. We used to be their friends since we were their initial point of contact on Earth."

Jared looked around them and recognized ground they'd covered earlier in the day. "We're not far from the ranger station," he said. "Does the fact that the siren quieted down mean we're safe?"

"For now," Kevin said, "but not for long. They always come back and try again."

"Hold your people here," Sara instructed. "I want to talk with Jared."

"You got it." Vivian settled on a large, flat stone. "None of us are backcountry travelers. I don't think I've gotten even one night's sleep since we hatched up this plan, and I'm beat."

Jared was glad Sara suggested a pow-wow, so he didn't have to, and he walked by her side to a fast running creek a few feet away. Jake trotted along, nuzzling Sara's hand.

She took off her pack and sat on it, patting the ground next to her. "What do you think?"

"Funny." He eased his pack off and sat next to her. "I was going to ask you the same thing."

"Well, they believe what they just told us. Even if I'm skeptical, I still think I owe humanity getting them to a place they can work undisturbed."

"It's more than one chopper ride. How many can you take at a time?"

"Maybe six plus me. So you're right about it being more than one trip. I suppose we could hike it, but it's a three thousand foot climb, and some of them look like they couldn't walk that far. Certainly not fast enough to stay out of harm's way. Once you hit the lakes, it's pretty exposed because it's above timberline."

"I don't like the odds of you making multiple trips with the helicopter." He laid a protective hand over one of hers.

She shot him a crooked smile. "Neither do I, but what choice do we have? I'm the only one here who can fly—"

"You don't know that," he broke in. "I just found you. I don't want anything to happen to you."

"Noted." She moved so her side pressed against his. "And appreciated, but I'll do what I have to. Chances of one of them being a chopper pilot are slim."

"True. Let's see. Twenty one of them means four trips."

"Not necessarily. Maybe some of them could walk it. If they could, that might cut it down to three. Maybe all of them don't need to be there to activate whatever technology they brought with them."

He pulled her into a quick, hard embrace. "I'd feel better if it were two—or maybe only one trip. Let's see what their minimal requirements are for whatever equipment and manpower they need to get this done."

Sara angled her face and brushed her lips over his. This kiss was brief and sweet, and it filled him with the need to protect her from every bad thing in the world.

He cupped the side of her face. "Sara. I don't want you risking yourself."

She smiled. "Silly. It's what I do for a living. You like who I am. Don't go all Neanderthal and try to change me."

"Good point." He grinned back. "Guess my first move—assuming we get back in one piece—will be learning to fly helicopters, so I can help out."

"Getting out of this unscathed is a pretty big assumption. Let's get through the next part first."

"Wise woman." His kissed her and got to his feet, extending a hand to help her up. She didn't need assistance, but he liked touching her. Jake licked his hand, and he ruffled the big dog's fur.

They made their way back to the group.

"I have a helicopter," Sara said without preamble. "Are any of you licensed pilots?"

Kevin shook his head. "Sadly, no."

Sara set her mouth in a determined line. "I can fly some of you up to the Muir Hut. It's made of stone, and it protected me from the ships. They couldn't sense me when I was inside."

Kevin's dour expression shifted for the first time. "That would be great. How soon could we go?"

"How many of you does the equipment require?" Jared asked.

"Twelve," Vivian said. "We have three mini-generators, and the timing of their output is critical. We need an A team and a B team, since one will sleep while the other mans the generators. Thirty-six hours is too long for anyone to maintain the level of attention these generators need."

"And Christine. We need her to monitor her early warning system," Kevin added.

Jared added the numbers. "So each generator needs two people to operate it." When Kevin nodded, he went on. "Two active and two resting times three yields the twelve."

"We hope that will be enough," Vivian said, sounding worried. "When we begin transmitting, there'll be a few hours when the aliens will panic. They'll know it's us and escalate their efforts to locate us."

"Well, they won't be able to find you in the Muir Hut," Sara said. "I'm confident of that."

"Yes, the thirteen of us there should be fine." Kevin spoke slowly. "This is likely a death sentence for the other eight."

"Is there room in the hut for all of us?" Vivian asked.

Sara started to nod, but Jared cut her off. "Probably, but the helicopter has limited capacity. Every single trip puts Sara at risk."

"Could some of us walk there?" Kevin asked. "How far is it?"

"Seven miles," Sara replied.

"That doesn't sound too bad," Vivian said.

"It's also three thousand feet of climbing," Sara added. "I could make it in two hours. It would likely take you five or six."

"That's too long," Vivian murmured.

"Why would Christine need to be in the hut?" Jared asked.

"Seems her radar system would do more good for those of you who aren't there."

"Of course you're right." Kevin clamped his mouth into a straight line. "I wasn't thinking. Or rather, I'm used to thinking of all of us together, since we each have specific tasks…" His voice ran down.

"Let's go back to the ranger station," Sara suggested. "Talk among yourselves and decide who will be in the first bird. It won't take long to fly to the hut, but you have to be ready to exit the bird immediately after I set it down, which means any equipment you need will be strapped to your bodies. That way I won't have to wait for you to hand things out."

"Got it." Kevin waved the others into motion and they headed toward the trail.

The rise and fall of his voice reached Jared, but he didn't work to sort out the conversation. He was too worried about Sara. Even though the logical part of his brain told him he was full of crap, the other side knew that if anything happened to her, it would be his fault for not protecting her.

He'd finally found a woman he could love, and he wanted to do everything in his power to keep her by his side.

SARA STOOD by the door of the chopper and counted as six NASA scientists, including Kevin, piled inside. The mini-generators were packaged into backpacks. Per Jared's suggestion, Christine remained at LeConte. In truth, she was too ill to do anything else. The radar unit would be with Sara while she flew, but she'd return it to Christine and the others once the flights were done.

She started up the chopper's ladder-like steps, but Jared gripped her wrist. "Do not take any unnecessary chances."

She flushed, pleased he cared, but feeling smothered. "I've been taking care of myself back here for a long time. Stick with our plan, okay?"

"You got it." He let go, and she vaulted into her seat, shutting the door behind her. The best plan they'd come up with was if she wasn't back in half an hour, he'd start up the trail with Jake and the other sidearm. Christine's radar sat next to Sara on the floor, mercifully silent.

Jake whined, staring at the closed helicopter door.

"I know." Jared petted the shepherd's head. "No room for you, plus you're safer here."

Jake barked once, the tone making it known he disagreed vehemently.

Sara leaned out the open window next to her seat. "Take care of each other."

Jared gave her a thumbs-up, and she engaged the engine. Once the rotors began thumping, she couldn't hear anything else from outside. She hoped Christine's warning system could be heard over the engine noise.

Guess I'll find out.

She checked her instruments and fed fuel to the chopper's engine. Her heart thudded against her chest. Once she'd returned from McClure, she didn't plan to use the bird again—certainly not this soon.

Kevin sat in the copilot's seat. "Thank you for doing this for us."

She glanced at him. "Did I have a choice?"

"Sure. We always have choices. You did the right thing."

"We'll be staying low," she cautioned him. "Just so it doesn't alarm you."

"Got it."

All too soon, they left trees where she might hide herself. Angling the bird, she almost clipped the top of Muir Pass before setting down.

"Watch the prop wash," she cautioned and jumped to the

ground, waiting for them to pile out. It didn't happen as fast as she wanted, but nor did she hear the whine of Christine's radar.

Sara didn't let herself think. She clambered back into the bird and let it drop below the pass. Though she scanned the horizon, she didn't see any other craft.

"One more trip," she muttered. "This one went okay. The next one will too."

Her hand slipped on the cyclic, and she realized it was slick with sweat. Moments later, she landed on the squared off pad next to LeConte. The minute she was out of the chopper, Jake jumped on her, and Jared pulled her into his arms.

"I love you guys." Tension thrummed through her as she petted Jake and hugged Jared. "But I'm only half done."

The second group streamed into the chopper. Not willing to be excluded a second time, Jake wriggled his way in, and she didn't have the heart to chase him out.

Vivian took the copilot's seat. Her face held a drawn look. "Jesus, but I want this to be over with," she said as the chopper gained altitude.

"That would be all of us," Sara said.

"You don't get it." Vivian shook her head. "This whole trade agreement was my idea. My baby. I pushed it through Congress."

"You couldn't have known," Sara protested.

"Maybe I wasn't looking closely enough." Vivian's voice was filled with recrimination. "I was so anxious to have a batch of aliens to study up-close and personal, I'd have done damn near anything to make it happen."

From its spot on the floor, the radar began its high, thin whine.

"Crap! Fuck! Shit!" Sara eyed where they were. Still in trees, but they'd thinned out. "I'm putting us down."

"What about the hut?" Vivian demanded. "Christine's device is just a warning they're close. They can't see us yet."

Sara wasn't listening, wasn't willing to take the chance. She dropped elevation and hovered, landing on uneven ground that made the craft tilt a bit to one side. At least the radar quieted.

She killed the engine and pushed the door open. "Everybody out," she called.

"What happens next?" someone asked.

Sara didn't answer until all of them were lined up next to the chopper. Jake remained inside, perched in the doorway, ready to come to her aid if need be.

"The way I see it," she eyed the group, "you have two choices. It's not a bad walk to the hut from here. Only about two miles, and we knocked off most of the climbing." She hurried on before anyone could step in with an opinion. "As I see it, the main problem is whether you take the radar unit with you, or leave it with me to protect the others."

"Radar stopped squealing," one of the men noted. "You could fly us the rest of the way."

Sara shook her head. "Not going to happen. It's too exposed above timberline. If one of their ships is close, I'm not willing to risk it."

"We'll be exposed too." Vivian's voice was quiet, resigned. "How long will it take us from here? An hour?"

Shame swamped Sara. It would only take her about thirty minutes, but she couldn't judge this group by her level of conditioning. "The radar thingie tells you direction too, doesn't it?"

Vivian nodded. She climbed back into the bird, moving around Jake and got back out clutching the device and studying it. "Says they're about ten miles that way." She pointed to the west.

"Okay. Get back inside." Sara's stomach tightened into a knot, and bile burned the back of her throat. She didn't have good feelings about this. "I'll get you closer. As far as the last lake basin."

Gratitude flowed from Vivian's dark eyes. "We'd appreciate any help. We'll leave the radar with you. The ones back at your station will need it worse than us, assuming we make it."

"Is there any way for the rest of us to know?" Sara didn't add the words *if you make it*. Vivian understood well enough without them.

Vivian nodded. "We have two-way radios. We haven't used them because it allows the aliens to triangulate our position, but if we get there, we'll key a mike."

"Good enough. You'll need to be outside the hut for the best transmission, but its line of sight, so it should go."

Sara hugged the ground and kept the radar device in her lap. It didn't go off again, and she let the group off at the lake before the final set of switchbacks to the hut. "Go as fast as you can," she instructed them. "It's not far. You can catch your breath later."

Skin crawling with tension and the fine hairs on her arms and neck quivering with apprehension, Sara waited until everyone was headed up the switchbacks at a dead run, only five minutes from safety—ten max. She'd just gotten airborne again when the radar in her lap erupted, blaring so loud, she set it on the floor.

Jake barked at it.

Did the dual tones mean aliens were closer? She peered at the readout, but was too close to the ground to take her attention away from flying the craft. Best thing she could do for the six human beings on their way to the hut was pray for them. They had guns. Hopefully, they'd put them to good use.

CHAPTER 27

*S*ara blessed her military training as she piloted the craft back to LeConte. She was shaking and sweating and strung so tight, she wanted to scream, but she was still flying the bird, goddammit.

Somewhere between the lakes below the hut and LeConte, the radar cut off abruptly. The mood she was in, its silence was almost as ominous as its shrieking had been.

Jared scaled the ladder and tugged the helicopter door open the second she touched down. "What happened?" he demanded, his features drawn and worried. "You were gone too long."

She handed him the radar unit and then crawled out of the chopper, only wanting to tell her story once. Jake hopped after her, sticking close.

The remaining seven from NASA huddled around Sara, peppering her with questions. Christine was too sick to move, so the group positioned themselves near the unconscious woman, in case she came around.

"Do any of you have your two-ways on?" Sara asked.

"No. Leads the bastards right to us," a bald man said.

"Well, turn one on now. I'll explain in a minute."

The man who'd spoken dug a radio out of an inner pocket and thumbed it on.

Sara held out her hand for it, staring at the display. At least it had battery power. Still holding it, she told the group what happened. "…I'm sorry I chickened out," she ended with. "I was just so certain if I brought the bird to the top of the pass, it'd get vaporized and all of us along with it. I know I was reacting, probably not thinking straight—"

"You did fine." A tall, thin woman with brown hair interrupted, training her blue eyes on Sara. "More than fine. Even if this second group sustains some losses, you got enough of us into position to fix things."

Sara didn't feel like she'd done *more than fine*. In truth, she felt she'd failed.

The radio in her hand beeped once, its display lighting.

"Hey!" the bald man beamed. "They made it." Cheers broke out.

Sara stared at the radio in her hand. She'd been so sunk in blaming herself, the significance hadn't registered.

The man grabbed the radio back, keyed it once, and shut it off. "There," he said. "Now they'll know we heard them."

Jared closed his arms around her. "It's okay. You did good. Come inside. I have hot water on the stove."

She pulled away from him. "Not yet. What happens next?" she asked the remaining scientists.

"The ones up top will begin transmitting," the tall woman said. "Worst part will be the next six hours or so." She swept the group with her gaze. We should take the radar and move away from here. Christine is helpless, and if we go, we'll lead the heat away from her."

Heads nodded, and murmurs of assent swept through the group.

"Some of the ones I left at the hut had guns," Sara said. "Do any of you?"

"Yes," the bald man said. "Look, we've been outrunning those slimebags for two weeks. We can manage for a few more hours."

"We'll meet you back here once the worst of it's over with," the tall woman said.

Without waiting for more conversation, the group left the ranger station after taking the radar unit from Jared.

Sara hunkered next to Christine. The woman's face was gray and her breathing labored. "Would you like us to move you inside?" she asked.

Jared squatted next to her. "She's unconscious, probably slipped into a coma. I asked her that same question, though, when she could still talk, and she said she'd rather die outside."

"Isn't there anything we can do?"

He shook his head. "IV antibiotics might help, but she needs a trauma center."

"I could fly her out of here once they're done with whatever they're doing in the Muir Hut. Fresno's not far by air."

Jared laid a hand on her arm. "You could. Odds of her being alive thirty-six hours from now aren't good." He straightened. "Come inside. You look about done in."

She felt more than *done in*. Running on fumes, she plodded up the stairs after him, Jake right behind her. He made a beeline for his dish and began crunching kibbles.

"Shit!" She rolled her eyes. "Wish I could just tuck into my dinner and forget all this."

He tugged a chair out for her and pushed her into it. She sat heavily and supported her head with one hand, elbow resting on the table. "I should be up at Muir with them," she said.

"Why?" Jared plunked a steaming mug of tea in front of her and poured a jot of booze into it. "No one asked you to stay with them. They seemed like a competent bunch, all in all."

"I suppose you're right." She blew on steam rising off the metal mug before taking a small sip. It burned her tongue, but it felt good going down, all heat with a bite of scotch. She glanced at

Jared. "I'm glad you didn't head up the trail after me. I'd have had no way to get hold of you. I have radios, but didn't think to drag them out."

"It's okay, Sara." He placed his hand over one of hers and dragged the other chair beside her, settling into it. "Yeah, I was close to leaving, but I didn't. Even if I had, I would've heard the chopper and doubled back."

"Oh yeah, huh?" She dragged her hand from beneath his and sifted fingers through her hair. "Guess I'm not thinking very straight."

"You have every right not to. You've had a hell of a couple of weeks."

"Do you suppose whatever they're doing up at the hut will really fix this?"

Jared shrugged. "They think it will. I don't see any reason not to believe them."

"Mmph. Guess all we can do now is wait."

He nodded. "I mixed up some freeze-dried glop from my pack. Saved you some on the back of the stove, so it's still probably warm."

She smiled weakly. "Sounds good. Haven't had anything since the oatmeal and energy bar we called breakfast."

He squeezed her shoulder and got to his feet, returning with a bowl of noodles in an oriental looking sauce. "I'm going to check on Christine. Be right back."

Jake padded to her side and looked meaningfully at her dish, whining softly.

"Sorry, dude. You had your dinner. This is mine."

As if he understood, he retraced his steps and laid next to his dish, head on his paws, watching her.

JARED BENT over Christine's inert form. She was still breathing, but beyond that, she'd sunk to a place she'd likely never surface from. Sweat beaded her forehead, probably fever from whatever infection was ripping through her body. He tucked a sleeping bag one of the scientists had offered more firmly around her and watched the sun heading for the western horizon.

LeConte was in a deep canyon, which meant it got the sun late and lost it early. This late in the year, the problem was even worse. Sara looked trashed. He wanted to give her something to help her sleep and tuck her into bed, but that wasn't a good idea. If anything happened, the last thing she needed was to be sedated to the gills.

He'd been frantic as minutes had turned to half an hour and she didn't return from the second trip up the mountainside. He'd just been gathering his pack when the *whump* of rotors sent him to the landing pad at a fast trot. It sounded like she'd had a damned close call. Good thing she'd followed her instincts— rather than her conscience—and not flown to the top of the pass on that last trip.

After a final check of Christine's pulse, which was fast and thready, he turned and mounted the steps back into the cabin. An hour had passed since the group left. If they were correct, after five more they'd be past the worst of repercussions from the aliens. Hell, just the thought of having them on the run made him smile.

Who knew what would be left of his old life, but it didn't matter. He'd built what he had from nothing, and he could do it again. This time with Sara by his side. He paused before opening the door. What if she didn't want him? Worse, what if she insisted on keeping her backcountry ranger job? When the answer came, it was so simple, it surprised him. No reason he couldn't be a backcountry doc for the Park Service. Surely they used medical personnel. Maybe he was a shred overqualified, but so what?

He pushed the door open. Sara still sat at the table sipping the tea and booze mix he'd given her.

"How is she?" Sara raised her gaze to him.

"Fading."

"Are you sure she wouldn't be better off in here?"

"She might be, but people have a right to decide where they want to die."

"Of course, you're right." She moved her eyes to the cabin's one window. "Want to go to the creek and watch the sunset? It's usually pretty dramatic when there are clouds."

"Sure." He tugged his coat off a hook and shrugged into it. "Temp is dropping."

Sara stood and zipped the parka she'd never taken off. "We can build up the fire after we get back."

He thought about calling the dog, but the minute Sara got to her feet, Jake joined her and headed out the door first. "He's a good boy."

"Yeah." Sara smiled. "The best. I haven't been nearly as lonely back here since I got permission to keep him with me."

If Jared had his way, she'd never be lonely again, but how to broach the subject? He walked next to her down a well-worn trail to the creek. It bubbled and burbled over stones on its way to the Pacific Ocean.

Sara sat on a large, flat rock and patted the place next to her. "All the ranger cabins are different," she said. "This one has a wild river that runs all year. The creek next to mine freezes over, but it has the hot spring."

Jared settled next to her and wrapped an arm around her shoulders. She leaned into him. "I've been thinking about after," he said.

"Wondering what'll be left out there?" She waved an arm toward the west.

"That, and trying to figure out how I can keep you in my life." There. He'd said it. He sucked in a breath, waiting for her response.

Her body stiffened where it rested against his, but she didn't pull away. "I suppose you could come into the backcountry and visit me," she ventured after a long silence.

"I could, but I want more than just visiting you." He paused long enough for a measured breath. "We're far from kids. I've been searching for a woman who loves what I do for a long time. We could be really good together, Sara. I know it."

She twisted out from under his arm and looked at him. The rays from the setting sun illuminated her face, giving her an otherworldly look that transcended beauty. "I've thought the same thing, and told myself I was being ridiculous. That we don't know each other well enough." Something like hope flared from the depths of her blue-gray eyes.

He laid his hand along her jawline, and she angled her face against it. "We may not know each other well yet, but we know ourselves. You understand why you're still alone, and so do I. If you think we might have a chance as a couple, and I believe the same thing, I'd say that's a really strong start."

"But how—"

"Anyway we want to. You can keep working. I could hire on as a doc with the Park Service during the summers. We could split the year up. Surely you're not manning McClure through the winter."

"No. I'm at Park Headquarters in Three Rivers then."

"See. Easy. I could move a branch of my lab there. Or I could move the whole thing. Depends how my staff feel about switching locations." He took a breath. God, she was the most beautiful creature. The bones in her face would've done a goddess proud. "Please say yes, Sara."

A smile split her face, making her even more stunning. "Just what am I saying yes to?"

"To giving us a chance."

She placed her hand over his, her fingers cold since she wasn't wearing gloves. "How could I not? I want to get to know who you are too."

He drew her into his arms and kissed her, soft and tender at first, but need raced through him, heating his blood with desire for the woman in his arms. She kissed him back as if her life depended on maintaining contact with his mouth. He recognized that level of intensity, twin to his own. It was how he approached everything in his life. Full steam ahead, throttle wide open.

He wove his hands into her hair and plumbed her mouth with his tongue. She opened for him, tasting of tea and scotch and Sara. She teased his tongue with hers and nibbled and bit his lips. He teased back, and she wrapped her arms around him. A chill wind tossed the last of the season's leaves from aspen trees growing by the creek, but he burned with an inner fire that consumed everything in its path.

Cupping a hand over a breast, he rubbed her nipple through multiple layers of clothing, and she moaned into his mouth. He broke their kiss. "I want to make love with you."

"Me too." She laughed, and color lent a rosy cast to her tanned skin. "I want you too."

"Should we go inside?"

"Do you want to?" She glanced at the top of the canyon walls where the sunset painted the sky in teal and violet and pink. "We'll miss the sunset."

"If you're sure you won't be cold, we can have it all. Each other and the sunset."

"Cold isn't much of a possibility with you next to me." She laughed again. "We can get fancier later, but this rock's looking like a pretty promising surface all of a sudden."

"We did warm it up sitting on it."

"See. The backcountry is full of possibilities." She grinned coquettishly, unzipped her jacket and drew his hand inside, atop her breasts, but still with fabric in between.

He took her hardened nipples between his fingers and tweaked them, using her moans as a roadmap for what to do more of. She snaked a hand out, settling it on his erection, and he pushed his free hand between her legs. Hunger snared him, and he wanted to sink inside of her with a desperation that turned even his live-on-the-edge world upside down.

Her boots would have to go, so he reached for one, but she said, "I have a better idea." Breathlessly jackknifing out of his grasp, she twisted away and undid her pants, letting them fall partway down her legs as she bent over the flat rock he still sat on. The perfect globes of her ass framed her sex in the rays of the dying sun, dark curls spiky with moisture.

He touched her folds almost reverently, tickling, teasing, rubbing until she gasped with delight, hips rocking against his fingers. Meantime, his cock swelled almost to a point of pain where it was trapped between his shorts and pants. She bucked her hips in clear invitation, and he stood and unzipped his pants, freeing himself.

Wrapping a hand around his erection, he guided it to the entrance to her body and steadied them with a hand on her hip. Slowly, ever so slowly, he sank inside her. Feeling the scorching heat of her surround him was ecstasy, and he clung to a ragged edge of control. She clenched her muscles around him, and he groaned with delight. Being inside her was amazing, incredible.

When he felt like he could move without pushing himself into an orgasm, he withdrew almost all the way, and then slid back inside. Reaching around, he rubbed her clit, while he continued his long, slow strokes into her molten core. She dissolved around him in a flood of liquid heat, and he felt the rhythmic contractions of her climax around his shaft.

It was tempting, so tempting to move up his tempo, to drive into her until he exploded, but he held back. He wanted to make her come again before he reached his peak, but wasn't certain his body would cooperate. In an effort to up the odds, he withdrew, missing the warmth of her vault immediately.

"Come back here." She twisted so she could look at him over a shoulder. "We're not done. Specifically, you're not."

"You had it right the first time."

Kneeling behind her, he bent so he could lick her pussy. The angle was awkward, and he tongue-fucked her while rolling her clit between his fingers. The tempo of her breathing escalated and she thrust her hips against his mouth and fingers, writhing beneath his touch. Her juices streaked his face, and her scent was intoxicating. When he was certain she was close, he straightened and pressed his cock back inside her.

She screamed her delight and shoved against him, forcing him into a rhythm that would topple him into release. The slow, cadenced lovemaking from earlier fled like chaff in a stiff wind and he slammed into her, hands on her hips, wanting nothing more than to take her, brand her, make her his.

Her pussy muscles milked him, clenching in spasms signaling her orgasm. He let himself go and felt semen judder out of him so hard a feral cry burst from his mouth. He gripped her so tightly, he prayed he didn't hurt her, but he needed intense contact with all of her.

They remained like that, her bent over the flat rock and him standing behind her until their breathing moved from gasps and pants to something slower. He pulled out of her and drew her to her feet, turning her to face him.

"Sara, darling. That was one of the most powerful experiences I've ever had."

"Glad it wasn't just me." She closed fingers over his exposed, still-erect cock, tucking him back inside his pants.

He tugged her trousers up her legs and helped her set herself to rights. Kleenex materialized from one of their pockets, and she blotted herself with it.

"Imagine what we could do with a double bed," he murmured.

"We had a bed inside," she reminded him. "We would've missed the sunset."

He glanced at the sky, still streaked with pink. "It sounds hokey, but it's like nature was smiling on us."

"She was. I'm sure of it. Every ancient religion held outdoor ceremonies where they blessed the earth by making love on it."

Jared pulled her close and kissed her forehead, her eyelids, her cheeks, and her lips. When he was done, he said, "Speaking of Earth, I wonder how things are going up in the Muir Hut."

"Well, we haven't heard anything...unusual, so maybe it's not premature to hope for the best."

Jake bounded out of some nearby bushes with something clamped in his jaws.

"Guess he burned up the time we were making love hunting." Sara laughed and leaned into Jared.

He loved how she laughed, wanted her to be happy for the rest of her days. "Ready to go inside?"

She nodded. "Yeah. We should check on Christine. I really don't feel right leaving her on that mat outside the cabin."

He latched an arm around her waist, and they walked back to the ranger cabin together, hips bumping against one another. Jake ran ahead, and began growling and snarling at something.

"Damn! What could it possibly be now?" Sara ducked from beneath his embrace and broke into a lope.

Jared ran behind her, ready for anything, and cursed having left his weapon in the cabin. In what was left of the daylight, he saw Sara stoop over the pallet where he'd laid Christine.

"Shit, aw shit." Sara turned to him, gesturing at Christine's inert form behind her.

"What?" Jared hastened forward, and stopped cold.

Where Christine had lain was...something else. He knelt and folded his fingers around what might have been a wrist, hunting for a pulse, but the thing before them was clearly dead.

"What the fuck is it?" Sara's voice took on a shrill note. "It doesn't look anything like Lonnie or Stuart."

"No. This looks like something out of *Close Encounters*. It's dead. It can't hurt us."

"I don't care about that. Why'd it change from Christine to this?"

"I have no idea."

"Did you notice anything odd while you worked on her?"

"No. Mangled tissue appears pretty much the same across species, though. Radius and ulna looked close enough to human, they didn't alert me." He stared at the body with a clinical detachment honed by long years in the lab. The humanoid was built rather like Christine, but with elongated limbs and almost elven facial features. He tugged an eyelid open and was met with a vertical slit pupil.

In the meantime, Sara was looking closely at the ground around the body. "No one's come or gone since we went to the river," she noted, "but I'm guessing that entire group probably aren't NASA scientists any more than I am."

Jared straightened slowly. "You believe the whole mess of them are some other kind of alien?"

Sara nodded. "Yup. I think we were played. No reason two groups of those fuckers couldn't have tag-teamed showing up on Earth. The only part that makes any kind of sense is that whoever the fake-NASA group is, they're on our side. And they needed our help getting rid of the other ones."

"Say more."

"Not sure there's more to say. I've read enough science fiction. If the human Christine required energy to maintain her illusory form, that energy would've dissipated after she died. Jesus! Can this whole mess get any more convoluted? I'm going inside."

"Sure. I'll be there in a few."

Clucking to Jake, she walked up the steps and into the cabin.

Jared stood staring at the corpse for a long time, trying to make sense of any of it and not doing a very good job. Sara's theory was logical, but there had to be more to it. Wondering if they'd ever get enough details to fill in the blank spots, he finally trudged up the steps to join Sara.

Sara fell into an uneasy doze cradled against Jared in the narrow bunk. Not exactly asleep, she wasn't truly awake, either. They'd tried to talk over possibilities, but ended up chasing their tails. Jake slept on the floor near the door, as if he sensed the need to keep watch.

A whine from the dog slammed her back to wakefulness. Running on instincts which rarely failed her, she bolted from the bed. Since she hadn't bothered to undress, all she had to do was zip her parka and stuff her feet into her boots, not bothering with the laces. Sara crossed the small space and pulled the door open, grabbing her gun off the table as she passed by.

Jake bolted through the door the second it opened, and his whines turned to full-fledged barks.

Sara recognized the bark pattern. It was the one that told whoever he'd cornered to stop in their tracks. She flicked the gun's safety off and barreled down the steps.

"Freeze," she yelled.

"What is it?" Jared joined her. Sleep fuzzed his question, but he had his gun in hand too.

Sara rounded the corner of the cabin in time to see three of the fake NASA group with Christine's body slung between. "Stop or I'll shoot."

"And what exactly would that accomplish?" The bald man turned to face her, motioning to the others to set Christine's body down.

"We need answers," Jared said.

"We sure as hell do," Sara seconded. "What are you? Why are you here?"

The tall, thin woman stepped from shadows. "It doesn't matter. You never saw us. No one would believe you anyway."

Jared blew out a weary breath. "I understand you came to get Christine—or whatever her name really is. You fucked up, though. She died—and transformed—before you returned for her."

"It was a miscalculation on our part," the bald man conceded. He exchanged glances with the dark-haired woman.

She nodded and moved a little closer. "We could wipe your memories, but you helped us, so we'll tell you a little. Probably not enough to satisfy you, but it will have to do. The deal is this. I'll talk. You listen. No questions. Not while I'm talking, and not when I'm done."

"Fair enough," Sara said. Figuring she wouldn't need her weapon, she clicked on the safety and stuffed it into a pocket. "But I do have one before you start. Were the rest of you successful at interrupting the harmonic that supported the other..." She stumbled over what word to use, but the woman saved her the trouble of questing about for something other than *aliens.*

"Yes. The ones who appeared to be large reptiles won't bother you any further. Last warning, though. One more question, and we'll simply leave."

"Got it," Sara said through tight lips.

"Me too," Jared seconded.

Jake stood between her and the group who'd come for

Christine, hackles raised, still growling. Sara called him to her side.

"Do you want to take this?" the woman asked the bald man.

He shook his head. "Your idea. Your party. If it would've been my call, I'd just have left. I never believed they'd shoot us in the back in cold blood."

The woman crossed her arms over her chest. "There are more varieties of intelligent life than you can imagine. The ones who wished to storm Earth for its mineral wealth were one. We're another, but don't make the mistake of believing what you likely learned about in school about there only being six of us."

Questions bubbled through Sara's mind. She wanted to ask if they really worked for NASA. If they'd infiltrated Earth so thoroughly they could blend in with humans, but she bit her tongue.

"I can read your mind," the woman said. "It's really quite useful. And yes, we do work for NASA, and we do live here. Have for generations. We were the ones who suggested the trade agreement, mostly because we wanted to study that particular species. We had no idea they'd would take it upon themselves to breach your boundaries, intent on establishing dominion. Once they did, we were the logical line of defense.

"If we'd established corrective measures sooner, we could've stopped them cold, but we argued among ourselves far too long. By the time we understood action was imperative, it was almost too late."

"Are there more like you?" Jared asked, followed by, "Sorry. Forget I asked."

"The less you know, the better," the woman said. "For now, it's enough to understand Earth is safe again. You'll return to some fallout, some destruction, but it could've been so much worse."

"Your best bet," the bald man spoke, surprising Sara, "would be to go through whatever process you usually follow and close up the ranger cabins for winter. By the time you return to civilization, the authorities will have things well in hand."

Sara nodded. "One thing I do need to know is if your colleagues are still at the Muir Hut. They had such a hard time getting up there, will they need assistance exiting the backcountry?"

"It's a fair question," the bald man said. "You don't have to worry about them. They're at the hut, but we're in contact with them. Remember, they needed to transmit for twenty-four to thirty-six hours. They'll leave once their task is done. We've dispatched a ship to pick them up. The atmosphere is difficult for us at altitude, but they'll be fine."

"A ship?" Jared said in a strangled-sounding voice. "You have spaceships too?"

The woman laughed. "Why wouldn't we? Our technology is lightyears ahead of theirs."

"Never mind. I really will keep my mouth shut," Jared muttered.

"We're leaving now," the bald man said. "Don't try to find us at NASA or anywhere else."

"Why not?" Sara asked. "There's still a whole lot I want to know."

The woman rounded on her. "Because some things need to remain secret. What would've happened to your precious planet if we weren't here, behind the scenes, ready to pick up the banner and fight for you?"

"You had a closer call than you realize," the bald man said. "Leave it at that. I would commit you both to secrecy, though. If you can't make a promise I trust, we'll erase your memory of us."

"You have my word." Jared squared his shoulders. "Look into my mind, or however you verify things."

"Mine too." Sara said. Life was full of unsolved mysteries. At least this one had a few answers.

"That was why Christine wanted to be outside," Jared blurted. "So you could retrieve her."

"Smart man." The woman bent and picked up one of Christine's legs. The others gathered more of their fallen companion and faded into the still, black night with her body suspended between them.

Jake sent a parting bark after them, looking pleased with himself. And why not? In his doggy brain, he'd chased off the intruders and kept his mistress safe from harm—again.

Sara sucked in a ragged breath, followed by another. "Jesus," she managed at length. "It's like something out of Robert Heinlein or Frank Herbert."

Jared tucked a hand under her elbow and guided her back toward the cabin's front porch. She walked up the steps, but turned and sat on the last one. "I'm not quite ready to go inside yet. You?"

"I'm good wherever you are." He sat next to her and fiddled with his gun, laying it on the porch.

The dog scrunched past both of them and curled in front of the door.

"Still trying to wrap my mind around all of this," Sara murmured.

"Know what you mean." Jared drew his brows together. "It's just so fantastic, my mind keeps skittering away from all of it."

"I suppose this means I can raise Park Headquarters from my radio at McClure."

"Probably, but why do you need to?"

She turned to look at him. "To check in. To let them know Jake and I are still alive. To see if there's anyone who needs help back here. To find out if anyone died beyond Lonnie and Stuart..."

He held up a hand. "Of course. I wasn't thinking. They're your family, and you want to find out if they're okay." He draped an arm around her shoulder and pulled her against him. "Once we're high enough, I can use my phone to do the same thing. Hopefully Donovan Enterprises is still in one piece."

"The NASA group said my dispatches were exaggerated." Sara stopped, thinking. "I want to know by how much." She smiled crookedly. "I may spend half my time out here, but it doesn't mean I don't appreciate having a world to return to."

"How about this?" He cradled her against his body, and she snuggled close.

"How about what?" It felt really, really good to be in Jared's arms. So good, she never wanted to leave.

"We'll go inside and sleep until dawn. Then you can fly us back to McClure. We'll soak in the spring to clean up, and then check in with the outside world. Once we have more information, we can plan what to do next."

"Sounds good. We should give the Muir Hut a wide berth for the next couple days." She glanced at her watch, clicking buttons. "October third. Normally, I'm back here until around the fifteenth —in case there are late season travelers, but I can fly you out if you need to leave."

Something tight coiled inside her. She'd offered him an out. It was the right thing to do. They'd had a lovely time earlier in the evening, but—

"Not on your life, sweetheart. I'll call in and make sure there's no reason I absolutely have to leave the high country, but absent a hardcore crisis, you're stuck with me, until we both leave for the winter."

A wellspring of warmth grew inside her, and her heart swelled with emotion. She stroked the side of his face. "Better watch it. You sound like you really meant that."

"Never been more serious in my life. Weren't you listening to me down by the river when we made love?"

"Sure, but we were both overcome by one another's charms."

"Darling. Sweetheart." He brushed his thumb over her mouth. "I'm still *overcome by your charms*. Probably always will be, but that doesn't mean I don't want all the things I talked about."

"Really?"

"Really." He kissed her nose. "Ready to go inside?"

"Yeah. We never did get much sleep earlier. At least I didn't."

"All the more reason to let Jake and me take over for a while. You won't have to fly so low it makes me not want to look, but I still want you rested before we leave here tomorrow." He paused a beat. "We've both been independent for a lot of our adult lives, so we're bound to butt heads. Let me take care of you, Sara."

"Only if I can take care of you back."

"Deal." He head out a hand. She shook it before he crushed his mouth down on hers.

Sara lost herself in that kiss. It felt like the beginning of a whole new life for her. Before she stretched out on the porch and invited him into her body, he scooped her into his arms as if she weighed nothing and carried her inside, kicking the door shut behind them.

As usual, Jake ran in ahead of them.

Jared laid her tenderly on the bed and crossed the cabin to toss wood into the dying embers in the stove. He moved back to her side and perched on the edge of the cot to lever off his boots. Next he unlaced hers and jockeyed them off.

"'Fraid I lured you in here under false pretenses," he murmured. "You can get all the sleep in the world, but not until after I've undressed you and made love to you properly."

She gazed at him in the flickering stove light. "What we did by the river was proper. Hell, it was damned hot."

"Yeah, it was all those things, but I want to look at all of you at the same time."

Sara wanted to look at him too. Not just glimpses of him in form fitting long underwear as he slipped into his sleeping bag. "Two can play that game." She unzipped his jacket and pushed it off his shoulders. Next came his vest and stretchy top. She traced the line of his nipples with their sprinkle of tawny hairs around them.

"Pretty man."

"Not as pretty as you." His breath hitched, and he pulled off her jacket and two layers of tops. She wasn't wearing a bra, and he filled his hands with her breasts while a feral, possessive sound flowed from deep in his throat.

She arched into his touch and undid her pants, pushing them down her hips and freeing her legs.

"Hey," he protested. "That's my job."

"What about being partners?" She grinned impishly and unfastened his belt and the button and zipper holding his pants in place.

He let go of her breasts long enough to stand and step out of his pants after they pooled around his feet. His shorts followed.

Sara let her gaze linger over the hard planes of his body. He was lean with muscled shoulders, arms, thighs, and calves. His cock rose from a mat of copper curls between his legs, a drop of semen glistening on its tip.

"Not just pretty." Her throat was dry with needing him. "Gorgeous. I could look at you forever and die a happy woman."

"Keep talking, sweetheart. I'm not cheap, but I can be bought."

"Get down here."

"Your wish is my command."

He lay next to her and wove his hands into her hair before he kissed her. Feeling him next to her naked, skin-to-skin, was electrifying. Suddenly, she couldn't wait. Never mind they'd just made love a few hours ago. Throwing a leg over his hip, she opened herself and reached to guide him inside her.

He thrust hard, sinking himself to the hilt, and she squirmed at the delicious sensations cascading through her. With his lips still glued to hers and her breasts squashed against his chest, she rocked against the cock buried in her sensitive places. When he reached between her legs and teased her swollen nub, she came, bucking and shrieking against him.

He turned her until she was beneath him and drove into her, his gaze never leaving hers. Color highlighted his chest and face, and his nipples were hard buds.

"Yes. Oh God yes, now. Come with me, Sara darling." He ground his pubes against her clit and held it there as his cock shuddered inside her.

The spasms of his release shot her over the edge a second time, and she clung to him, wanting nothing more than the man in her arms and for the moment to last forever.

"That was even better than the first time." His voice rumbled against her hair, and he kneaded her back with strong fingers.

"Flattery will get you—"

"All it needs to get me is more of the same. I'm falling in love with you sweetheart." He smoothed hairs away from her face. "Sleep. Tomorrow's soon enough to face whatever's left of the world."

"World aside, I'm falling in love with you too. It's hard to believe, though."

"For me too, so we'll just have to write the script as we go."

"Sounds good to me." She smiled and he grinned back.

Trusting, really trusting, another person for the first time in a long time, Sara relaxed in his arms. They'd face whatever they had to together. It felt right in a way nothing had in years. With her heart full of hope for their future, she dozed against him.

"One more thing." His voice roused her.

"Yeah?"

"If there's no pressing reason for either of us to go back right away, maybe you and Jake could walk out to Whitney Portal with me."

A giggle started deep in her chest. Minutes later, it turned into a full-blown laugh. "You want to finish the Muir Trail. After everything that's happened, you still want to finish the trail."

"Wouldn't you?"

She nodded. "Of course. I understand perfectly. The logistics are wonky since we can't leave the chopper in here all winter, but we'll figure something out. Maybe we could fastpack up to Trail Crest, snag Whitney's summit, and then return to LeConte."

"There's my girl." He kissed her eyelids and mouth just before they both fell asleep.

You've reached the end of the first three Alphas in the Wild books. There is a fourth, Fire Moon. Keep reading for a sample.

ABOUT THE AUTHOR

Ann Gimpel is a national bestselling author. A lifelong aficionado of the unusual, she began writing speculative fiction a few years ago. Since then her short fiction has appeared in a number of webzines and anthologies. Her longer books run the gamut from urban fantasy to paranormal romance. Once upon a time, she nurtured clients, now she nurtures dark, gritty fantasy stories that push hard against reality. When she's not writing, she's in the backcountry getting down and dirty with her camera. She's published over 50 books to date, with several more planned for 2018 and beyond. A husband, grown children, grandchildren and three wolf hybrids round out her family.

Keep up with her at www.anngimpel.com or http://anngimpel.blogspot.com

If you enjoyed what you read, get in line for special offers and pre-release special reads. Sign up for Ann's newsletter on her website or her blog.

FIRE MOON, CHAPTER ONE

"Damn!" Cara Carlisle coughed and pulled the moistened bandana up over her nose again. It didn't help much, but anything was better than nothing. Squinting against the ever-present smoke, she wriggled to make her position on the narrow ledge more comfortable and checked her single piece of climbing hardware. It didn't budge when she tugged on it. Sweat dribbled from beneath her snug-fitting helmet and stung her eyes.

Piton's secure. What happens when I run out of water? Will the smoke do me in before thirst drives me mad?

"Climbing!" John's voice echoed off the canyon walls.

"Take your time. Be careful," she yelled. "I've only got a single pin in. It's okay for me, but..." As soon as the words were out, she rapidly hammered in another piton a few inches farther up, looping the rope through a second locking carabiner. The clatter of aluminum hanging off John's gear rack told her he was getting closer. More to kill time than anything else, she examined the rock face. The crack she'd chosen to defeat the thousand-foot wall zigged upward as far as she could see, but she couldn't see all the way to the top, not even close.

Fire raging through Kings Canyon National Park spread below them and made this route irreversible. They couldn't retreat, so she crossed her fingers and breathed a silent prayer she'd chosen well.

Fires weren't all that unusual. They rampaged through the Sierra Nevada Mountains every summer, especially as run-off from the last season's snow diminished to a trickle, but some idiot of a work crew boss must have brought in explosives to finish needed trail repairs. One of the fires had likely gotten too close, a stash of dynamite detonated, and the autumn-dry forest went up like a torch.

Cara had been high on the eastern escarpment of Dragon Peak watching it happen. To escape, she'd led her clients—there'd been three of them then—over an unknown, and as far as she knew previously unclimbed, route down toward Rae Lakes. They'd ended up miles from their camp on the wrong side of a thirteen-thousand-foot ridge. Wind had thwarted her, fanning the fire with breakneck speed, and narrowing retreat possibilities.

"Ah shit," she muttered through clenched teeth as memory jabbed her mercilessly.

Her next route choice had been a mistake, forcing them high onto this rock wall. So many other mistakes peppered her slightly less than thirty-five years, she winced. Having kicked the door-to-looking-back wide open, she stood at the lintel, an unwilling witness to her travesty of a girlhood. About the only thing she hadn't done wrong back then was running away from her drug-addled mother and Betty, her mom's bitch of a partner, the second she finished high school.

She still remembered that afternoon, saw herself as a gangly seventeen-year-old, ratty valise clutched in one hand, trying to rouse her mother enough to tell her goodbye. She'd finally given up. It didn't matter much one way or the other since her mother wouldn't remember. Goodbyes were for the living, and drugs had killed her mother's humanity.

Betty's words slammed against her as she headed out the door. "You'll never amount to nothing. Nope, nothing but trouble from you. Your ma'd be better off if you was dead."

Cara shivered, swallowing around a lump that formed in her smoke-sore throat. Once the memories wakened, it was pointless to stem their tide.

Might as well let 'em roll.

In rapid succession, she shuffled through her years of waitressing and a brief stint with a cruise line she'd left the minute it became clear other things were expected of their hostess staff. After that, she'd found Leif—or he found her. She'd never been sure quite which. Crack climber, ace skier, Leif had been a mountain man to the core. He was also a drunk and a womanizer and nasty as all get out, but he had taught her about the mountains. It had been Leif—nagging, pushing, and criticizing—who'd seen she got her certification as a guide. If it wouldn't have been for the avalanche that obliterated the entire group he'd been leading up Annapurna, she supposed she'd still be with him. Miserable, but at least not alone.

After Leif's death, she'd pretty much shunned men. She snorted under her breath, and her face contorted into a scowl.

No matter how far I run, I can't get away from Ma and Betty.

Cara squeezed her eyes shut tight and forced herself to focus. Wallowing in the past was an indulgence. She tucked her raggedy black braids more firmly into her bright red windbreaker. Hair caught fire fast. Her helmet protected most of it, but it was best if she kept the rest covered. Looking at the flames raging five hundred feet below, she felt an almost unbearable urge to just let go and finish things off.

"Bad call, sister!" she hissed. "I have to stay in the moment. I lost the other two. I owe it to John to hold it together." A flash of pain tugged at her attention and she realized she'd bitten through her lower lip. The jangle of John's hardware grew louder, and movement intensified on the rope.

"Easy, now," she called down. "You're close. Here, let me just scoot up to the next ledge."

"Not yet," he rasped. She heard an odd undernote in his voice, and he was panting. Not good. "I just have to—"

"It's all right, John. Take all the time you need." Cara tried to infuse confidence she wasn't feeling into her voice. She was good at what she did, had been leading and training climbers for over ten years, but this was one of the worst situations she'd ever landed in.

If you're so good, an inner voice—Betty's voice—mocked, why aren't Ruth and Christopher still here?

"Because," Cara snarled, "they didn't follow my instructions. They panicked and ran for the ranger station, right into the heart of the fire."

You didn't follow them. The implacable voice continued. You were their guide. They paid you to take care of them.

"I may have been their guide, but I didn't sign up to follow them into Hell." Control fraying dangerously, Cara tightened her hold on the rope until her hands hurt. "What the fuck am I doing talking to myself?" she muttered.

"Cara? Who are you talking to?" John's sooty face appeared out of nowhere at the level of her boots; his blue eyes were red-rimmed and bloodshot from the smoke. He sounded even more uncertain—or maybe concerned—than he had earlier.

Of course he's concerned. He just heard me talking to myself, sounding like a crazy person.

"It's okay, John. I'm okay." She stretched out a hand and helped him onto the ledge. "Ready to settle in? I'll get us up the next pitch."

"How many more do you think?" He coughed, choking on the smoky air. His flame-colored hair fanned around his gaunt face and stuck out at odd angles beneath his orange climbing helmet.

"Pitches?"

He nodded, licking his dry, chapped lips. "Yeah, can't quite see the whole crack from here."

"Uh, maybe half a dozen. I can't see the top from here, either."

"Around the corner—" he jerked his thumb behind him "—I thought I saw a way off here in, maybe, only a couple hundred feet." He hesitated. "You probably didn't see it because you were just looking at this crack."

"There's a different one?" she asked, nonplussed. How could she possibly have missed it? She had looked. In fact, she remembered looking. Leif had taught her to always look. It wasn't that his lessons were wrong, but they'd turned brutal fast if she didn't respond immediately to all his directives.

John nodded again and then croaked out, "Yes."

"Did you see a way from this crack to that one?"

"Not exactly. But I don't see things the way you might. It's worth the time for you to take a look, though."

"Okay." She blew out her breath. "Can't hurt. Belay me. I'll rap down a little and see if I can't pendulum over to it."

"What happens if you like it better? We need a plan while we're close enough to talk without yelling. Don't know about you, but my throat is trashed from the smoke."

"Mine is too. If there's a better crack, I'll position myself above where we are. Once I'm there, I'll swing my second rope over and top rope you up to me." Struggling to keep exasperation out of her voice—because she was certain there wasn't another way off this wall—she added, "Look, John, we have to move fast here. I don't know about you, but the smoke's really getting to me. My eyes feel gritty, and I'm nearly out of water. We've got at least a few hundred feet to go yet. If we can just get over the shoulder of Mount Rixford, there's an easy way down the other side to the Kearsarge Pass trail. We can get out from there."

Maybe. If Onion Valley's not on fire too.

"Okay, I'm good here," he said, his voice carefully neutral, as if he sensed she didn't believe him and didn't want to push things.

She watched as he went through the same wasted motions she had trying to carve something approximating comfort from their slender ledge. A rustling noise caught her attention. She sought its source and watched a small group of kites rise out of the smoke, their long graceful wings spread as they tried to escape the inferno.

"Too bad we can't fly," she said wryly, pointing at the raptors.

"Do you suppose they're coming for us?" The question was casual, but John stared at the birds through eyes narrowed to slits.

His question was so off-the-wall, she twisted to look at him. "Why would you even say that?"

Color flooded his sharp-boned face. "There's an old Indian legend about kites being spirit guides. About them showing up to cull the warriors from the cowards." He looked away, obviously embarrassed. "I know I don't look it—" he tugged at a coppery chunk of hair "—but my dad and grandmother are Lakota Sioux. She told me lots of stories growing up, because she said a man without history is like wind on the buffalo grass."

Cara forced out a laugh to cover sudden discomfiture. John's words creeped her out, and the last thing she needed right now was one more impediment. Something else standing between them and escape.

"John. I need you to focus." She infused a stern, no-nonsense note into her voice. "Those birds don't mean a thing. They're trying to get out of here, just like us."

Taking a deep breath, she pounded in another piece of hardware, pulled up the rope, and threaded it through a breaker bar into a figure eight. Double-checking everything, she moved one hand behind her and rappelled down about twenty feet to where she could see something. Breath whistled loudly through her teeth when she located John's crack.

"Jesus, how could I have missed that? It's practically a chimney," she snapped, furious with herself.

"Tension!" she yelled, as she began swinging the rope back and forth. Cara reached, lunged, extended her fingertips, but the crack remained stubbornly out of reach. She squeezed her eyes shut tight, sure the smoke was playing tricks on her. The crack seemed like it was moving away. Just when she was certain she'd have it this time, she missed by centimeters.

Panting and sweating, she let herself hang in her harness and stared at the elusive crack. Damn if it didn't look close enough to touch—except she knew better. She rapped down a few more feet to give herself more rope and a longer reach. She'd be worse than a fool if she let herself get caught up in believing the crack held some sort of supernatural power. This was a granite face. Solid granite. And that was just one more crack, although it was a damned promising one.

If she could just reach the fucking thing.

She pushed her body from side to side, using her feet against the rock to establish momentum. Each arc back and forth widened her reach. Penduluming could be a risky maneuver, and she hoped to hell it wouldn't place her square in the path of rocks falling from above. Reaching with the fingers of the hand that wasn't holding her rappel position, she flattened her body, stretching, making herself as long as she could.

Please, she sent up a prayer to the mountain gods. All I need is a couple more feet.

Aha!

The tips of her fingers grazed the edge of the crack. So much for her moronic occult theories about the damned thing teasing her by moving away. Next swing, she'd have it. Sending every second of her years of experience into her fingertips, she felt them connect with the edge and clung to it like a limpet. Triumph soared, but she didn't let herself relax until she'd jammed a foot into the crack.

She was getting ready to call over to John when she heard wings rustle again and felt a stab of pain in her rappel arm.

Surprised more than anything, thinking a rock must have fallen, hitting her in the forearm, Cara looked over—and froze.

One of the birds had landed on her. Its sharp black beak was firmly buried in the folds of her jacket, and the pain was excruciating. Shocked and sickened, she put her other foot atop the first one to stabilize her stance and tried to shake the bird off, but its talons only tightened.

"Okay," she said in measured tones. "Take that you son of a bitch."

Cara flung her arm hard against the wall. The bird's head cracked open on the granite, and it dropped like a stone. Red bloody pulp and black feathers joining the deeper red of the hungry flames.

Examining her jacket, Cara found bloody tracks where the kite's talons had dug deep into her flesh. John's words about the birds coming for them slapped her hard.

Aw shit, we don't need any more problems. It's not like there aren't enough of them already.

Stop it. Just stop right now. Those birds aren't any weirder than this crack was. Get a grip for Christ fucking sake.

"Cara?" John shouted. "The rope's slack. You okay?"

"It's good. The crack's going to work," she shouted, controlling her sense of outrage and anxiety about her latest assailant—and kicking herself for not alerting John as soon as she no longer needed his help. "Off belay. Coil the rope. Give me a couple minutes to shinny up this crack and I'll get my rope down to you. This will sound bizarre, but watch out for the birds."

"What?" He sounded wary, but not surprised. "The ones near me flew away."

Cara took a deep breath. Warning him was the right thing to do, no matter what kind of nut-job it made her sound like. "Watch out for the goddamned birds. Either you might've been onto something with your Native American legend stuff, or the smoke's made them feral. Put on an extra jacket if you have one. Do it before you rescue the rope."

She worked her way up the crack, which widened slightly as she climbed. Unfortunately, it was angling away from where she'd left John. If she went much higher, the rope wouldn't reach.

"Okay," she called out. "I'm going to snake the rope your way. Be ready."

"'Kay. Hurry, Cara. Those fucking birds are back, and they're dive-bombing me."

"Why didn't you say anything?"

"Just hurry."

A flat, dead tone underscored those two words. It chilled her and she swung the rope, gratified he caught it on the first try. "Got you," she shouted. "Give me a minute to secure you to this piton. I'll tell you when to come. Double check your knots."

There was a brief pause and she heard him call, "Now?"

"Not yet. Wait for me to tell you."

"Got it."

He sounded like he was holding on by the thinnest of margins, but covering it with bravado. She got set up for him as fast as she could. The sooner they got to the other side of Mount Rixford, the better she'd like it.